The
Last Witness

www.jerryamernic.com

Story Merchant Books
400 S. Burnside Ave. #11B
Los Angeles, CA 90036

www.storymerchant.com/books.html

Book design ©2014 Leslie Taylor, buffalocreativegroup.com

Los Angeles / Jerry Amernic

ISBN 978-0-9904216-5-8

Printed in the United States of America

The
Last Witness

Jerry Amernic

STORY MERCHANT BOOKS
LOS ANGELES / 2014

THE STORY MERCHANT

One

New York City, 2035

He was a tough sort. Ninety-five years old with elastic skin stretched across his bones like taut canvas, he was supposed to be an easy mark. Fragile and weak. A pushover. Albert Freedman lived by himself in a flat on the upper East Side, and when they came for him they didn't expect any trouble. Albert knew something wasn't right when the second one walked in, but the voice was soft and reassuring.

"We're here to change your palm reader," he said through the door. "We're doing all the apartments on your floor today and you're the first. It won't take five minutes."

"You're here to change my what?"

"Your palm reader."

"I donno what yer talkin' about. Go away!"

"You don't understand. There's a problem with the sensor. You know, the thing that opens your door when you put your hand in front of it? The palm reader?"

"What?"

"It scans your hand. Your print. Then it lets you in."

Nothing.

"Look," the man said, more softly now. "Mr. Freedman? You are Albert Freedman, aren't you?"

"Yes."

"I realize you don't want to be bothered but this is for your security. It's like putting a new lock on the door."

"A new lock?"

"That's right. The sensor in your palm reader is ten years old."

"It is?"

"The year's inscribed on the side of the door. It says 2025. See for yourself."

Albert looked, but he didn't see anything. His eyes weren't good. "Where does it say that?" he said.

"On the side of the door. It might be hard to read. The numbers are small."

"Where are they?"

"Trust me. The thing is ten years old and it's not working right. But we have new ones now that are much better. But it's not only that. You see there was a break-in last week and they want everyone's palm reader changed. That's why we're here. You're the first one on our list, Mr. Freedman. We'll be done in five minutes. Can we come in?"

"Five minutes you say?"

"That's all it takes."

He started jiggling the latch from the inside and then he stopped. "Wait a minute. Why am I the first one? This isn't the first flat on the floor. You should be down at the end of the hall. Unless you're doing it alphabetically and then you wouldn't be starting with me. Why am I the first one?"

He was ninety-five years old. He wasn't supposed to be asking questions like that. He was just supposed to open the door so they could kill him and make it look like a robbery.

There was an audible sigh from outside the door. "Look Mr. Freedman. It's like this. Doing all these sensors isn't going to be much fun for us but the landlord said you're a nice guy and we thought we'd start with you."

At first nothing and then the jiggling from inside the door started again.

"All right. Come in. But make it fast."

Albert released the latch that was linked to a sensor that had nothing wrong with it in a building where there had been no break-ins the past week, the past month or the past year. The first man through the door was short and slight, thirtyish with close-cropped hair and a soothing voice. He had a tattoo on his arm that looked like a snake, and if Albert had seen that he wouldn't have opened the door. But then it was too late.

"Thank you," the man said with a disarming smile.

The one behind him, younger and bigger with straggly hair and brown skin, burst through the door and pushed Albert out of the way. Old Albert fell against the wall and managed to brace himself with his hand, but the sudden impact jarred his wrist. The arthritis. Then the girl appeared, tall and skinny, dressed in black. Albert never got a good look at their faces, but it didn't matter. He would be dead before they left.

"Where do you keep the money?" the girl screamed at him. "Tell us!"

The small slim man with the snake on his arm turned, retreated into the hallway and closed the door behind him. In his hand was a little gadget with a screen on it. He touched the screen and a list of names came up. He ran his fingertip over the last name – Albert Freedman's name – and it disappeared. Then he was gone.

The girl began riffling through Albert's cupboards and drawers. Albert was confused. He didn't get many visitors.

"Where do you keep the money?" the girl said again.

"What do you want?"

"Your money!"

The man who was now inside Albert's flat didn't waste any time. He came for him with his fists clenched. He hit him in the face and knocked him to the floor. Albert fell on his side, his hip, but was close enough to the door so he could reach behind it for his cane. The one with the heavy metal handle. He always kept it there. Blood dripping from his nose, he scrambled to his knees, brought the cane back over his head, and with every ounce of strength he had walloped the intruder or thief or whatever he was across the ankles. There was a loud cry, but Albert wasn't finished. He got to his feet, straightened up, and brought his cane back a second time. Now he turned on the girl and landed that metal handle square on the back of her shoulders.

"I'll kill you both!" he said.

But Albert was old and the man was enraged now. He tore the cane from Albert's hands and started hitting him with it. He hit him on the head. He hit him on the chest. He hit him on the arms. Albert tried to shield himself with his flailing hands, but the blows were relentless. They kept coming and coming and coming. The girl was going through his drawers, throwing everything she found on the floor. Albert always kept his place neat and he didn't like that, but he could barely see through his eyes now.

"Here's his wallet," she said. "Get it over with."

The beating took less than a minute. Albert, barely conscious, lay on the floor, bloodied and battered to a pulp, a near corpse of broken bones. He couldn't move and the only thing to feel was pain. The man with the brown skin and straggly hair turned him over so he was face down and all there was to see was the cold dusty floor. It was the last thing Albert would see in his ninety-five years. He sniffed at the acrid air as a knee went deep into his back and the cane came up under his chin. Albert gurgled a few times, there was a crack, and his body went limp.

Two

The message said '*Happy 100th Birthday, Jack.*' The column in the middle of the lobby was wider than the others, on each side a monitor with the news of the day rolling down to the floor before starting up at the top again. There was the coming bingo tournament, the time and route for the walk through Washington Square, and a short bio on the pianist who would perform that night in the Grand Hall.

'*Happy 100th Birthday, Jack. The staff, executive board and residents of the Greenwich Village Seniors Center are pleased to announce the 100th birthday celebration for resident Jack Fisher to take place December 1st, 2039. Please join us in the recreation room on the lower level at 2 p.m.*'

The letters looked like they might have been drawn by a deft hand, but you couldn't tell for sure. They were crafted in a golden script with long curly stems, the '100' bigger than everything else to show the accomplishment of living for a whole century. Not that it was unusual. Lots of people around here had made it to a hundred. Jack was merely the latest. But as the words said, it was a celebration and you can't have enough of those in a building for the old.

Jack had slept through his alarm. It went off every morning at seven o'clock sharp. Seven o'clock and that thing that looked just as old as he was released its piercing blare from atop the night table next to his bed. Sometimes he got up and sometimes he didn't. Today he didn't because of the old pain in his shoulder, a subtle reminder of getting whacked with the butt of a rifle when he was a little boy. It had been going on all these years, but he was lucky. Awfully lucky. The madman who hit him, one of countless many in a sea of unending insanity, didn't bother to shoot. Still, after all this time, it hurt.

December 1st was a special day for Jack and he took extra care combing his hair. It was ashen white, but for a man one hundred years old having any hair at all is a victory. He opened his closet and chose the fancy shirt with the long, button-down sleeves, a French brand he had never heard of but they said it was the best cotton shirt around. It had solid gray lines running up and down, and in between them thinner lines. It was the kind of shirt that went with a suit, but Jack didn't wear suits anymore. They were stifling. The shirt with a sweater on top would be fine. It was his birthday, December 1st, and the chill of winter filled the air. He put on his glasses and washed his face.

His two sons were coming with their families. Ralph lived in East Rutherford, so Manhattan was no problem for him, but Bill was coming from Canada and that would be a treat. They would have their wives and their kids – Jack's grandchildren – and in Ralph's case his own grandchildren, which made them Jack's great-grandchildren. Jack was never one to crave attention, but having them all around would be nice. Unfortunately, Bill's two granddaughters couldn't make it. The older one, Tiffany, had a little girl of her own, which made this one Jack's great-great-granddaughter – five generations, pretty amazing all things considered – so Tiffany was at home tending to her daughter. As for her younger sister Christine, she was a schoolteacher whose job always came first, but even though Christine couldn't attend, she didn't disappoint.

Christine never disappointed Jack.

Her call woke him after he had slept through his alarm and it wasn't the ring that roused him but the flashing light on the console. Jack's eyes weren't good, but they were still better than his hearing. His hearing had been waning for years now. He reached for the phone on his night table and it was her. Christine. The first thing she said was, "Happy one hundredth birthday, Jack!" It would be the first of many such greetings that day. Then she said she had sent him a 3D e-mail. A *3DE* she called it. Last Christmas she had bought him one of those little box things. It came with some newfangled medical device that let him self-diagnose his blood pressure and heart rate and a host of other indicators that confirmed he was alive for yet another day. Once he got the all-clear, he would pop open the lid, hit *receive*, and see and hear his messages three-dimensionally. She told him to look for it. She said good-bye and apologized for not being there.

After getting dressed and combing his hair, he perched himself on the chair in front of the box. He checked his blood pressure – 160 over 90. Heart rate 74. He popped open the lid, pressed the button and *Happy Birthday to You* started up. Then there she was. Christine. All of her. A perfect likeness no more than a foot high. All dressed and ready for school to begin her classes. Living. Breathing. Talking.

"Good morning, Jack. Well what can I say? You're the first member of the Fisher family to reach one hundred and I'm so proud of you but I feel guilty for not being there but this week has been just impossible. It's not so much my students but those bureaucrats at the school board. You know what I mean. We've been there before, you and me, and you always say to keep fighting so that's what I'm doing. Fighting them tooth and nail. I told them about you ... it's not the first time ... and they don't care. Some of them don't even think it's true. Can you believe that? And this is a school

yet. Indifference remember? That's how people are. But I just can't accept it. I never will. Anyway I'm seeing my department head this morning and I'm going to give him a piece of my mind. Whatever piece is left. To tell you the truth I'm not doing too well with this condition of mine. I'm so dizzy every morning. Twenty-five and I feel like an old woman. It's really starting to wear me out and if not for you I'd probably feel sorry for myself but one thing you always taught me, Jack, is never to do that. When I look at you, well, that's why you're my inspiration but then you always have been. Because of you my life is one big mission and that's why I feel terrible about not being there today. I'm so sorry about that. I really wanted to make it. Still I can wish you a happy hundredth, can't I? Say hello to everyone for me. You have a great day!"

Jack smiled at the diminutive likeness of his great-granddaughter. She was so real that for a moment he forgot it was just an image – a three-dimensional image – and started speaking to her.

"Christine I ..."

But she wasn't finished. Not yet. Her hands clasped behind her back, she raised her head and made eye contact with him once more.

"By the way, you're going to get another message from me and you'll be amazed at what I found. I can't wait to tell you about it. Meanwhile, I have some unfinished business to attend to but I know you'll get along fine without me. You always have. Always remember that I love you dearly, Jack. Your little Christine."

Three

"That's the guy. Jack Fisher. He's a hundred years old and he's supposed to be the last one."

"You sure about that?"

"I have an aunt, I mean a great aunt, and she knows everyone in this place. That's what she said."

"How old is your aunt?"

"Great aunt."

"Okay. How old is she?"

"Eighty-two. She's one of the younger ones around here but still pretty spry. She wouldn't make it up."

"Maybe I should meet your aunt first. Great aunt I mean."

"We can do that."

The two NYU students, eighteen and nineteen years old, walked across the floor of the lobby of the Greenwich Village Seniors Center and headed for the reception area, a bit dumbfounded to be in a place like this. A stout, middle-aged woman was behind the desk.

"We're here to see Jack Fisher. Is he around?"

"Jack Fisher? Where would he be going? He's our next

member of the Hundred Club, you know. In fact, today is his birthday." With that, she motioned to the big column in the middle of the lobby. "It's all there." She had a hint of a drawl and skin as black as night.

"We saw it."

She nodded. "The cards and e-notes started coming real early for him. Over a month ago. The man has a lot of relatives. You family?"

They looked at each other. "Not exactly," one of them said.

"What are you then?"

The second one, whose great aunt was not a resident in the building, replied. "We're from NYU and I write for the *NYU Hotline*. It's a blog. We want to speak to him." He pulled out his mini. It was the latest model.

"I haven't seen one of those," she said.

"Pretty compact, isn't it?" He brought it close to her face and showed it to her. He rubbed his thumb on the little screen and it doubled in size. "You could write a thousand ezines on this thing. The chip will last forever."

"Isn't that something. So you want to see Jack Fisher?"

"Yes we do."

"And you're not family?"

"No."

"And why do you want to see him? Because he's a hundred?"

A hesitation. "Yes. Because he's a hundred years old. That's why."

"It's not so unusual. We get more of them all the time now. What's so special about Jack Fisher?"

A shrug and a nod to his friend. "Well his aunt ... his great aunt ... lives here and she said he's an interesting guy. Besides, I never interviewed someone who's a hundred years old before."

"He's a novelty then?"

"Maybe and I think he may have gone to NYU."

"He did? Jack?"

"Yeah. About eighty years ago." The one who was doing the talking laughed and his friend's face hinted it might not be true, but she didn't catch it and joined in the chuckle.

"Is he expecting you?" she asked, more seriously now.

"Yes." He lied again.

They waited as she called the room. "I'm afraid no one answers but Jack's hard of hearing. I guess that's what we all got to look forward to when we get to be a hundred. I'll call the nurse on his floor. Hold on a minute."

"Thank you."

Another wait. Longer this time.

"I'm afraid no one's there. Would you mind taking a seat?"

The two of them sat down and looked around the cavernous lobby where old people were milling about in all directions, some of them in mobilers – high-powered wheelchairs – while others had walkers, and those ones moved at their own speeds. All of them slow. Their bodies were at different angles, the more adept among them upright and walking with a steady gait, but those with a stoop to the back were methodical at best. A few were bent over at ninety degrees. It was bizarre watching them inch their way across the floor, pushing their walkers as if steering ploughs through dense brush or muck. A relentless, plodding army going nowhere in particular.

"You sure he's the last survivor?" said the one with the mini in his hand. He was already growing impatient.

"That's what she said. The last living survivor of the holocaust."

"What holocaust was that again?"

"The Jewish one. You know. With the six million dead."

"My uncle said it wasn't like that. That it's exaggerated."

"Some people say that."

"What if they're right?"

"She wouldn't lie about something like that."

"Who?"

"My great aunt. She says it happened just like they say."

"But how does she know? She wasn't alive then, was she? You say this guy Jack Fisher might be the last one ... the last survivor ... "

"The Jews say it happened."

The nineteen-year-old who wrote a blog for the *NYU Hotline* was playing with his mini, checking his 3DEs. "Of course they do. But ask people who aren't Jews and what do they say?"

"Like your uncle?"

"Yeah."

"But there's all kinds of stuff about it. Information I mean."

"Look, I can find information about a lot of things ... even things that never happened. Once I was supposed to write this bit about a leopard that escaped from the zoo. People said it was running through Central Park. There were even sightings! We checked it out and it never happened. There were never any leopards in the zoo but still there were sightings! People called the police. They said they saw it."

"So did they?"

"They think they did. Someone hears about it and the next thing you know you got witnesses. It's like things from outer space. You remember all those reports about aliens right after the Mars mission? I mean the first manned one? Remember that?"

His friend nodded with an agreeable sigh.

"Exactly. People see what they want to see and they believe what they want to believe." He passed his thumb over the surface of his mini as he talked, 3D images popping up by the second only to disappear a moment later.

"Those death camps were supposed to be real."

"I don't know if any of them are around anymore and just because they were doesn't mean that's what they were for. Killing people, I mean. They could've been used for anything."

"Like what?"

"A factory. There was a war going on, right? They had tanks in those days. Maybe they made tanks there. Or guns. It could have been anything. A munitions factory. That doesn't seem so far-fetched."

"Wait a minute. You're forgetting something. We're talking about *millions of people.*"

"Yeah but if you want to kill *millions of people* why round them up and stick them in camps? Why not put them in one place and drop a smart bomb on them? Boom! They're gone and it's all over." With that, he keyed in 'smart bomb' on his mini. "Here. Look. It tells you how to make a precision-guided missile with a laser sensor." He held up his mini and in the air was a 3D image of all the components for a smart bomb. "See? Like I say. Boom and it's over."

"You're forgetting they didn't have stuff like that in those days," said his friend, nodding to the mini. "Besides, it would take a lot of smart bombs to kill that many people."

"Not if you got them altogether in one spot."

"You mean a stadium or a place like that?"

"Maybe."

"You'd need a lot of stadiums."

"You would. But say you put a hundred thousand people in there. The next day you bring in another hundred thousand and the next day another hundred thousand. In ten days you kill a million people. It's possible. Do that six times and you have your six million."

"But the stadium would be gone too."

"Not if you use gas. All the people are dead but the stadium is ready for the next day."

"It would have to be enclosed."

"So enclose it."

"But you think moving a million people is so easy? You don't know how many people that is. It's a whole city. But maybe that's what they had those camps for. To organize them. Before they killed them, I mean."

"I don't know but let's talk to this guy and see what he says."

"Don't forget he *is* a hundred years old. Who knows what he can remember? And if his hearing's gone maybe his memory is too."

The woman at reception tossed them a wave and said she got through to the nurse's station on Jack Fisher's floor. That would be the sixth floor of the Greenwich Village Seniors Center. Fair to limited mobility. Mild to severe osteoarthritis. Early onset stages of dementia.

"Jack is resting in his room right now. At his age he's always resting. I guess he didn't hear the phone but like I say he's hard of hearing. He's a real sweetheart though. He always says hello and he always asks how I'm doing."

"So can we see him?"

"You're lucky. It's a good time for him right now because it's between breakfast and lunch. You see their day ... their whole life ... revolves around meals so here's what I'm going to do. I'm going to have Mary Lou Bennett ... she's our Director of Care ... take you up but you may have to wake him. He tends to fall asleep real easy. God I wish I could do that."

"No problem."

"Mary Lou will stay in the room with you a few minutes just to make sure he's comfortable. You don't mind, do you?"

"No. We don't have any secrets. We just want to see what NYU was like eighty years ago, that's all."

He smiled and she smiled right back. "Jack at NYU. That's a good one. I like that. Mary Lou will be right with you."

Four

Christine Fisher rushed through the hall of her school to the parking lot. She was in a frenzy. She was carrying a hardcover book – a dinosaur – and a bag with her portable e-book reader. There were hundreds of titles in it. She climbed into her car and threw everything into the seat beside her. She had charged the power cell that morning with just enough mileage for this trip. Christine was always frugal that way. Never one to waste. She got behind the wheel and waited for the onboard computer to recognize her.

'Hello Christine. Driving conditions are ideal today.'

The car started itself and she was off. She took Regional Road 22 out of town, crossed the Conestoga River and headed north through the rolling hills and farmers' fields, the silos and barns, the signs advertising fresh maple syrup and the lonely cows on either side of the road. The hills soon gave way to flat open land and she liked the fact she could get lost in the country in fifteen minutes flat. Up a bit more and the image of a deer appeared on the screen of her dashboard. The voice of her computer came on again.

'Be careful. It's not far off the roadway, about two kilometers up number 22.'

Sure enough, a moment later the deer appeared at the side of the road, but one glimpse of the car and it ran off, disappearing through the grasses. Christine watched and then there was that familiar sign – 'Christ died for the ungodly' – and further up the road another sign. It marked the boundary of the town of Salem, or as it more accurately noted, the Historic Hamlet of Salem. A few minutes longer and she pulled into the next town.

Elora.

It was a quiet community in the Southern Ontario countryside, an hour's drive west of Toronto. Christine had been here countless times and was familiar with the old stucco homes that sat beside the road not too far off, but then again they were, and for all she knew they could have belonged to the original settlers. They looked ancient enough.

She was twenty-five, a teacher at Williamsburg Senior Public School, part of the Upper Grand District School Board, and she was a very good teacher, too. At least, she wanted to be. If only they would let her. She often wore a sharp edge about her, but today it was a razor.

Christine loved the drive to Elora. It was an escape, a respite from the hustle of the busy work week at school, and she liked the people here. They were different, not in as much of a hurry, and she knew all about them. She had always been a voracious reader and more than anything it was history that intrigued her. People intrigued her. Where did they come from? What did they do? How did they handle their hardships? But for people in Wellington County, life was good. The area was teeming with families that went back one and even two centuries. Elora was typical.

It was full of stone buildings, shops and eateries with names resonating from the past. Antiques Arts Books. Shepherd's Pub. The Yarn Bird and Kids Boutique. In the center of town they all came one after the other in a streetscape that looked make-believe. The shops were connected in a long building that rose from the ground on a base of stone slabs and brick. There were creaky doors and window frames of weathered wood, and signs for businesses hanging from wrought-iron arms that swayed effortlessly in the breeze. The sidewalk in front of the shops was uneven with a gentle slope leading to the street, its stylish bricks sitting as pieces of a puzzle, the odd piece missing, and behind this ramshackle collection was the unmistakeable sound of rushing water from the Grand River.

Christine knew the corner of Metcalfe and Mill Streets well. Right across the road was the Elora Mews with more shops still. A kabob house called Jenny's Place. The Enduring Elegance Gift Boutique. The Karger Gallery with its fine pottery and artwork. All of them had been around for years. Beyond the shops was the Elora Mill Inn where the water was loud and the wind strong. She spotted an elegant swan riding the current to where the water began to drop and it looked as if it might go over the edge and down the waterfall, but at the last moment it turned around and swam back the other way. Like most everything in Elora, the five-storey inn – a veritable skyscraper in these parts – stood on a foundation of stone. One glance and anyone could tell it was old with long meandering vines climbing up the side all the way to the roof.

This was the site of the original mill dating from the nineteenth century. Christine knew all about it. In 1832 the founder of the town purchased fourteen thousand acres near the falls for two and a half dollars an acre. He wanted to build a mill, but died. Ten years later, when the village had two dozen families, a carpenter became the fledgling community's first miller and did his thing on two acres set aside for him. These two acres. When the U.S. Civil War broke out south of the border, Elora had a thriving population of twelve hundred people. It was all there in the historical record, and Christine knew as well as anyone that history mattered.

Further along where the water was even louder – its dull rush had mushroomed into a boisterous thrashing – stood the gates to the lookout. Here, amid the pungent smell of lavender and the mighty roar of rapids below, she could peer out onto the gorge. It was spectacular, but not as spectacular as further to the west where the Grand and Irvine Rivers met. If you had never seen it before, the site was something to behold.

Christine parked her car and grabbed the old hardcover book she had placed in the seat beside her. She walked into the old building where the mill once stood and headed downstairs to the dining room with the rushing water running just outside the window. She could hear it. The sign on the doorway with Rules of This Tavern bid a quaint hello to all who ventured in:

Four pence a night for Bed
   Six pence with Supper
   No more than five to sleep in one bed
   No Boots to be worn in bed
   Organ Grinders to sleep in the Work house
   No dogs allowed upstairs
   No Beer allowed in the Kitchen
   No Razor Grinders or Tinkers taken in.

It was called The Gorge Lounge and its stone walls, cosy fireplace and grand piano offered the ambiance of a country retreat. The waiter arrived and Christine ordered her favorite meal – organic green salad, a main course of tomatoes filled with chickpeas and spinach, all of it washed down with a glass of red wine. So delicious and sad. The wine tasted good and made her a bit queasy, and then she was finished, leaving not a thing, not a morsel, and it was almost as if no one had eaten off the plate at all.

She placed her tip on the table, left the building and walked two minutes up Mill Street before turning onto Metcalfe. One block north she turned again, passed a string of old homes and ventured into the park. She waded through the thick underbrush, dodging in and out among the long narrow trees, and headed for the gorge. A wire fence was at the pathway's edge, but it was easy to lean over and look onto the rocks below. There was a warning. UNSUPERVISED AREA – USE AT OWN RISK. Then she walked down the six slab steps to the end of the concrete where a low-lying, stone wall served as the barrier.

It was called Lover's Leap Lookout, but that was just a name. Still, Christine knew that people had jumped into the gorge. It was a serene place to end it with the trees, the sky and the water. She was all alone, accompanied only by her thoughts.

Her great-grandfather Jack was a hundred years old and he more than anyone inspired her to become a history teacher. He had so much history in him, a hundred years of it, and while much of it was good – the life he had built, the family he and his wife had raised, the grandchildren and great-grandchildren – there was that other part. The nightmare. That was how he once described it to her. The total nightmare of his childhood. But then it wasn't a childhood, was it? That had been stolen from him, cut off and snuffed out before it even began. When he first told her about it, she found it hard to believe. Who could believe such things? Who would *want* to believe such things? No one wanted to think things like that really happened. It was better, safer, easier to simply forget and pretend it wasn't so.

She had the book, the one she hated so much. She lifted it over her head as if passing sentence, and with smug satisfaction tossed it over the wall right into the gorge. The pages filtered through the air, slowing the speed of descent, and it seemed such a long time to drop a mere hundred feet or so. Such a long time to die. She watched the book strike the rocks and skip into the water before disappearing below the surface. She heard it, too. The fluttering of the windswept pages as the book fell. The harsh *thud* when its spine hit the rocks. The soft, but sharp *plop* when the river swallowed it whole. She stood there, looking into space, drawn to that familiar stone wall, and realized just then that the time had come.

A young girl was sitting on the ground behind the trees eating a sandwich. Off in the distance through the thick brush, she could see someone standing at the edge of Lover's Leap Lookout. She thought it was a woman. The girl saw her throw something into the gorge, but she didn't know what. Peering through the trees, through the slender rising columns of bark and panoply of leaves, the girl watched the solitary figure stand there for the longest time and then she saw her climb up onto the ledge. The girl put her sandwich down.

Standing on the narrow ledge, Christine steadied herself with her arms at her sides as if she were a bird. That's what she was. A bird. It wasn't easy, but then she knew it wouldn't be. She had always known that, ever since she was little. How odd that one's sense of balance is suddenly so precarious when you look down and it's such a long way to the bottom.

The girl watched as the solitary figure kept standing on that uncertain ledge. It was hard to see. And the girl stared in disbelief at what happened next.

For a few seconds, Christine's life hung suspended between two worlds. It was an in-between place. She would never know if it was a sudden rush of wind that came from behind or what, but it was just enough to lift her into that space where her arms became her pages. Her wings. Just like the book, they, too, fluttered in the air, and for one precious moment engulfed in absolute peace she found herself in a state of complete euphoria. It was perfect. Nothing but sheer freedom with only her body and the air to guide her. How wonderful. How strange. And just like that it was gone.

Five

The knee was made of titanium. It wasn't a new substance, but it was still the best. It had been a few weeks since the surgery and the thing felt stiff, but the doctors said it would be like that. The pain had been terrible the first few days, but has since subsided and now the biggest problem was getting used to the feel of a new joint. It didn't feel like the old one. The old knee was in bad shape, tired and worn out from holding up that big load all those years, and why it was the right knee and not the left no one ever knew. There was constant pain in that knee from the arthritis – severe arthritis they called it – and one thing they all agreed on was that it wouldn't get any better. A knee replacement was the only tangible option – the surgeon had stressed the word *tangible* – and besides, Jack Hodgson still had a lot of years left.

"How are we doing, Lieutenant?" the doctor said.

"Not bad. Considering I have a new leg."

"Not a new leg. Just a new knee. I don't do legs."

Hodgson squeezed his massive frame into the chair. It was a chair built for a normal human being, not a man who stood six-foot-five and weighed three hundred and thirty pounds.

At least, that was what he weighed before the surgery. Walking into the room, he dwarfed the doctor – he did that to people – and it wasn't so much his height but the bulk that he carried around with him. It was his ball on a chain. The load had become his prison.

"Eating well?" the doctor asked.

Hodgson nodded. "Back to normal."

"Then that's not good. The whole point was to eat better, exercise and get control of your weight. I believe our goal was two-seventy-five."

"Our goal?"

"You know what I mean. It was two-seventy-five, wasn't it?"

"Doc, I haven't weighed that since I was eighteen."

"Look Lieutenant, I gave you that chart. Have you been following it? With all the fruits and vegetables?"

"I eat fruits and vegetables."

"Yes but what else are you eating?"

Hodgson didn't say anything. The doctor smirked.

"Let's check your weight," he said.

"Not on that scanner. I don't like that thing. It takes half a second and tells you how much you weigh. It doesn't give you any time to prepare yourself."

"I have a scale if you like. It still works. Want to use that?"

Hodgson said he did. The doctor led him into the next room and said to take a seat. The old scale was on wheels, and apart from a little dust, in good working order. The doctor took a cloth and wiped it off before giving a nod to Hodgson who grudgingly got up from the chair. His right knee with the new titanium joint didn't take to the task with the dexterity of his left.

"I think I need a little oil in there," Hodgson said, climbing onto the scale with the two balance beams.

The doctor slid the first weight over to the far end of the scale, the three-hundred-pound marker. Then he started playing with the smaller, second weight. He kept nudging it across. Bit by bit.

"Let's see what we have here. Uh-huh. Three hundred and twenty-seven pounds. And you were what? Three-thirty before the operation? You have a knee replacement which is pretty invasive surgery and after all is said and done and you're starting to feel better we've lost a grand total of three pounds."

"We?" said Hodgson, staring at the two weights in front of him. "At least that's something."

"Lieutenant, you don't fool me. We both know you lost a good twenty pounds after the cut and now you're putting it back on. You're not following that chart, are you? What did you have for breakfast this morning?"

"I didn't have breakfast. Just coffee."

"One coffee?"

"Two."

"Sugar?"

Hodgson didn't say anything. He was still looking at the two weights.

"Lieutenant, a knee replacement is serious business. You put your life on hold. You put your job on hold and I'm sure you want to get back to being a cop, don't you?"

"That's for sure. The past few weeks I've been going crazy sitting around doing nothing but I'm pretty well healed now. Tomorrow is my first day back."

"Well that's good news but it's not so good if you don't follow the rules. And the first rule is to gain control of your weight or you're going to be right back in here with your other knee."

"My other knee is fine. It was always the right one that bothered me."

"Lieutenant, believe it or not they're both connected to the same body and your body is just too damn ..." He searched for the word. "Huge. It's too huge for your own good. That's what got you into all this trouble in the first place. Your weight."

He glared at the big man.

"Doctors call it morbid obesity but that's really a fancy way of saying you eat too much. Too much of the wrong food. And you don't get enough exercise. Not nearly enough. You're still a young man. You're only ..."

"Fifty-four."

"Fifty-four years old and you have a knee replacement. What's it going to be like when you're sixty-four? Or seventy-four? We'll have to do your whole body over with new joints and that won't be easy. Not for a man your size. Why I think that knee of yours was the biggest one I've ever done. What are you smiling about?"

"What you said. About doing my whole body over. I'd be a cop made of titanium. Think of the possibilities."

The doctor shook his head and told him to step off the scale. It was a good thing because Hodgson didn't want to keep looking at that number with the two threes and the zero staring him in the face, the smaller of the two weights a crack to the left of the 'thirty'. Three hundred and twenty-seven pounds. He dropped his great bulk into the chair.

"Lieutenant, you have weak quads. Those are the muscles in front of the thighs. You have to build those muscles up and you have to lose some weight. That's the only way you're going to avoid having another knee replacement."

"I hear you, Doc."

"But what are you doing about it? Hey it's your life. If you want to be back here in two years for your other knee I can always use the work. Are you still wearing those compression stockings?"

"No. I got rid of them after a few days. As soon as the pain started going away. Actually, the knee feels pretty good now. Just a little stiff. That's all."

"That's normal. It'll loosen up. What about the cane?"

"Gave that up too. After a couple weeks."

The doctor took out a light pen and scribbled on his mini before closing the file on Lieutenant Jack Hodgson of the NYPD.

"It's up to you, Lieutenant. Make some changes in your life and you won't be coming back here to see me again."

He stuck out his hand. Hodgson's thick fingers embraced it and the doctor's hand all but disappeared.

Six

The *NYU Hotline* was a daily blog for students. It had views on a wide range of issues, everything from the value of a college degree to how current economics impacted one's ability to pay for tuition. The price of tuition was always too high. There was a piece about how the presence of a Christmas tree in the Steinhardt School of Culture, Education and Human Development – a proud faculty whose beginnings went back to 1890 – impinged on the very human development that was supposed to take place within its hallowed walls. There was a profile on the new President-Elect of the United States and a short piece about an old man who claimed to be a survivor of the Jewish holocaust from the Second World War. Jack Fisher was a hundred years old, and the writer made it clear at the outset of his article that anyone of such advanced age could expect to suffer from memory lapses.

As he recalled these events of 95 years ago, I was immediately thrown into turmoil. Are his brain cells in crisp working order? Is his concept of time suspect? Should I just believe everything he says and not dispute any of his claims, as incredible as they may sound? Should we all accept that less than a century ago, not long in the human scheme of things, one of the most advanced societies on earth, Germany, selected all the Jews of Europe for extermination while the rest of the world just watched and did nothing? Even if you accept all that he says and trust the writings of those who agree, the figure he mentions of six million people dead ... murdered ... is beyond comprehension. It's more than 120 times the number of Christians killed in the Great Holocaust of 2029. One hundred and twenty times! The year 2029 is imprinted on my memory as the darkest chapter in human history and anyone with a conscience would agree. It would be a travesty for that to be expunged by stories, facts and figures about another event that still remains open to scholarly debate. Let us not forget that there are substantive arguments about this issue in terms of just how severe it was and when that is the case the truth is often somewhere between two extremes. Let us also not forget that the Great Holocaust of 2029 targeted Christians. No one else. It leaves the door open for non-Christians to forever dwell on what may have befallen them in earlier times for fear of being relegated to second tier in the annals of modern history.

The article was the alarm that triggered a heated reaction from NYU's student body, but only a small portion of that student body. The Jewish Law Students Association, representing a formidable group within the NYU School of Law, countered with its own piece citing sources and statistics to document the claims of one Jack Fisher. If that wasn't enough, the president of the Jewish Graduate Students Association challenged the writer of the original article to a debate about the *veracity* of the Jewish Holocaust. That was the word used – veracity – and just to make a point, the 'H' was capitalized. But there was nothing from anyone else. Not a word.

Seven

The summer of 2031 was Christine's last one before she would start university. She wanted to pursue a degree in English, but tuition was expensive, and while her parents would help pay her way she needed a job. Jack, her 91-year-old great grandfather of all people, gave her an idea.

"Why don't you work as a reporter?" he said. "You like to write. Here's a chance to get paid for it."

He always seemed old to her. The day she was born he was already seventy-five, and by the time she started to discern the meaning of age, he was well into his eighties. The very number seemed ancient. *Eighties.* Especially to a child. He was the oldest person she knew in the whole world and when he turned *ninety*, well, that was something else again.

"Old Jack will live forever," they used to say. His heart was good, his lungs were good, but even back in those days he never smoked. His blood pressure sometimes acted up, but was regulated with the latest beta blockers, and aside from his arthritis and that bad shoulder he always complained about, his health was pretty good. But then his wife Eve – Christine's great-grandmother – died and it was a shock. She went quickly. It was an aneurysm. They were married so long no one could picture Jack without her, but he surprised them, even those who were closest to him. His children. His grandchildren. His great-grandchildren. That Jack was one tough character.

"He's made of deep moral fibre," said Christine's Uncle Ernie, who was her father's younger brother and one of Jack's grandchildren himself. "He has seen a lot."

Christine would visit with him at family functions. Weddings. Anniversaries. Christmas. He was a slight man in stature, and Christine knew why he was short. His roots were Polish, and for some reason people from Eastern Europe just weren't as tall as those from the West. Weren't the Dutch the tallest people on earth and weren't the Scandinavians right behind them? But Poles? Forget it.

Christine's father Bill was Jack's grandson, and not that big either. Luckily, on Christine's mother's side there was some height, which no doubt accounted for Christine's size. Indeed, by the time she was thirteen she was taller than Jack, and it wasn't long before she outweighed him, too. But he was strong and surprisingly agile for a man his age. He got around without difficulty even after hitting ninety. For as long as Christine could remember, he could lift her up, perch her body on his hip, and tickle her behind the ears. And she always called him by his first name.

Jack.

"Why don't you work as a reporter? You like to write. Here's a chance to get paid for it."

It sounded like a good idea.

The biggest news journal in Wellington County was the *Kitchener-Waterloo Record* with more than 150,000 e-readers daily. But Christine never got further than the human resources department, so she set her sights a little lower and talked her way into a job with a local community newspaper. *The*

Reflector. It still had a newsprint edition, the only one left in Wellington County.

"We don't have an office manager right now so that position is open. You'd handle reader correspondence and keep the place clean. Make everyone happy. And if you can string a few words together you could do some features."

The hard copy version of *The Reflector* was distributed to a few hundred rural subscribers, who lived outside the perimeter of Kitchener-Waterloo, two small cities in Southern Ontario that had grown on either side of the same street and were forever destined to share a hyphen. The readers were largely Old Order Mennonites, most of them farmers and owners of small businesses, and the modern world had passed them by. They still wanted their newspaper. They and many others in the area had deep roots in these parts.

There were four types of features that Christine would write for *The Reflector*. The Events Calendar was straightforward. People sent in news about their coming bake sale or fundraiser, and it went into the calendar.

'Antique auction sale at 40 South St., Elmira. Antiques and collectibles include small pine storage cupboard 175 years old, and a stove, a high-quality teak sideboard, and three good teak lamps.'

The Personals column wasn't much of an exercise in writing either, but it was a good way to learn about people. Readers filled out a form and added a few words, which often had to be rewritten. The Personals came in different categories: Projects and Causes, Personal Development, Travel Plans, Miscellaneous, and the best one of all – Friends and Companions.

'Beautiful, well-educated woman, mid 30s, tall and slim, with oodles of energy and a curious approach to life, searching for a gentleman to share long-term relationship.'

Then there was the Genealogy column, which allowed readers to explore their family trees. Christine liked doing that because she could delve into the old shipping lists. Records still existed from a steamboat passenger line. The steamers picked up travellers, who had come across the Atlantic, and took them to Quebec City and Montreal where they would stay, go south to the United States or continue west to what was then called Upper Canada. Most of them were immigrants making a new life. What with the winds and tides along the St. Lawrence River, the passage from Quebec City to Montreal could take thirty hours. It was all there in the ship's list.

One steamer, the *Malsham*, arrived in Quebec City on July 3, 1819. According to the passenger records, the prime occupant of the stateroom on that trip was the Earl of Dalhousie, who had come from Halifax aboard *H.M.S. Mersey* on June 30 with his wife Lady Dalhousie. She had her own suite because all the other stateroom dwellers were men. There was Lord Ramsay, Mr. Temple, Lord S. Kier, Major Cooper, Captain Collier who was the captain of *H.M.S. Mersey*, Mr. Hays, Mr. Woodford and Lieut. Torrians. There were one hundred and nine people on that steamship, and the surname of every one of them was recorded in the ship's list. Christine's job was to check those names against families still living in Wellington County and then contact these people. Every week she would focus on a different family.

It was a revelation to find that Veronica Hays, who worked at the university, was a descendant of that same Mr. Hays or that Pete Collier, chef at one of the Salem diners, could trace his lineage back to Captain Collier of *H.M.S. Mersey*. There were many old steamers and lots of lists, so Christine was never wanting for material.

But the best part about the job was writing obituaries, and Christine's instructions were clear. Make sure the name of the deceased was spelled correctly, mention what kind of work they did, and include whom they left behind. That was it. It was an impersonal way to report on one's passing, but space was limited. Then she came across an old British writer, Hugh Massingberd, who by the time his own obituary appeared in 2007 was best known as obituaries editor for *The Daily Telegraph* of London. Massingberd had made a lasting impression. In fact, he made the obit an art form. He single-handedly changed how the obit was written, hastening its evolution from a dry, paint-by-numbers summary to a personal, often witty essay on what made the deceased unique. In short, he made the person human, and because readers flocked to what he did, he was given more space. Christine wanted to write obits like that, too.

But there was a process and like the Personals it started with a form. Along with the photo was the name of the deceased, their age, dates of birth and death, where they died, occupation, names of any predeceased, and survivors. If the person was old and had left their mark, the number of survivors could go on forever. But the whole thing was flat and without substance, every obit pretty much the same, and it left Christine hungry for more. She wanted to know how the person died, whom they influenced, where they traveled, what kind of contribution they made to the world, or whether they were known for a certain trait or turn of a phrase. Something, anything, to identify them as an individual. So she asked about expanding the obit and they said no. Space was limited. Then came the tragic death of a two-year-old boy, the son of a couple who ran the bakery in Salem.

It broke her heart.

What arrived was a 3D email relating how little Brian Shepherd died of leukemia after a long hospital stay. In the 3DE, Christine could see the pain and sorrow oozing from the face of the boy's mother. She had provided the form with all the blanks filled in – name of deceased, the tender age of two, and the list of family members left behind. There was a photo – a head shot with big brown eyes and cherubic cheeks.

Christine called the family to see if there was anything about him they might like to include and indeed there was. Brian loved animals. They said when he was in hospital they would take him outside where he chased the squirrels, listened to the sparrows, and was mesmerized watching the geese. The family also had a dog, a Dalmatian named Spotty, and 'Spot' or rather 'Pot' was the first word Brian ever said. What's more, ever since his passing, the bewildered dog had been going around the house sniffing for him and coming up empty. The Shepherd family was more than happy to talk about their son – it was a way of healing – and they spoke to Christine for a long time. She decided to go for broke.

On October 24th, 2029, Brian Shepherd was welcomed into the family of Richard and Anne Shepherd, long-time proprietors of Shepherd's Village Bakery in Salem. He was born on a beautiful day when the autumn leaves were full and he was the best friend of the family's Dalmation Spotty. In fact, Brian's first word was when he called the dog 'Pot.'

Brian was a happy child, but at sixteen months he was diagnosed with leukemia and for the next nine months he spent most of his time in hospital. He never complained, preferring to treat the hospital stay as an adventure where he met interesting people and fascinating creatures, which were plentiful in the luscious gardens of the hospital grounds.

Brian's favourite time was going for walks with his family and Spotty. He scampered after the squirrels, always stopping at the foot of whatever tree they climbed, staring at them dumbfounded. He liked sharing his snacks with the sparrows and learned that breadcrumbs would bring them around in an instant. While he never got close enough to the geese, the arrival of a new friend on his second birthday, a toy figure named Mr. Goose, made him content. That same Mr. Goose rests with him today.

Brian's last visit at home was a traumatic day for Spotty, who knew something was amiss. No sooner was Brian out the door that the dog stuck his nose into every corner of the house, relishing the scent that would no longer be. Brian died in his sleep on November 6th, 2031 with his family around him. They don't know what he might have become or the wonderful things he would have done, but in his brief life he brought love and joy to everyone he knew. The squirrels, sparrows and geese, and a special dog named Pot, have all lost a friend.

At a tad over three hundred words, that wasn't the standard obit. It was an article. But Christine controlled what got into the obit section and what didn't, and since that was the only entry this time it stayed. It immediately prompted a letter suggesting that the practice continue. Then came another letter and yet another. Three letters from readers about the same thing was enough for the editor to take notice, and soon more space was made available for Christine's obituaries.

"We're going to expand the Obit section. Do one in every issue. Keep it the same length."

Deaths of young people always aroused the greatest sorrow. One of them was an infant who hadn't yet spoken her first word, so Christine made that part of the story. She wanted to make that little baby human. Soon her obituaries became a popular staple in *The Reflector.*

"I loved your piece on Jeannie Bremmer. I knew her. She was a lovely lady. You summed her up perfectly."

"I know the family of Andrew Blinkney who was killed in the Turkish uprising. A fine young man. What a horrible loss. But you captured how everyone feels."

Andrew Blinkney was an army platoon commander. A local boy from the town of Fergus, he was part of the international peacekeeping team in the troubled Malatya province of southeast Turkey. Tensions against minority Christians in that part of the country, which sat on the Syrian border, had been bubbling over ever since the 2029 attacks grew into full-scale hostilities. What set things off in the first place were Muslims converting to Christianity.

This was a military death and that made it different from the others, but the family still wanted to talk. They always wanted to talk. Christine learned that the soldier's death occurred a mere two weeks before he was to come home. He left behind a little daughter.

Andrew Blinkney's death in Malatya, where he was serving with the 2ⁿᵈ Battalion of Prince Patricia's Canadian Light Infantry, came two short weeks before he was to return home from his final tour of duty. Eagerly waiting for his safe return were his wife Joan and daughter Felicia, who is three.

Andrew was the son of Sean and Andrea Blinkney, long-time residents of Fergus. Sean has coached minor hockey and baseball for fifteen years and coached all his boys. The Blinkneys, who have been a fixture at the local arena since their sons first put on skates, have deep roots in the military.

Andrew's grandfather William Blinkney served in Afghanistan after the turn of the century and while his father Sean never served overseas he did help develop a fitness training program for new recruits at an old military base out west.

Andrew was a fierce competitor as an athlete and a soldier. Early in his second tour of duty, he once saved the life of Private Mike Rickey who was wounded by sniper fire. Directed by the chief surgeon over his radio, Andrew managed to stop the bleeding after applying a tourniquet to Pte. Rickey's leg. He also helped treat other casualties.

Known by the nickname 'Muckraker' because he liked to get down and dirty, he was a loving father to his little girl Felicia, despite being away for much of her life. This newspaper ran a photo of Andrew holding Felicia before his most recent departure a year ago.

A yellow ribbon has been tied around the tree in front of the Blinkney home in Fergus. Andrew's mother Andrea said her son always wanted to be a soldier. While his life ended in sacrifice, he brought honour and a great sense of pride to the community. The town of Fergus and people of Wellington County will miss him.

The accompanying photo of a handsome, square-jawed man in uniform was serious, but not stern. After penning the obit, Christine hoped the Blinkney family would like what she wrote and, hopefully, so would the spirit of Hugh Massingberd. But still, it was the little girl Felicia who tore at her heartstrings. A little girl now without a father. Through no fault of her own. Christine thought a lot about that, and kept asking herself why such things happen.

Eight

Christine's first inkling about Jack's early life came at the train station. Her sister Tiffany was getting married, the wedding was taking place in Kitchener, and Jack the family patriarch would be there. But his blood pressure was acting up and his doctor thought it best that he not fly. Of course, the trains were almost as fast. The sleek electric rockets roared along the rails at 300 kilometers an hour and did the New York-Toronto route in two and a half hours flat, and then it was another half hour to Kitchener, so the time difference was minimal. Jack arrived with his son Ralph, and Ralph's wife and kids, who were all grown up. Ralph was sixty-eight, and like his father lived in New York. This was Jack's first trip out of the city since Eve's death, and a group of family members were at the station to meet him.

"He's not feeling well," Ralph said as they got off the train. "It was a long ride for him."

Jack never came out and said as much, but Christine was his favorite. He knew it and so did she. She hadn't seen him since her great-grandmother's funeral. She watched him step off the train onto the platform. There were hugs and kisses, and the little ones with their shy greetings of 'Great Grandpa Jack,' and then it was Christine's turn.

"Christine," he said. "My little Christine." He had always called her that. My little Christine.

"How are you, Jack?"

He looked wearier than the last time, but was the same old Jack with the soft, gentle exterior masking that inner tenacity. His ashen hair neatly parted, he was very much the gentleman.

"I made it," he said.

It was a gray, dreary day with the rain coming and going in spurts, leaving a trail of puddles on the ground and black clouds overhead. Jack didn't like canes to help him with walking, but he had one this time. He was slogging along the walk at the train station with Ralph on his arm, using the cane for support, and Christine could see the fatigue draped over his frail body. There was a loud rumble and the ground began to shake as the train on the next track started pulling away. It slowed and screeched to a halt, then pulled away again, and something happened. Jack stopped, he lifted his head, his face went white, and his hands began to shiver. His eyes straight ahead, full and still, he didn't seem to be breathing. Christine had never seen him like that before; he looked like a feeble old man. Her mother Emma, who was a nurse and always let everyone know it, cried out, "I think he's having a heart attack!" But Ralph knew better.

"Jack has the heart of an ox," he said of his father. "He's just tired. It was a long ride. And seeing everyone like this. It's a lot for him."

Ralph put his arm around him and led him to the men's room inside the terminal. Ten minutes later they were back, and Jack looked fine. Everyone was waiting for him. Jack scanned the group, spotted Emma and walked over to her. He peered right into her eye.

"I have the heart of an ox," he insisted and thumped himself on the chest.

Except for Emma, everyone figured it was just as Ralph had said. The excitement of seeing the family again. The long train ride from New York. His first family function without Eve at his side.

"He'll be all right," Ralph said.

That evening after dinner the whole family gathered at Christine's. There was her father Will, her mother Emma, her sister the bride Tiffany, and Tiffany's husband-to-be. The groom's family was there, too, along with Christine's grandfather Bill, who at seventy was Jack's older son. Bill and his crew were locals who lived in Kitchener. Jack was sitting in the den, drinking a glass of soda, leaning on his cane.

"It was a good dinner, wasn't it?" said Christine.

Jack patted his stomach. "I'm going to burst," he said.

She got beside him on the couch. "Are you excited? About tomorrow I mean? Tiffany getting married? I can hardly believe it. My sister."

He nodded his head. "It is hard to believe."

Christine nudged closer, making herself comfy. "Jack, what happened at the train today?"

He put down his glass of soda.

"What was it?" she said.

He lowered his eyes and stared into his lap.

"Jack? Can you hear me?"

Everyone kept saying how his hearing was going. Christine hadn't noticed, but then she didn't see him every day.

"Jack can you ..."

"It was an ugly day," he said. "Overcast. Rain. The air was damp and cold."

"So that was it? The weather?"

"Maybe. No. Not really."

"What was it then?"

"The noise the train made. The sound."

"What about the sound?"

"It's been a long time since I was on a train. But it made me think of the first time. I was just a little boy. Four years old."

"You were on a train when you were four years old?"

He nodded. She smiled.

"What year was that?" she said.

"It would have been around 1944. Thereabouts."

"I bet it was a lot slower in those days."

"It was the sound."

"What about the sound?"

He lifted his head. "How old are you now, Christine?"

"Fifteen."

"My little Christine. Fifteen."

"It rhymes."

"What rhymes?"

"My little Christine. Fifteen. You made a poem, Jack."

He smiled. "It was the sound," he said again.

Christine knew precious little about her great-grandfather. She knew he was born in Poland and came to Kitchener as a boy. He grew up, got married and raised two sons – her grandfather Bill and her great uncle Ralph. Jack was good with his hands, and in his younger days he was a tailor. Then came an opportunity in New York City. A shop with all kinds of sewing machines was going out of business, so he bought it. Everyone always said he knew a lot about sewing machines. There already was family in New York and, as time passed, plenty of Fishers would be on both sides of the border.

"What about the sound, Jack?"

"It reminded me of ..."

She waited. "What?" she said.

"Auschwitz."

It was only a whisper. He raised his head as if to say more, but no words came. Christine could see something was bothering him. She wrapped her hands around his and gave them a squeeze.

"You want to tell me about it?" she said.

He shook his head up and down. "Like I said it was 1944. I was four years old. I was with my mother and my father and they took us by train to this place. *Auschwitz*. I didn't know what it was."

"It was in Germany?"

"No. Poland."

"You were born in Poland, weren't you?"

"Yes."

"Where exactly?"

"Lodz."

"Where is that?"

"It's a city in the middle of the country. But when I was born it wasn't called *Lodz*."

"What was it called?"

"Litzmannstadt."

He didn't say it the way an English-speaking person would say it. He said it as if he was German. It was strange hearing him talk like that.

"That's German, isn't it?" she said.

"Yes."

"Why was it called a different name?"

"Because the Germans occupied the city and changed the name. They occupied the whole country. All of Poland."

"Why did they take you there?"

"Where?"

"To that place. What did you call it?"

"Auschwitz."

Another whisper.

"Why did they take you there?"

He sipped his soda water, put it down and looked at her. "Because ..."

"Because what?"

"Because we were Jews."

Christine was dumbfounded. "Jews? What do you mean?"

"I never told you about this."

"You were Jewish?"

"At one time."

"How could you be Jewish? You're Catholic. We're all Catholics."

"I was a Jew first."

She was bewildered and he could tell how bewildered she was.

"I don't understand," she said.

"Christine."

"You were Jewish?"

"Yes. At first."

She looked confused. She opened her mouth and just stared at him. He looked her in the eye and didn't say anything.

"But if you were Jewish why didn't you ever tell us? How could you hide something like that? Were you ashamed of it?"

"Ashamed? No. I wasn't ashamed. But I didn't want to remember. I wanted to forget. You see ..."

She was listening.

He looked up to the ceiling, searching for something, and then shook his head from side to side. "You have to understand. Those were the worst memories of my life and they happened before I was five years old. In the ghetto and then *Auschwitz*. It was a horrible place. The most horrible place on earth. And the train today brought it back but it wasn't just the train. It was the sky ... the clouds ... the rain ... the muck."

"What are you talking about?"

"There was so much muck."

She felt his hands. They were cold. Like ice.

"Jack, you're here with all of us now," she said. "Your family is all around you. Tiffany is getting married tomorrow. Just think. You have a great-granddaughter who's getting married." Her thoughts turned to her great-grandmother. "I know it's hard without Eve but ..."

"I survived. I survived the ghetto and I even survived the camp. But I shouldn't have. I had no right. My parents didn't. No one in my family did."

She was hanging onto his every word.

"Your grandfather Bill, he knows and so does Ralph. They both know. But we never spoke about this to the grandchildren. It was a new life here. We didn't want to bother them."

"You didn't want to bother them?"

"Well ..."

"You're telling me you were born a Jew. My great-grandfather. That there is Jewish blood in my family. In me! I think that's important Jack and I want to know about it. Whatever happened to you when you were a boy, that's part of me too. Isn't it?"

"Christine, my little Christine. You've always been special to me. Ever since you were a little girl. There was something about you but ..."

"But what?"

He heaved a deep sigh. "One thing I will never be able to understand is how people can treat other people the way they do just because they're different. How people can kill other people just because they're different. It makes no sense."

"I know what you mean. Just a few months ago in Turkey. The Great Holocaust. More than fifty thousand people killed by Muslims just because they were Christians."

"The Great Holocaust. Yes that was a terrible thing. Terrible. But sometimes the Nazis killed fifty thousand Jews in a day."

She looked at him, mesmerized by what he just said.

"It was hot inside that train. I was four years old and I still remember how hot it was. Everyone was filthy and sweating. We were in boxcars. I don't know how many people were in the car. Maybe a hundred. That's what they said. We were like cattle. Worse than cattle. You couldn't see outside. I was little so I couldn't reach the window but nobody could see anything because the windows had barbed wire over them. There were so many people there was no room to move. And the smell. It was terrible."

"What kind of smell?"

"There was no place to relieve yourself."

"What do you mean?"

"There was no place to go. They gave you a bucket ... one bucket ... for a hundred people. It got full ... and you still had to go."

"You mean ..."

"I remember telling my mother I didn't want to do it but what could you do? And it wasn't just the children but the adults and the old people. There was a lot of old people."

Christine had her mouth open again.

"When we got to *Auschwitz* German guards were watching us with their rifles. They all had rifles. Every one of them. We got out of the train and one old man ... I can see his face even now ... he had to pee because he was holding it in on the train and he couldn't hold it in anymore. They pulled down his pants and made him go right in front of everyone. They liked humiliating people but that wasn't the worst part."

"What was the worst part?"

"People died on that train. There were dead people on it. Corpses. They were there with the rest of us. I remember dogs barking and the orders. *'Heraus! Heraus!'* It was crazy. And there were these people in striped clothes. If you didn't get off the train right away they just threw you off. Even if you were an old woman. It didn't matter. Nothing mattered to them."

Christine found it strange hearing him speak these words from another language and, as before, it was perfect. This perfect German coming from the lips of her great-grandfather.

"You said something about a ghetto?" she said.

"Yes."

"What was it?"

"What do you mean what was it?"

"What was it? The ghetto."

"What was it? It was where we lived and they kept you like a prisoner. All the Jews were kept in a small section of the city."

"What city was that again?"

"*Lodz.*"

"Ladhz?"

"No not like that. *Lawdge.*"

"Loj."

"That's better. You almost sound Polish now."

"Is that what you were? Polish?"

"What do you mean?"

"I mean your identity. You were a Jew but you were also Polish."

"A Jew was a Jew."

"But you were born in Poland. That makes you Polish, doesn't it?"

"You don't understand. The Poles were Poles and the Jews were Jews. They were different. Look, my name was Jacob. You would pronounce it like that. Jacob. But in Jewish or Yiddish it was *Ya-koov.* That's what my parents called me. *Ya-koov.* But when I was on the Aryan side ... the Polish side ... I had to change my name to the Polish *Jacub.* It was different."

"Your name was Jacob? Not Jack?"

"That's right."

"I don't understand what you're talking about."

"Look, when I was a boy I spoke Polish and a little Yiddish but I also spoke German because you had to speak German. The Germans controlled everything and you weren't allowed to speak anything else. But we were still Jews."

"So that was your identity? A Jew?"

He laughed, but then was it really a laugh? She couldn't tell.

"Let me explain something to you, Christine. When they make you wear a Star of David, when they don't let you stay out after a certain hour, when they take away your business and your job and they don't let you ride the bus and they let you eat only so many calories a day ... and it's all because you're a Jew ... what else are you?"

"You remember all those things?"

"Of course. Everyone had to wear the star. It marked you as a Jew and you could never leave the ghetto. It was our prison and it was small."

"How small?"

"A few blocks in the old part of the city. You had maybe a hundred thousand people ... maybe more ... living in just a few streets."

"What do you remember about it?"

"What do I remember? Nothing and everything. You have to understand I was a little boy ... three ... four years old. Memories are sketchy when you're that small but powerful things they stay with you."

"Like what?"

"I remember it was always crowded. There was no space. I remember people being sick and dying from disease. All the time. I remember never having enough food to eat. We were always hungry. And there were broken windows everywhere. Another thing sticks out too."

"What's that?"

"Everyone seemed angry."

"You were angry?"

"I was too little to be angry. I didn't know anything else. But I remember the police ... the Polish police ... they were always angry. The Gestapo were always angry. I think it was in their DNA. Even the Jewish police were angry."

"There were Jewish police?"

"The only man I don't remember being angry was my father. I think he was too tired to be angry. You see, he had a business ... he was a tailor ... and they took it away from him. He had his own home and then he had to leave it. He had food and then there wasn't much food. When I think about it now ..."

"What?"

"Maybe that's why he was so tired. There was no fight left in him. How can you fight when they take everything away from you?"

"What else do you remember?"

"I remember all the Jews had to wear the star over their chest. It was a big star and it marked you as different. And the German police ... the Gestapo ... the soldiers ... they were different too because they all had uniforms and they had the *swastika* on their arm. Right here." Jack touched his arm just above the elbow. "It was big. To me it looked like a spider and I remember thinking it was a strong spider. Jews with the stars were weak and Germans with the spiders were strong. Even a little boy can see those things." He stopped talking, but his mind kept racing.

"Go on," Christine said.

"There was a lot of sickness and anger and death. All the time. Every day. A lot of death. It was everywhere." He looked out into space. Staring at nothing. "I grew up with death. Death was part of my life. It's always been part of my life."

He took a deep breath.

"Well, those are the earliest things I can remember. It meant you had to think for yourself and do things for yourself or you wouldn't survive. I was just a boy but I was very independent. Quick on my feet. Enterprising. I had to be. I would steal things. For my family."

"Steal things? Like what?"

"Anything I could get my hands on. Food mostly."

Christine put her arm around his shoulder and took his hand. "I'm glad you're telling me this, Jack. I never want you to keep secrets from me again. Never. I'm your great-granddaughter, remember? Your little Christine. Who's now fifteen."

He gave her a smile.

"What is it?" she said.

"You just made a poem."

Nine

The Lodz Ghetto, 1944

A pile of newspapers was in the middle of the lane behind the two-storey building on Bazarowa Street, and something was underneath it. There was a bulge. The little boy brushed away the newspapers on top and saw a button and what looked like an overcoat. A *kaftan*? He threw off more papers and found a man sleeping with his eyes open. The boy poked him once, twice. Nothing. He wondered what to do, but it didn't take him long to decide. It was a cold day and the building had no heat. He quickly undid all the buttons.

The man was more than twice his size and rolling him onto the side was difficult, but with some twisting and tugging the boy got an arm out. Then he pushed with all his strength to roll him onto the other side and got the second arm out, but even then he couldn't remove the coat. With both his hands on the man's back, he pushed and pushed until the man rolled onto his front. Finally, the coat came free.

After covering him up with the newspapers, the boy put on the coat. It was old and heavy and much too long, but when he fastened the buttons it kept his back and shoulders warm. It was the first thing Jacob Klukowsky ever took that didn't belong to him. He stole a glance at the sky and felt the soft breeze touch his face before sneaking back into the flat. When he got there his mother took one look at him and asked about the coat. He told her a man covered in newspapers was sleeping in the lane and didn't seem to mind.

"*Mashugga!*" she cried and went into a frenzy.

Jacob knew he shouldn't be going outside, but he only wanted to taste the air. She told him again what would happen if they saw him. She said they would whisk him off to the hospital and take his blood for their soldiers at the front until there was none left. That was what the Germans did with Jewish children, she said. It was the same for his cousins Zivia and Romek. They were the children of his Aunt Gerda, his mother's sister, and lived in another room down the hall. Like Jacob, they were hidden children. Zivia was ten and Romek was seven. Jacob at four and a half was the youngest. Gerda's husband Israel had died from TB – a disease, one of many in the ghetto – but Jacob had no memories of him. The only thing he ever knew about Uncle Israel was that he was dead. He had always been dead.

Jacob slept inside an old armoire with the drawer open at night, but the air was stale. That was why he went out. His mother wouldn't say another word to him until his father Samuel came home. He, too, had seen the man in the laneway.

"Bela," he said to his wife. He looked up and told her that Shmuel Zelinsky was dead.

"*A mentsh on glik is a toyter mensh,*" she said.

An unlucky person is a dead person.

She said there was nothing anyone could do and they will come for him. Later, Jacob watched through the window as two men picked up the body and flung it onto an open wagon that was full of others just like him. They came twice a day like that. He asked his father if all those people were sleeping.

"They are sleeping," Samuel said.

"They aren't sleeping," Bela replied. "They're dead. All of them are dead."

Jacob couldn't remember the last time his parents smiled. His mother was pregnant and when they found out about it there were no smiles then either. The three of them shared a room of two square meters in the basement of a run-down, tenement building on Bazarowa Street in the old section of Lodz, the ghetto, but it wasn't Bazarowa Street anymore. Now it had a German name. *Basargasse*.

"Jacob, if you ever go outside again and the Gestapo don't catch you ..."

His mother glared at him, her eyes hostile and still. He was her only child. She told him again that he can never be seen or the Germans will snatch him. She said they would take his blood and throw what's left to the dogs. Jacob had seen the dogs and they were big. It had been like this for two years, ever since the *Kinderaktion*, the roundup of all Jewish children under the age of ten.

"Did you shake out that coat?" she asked before grabbing it and going out the door where she beat it with a broom. She did this for a long time and when she came back she was out of breath, but she had to get rid of the lice.

That night he overheard his parents talking about there not being enough food. The Germans had just reduced their rations again. They talked about the baby that was coming and how they would feed it. Jacob knew that Josef Karasik, who was twelve and not hidden, helped his family by sneaking into the Aryan section to smuggle food. Jacob was always told that smuggling and stealing were bad, but if Shmuel Zelinsky was dead and got carted away on the wagon, then he had no more need for that coat, so that wasn't really stealing. Besides, Josef once said that taking food from the rich *machers* who lived outside the ghetto was the right thing to do. He said what he took wasn't much anyway. Just *bobkes*.

The next day Josef came to their flat and Jacob told him he wanted to go with him into the Aryan section. Josef knew that Jacob with his blue eyes could pass for an Aryan boy. Then Josef emptied his pockets and showed his cigarettes. Jacob asked him if he smoked and he said no. He explained how he went about his business. Josef said he took some of his mother's forks and spoons – she had plenty of them – and sold them on the street for cheap cigarettes. He said he had lots of cigarettes. Then he would sneak into the Aryan section and sell the cigarettes to farmers, who were busy manning their stalls in the market. They all smoked, but could never leave their stalls.

"You sell a hundred cigarettes and make enough money to buy a loaf of bread," Josef said. "You could get through the wall. You're small." He called him a *pisher*.

Jacob was short and slight, the ghetto was the only thing he had ever known, and food was something there was never enough of. There was never enough of anything his family wanted. Never enough food, never enough water, and never enough clothes, especially in winter when the air was so cold it crawled down your back and legs before turning your blood to ice. He didn't know what was worse – taking a crap in the outhouse in summer when the smell was so bad that it parked in your nostrils or taking one in winter when you just froze to death.

"I'm hungry," Jacob said to his parents. It was his first thought in the morning and his last thought at night. Every day was the same.

Josef was right about the wall and the hole. Jacob climbed through it easily, and when the Polish police and German guards filled it in, the boys just made another one by chipping away at the bricks with the knives and forks they got from Josef's mother. Or they went over the top of the wall by scaling the brick, but had to be careful because of the crushed glass that was ground into the cement along the top, so they laid out rags to protect their hands and knees. Then they would jump down to ply their trade. They were good at it. The stores were closed on the Aryan side on Sunday and Saturday was the Sabbath, so they couldn't work then, but all other days were fair game. The first day that they went out they came back with bread and sauerkraut wrapped in pillow cases. Jacob's mother was furious.

"*Got in himmel!*" she cried in despair.

But Jacob told her that he looked like an Aryan boy and spoke good Polish. No one on the other side knew he was Jewish. His parents talked long into the night, but his mother was dead set against his sneaking across the wall. If he was taken for a Jew, even once, they would never see him again, she said. His father didn't say much, but his eyes told Jacob that the family couldn't exist on the meager rations they got from the Germans, so the boys went out again and again, and with each venture they grew more confident.

"Why bother with cigarettes and smuggling food when we can just steal?" Josef said.

The next time they went to the farmers' market, they didn't bring cigarettes. Jacob did as he was told. He leaned against a cart that was filled with apples until the legs of the cart gave way and the apples flew everywhere. In the commotion that followed, the men working the stalls helped him to his feet, but they weren't ready for a second boy. Josef. He stuffed the apples into his pockets – and down his pants and down his shirt – and ran off. Later, the boys did the same thing at another stall, only this time it was pears. When they got back to the ghetto, they had two pillow cases filled with fruit under their arms. It was more fruit than their families had seen in a long time.

One day things didn't go as planned. The boys were at another market, further from the wall than they had ever been before. After they played out their routine, one of the stall keepers wrung his arm around Josef's neck so he couldn't get away. Jacob did, but not Josef. Jacob didn't see his friend until the next day and his face was covered in bruises. The farmer had turned him over to a Polish policeman, who beat him with his rubber truncheon. All the Polish police carried these things. Jacob decided then that he could work better alone.

He knew he didn't look Jewish. His features were fine and narrow like his father's, and his eyes were blue like his mother's, so he could pass for an Aryan. With his command of Polish, those on the other side would think he was a Polish boy. A gentile.

In the weeks and months that followed, Jacob learned more about stealing and even more about people. Guards could always be bribed as long as you had something they wanted. Money. Cigarettes. Give them that and they would look the other way. It was the same with his father, who looked the other way when Jacob came back with his day's catch. What people thought or believed was readily sacrificed for need. Need was paramount and the biggest need was putting food in your mouth.

Jacob's father was a man who dressed well when he went out, even in the ghetto. He always wore a good pair of pants and a well-fitted jacket. He didn't have many clothes, but what he did have he kept clean and pressed. He used to be a tailor until he wasn't allowed to be a tailor anymore. When they first rounded up all the Jews and confined them to Baluty and the Old Town of Lodz, an area of four square kilometers, Samuel had been a relatively prosperous man. He was a skilled tailor and knew how to fix sewing machines.

The Jews always wanted a *Singer* sewing machine, while the Germans preferred a German brand. *Pfaff.* After the ghetto was formed, sewing machines became scarce, so Samuel got an idea. No matter what brand came in to him, he made sure that what went out was a *Singer.* Except for the label, people couldn't tell the difference. None of them could. So if he got his hands on a *Pfaff* sewing machine, he would remove the word *Pfaff* from the label and replace it with *Singer*, but if a German wanted a sewing machine and some did in the early days of the ghetto, Samuel made sure they got a *Pfaff*. It was all explained to Jacob one day when he saw his father scratching away at the label of the latest sewing machine that just came in for repair. The story brought a smile to Jacob's lips and he was sworn to secrecy. His father said it was all about getting some extra food or money. *Gelt.*

Soon the size of the ghetto shrank. The Germans took the blocks bounded by the streets of Drewnowska, Majowa and Jeneralska, and made all that part of the Aryan section, so now Jews were restricted to even less space than before. At the entrance gate was a sign: 'WOHNGEBIET DER JUDEN BETRETEN VERBOTEN.' Jewish residential area. Entry forbidden. The word 'JUDEN' was in big letters. It was the first German sign Jacob ever saw.

CHAPTER TEN

Ten

Mary Lou Bennett, Director of Care at the Greenwich Village Seniors Center, knocked on the door. "Hello? Is that the newest member of The Hundred Club? It's me. Mary Lou. Can I see you for a minute?"

"Come in," said Jack.

She found him curled up on his bed, resting.

"May I sit down?" she said.

"Sure," he said, pointing to the armchair in the corner of his room. "And to what do I owe this visit?"

Jack was always such a charmer, especially with the ladies.

"Jack, we're getting calls from people who want to talk to you. Ever since that NYU thing appeared. Did you see it? The one by that student who came to see you?"

"It was a young person," he said, waving his hand dismissively. "What do you expect?"

"I know but we've got real journalists calling now. This morning it was someone from the *Times*. *The New York Times*. Did you hear what I said?"

"A very fine newspaper. At least it was when I used to read it."

Mary Lou smiled. She had never seen Jack reading anything. "When was that?" she said.

"When they had a print edition. But that was a long time ago."

"I'll say. I can't even remember. So how do you know it's still a fine newspaper?"

"I know it on reputation."

She chuckled. "But it's not just them. The other day it was a crew from one of the ezines. They want to shoot you."

"Shoot me?"

"Bad choice of words. You know what I mean. They want to do a clip on you. A story."

"Hmm. I heard something about a debate at NYU. Do you know what that's all about?"

"Yes. After that article there was a backlash from some people at the school. Somebody challenged the writer to a debate but now it's not going to be a debate. It's going to be a panel."

"What does that mean?"

"It means a few people have agreed to sit on a panel and they're going to talk about the Second World War."

"A few people?"

"A professor. Head of the students' union from the law faculty I think. And the head of a Christian organization. He's going to talk about the holocaust."

"The holocaust from the Second World War?"

"No. The Great Holocaust of 2029."

Jack shook his head. "People do get their holocausts mixed up these days."

"Look, I don't want to do anything that's going to upset you. If you don't want to see these people you don't have to. You have every right to keep these things to yourself."

"What things?"

"Your memories. But they did call so what should I tell them?"

Jack got up from his bed and steadied himself. He checked

the alarm clock on his side table. It said ten to twelve. "It's almost lunch time," he said. "I'm hungry. What's on the menu today?"

"I don't know but I'm sure it'll be good."

"Last time it was shepherd's pie and it wasn't so good at all. It was too dry. The peas were hard. Like marbles. I hope it's not shepherd's pie again. My mother used to make that and it was delicious. You know how she made it?"

"Tell me."

"She would take a diced onion and add a tablespoon of olive oil. Then a pound of minced lamb. Then she'd take a clove of garlic, a carrot and it was a big carrot, and some beef and then she'd chop some tomatoes, add a little corn flour, a pinch of salt and pepper, and two pounds of potatoes."

"You mean grams. People don't talk about pounds anymore. Not for food anyway."

"It was pounds then. That's how I remember it. Then she'd put in some butter and mix it all up. Oh and one more thing."

"What?"

"Worcestershire sauce. She would add Worcestershire sauce."

"It's incredible you remember all that. The recipe I mean."

"I used to make it too. It was a lot better than the stuff they serve around here."

Mary Lou laughed.

"My mother would make it," he said. "It was good."

"Your mother?"

"My adopted mother. My real mother died when I was a little boy."

"Jack, I know this is hard for you."

"No it's not. It's good to remember. I like to remember my parents."

"How old were you when you lost them?"

"Four."

"Four? Four years old. How terrible to lose your parents when you're so young."

"When you're that young it's your whole world." Jack looked up and thought for a moment. "You don't think I'm making this up, do you?"

"I don't think you made up that shepherd's pie recipe."

"I can still taste it." He licked his lips.

"No Jack, I don't think you're making anything up."

"But those students. They think I'm crazy."

"What do they know?"

"Not much. I wonder what they learn there."

"Where?"

"At school. They think history is the last ten years and that's it. Did I ever tell you that my great-granddaughter is a history teacher?"

"No. You must be proud of her."

Jack nodded. "The other day she sent me one of those 3D things."

"What?"

"An email. By 3D."

"You mean a 3DE?"

"Yes that's it."

"So Jack what do you want me to tell these reporters? The one from the *Times* and the people at that ezine. They all want you."

"Tell them I'm here and I'd be happy to talk to them."

"You sure?"

"Why not? They've already got a good story, don't they?"

"What's that?"

"I'm a hundred years old. Or did you forget?"

Eleven

Kitchener, Ontario, 2036

The Upper Grand District School Board met every month, and while schoolteachers didn't take part in the proceedings, Christine Fisher was a special guest since the board was going to hear her out. She had sent them a 3DE objecting to the standard issue text – *An Overview of the Twentieth and Twenty-First Centuries* – for her Grade 8 history course. This being her first year of teaching, she had hoped the message and her appearance before them wouldn't put her in bad stead with the members. They were all seated around a long, rectangular table at the education administration building.

Christine recognized the woman who served as Chair, a high school principal with over thirty years of teaching to her credit. Christine also recognized the face and knew the name of John Salmon, head of the history department at one of Wellington County's high schools. He had helped set curriculum for the board's history program. The others she didn't know.

"Christine Fisher teaches Grade 8 history at Williamsburg Senior Public School," said the Chair. "Her 3DE to the board asked that we reconsider the text being used for her course. I believe all of you were copied?"

Everyone said they were.

"Good. Well we'd like to welcome you to the board. I understand this is your first year of teaching?"

Christine said it was.

"So you have not yet taught a full term?"

"That's right."

"So my question is this. How can you come to us recommending a change to the curriculum when you have yet to see the benefit of how your students react to the program? Don't you think it's a little premature?"

There were chuckles around the table.

"I mean you haven't even got your feet wet," the Chair said.

Christine hesitated before responding. "The course I teach is history in the twentieth and twenty-first centuries," she said. "And that includes the First World War and the Second World War from the last century. The text for this course doesn't mention the holocaust at all and I think that is a glaring error of omission."

"Why?"

The question was posed by John Salmon, long-time member of the school board.

"Why?" said Christine. "Because it is. The holocaust was one of the most significant ... probably the most significant event ... of that entire war."

"I don't think so," Salmon said. "The Second World War was about the defeat of Nazi Germany by the Allies and the Russians. It was about an imperialist authoritarian regime that wanted to enslave all of Europe. I've taught it for twenty-five years and the prime pedagogical requirements of that episode of the twentieth century are that the Allied forces fought Germany and its fellow

Axis nations on the western front and the Russians fought them on the eastern front. It's military history."

"Yes it's military history," said Christine, "but ..."

"For many years the suffering of the Jews at the hands of Nazi Germany was included in how this period was taught in our schools," said Salmon, his eyes moving around the table, connecting with each board member. "But the teaching of this period has changed over the years and I think that's a good thing."

"Yes it has changed," said Christine. "I have some of the old textbooks with me and it's very clear what's been happening."

"What's been happening?" the Chair asked.

Christine took out three books. Hardcover books.

"I haven't seen one of those in a long time," said one of the members. "How old are they?"

"This one was published in 1988," said Christine.

"An antique."

"Well antique or not it has over four hundred pages and at one time it was a primer on the twentieth century."

"A very poor text that one," Salmon said.

Christine let it pass. "If you look at the index you can see there are thirteen pages devoted to World War I," she said. "That's what they called it then. And for World War II ... or the Second World War ... only eight pages. That was it. As for the holocaust ..."

"Let's get something straight," Salmon said and he pointed to Christine. "You are referring to the Jewish holocaust, I believe. In the current vernacular the word *holocaust* refers to the massacre of fifty thousand Christians seven years ago. The Great Holocaust of 2029. That of course was the Middle East crisis precipitated by a group of Muslims who had been converting to Christianity in the Malatya province of Turkey and who then began publishing biblical literature and proselytizing. It was the Syrians in particular ... and they're right across the border ... who became very upset with that and started slitting throats."

My God, Christine thought to herself. The man is an encyclopedia.

"Please continue," said the Chair, motioning to Christine, who could only say that she had lost her train of thought. "You were referring to this 1988 text book and its shortfalls."

"Yes that's right. As for the Jewish holocaust there was only one paragraph ... one paragraph about the extermination of six million people."

"Extermination?" said Salmon. "You speak of them as if they were termites."

"Well they ..."

"Now hold on a minute. When we teach history to young students and we're talking about Grade 8 here we must stick to the facts. The known facts. There is no doubt that Jews were persecuted by Nazi Germany. But there is considerable doubt as to the magnitude of that persecution. Our history text books should not be in the business of perpetuating religious dogma."

"Religious dogma?" said Christine.

"It's a history class. Not a religion class."

The chair interrupted. "Mr. Salmon, this young lady has brought several of these old books with her. Why don't we hear what she has to say and then we can discuss the matter? Please proceed."

"Thank you Madam Chair," said Christine, convinced by now that she had alienated the section head of the history department. "As I said this textbook from 1988 had one paragraph about the holocaust ... the Jewish holocaust ... and incidentally on page 155 it does mention the figure of six million dead."

Salmon was shaking his head back and forth. Christine went on to the next text.

"Now if we go to 1996 we have this textbook. There is a chapter on World War II ... I mean the Second World War ... and two full pages on the Nazi death camps." She opened up the book to a two-page spread. On one side was a photograph of

Jews in striped clothes standing behind a barbed-wire fence. "It talks about the Final Solution. It talks about the death camps at Dachau and Bergen-Belsen."

"There is a lot of scholarly debate about that," shot back Salmon. "On one side you have the point of view that these were death camps, pure and simple, and on the other side something less than that. The term has often been mentioned but ..." and his voice trailed off.

Christine tried to plod ahead with her argument, but felt she was sinking into a quagmire. "This book talks about Treblinka, Sobibor, Maidanek and Auschwitz ... and these ones were all death camps." A surge of confidence and she tossed a glance at Salmon. No reaction. "It talks about the gas chambers and how the Nazis dropped Zyklon B gas through an opening in the ceiling."

"Does it say how many Jews were killed by the Nazis?" asked Salmon.

"Yes," said Christine, consulting the book. "It says right here. *'It is estimated that six million people were put to death.'*"

"Estimated."

"Yes."

Salmon looked over to the Chair. "Can I say something?"

"Go ahead," said the Chair.

"Having this kind of material in a history class ... any history class ... but especially for kids in senior public school can be very damaging. It uses estimates ... she said so herself ... and innuendo. Estimates and innuendo do not belong in a history text."

All around the table were nods from the other board members, and then one of them interjected.

"That photograph," said a woman, pointing to the book in Christine's hand. "I have a problem with a photograph like that."

"Why?" said Christine.

"It's in bad taste. We're talking about thirteen-year-olds. I don't think they should be seeing things like that. It's bad enough we're talking about war. We aren't showing them pictures of bodies being ripped apart, are we? I'm glad we don't have photographs like that anymore, never mind 3D images in the e-readers we use now. That kind of thing was traumatic for those kids. I don't think we should be in the business of upsetting them."

"I tend to agree," said Salmon, "provided we don't shortchange history."

The Chair nodded in approval. She looked at Christine. "You have other books with you?"

"Yes I do. This one here is from the year 2000. It lumps in the Great Depression and World War II ... sorry ... the Second World War ... into one chapter. There are three pages on the holocaust ... the Jewish holocaust ... so we can see a trend here. As we proceed from one book to the next ... and I'm talking about forty years ago ... the teaching of the holocaust was actually increasing but ever since 2000 the opposite has been happening." Christine put another book on the table. "This is the standard history textbook from 2012. It has four pages on the Second World War and one paragraph on the Jewish holocaust. That was the last hardcover. Now this is the text from 2018. It was the first e-reader issued for this course. A pocket kindle."

"Another antique. Look how big it is."

It was the same person who had denigrated the old textbook earlier.

"There is but one line ... one sentence ... on the Jewish holocaust," said Christine.

"That thing is so big it wouldn't even fit in your hand."

"It was almost twenty years ago," said Christine.

"Yes," said the Chair. "When that came out it was revolutionary but look, we're not here to discuss technology. We're here to discuss content. Are we not?"

Christine gave her a nod. "That's right," she said. "But the point I want to make is that first e-reader or not, there was only one sentence on the Jewish holocaust. One sentence. And this here is what we're using now."

She took out her latest mini kindle. It contained all the books and source materials for Grade 8 students.

"The text for the course is called *An Overview of the Twentieth and Twenty-First Centuries* and it was released just last year so it's new. There is absolutely no mention of the Jewish holocaust in it ... nothing at all ... but there are several pages about the Christian holocaust of 2029 in Turkey."

"*The Christian holocaust*?" said Salmon. "You mean *the* holocaust, don't you? The Great Holocaust."

Salmon looked like he was getting angry.

"Look," said Salmon. "This whole thing is ridiculous. We're talking about the teaching of *history*. When we teach Grade 8 history do we tell them about the persecution of early Christians at the hands of the Romans? No. And if we did that would belong in a religion class in a private school setup. They can teach that in a bible class or in a Jewish school if they want but certainly not in a public school. It has no place in a public school. When we teach Grade 8 history do we tell them about the genocide of Armenians at the hands of the Turks during the First World War? No. The government of Turkey has never even acknowledged that such an event took place. When we teach Grade 8 history do we tell them about massacres in Africa where tribalism is rampant even today? No. Places like Rwanda and Darfur and Zimbabwe hold little meaning for kids in Grade 8. They couldn't even find these places on a map. Lots of them couldn't find Africa on a map."

"What about black kids in Grade 8?" one of the board members asked.

"That is a good question," Salmon said. "But we don't have many black kids in Grade 8 in our schools. Not here in Wellington County. The point I'm trying to make is that history has to be relevant to our students and even if they are black kids are you suggesting we turn around the curriculum in order to meet their needs? Just because they happen to be black and because many

generations ago their ancestors might have come from Africa? If
we did that then we'd have to do the same for every other kid and
consider where they came from. Why you would be teaching a
different course for every student."

The Chair nodded her head in agreement. Salmon went on.

"In a history class and in a history text we should stick to
known facts and not become engaged in hyperbole. The fact of
the matter is nobody knows exactly how many Jews were killed
by the Nazis a hundred years ago. It's impossible to know."

"Do we even know for certain if there was a program designed
to kill Jews?"

It was a man not much older than Christine.

"Of course there was," said Christine. "That goes
without saying."

"How do we know that?" he said. "How do *you* know?"

Christine didn't want to get into it, but they weren't giving
her much choice. "My great-grandfather is a survivor of the
holocaust," she said. "The Jewish holocaust. He was born in
Poland in 1939 and he was in a camp. Auschwitz. I know first-
hand what he went through."

"You know first-hand?" said Salmon. "How is that?"

"He told me."

"Ah he told you. And as a teacher do you believe everything
that everybody tells you?"

Christine was taken aback with that one.

"I see what the situation is now," said Salmon. "With this
young lady the problem is ... personal. She's Jewish and ..."

"Who said I was Jewish?" Christine said.

"You did, didn't you?"

"No. I'm Catholic and so is my great-grandfather. But he was
born a Jew and he was at Auschwitz."

The Chair broke in. "This man, your great-grandfather, he's
alive today?"

Christine nodded.

"How old is he, Christine?"

She was calling her Christine now. Not a good sign.

"He's ninety-seven."

"Ninety-seven?" repeated the Chair.

Salmon was smiling. "He'd have to be if what she says is true. So I gather he would've been one or two years old when he was at Auschwitz which begs the question. How can he remember things if he was only one or two years old at the time?"

"He was four years old," said Christine.

"We are splitting hairs," Salmon said.

"I think we are too," said the Chair.

"Wait a minute." It was the woman who had objected to the photograph from the old text book. "A lot of terrible things have happened in history with people having absolutely no regard for other people. I don't think the purpose of Grade 8 history is to horrify young minds with the brutality of the human race. If anything we want to give them hope. We don't have to spell things out graphically like they used to years ago. That was wrong and that's why the practise was stopped. Even when our texts tell them about the Great Holocaust ... and I think we have an obligation to tell them about that ... we don't have to do it graphically."

"So this is all about sanitizing the Jewish holocaust?" said Christine. "Is that it?"

"No." Salmon again. "It's not about sanitizing anything. It's about reporting known facts in a way that young minds can process. Six million Jews dead at the hands of Nazi Germany is not a known fact. Neither is five million dead or three million dead. We just don't know. We do know however that fifty thousand Christians were slaughtered in Turkey by fundamentalist Muslims. It's all documented and it's recent history."

"The Jewish holocaust was documented too," said Christine.

"My dear young lady," said Salmon, "let me tell you something. For every fact you claim or source you can give me about the

Jewish holocaust I can provide another one to contradict it. I can give you sources explaining how it was impossible that so many people were killed. Impossible. And today, as I'm sure you know, a number of international scholars question the very nature of that particular event. Not just the magnitude of it but the *very nature* of it."

"What do you mean the very nature of it?" said Christine.

"They are questioning whether it even happened," said the young man who had spoken before.

"Whether it even happened?"

"That's right. I've read a lot about this myself and it does get you thinking. But isn't that what education is supposed to be about? To make people think?"

"What kind of thinking is it when you deny something happened when we know perfectly well that it did?" said Christine.

"The point," said the Chair, "is to let people think for themselves and allow them to reach their own conclusions."

"May I?" Salmon again. The Chair gave him a nod. "Current scholarship holds that Jews were persecuted by Nazi Germany. There is no debate about that. But there is debate ... considerable debate on this matter I might add ... as to how many were actually killed and also *how* they were killed. There is one view that says the Nazis never used gas chambers to kill Jews and other people. Let's not forget that we're not only talking about Jews. We're also talking about Poles, Catholics, members of the clergy, homosexuals, intellectuals, communists, Gypsies ... a lot of different people. It's not only about the Jews."

It was a speech.

"What about ovens?" said Christine.

"Oh please," said the young man at the far end of the table.

"What about ovens?" Christine said again.

"I see where you're going with this," said Salmon. "At one time there were reports that scores of people were disposed of in ovens ... burned alive ... and that horrible experiments took place but many of those reports have since been discredited as being inaccurate or exaggerated. Why even the sworn testimony of some survivors themselves was shown to be full of inconsistencies." He stopped and heaved a long sigh. "History evolves. It always evolves and the scholarship evolves as well. As more things come to light we are able to look at history ... any period of history ... with a more enhanced open mind." Salmon looked straight at Christine. "Surely you're aware that in some societies teaching of the Jewish holocaust is against the law?"

"You mean Arab countries?" Christine said.

"Yes and even in some school boards in the United States and Great Britain. For over thirty years now a number of boards in the United Kingdom haven't taught anything about this matter at all for fear of upsetting an ever increasing number of Muslim students. Muslims comprise a large percentage of the student body in some of these boards and the students' parents vehemently object to this sort of thing being taught in much the same way that you object to using this particular text in your history class. That's what happens when we allow history to become ... *personal.* What's that text called again? The new one?"

"What text?" said Christine.

"The one you so strenuously object to using."

"You mean the one we're using now?"

"Yes. That one."

"An Overview of the Twentieth and Twenty-First Centuries."

"I see." Salmon clasped his hands together and placed them on the table in front of him. "And who is the author of this book?"

Christine picked up the mini kindle and advanced her thumb through the pages to the front cover. "Oh my God," she said.

There in small type was the name of John Salmon. One and the same.

"You wrote it?" she asked him.

"I'm afraid so."

The Chair couldn't hide her chuckling. "We have many items on our agenda today and I think we've given this piece of business more than due course. Christine Fisher has drafted a motion that will be tabled for consideration by the board. All of you have this draft at your disposal. Her draft motion is to replace the current Grade 8 history text and to begin searching for a new text from another publisher."

"Can't we just vote on it now?" said Salmon. "We all read it."

There were nods around the table.

"Fine then," said the Chair. "Let's have a show of hands. All those in favor?"

Christine raised her hand, a meek form of protest. It was the only hand that went up.

"I'm afraid you don't have a vote," said the Chair. "This is confined to members of the board."

"Sorry."

"Opposed."

It was unanimous.

"The draft motion is defeated."

The Chair, implicit matriarch of the Upper Grand District School Board representing one hundred elementary and secondary schools in Wellington County, showed Christine a wan smile. "You'll have to keep using that same text, I'm afraid. John's. It might not be perfect but it's the best one we've got. Thank you for coming today."

Twelve

The yellow taxi pulled up just past the front doors of the Greenwich Village Seniors Center. The driver spotted an elderly woman with a cane standing next to a man who looked even older than she was.

"Taxi?" he said.

The woman raised her cane, and the driver backed up his car to get as close as he could to them. She saw that he was middle-aged with a dark complexion. The side door of the taxi opened. The driver stayed behind the wheel, watching through his rear-view mirror as the old man helped the old woman navigate into the back seat.

"Arabs," the woman whispered to the man. "They would never dream of getting out to help you into their cab. Not in a million years would they offer a hand."

With the two of them inside and the car doors closed, the driver looked over his shoulder, awaiting instructions. A thick pane of glass separated the front of the car from the back.

"New York University School of Law, Forty Washington Square South. The building is called Vanderbilt Hall," said Jack's voice through the car's speaker system. "It's in Greenwich Village."

"We're in Greenwich Village," said the driver.

"I know," said Jack. "It's not far."

The driver smirked, slighted at the prospect of such a short fare. With the one-way streets and bumper-to-bumper traffic, it would take ten minutes for the trip and that only if he stretched things out. Walking would be faster, but this couple wasn't walking anywhere.

"It's the main building of the law school," Jack said. "It's the whole block between West Third and Washington Square South."

"I know where it is," said the driver.

"I'm glad you know."

The woman steadied her cane between her knees, her hands clasped around the top. "This should be interesting," she said to Jack as she settled in. "Do you think they'll know who you are?"

"Why would they know me?"

"My nephew's son knows who you are. He met with you, didn't he, when he wrote that article?"

Jack nodded.

"That was a terrible thing he wrote and I'm going to tell him that."

"He's young. He doesn't know any better."

"Imagine writing what he did after all the things you told him."

Jack shrugged.

"It's not right. They think just because you're a hundred years old you don't know what you're talking about."

The sound system was picking everything up. The driver peeked into his mirror, and scrutinized the face of the man in the back. "You're a hundred years old?" he said.

"What was that?" Jack said, raising his head.

"You're a hundred years old?" the driver repeated in a louder voice.

Jack smiled. "Yes I am. They had a big party for me the other day but that was the other day. I'm working on my second hundred years now."

The driver laughed as he inched his cab onto the roadway. The traffic, full of small electric taxis like his, was barely moving.

"Didn't you tell him about Auschwitz?" the woman said to Jack. "And how everyone was starving to death? And about the gas chambers and the crematorium?"

"I did but I guess he didn't believe me."

The driver looked into his mirror again.

"I don't understand how people can be so ignorant," the woman went on. "And university students yet. What makes it so bad is he's my nephew's son. I wonder what's going to happen at the debate today."

"It's not a debate," said Jack. "It's a panel discussion. But that's why we're going. To see what they have to say."

"I'm not terribly hopeful."

"They're going to have some professors there and the president of the Jewish students association or whatever it's called."

"One would think he'd have something to say about it."

The cab wasn't moving. None of the cars were moving. The driver stared into his rear-view mirror.

"What was that you said about gas chambers?" he said.

"I beg your pardon?" said Jack.

"She said something about gas chambers."

The woman lifted her cane and tapped it twice against the glass directly behind the driver's head. "This man," she said, motioning to Jack, "is a survivor of the Nazi death camp at Auschwitz. You've heard of Auschwitz, haven't you?"

The driver just shrugged.

"My God," the woman exclaimed at his apparent indifference.

"Can I ask you a question?" said Jack, leaning forward.

"Sure," said the driver.

"Where are you from?"

"Iran."

"When were you born?"

"Nineteen-ninety-five."

"How long have you been in New York?"

"Nine years now. Almost."

"And you've never heard of Auschwitz?" the woman asked him.

"Well ..."

"Well what?" said the woman.

"I heard rumors."

"Rumors?" the woman said.

"Yes. I heard a few things but that was only after I came here."

"What about over there?" said Jack. "In Iran. Did you go to school in Iran?"

"Of course."

"Did you ever learn anything about the holocaust or about the war when you were in Iran?"

"Which war? There are lots of wars."

"World War II. Back in the nineteen hundreds."

"World War II?"

"The Second World War. Isn't that what they call it now?"

"No. We never studied that but the Great Holocaust? Sure. That happened the year before I came to America. Everyone knows about that but even that is exaggerated."

"What do you mean?" said the woman.

"What you read in America isn't what you read in Iran. There they print the truth. Over here it's all propaganda. Can you deny it?"

"You're talking about the Christian holocaust?" Jack said.

"That's the only holocaust I know about."

"And you think it's exaggerated?"

"Of course. They say hundreds of thousands of Christians were murdered but that's not true. Yes there were a few murders when some Christians started preaching about Jesus to the

Muslim community but that's all. It was only a handful."

"I believe the number they claim is fifty thousand."

"It's not true. It's all exaggerated. But they should never have been preaching to Muslims in the first place."

"And what about the other holocaust? The Jewish holocaust."

"I don't believe it."

"Why not?"

"I never heard a thing about that until I came to this country. Now why is that the case? Maybe because it's an American invention?"

The traffic was crawling along, giving the driver plenty of time to keep glancing into his rear-view mirror.

"This man is a survivor of the Jewish holocaust," the woman said, raising her voice. "And that was the big one. Six million people."

"I'm sorry," the driver said, "but I don't believe it. Look. If six million Jews were murdered how come there are so many Jews today? Where did they all come from? There must be six million Jews in New York City."

"What kind of logic is that?" said the woman.

"There is another holocaust too," said Jack. "More than a million Armenians were killed by the Turks in the early nineteen hundreds."

"By Turkish Muslims?" said the driver.

"Yes."

"Of course. What do you expect? It's all lies. All of it."

The woman was shaking her head from side to side.

"Do you mind if I ask *you* a question?" said the driver, looking into his mirror at the reflection of Jack.

"Sure."

"How come no one here ever talks about Jews killing Muslims? What about that holocaust?"

"I don't know what you're talking about," said Jack.

"I'm talking about Jews killing Muslim babies. Muslims have

lots of children and Jews try to kill as many of them as possible to keep the population down."

"Where does this happen?"

"Wherever there are Jews."

"I don't think so," said Jack.

"So you don't believe it?"

"No."

"And the same way I don't believe the story about your Jewish holocaust either. It's not true."

The woman piped up. "Show him your arm," she said to Jack.

"What?"

"Show him your arm."

"I don't want to."

"What about your arm?" the driver said, glancing back again.

"He has a number stamped on his arm. It's from the camp."

"Really? Let me see it."

"Show him," she said to Jack. "Why don't you? Then maybe he'll believe you."

Reluctantly, Jack removed his coat, peeled off his sweater, and rolled up his shirt sleeve. The driver had the cab at a complete standstill now. He turned around and looked through the glass partition.

There," Jack said.

High up on his right arm was a letter followed by five numbers.

A-25073.

"How did you do that?" the driver said.

"He didn't do it," the woman said. "The Nazis did it."

"How?"

Jack rolled his sleeve down and put his sweater back on. "They stuck a needle in me. It hurt."

"You remember?" asked the driver.

"Of course."

The woman seemed satisfied, but she didn't know what the

driver was thinking. He turned around to face the front and put his hands back on the steering wheel. Jack looked at his watch.

"The meeting is going to start soon and we're stuck in all this traffic," Jack said, leaning forward. "When are we going to get there?"

"We'll be there in a few minutes," the driver said. "There's a lot of traffic. I can't do much about that. Can I ask you something?"

"What?"

"If what you say is true how did you get out?"

"Now *that* is quite a story," the woman said.

"You want to know?" Jack said, sliding his coat over his shoulders, and the driver said he did. "All right. If you want to know I'll tell you. It was like this. I looked like an Aryan boy."

"What's that?"

"An Aryan? It means you've got blonde hair and blue eyes. A true German. When I was in the ghetto I used to sneak out to the Aryan side to steal food and other things for my family. If anyone stopped me I just gave them a Hail Mary."

"What's that?" the driver said.

"Hail Mary," Jack said.

"I don't know what you're talking about."

Jack went right into the Latin.

"Ave Maria, gratia plena, Dominus tecum. Benedicta tu in mulieribus, et benedictus fructus ventris tui, Iesus. Sancta Maria, Mater Dei, ora pro nobis peccatoribus, nunc ete in hora mortis nostrae. Amen."

Every syllable, every letter, was perfect. Jack sounded like a priest at mass. His woman friend was impressed, but she didn't know about the driver.

"What's that mean?" the driver asked, so Jack told him.

"Hail Mary, full of grace, the Lord is with thee. Blessed art thou among women, and blessed is the fruit of thy womb, Jesus. Holy Mary, Mother of God, pray for us sinners, now and at the hour of our death. Amen."

He said it without thinking. It was automatic. The driver was confused.

"Why would a Jew know something like that?" he said.

"Well," said Jack, "in the ghetto at *Lodz* ... that's the city where I lived in Poland ... I used to slip into a church on the Aryan side. It was one street over. Like I said I could pass for an Aryan boy so it wasn't difficult. In the church there was a priest ... Father Kasinski ... a wonderful man ... and he taught me the prayers. He baptised me. He taught me about Catholicism and it's a good thing because that's what saved my life."

"You mean Jesus saved your life?"

"Yes he did and I never forgot it."

"And you learned those prayers?"

"I never forgot them."

"Tell him how you got into the church," the woman said.

"I went through the sewers," Jack said.

"The sewers?" said the driver.

"I learned how to go through the sewers but then the Germans found out about all the Jews hiding in the sewers and they found us. My family ... my mother ... my father ... my aunt ... my two cousins ... we were all sent to *Auschwitz* and they died there. Every one of them. Except me. I lived."

"Why did you live?" said the driver.

"I was lucky. I knew the prayers."

The driver was listening intently, but now the car was near Vanderbilt Hall. He pulled his taxi up to the entrance. "That's quite a story," he said. "It really is. But is it true?"

Jack took out his wallet to pay for the fare. "I don't know if you're aware of this," he said, "but on this trip you've been trying awfully hard *not* to earn a good tip from us. Did you know that?"

The driver shrugged and tossed Jack a smile. "It was a short ride. But I enjoyed your story."

Thirteen

New York City, 2037

Miriam Abraham was ninety-seven years old and in bed every night by nine o'clock. When her husband was alive, the two of them would retire with a nightcap of green tea and hit the lights by ten-thirty, but since his death the evenings were long and empty. So she got into the habit of going to bed earlier. This night was different. It was Wednesday. Her card night. She was at a friend's apartment in New Jersey, and arranged to have her daughter pick her up and drive her home across the George Washington Bridge. She always liked going over that bridge. It was pretty, especially at night with all the bright lights from Manhattan, but then she got a message. Her daughter's garage had been broken into and her car vandalized. What's more, the charger wasn't working, and now she was waiting for someone to come help, but it was late and who knew how long that would take? Would Miriam mind calling a taxi for the trip home? Her daughter even said she would pay for it. Miriam called back and said she would summon the taxi, but being an independent sort she insisted on paying herself.

The taxi took its time and didn't arrive until past eleven. It was late and Miriam was tired. "Are you the lady who called?" the driver said as he helped her into the car. She gave him her address and on they went. She didn't notice anything peculiar about him except for the tattoos on his arms.

"Are those snakes?" she said and the driver said they were.

"But they're not just snakes," he said in his soft voice. "They're cobras. The cobra is the king."

"What do you mean?"

"Cobras eat other snakes."

Ten minutes later they were approaching the GW Bridge, as everyone called it. During the day it was packed, but now traffic was light.

"Can you take the upper level?" Miriam said to the driver. "You get a much better view of the lights up there. I like to look at the city."

"I can take the upper level," he said.

He slowed down, the car and its license plate got scanned, and then he stopped to pay the toll. Miriam was glad he was taking the top level because it was higher there and she could see better. This was the way her daughter always went. Miriam would look out the window and see the lights of Manhattan. It was a beautiful clear night with more lights than she had ever seen before. When they were halfway across – right at the border between New Jersey and New York State – the driver pulled over to the side.

"What are you doing?" she said.

"I'm afraid we have a problem with the tire."

"Oh dear."

This wasn't turning out very well, Miriam thought to herself. First her daughter's car was vandalized. Now this.

The driver got out to inspect the rear tire on the passenger side. Then another car pulled up and stopped right behind them. A moment later, Miriam's door opened and a different man appeared.

"Are you Mrs. Abraham?" he said. "Miriam Abraham?"

"Yes."

"Can you come with me please?"

Miriam didn't know what was going on. Except for those snakes on his arms, the driver looked neat, but this man was anything but. Younger and bigger than the driver, he had straggly unkempt hair, and though it was hard to tell in the night, dark skin.

"Where are we going?" she said from inside the car.

He opened the door and helped her out.

"Where are we going?" she said again.

"Nice view, isn't it?" he said, pointing off in the distance to the lights of Manhattan.

"Yes it's very pretty but ..."

"This will just take a minute. I want to show you something."

The driver was standing beside the car, looking one way, and then the other. Back and forth. Back and forth. He dropped some chewing gum into his mouth and pulled out his mini. A touch of the screen and a list of names appeared. He ran his fingertip over the last one and it was gone. Then a line of cars approached and he watched them go by. One by one. When they passed, he nodded to the man with Miriam, who took her by the hand and led her across the sidewalk that ran parallel to the roadway on the bridge's upper level. Before Miriam knew what was happening, he picked her up and was carrying her in his arms. She was a small woman and not very heavy.

"What are you doing?" she said. "Put me down!"

He carried her to the end of the roadway, to the far edge of the bridge, and sat her on the railing. He just sat her there, plopping her down as if she were a bag of groceries. Right on the edge overlooking the water. She was scared and started grappling with him. Kicking with her feet. Flailing away with her arms.

"What are you doing? What are you doing?" she cried.

"I want to show you the view but you have to be careful. It's dangerous, you know. You could fall from here."

She relaxed for just a moment and that was his cue. He gave her a push and she tumbled over the side. It was a long way down. He heard a gasp. It wasn't a scream. There wasn't time for a scream. A few seconds later and her body was floating in the deathly cold waters of the Hudson River.

Fourteen

"Dad? It's me. Ralph."

"Who?"

"Ralph. How are you? Are you all right?"

"I'm fine."

"I wanted to see how you're doing."

There was something in Ralph's voice. Jack could tell.

"I'm doing fine," Jack said.

"How was that debate you went to?"

"Debate? It wasn't a debate at all. It was a panel discussion. I'll get the program and tell you about it. Hold on."

"No it's all right. Hello? Hello? Are you there?"

A moment later and Jack was back. "Here it is. Let me get my glasses on. You want their names?"

"What names?"

"The names of the people on the panel."

"It doesn't matter."

"Hillel Schwartz from the Jewish Law Students Association. He was on it."

"Dad."

"Christopher Lawrence from the ... let's see ... the World Community for Christian Meditation and Fellowship."

"Dad."

"Now this guy ... Khalid Khan ... the Islamic Chaplain at NYU. He didn't believe anything unless it came direct from the prophet Mohammad. And David Tipwell from the *NYU Hotline*. He's the kid who came to see me. The one who wrote that article and didn't believe anything. He still doesn't believe any of it. He thinks I'm senile."

"You're the last person in the world I would call senile."

"There were supposed to be some professors but none of them showed up. I guess they had better things to do. And there weren't many people there either. People just aren't interested. They don't care."

"I'm not surprised. Listen, I have something to tell you. It's about Christine."

Jack perked up.

"Nobody seems to know where she is."

"What do you mean?"

"You know she teaches in that little town outside of Kitchener? Well, after one of her classes she left. No one has seen her."

"What are you talking about?"

"Just that. No one knows where she is and that's why I'm calling. Has she been in touch with you?"

"Christine?"

"Yes."

"With me? No. Wait. Yes she called the day of the party they threw for me. First thing that morning. I remember now. She woke me up."

"She called you?"

"She sent me an email too. One of those 3D things."

"Do you remember what she said?"

"Only that she was sorry she couldn't come."

"Anything else?"

"Let me see. I'm trying to remember. What do you mean no one has seen her?"

"I'm sure she's all right. But no one has heard from her and her mother is worried crazy. It was Bill who called and told me. That 3DE she sent you ..."

"What?"

"That message she sent you. Have you still got it?"

"I think so. Why?"

"Listen to me. Don't delete it. Somebody may want to talk to you about it."

"I don't know how to delete it."

"Good."

"Who wants to talk to me about it? Hello? Ralph?"

"I'm here. Don't delete it. Okay?"

"I won't touch it."

"I'm sure everything is fine. We all know Christine is a responsible kid."

Fifteen

It began with a phone call from reception. A police officer was in the lobby and he wanted to see Jack. He came up to the sixth floor with a nurse, who rapped on Jack's door. Jack was waiting for them.

"Mr. Fisher, I'm Lieutenant Jack Hodgson of the NYPD."

The man was enormous. When Jack was younger, he stood five-nine, but now he was closer to five-seven and his weight had settled in at a hundred and forty pounds. But this man before him was at least two of him and maybe three. His hulking shoulders filled the width of the doorway. A massive torso and an obvious bulge in the gut. But then it was hard to tell where one part of his body ended and another part began.

"NYPD?" said Jack looking up.

"New York Police Department," the giant said.

He wasn't just tall – a full head over the suddenly diminutive Jack – but big. Everywhere. More than big even. It was his frame.

"My name is Jack too," Jack said.

"We have something in common then. Can I come in? I want to ask you a few questions. It won't take long."

He was wearing a suit, which like the body inside was huge. Jack told the man and the nurse to come in. The nurse immediately checked his blood pressure. She made some small talk, then gathered up her equipment and left. Now the two men were alone. The police officer remained on his feet, Jack sitting on the edge of his bed. It was then that Jack noticed his shoes.

"Something wrong?" Hodgson said, seeing how the old man was staring at his feet.

"What size are those?" Jack asked.

"What size are what?"

"Your shoes."

"Fifteen."

"Fifteen?"

"That's right."

"I didn't know they made shoes that big."

"They do but you can't buy them just anywhere. It's like that with all my clothes."

Jack looked up at him from the bed. "It must be difficult when you're that big. With clothes I mean."

"It can be but my wife has all my measurements and she knows where to go. I'm not much for shopping."

"That makes two of us."

Hodgson the police officer smiled and it was a warm, friendly smile. He showed his badge.

"That's all right," Jack said. "I believed you when you said you were a cop. They wouldn't let you in here unless you identified yourself."

"We went through that in the lobby. They told me you were a hundred years old. I must say you're not what I expected."

"What did you expect?"

"Someone who might not speak too clearly and who might not be too sure about himself. But you don't strike me like that. You look pretty sharp to me."

"My hearing isn't that great."

"I understand they had a birthday party for you."

"That's right. It was nice. Lots of family and friends."

"That's something. To be a hundred years old. You must have good genes."

"I wouldn't know."

"You wouldn't know what?"

"About my genes."

"How old was your father?"

"You mean when he died?"

"Yes."

"Young."

"Compared to you young could be eighty-five or ninety."

"He was more like thirty."

"Thirty? What was it? Cancer?"

"No. He was just in the wrong place."

"Sorry to hear that. Look, you have a granddaughter named Christine Fisher?"

"She's my great-granddaughter."

"Your great-granddaughter then. She lives in Canada and her family hasn't heard from her for a few days. I understand the two of you are pretty close."

Jack nodded.

"Your son Ralph told me Christine called you on the morning of your hundredth birthday. Is that right?"

"She did. She phoned."

"He also told me she sent you a 3DE."

"Yes. One of those things."

"Would you mind if I had a look? It might be helpful."

"Has something happened to her?"

"We don't know but when a family puts in a missing person report we have to investigate. We're assisting the Canadian authorities on this one. They'd do the same if someone was missing here and it was believed there was some connection up there."

"Some connection?"

"The 3DE. She sent you a message. If you've still got it I'd like to see it."

"I've got it. I don't know how to delete them."

Jack got up from his bed, went over to the box and opened the lid. He started going through the folder for incoming messages, but there was only one. The one from Christine.

"Good morning, Jack. Well what can I say? You're the first member of the Fisher family to reach one hundred and I'm so proud of you but I feel guilty for not being there but this week has been just impossible. It's not so much my students but those bureaucrats at the school board. You know what I mean. We've been there before, you and me, and you always say to keep fighting so that's what I'm doing. Fighting them tooth and nail. I told them about you ... it's not the first time ... and they just don't care. Some of them don't even think it's true. Can you believe that? And this is a school yet. Indifference remember? That's how people are. But I just can't accept it. I never will. Anyway I'm seeing my department head this morning and I'm going to give him a piece of my mind. Whatever piece is left. To tell you the truth I'm not doing too well with this condition of mine. I'm so dizzy every morning. Twenty-five and I feel like an old woman. It's really starting to wear me out and if not for you I'd probably feel sorry for myself but one thing you always taught me, Jack, is never to do that. When I look at you, well, that's why you're my inspiration but then you always have been. Because of you my life is one big mission and that's why I feel terrible about not being there today. I'm so sorry about that. I really wanted to make it. Still I can wish you a happy hundredth, can't I? Say hello to everyone for me. You have a great day!"

Hodgson had a notebook with him and it was the old-fashioned kind, but he wasn't writing anything in it.

"Your granddaughter thinks a lot of you," he said.

"She's my great-granddaughter. Her father is my grandson."

"Oh I see. That's right. But then you are a hundred,

aren't you?"

"That's what everyone keeps telling me."

Hodgson laughed.

"She's not finished," Jack said. "There's more."

"By the way, you're going to get another message from me and you'll be amazed at what I found. I can't wait to tell you about it. Meanwhile, I have some unfinished business to attend to but I know you'll get along fine without me. You always have. Always remember that I love you dearly, Jack. Your little Christine."

Hodgson was busy jabbing his pen – that was old-fashioned, too – onto the pages of his notebook, but he still wasn't writing anything. Jack was looking at the notebook.

"I didn't think police used those things anymore," Jack said.

"Not many of us do. Almost everyone I know has their own personal mini. A PM. It's portable. You can put it in your pocket or it works on battery and it's small. Tiny little thing."

"So why do you use that?" Jack said.

"Why? Because it works if the power goes out. It doesn't need a battery. And if you drop it you'll know about it. It's not tiny. Besides, I like pens. I'm a pen-and-ink kind of guy."

Jack said he was, too.

"So tell me," Hodgson said. "Do you have any idea what this unfinished business is she's talking about?"

"No."

"She said she's going to send you another message. Did she?"

"I haven't received anything."

"What about this business with the bureaucrats on the school board? Know anything about that? What does she do for a living?"

"She's a teacher."

"What does she teach?"

"History."

"I see. And she's fighting the school board?"

"She is always fighting the school board. It's been like that ever since she started teaching."

"What is she fighting them about?"

"The books. She doesn't like the books they use."

"Why not?"

"Because they're not accurate."

"I don't understand."

"Can I shut this thing off now?"

Hodgson said he could, but he told Jack that he wanted to forward Christine's message to his office. Jack said he didn't know how to do that. Not to worry, said Hodgson. He said he could do it himself, so he pressed a couple keys and it was done. Jack just shook his head.

"It's that easy?" he said.

"It's that easy."

"But I still don't know how to do it."

"You want me to explain it to you?"

"Not really. To tell you the truth I don't get many of these messages anyway. Who's interested in an old man?"

"Your granddaughter obviously is."

"She's my great-granddaughter. Her father is my grandson."

"You said that before."

"And I'm going to keep saying it until you get it right."

Hodgson had been a cop for over thirty years. He had seen it all and considered himself a good judge of people, a quick study, and he liked this old man.

"So what's this about those books not being accurate?" he said.

"She teaches history of the twentieth century. The wars. And the holocaust. The Jewish holocaust."

"So?"

"So nothing. The book they want her to use doesn't have anything about the holocaust."

"That's it?"

Jack went back to sit on his bed. "That's it."

"And why is she bothering you with all this?"

"She's not bothering me."

"Why is she telling you about it then?"

"Can I ask you a question?" Jack said.

"Go ahead."

"How old are you?"

"Fifty-four."

"A native New Yorker?"

"Can't you tell?"

"I could tell right away. As soon as you said your name."

Hodgson smiled.

"So," said Jack, "you would have been born in ..."

"Nineteen-eighty-five. December. In fact my birthday is next week." Hodgson smiled. "You and I have something else in common, Mr. Fisher. We have the same first name and we were both born the same month. December."

"But you were born in New York in 1985 and I was born in Poland in 1939. As a Jew."

Hodgson looked Jack in the eye and started jabbing the tip of his pen onto his notebook again.

"I was born in the ghetto and then I was sent to a camp," Jack said. "My mother and father died there. And my brother too. And everyone else in my family. All of them."

Hodgson began jabbing his pen onto his notebook faster now.

"Not many children survived I can tell you. I was lucky. Six million others weren't so lucky. That's why Christine thinks this should be in her book."

"And that's why your father was thirty when he died?" Hodgson said.

"I think he was thirty but I don't really know."

"Do you know how he died?"

"The gas chamber probably."

"And your brother?"

"He was suffocated."

"Suffocated?"

"We were hiding in the sewers. All of us. He was just a newborn baby and he was crying. If they heard him they would have known we were down there."

"Down where?"

"In the sewers."

"Who would've known?"

"The Germans. But he was crying and that put us in danger. It was my aunt who did it."

"I don't understand what you're talking about."

"Look ... my aunt ... my mother's sister ... she took my brother and put a blanket on his face to make him quiet."

"To make him quiet?"

"To protect the rest of us."

Silence. A long, drawn-out silence.

"Lieutenant Hodgson," Jack said.

"You remember my name."

"Yes I have a good memory. Please tell me what happened to Christine."

"We don't know. Probably nothing. But no one has heard from her for a few days. She hasn't contacted anyone that we know of. Just you." Finally, he stopped jabbing the pen onto his notebook. "In her message she said something about a condition that she has. What condition might that be?"

"She hasn't been well."

"What's wrong with her?"

Jack bit his lip.

"What's wrong with her?" Hodgson asked again.

"She has a health problem and there's nothing they can do about it. She's twenty-five."

"Is it serious?"

"Lieutenant Hodgson, you're a police officer?"

"Yes."

"Do you ever have a problem that's not serious?"

Hodgson thought for a moment. "Offhand I'd say any problem is serious. Otherwise it wouldn't be a problem, would it?"

"We're on the same page then."

There was something about this old man who had a hundred years under his belt. It was something Hodgson admired.

"I'm sorry," he said.

"Don't be. She isn't. She even said so in her message."

"She did, didn't she? But she also said she has some unfinished business to attend to and you have no idea what that might be?"

"I wish I knew."

"Mr. Fisher, I'm going to give you my card. It's a smart card with a chip so you can plug it into ..."

Jack waved his hand in front of him. "Lieutenant Hodgson, you're a pen-and-ink kind of guy, right? You don't do minis?"

"No I don't."

"Well I don't do chips and smart cards. Oh I know they're supposed to make my life better and my wallet is teeming with smart cards about this and smart cards about that but between you and me I just find all these things to be a pain in the ass."

Hodgson broke out into a long, slow smile. "I understand," he said. He showed Jack the back of his card. "My address and phone number are on this side. Can you read it all right?"

Jack brought the card close to his eyes. "Yes I can make it out but it would be nice if they used bigger print." He put the card down and looked up at Hodgson towering over him in those size fifteen shoes of his. "The people who make all these things forget about people like me. I mean old people. Who can't see so well. They don't think about us when they make these things. They don't understand that a lot of older people just don't get it. They ignore us. I guess it's like the problem you have with clothes. The manufacturers forget there are some people who weigh three hundred pounds."

"I only wish I did weigh three hundred pounds."

"You're more than that?"

"The last time I checked it was three-twenty-nine which means I just gained another couple pounds and if I go over three-thirty my doctor is going to kill me." With that, Hodgson bent down and rapped on his right knee. "You hear that?"

"Hear what?"

"That's not bone in there."

"What is it?"

"Titanium. I had a knee replacement. It's still a little stiff."

He straightened up and put his arms at his sides, which made him look even bigger than before. Now he was so big he almost took up the whole room.

"If you remember something ... anything ... about Christine I mean ... give me a call. I don't care what time it is. Okay?"

Jack said he would. Hodgson started moving toward the door.

"Lieutenant Hodgson," Jack said.

"Yes?"

"If you find out anything about Christine you will tell me, won't you? I want to know what's going on. She's my great-granddaughter. I don't want you to think you should spare the feelings of an old man." Jack pointed to the side of his head. "I still have it up here, you know. I know you're fifty-four years old. You're from New York City. You wear a size fifteen shoe and you weigh three-hundred and twenty-nine pounds. And ..."

He looked at Hodgson's legs.

"You have a titanium knee."

Hodgson chucked. He really liked this old man. "Not much escapes you, does it?" he said.

"I told you. I have a good memory."

"If we hear anything I'll let you know. You have my word."

Hodgson turned around again and went through the door. Then he stopped and glanced over his shoulder.

"Mr. Fisher," he said.

"Yes?" said Jack.

"It was a pleasure meeting you, sir."

Sixteen

The Lodz Ghetto, 1944

The Church of the Virgin Mary was one street over from the ghetto. Jacob had passed it many times and didn't take much notice until the time he smelled the onions from the garden. There was no mistaking the smell of onions. One day when he was about to lose himself in the Aryan section, he saw a man standing by the church door. He was tall and thin, and wearing a black robe with a white collar around the neck, smoking a cigarette. The man saw Jacob and smiled as if he knew him, but Jacob didn't know what he wanted. Didn't everyone want something? When the man opened the door and motioned for him to come in, Jacob weighed his options. If he succumbed to his curiosity and went in, the door might be shut behind him, and then what? But if he trailed behind the man, he could have his look and run. However, after following the man with the collar through the door, he didn't turn and run because one look inside and he couldn't stop looking. The ceiling was higher than any ceiling he had ever seen, but then he had never set foot inside a church before.

There were two rows of benches, at the very front the life-size figure of a man on a cross high on the wall. Jacob had seen crucifixes because Poles wore them around their necks, and he knew about Jesus, but had never seen anything like this. Even higher on the wall behind the cross were faces, and along the sides were windows, but not the kind of windows Jacob recognized. These were in brilliant color and they depicted scenes of a rising sun, a mountaintop, and a man with his arms in a gesture of welcome. Jacob was mesmerized. The man in the collar saw the look of awe on his face and put his hand on his shoulder. Speaking Polish, he asked if Jacob was Catholic.

Jacob was about to say no, that he was a Jew who lived in the ghetto, but admitting this to anyone on the Aryan side was a mistake. It could mean a beating like the one Josef got. It could mean the end of his stealing and worse. He could be taken away and never seen again.

"What is your name?" the man said.

Should Jacob tell him? No, he shouldn't tell him anything.

"Do you live over there?" the man said, pointing to the ghetto.

Jacob was frightened, but there was something about this man that wasn't threatening, and so, he nodded.

"Where is your star?"

All Jews wore the *Mogen Dovid*. They had to, but Jacob never wore it in the Aryan section because that would mark him as a Jew and everything would be ruined. Boys like him weren't even supposed to be in the ghetto. Two years earlier the order had come that all children under the age of ten and anyone over sixty-five would be resettled outside the ghetto. Twenty-five thousand people. But the Germans didn't get that many because the Jews hid their children. At least, they tried to hide their children. The alternative was the death camp. A place called *Chelmno*.

Jacob told the man that he never wore the *Mogen Dovid*. In

the ghetto he was in hiding, but here on the Aryan side he was free and could wear this coat, Shmuel Zelinsky's coat, and not even the whole coat because his father cut off the bottom so it wouldn't drag on the ground. But still the coat was too big for him. Even with all the buttons done, there was enough room for two Jacobs inside it.

The man ruffled his hair and smiled. "Are you hungry?"

Jacob said yes. He was led into a small room that looked like a kitchen. The man took two pieces of bread, cut a hunk of salami and made a sandwich. Then he sat Jacob down at a table, and watched him devour it.

"I have seen you before. You come by the church with nothing and on your way back your arms are full. Where do you get the food?"

Jacob didn't answer.

"Listen, from now on when you're hungry come here and I will give you something to eat."

"Then I will be here every day," Jacob replied in Polish, his teeth tearing through the salami.

The man laughed and said his name was Father Kasinski. Jacob asked if he was Jewish, which prompted another laugh. He said no. He said he was a priest.

"These are insane times. But I am your friend so next time you're on the street come here and I will make you another sandwich. *Farshtaist?*" That was a Yiddish word. He ruffled Jacob's hair again and said he knew many Jews. He said he even had friends who were Jews, but didn't see them anymore because they were all in the ghetto. "I told you my name. Now what is yours?"

Jacob told him. It was the first time he ever spoke his real name on the Aryan side.

"Can I give you some advice?" Father Kasinski said. "I have no problem with the name Jacob. In fact it's a very good name but it's a Jewish name. When you come here you should call yourself something else. How about *Jacub* which is Polish? So when you're back home over there you will be Jacob and when you are here you will be *Jacub*. Can you say that?"

"*Ya-coob*," Jacob said, and he said it the Polish way.

"Good," said Father Kasinski. "Now if anyone asks your name tell them you are *Jacub*. *Farshtaist?*"

Jacob nodded. For a sandwich with meat in it, he would let Father Kasinski call him anything he wanted. The next day Jacob was back, but Father Kasinski wasn't outside the church. Jacob boldly opened the door and walked in. There was Father Kasinski.

"Are you hungry?" he said.

What impressed Jacob most was that Father Kasinski made him something different every time he came. First it was salami, then sausage, and after that cheese. He even had butter to spread on the bread and Jacob's parents never had any of that. One day Jacob was back in the kitchen eating another sandwich when Father Kasinski asked him his name. He was about to say Jacob, but stopped himself.

"*Jacub*," he said.

"Good," said Father Kasinski. "When you're finished I want to show you something."

After eating the sandwich, Jacob let Father Kasinski lead him through a side door off the kitchen to an alleyway behind the church. They passed the garden with the pungent smell of onions, and then stopped in the middle of the alley where there was a manhole cover. Father Kasinski lifted it off and pointed into the hole. He said this would be a safer way to travel between the ghetto and Aryan section because Jacob wouldn't have to sneak through the wall or go over the top. Then he led Jacob down a steel ladder inside the hole. At the bottom leading off in all directions were tunnels and sewers. It was an underground city. Father Kasinski showed Jacob how to get from directly below the Church of the Virgin Mary to a building on the next block in the ghetto. All he had to do was bring a stick so he could push up the manhole cover, but when he tried, he couldn't do that. He wasn't strong enough, so Father Kasinski said he should come with a friend. Jacob immediately thought of Josef, who was bigger and stronger.

"How old is your friend?"

"Twelve."

"Bring him with you next time. What is his name?"

"Josef Karasik."

"He also needs a new name."

Jacob was thinking. He wasn't sure how to tell Father Kasinski what he wanted to say. "It won't work," Jacob said.

"Why not?"

"Josef doesn't look like me but I know another boy with blue eyes and light hair." Jacob said this boy was also twelve, but even bigger than Josef.

"You don't have light hair either," Father Kasinski said. "Would you like some?"

Jacob didn't know what he was talking about. Father Kasinski took him back inside the church, sat him down in the kitchen and brought out a bottle. He poured the contents into another bottle with a spray on top and then he mixed the concoction he had created with tap water. Jacob watched as the water poured from the faucet. There was no tap water in the ghetto; there was no running water at all. In the ghetto, Jacob's mother collected rainwater in barrels outside their building, so they could wash their hair and clothes, but here on the Aryan side there was plumbing. Father Kasinski said the clear liquid he just made was *peroxide*. He shook the bottle, told Jacob to close his eyes and then sprayed his hair with it. Then he ran a comb through Jacob's hair over and over. Ten minutes later he had him rinse his hair in the kitchen sink. It was a miracle. Jacob's hair was blonde.

"Now you have a new name, you have light hair and you have a safe way to get out of the ghetto and go back home as long as you bring a friend. But there is one other thing you need." Father Kasinski dug his hand into his pocket and fished out a coin. "Take this. It's Russian. And it's gold."

Gold?

"It's worth ten Russian roubles which is a lot of money but I don't want you to take it for the money. I want you to take it so you'll remember that even during this darkest time you had a friend." He put the gold coin into Jacob's hand and closed his fingers around it. "Never let anyone know about this. You see, Jacob ..." – he didn't call him *Jacub* but Jacob – "... they would kill you for a *chervonets*. They wouldn't care that you're just a boy. That's why I want you to hide it in your shoe. Inside the heel. Do you have glue?"

Jacob said his father had glue for fixing sewing machines.

"Good. Put it inside the heel then glue the heel back on the shoe. *Farshstaist?*"

"*Ich farstai.*"

Jacob gave him a smile and he didn't know it then, but it was the only time Father Kasinski would ever see such a thing from him.

Now Jacob didn't have to sneak through holes in the wall, and watch for the German Gestapo and Polish police. From what he could tell, one was as bad as the other. He saw them hit people with their truncheons and fists. He saw them hit men and women and old people and children. They were always angry.

There was a young Gestapo officer who always patrolled near the wall. He was short and squat with thick jowls, a wide neck, and a brown shirt that would look neat on Jacob's father. He had a cap and looked like a schoolboy, but the black spider on his red armband – the *swastika* – meant he was dangerous. He saw Jacob a few times, but never said a word. He stood with his feet pointed to the sides, one hand resting on his belt, a look of power and self assurance about him, and it was different from anything Jacob saw from the Jews in the ghetto. The Jews always followed orders.

But even the young Gestapo officer gave way to the German soldiers, especially the older ones who walked like kings with their gray jackets, peaked caps and Iron Crosses hanging from their chests. Jacob figured all Germans were rich.

The older boy who came with Jacob the next time was Shimek Goldberg and he didn't take kindly to Father Kasinski. He said it was fine if the priest gave them food and didn't tell anyone how they came through the sewer into the Aryan side, but he said not to trust him.

"He is a priest and he hates you because he thinks you killed Jesus," Shimek said.

Jacob didn't know what Shimek meant. He only knew that Father Kasinski was kind to him. Then one day there was another roundup in the ghetto. The Gestapo, aided by the ever-present Polish police, went door to door and marched off with men. There was no rhyme or reason to it. They went into one building, but not another. They took Shimek's father, they took Josef's father and they took Jacob's father, too. No one knew where they were going.

"*A klog iz mir!*" cried Jacob's mother, who went hysterical after the Gestapo walked off with Samuel. She pounded her fists against her head until her skin turned blue. She was several months pregnant by this time and feared she would never see her husband again.

Jacob had told his parents about Father Kasinski. He had to after the blonde hair, but he never told them about the sewers. They thought he was still going through the wall.

"I will ask Father Kasinski about Papa," Jacob said to his mother.

When Jacob told him what happened, Father Kasinski said he would ask around and a few days later Jacob's father came back. He was wearing the same clothes – the same pants, shirt and jacket – but they were creased and dirty, and if he had style when he left he didn't have it now. He didn't say where he had been, but was glad to be reunited with his wife and son. Even if it was the ghetto.

The next time Jacob and Shimek came up through the sewer, Father Kasinski was waiting for them. He said he had to speak with Jacob, so Shimek went on alone to the Aryan side.

"It's getting more dangerous for you and your family," Father Kasinski said. "It's getting more dangerous for all Jews. You must start learning." He took Jacob into the kitchen and closed the door that led to the chapel. "I want you to listen carefully," he said and then he spoke a language Jacob never heard before.

"Ave Maria, gratia plena ..."

It rolled off his tongue like music. The last word he said was 'amen' and Jacob knew that from his Hebrew prayers.

"Now you say it," Father Kasinski said.

"Say what?"

"A-ve ma-ria ..."

"A-vuh ma-reeyaa."

"... gratia plena ..."

"Grah-teeya play-na."

"Good."

Father Kasinski said learning this prayer was important. He said it could even save Jacob's life. It was Jacob's first Hail Mary and he learned it quickly. Father Kasinski said he would teach it to Shimek as well, but Shimek wouldn't want anything to do with it.

From that day on, every time the two boys came up through the sewer Jacob went into the kitchen with Father Kasinski to study, while Shimek headed off to the Aryan side. Jacob would eventually join up with his friend before coming back several hours later, and the boys would then return to the ghetto. One day Father Kasinski said Jacob had to be baptised. Jacob asked him why.

"To protect you."

Inside the empty church, he took Jacob to the altar where he had him bend down and kneel. He poured water – holy water he called it – over his head. "I baptise you in the name of the Father and of the Son and of the Holy Spirit." Father Kasinski said Jacob was now a Catholic, but Jacob insisted that he was a Jew.

"You are forgetting something," Father Kasinski said. "When you are on the other side you are a boy named Jacob who is a Jew but here on this side you are *Jacub* and *Jacub* is a Catholic. Now say it."

"Ave Maria, gratia plena ..."

Jacob knew it perfectly and in this way he learned about being a Catholic. He also learned the words to the Apostles' Creed and the Lord's Prayer. Much to Father Kasinski's delight, he had many questions. One of them was this business about forgiveness. Jacob asked whom he should be forgiving. Father Kasinski said he should forgive anyone who sins, so Jacob thought of the German Gestapo and Polish police.

"Should I forgive them?" he said.

"You should forgive anyone who has forgotten how to behave like a human being."

"Even them?"

"Even them."

"What about people who steal? Like *Jacub*."

Jacub had become Jacob's alter ego. Another person.

"*Jacub* is only trying to feed his family," Father Kasinski said. "It is not stealing to try and stay alive."

"Should I apologize to Shmuel Zelinsky for taking his coat?"

"You should apologize and also ask for his forgiveness but I think he will understand."

One time after many hours in the Aryan side Jacob was back in the alley behind the Church of the Virgin Mary. He didn't go into the sewer with Shimek, but marched straight into the church where he saw the priests. He asked for Father Kasinski and a moment later he appeared. He took Jacob into the back and shut the door. Jacob was very upset.

"I cannot forgive the Gestapo," he said and the tears streamed down his face. "A man was walking on the sidewalk and they told him to walk in the gutter where all the Jews have to walk but he said he wouldn't do that anymore so they shot him. They shot him right on the sidewalk. I watched him die."

Father Kasinski cradled Jacob's head in his arms. The boy wasn't even five years old. He should be in school, but there wasn't any school for him. Father Kasinski held Jacob until he stopped crying, ruffling his fingers over and over through his blonde Aryan hair.

....

The sewers were another world where it was always dim. The only light came from light bulbs hanging from above, but they were spaced apart from one another so the shadows followed you wherever you went. Dim was good because it meant perpetual night and the night offered protection, but it was always cold and damp. Jacob came to know the sewers below the church very well and how to follow them into the next block where the ghetto began. Beyond that there were no sewers at all because the ghetto was the oldest part of Lodz. The best thing about the sewers was that no Gestapo or police watched your every move. The worst thing was the rats.

Father Kasinski gave Jacob long, wool underwear and boots to keep warm, and they helped as long as he stayed dry. The first time Jacob ventured into the sewers with Shimek he was walking on a ledge where everything was wet. He slipped and fell knee-deep into the water. It was cold and dirty and it stunk. He regained his footing just when a hideous creature – half a meter long from its nose to the tip of its tail, and with flashing teeth and whiskers – scurried right in front of him on the ledge. From that moment on, Jacob kept a watchful eye out for the rats.

July came and his mother was almost bursting. The baby

was due any day and Jacob's parents were trying to hide the pregnancy. If the Germans knew a woman was expecting, they would take the baby at birth, and that was why his mother stayed indoors. The only people she ever saw besides Jacob and Samuel were her sister Gerda, her niece Zivia, and her nephew Romek. There was talk of a midwife, but then word might get out about the baby. Another pregnant woman had been taken away from her family and never seen again. There was talk about this place *Chelmno* where they say Jews were being exterminated.

"With the Gestapo it is best to think the worst," Jacob's father said and he asked about the sewers. He said they should leave their flat and escape to the sewers before the Gestapo come for them. And so, a decision was made. The Klukowsky family – Jacob, his mother Bela, his father Samuel – and the Zaltsman family – Jacob's Aunt Gerda, and his cousins Zivia and Romek – would move to the sewers. One man, two women, one of them about to give birth, and three children.

Zivia was ten and showing signs of blossoming into a young woman. She looked like her mother, Jacob's Aunt Gerda, but without the cold stern spine of a Jewess who had lost her husband and was left lonely and bitter to fend for herself with two children. Jacob figured Zivia, who was six years older than him, was wise. She could prepare food and clean and look after her little brother Romek. No one had to tell her to do these things. Romek was also older than Jacob, but shy and withdrawn, and he never joined his younger cousin on his trips to the Aryan side. He was too big to get through the hole in the wall and lacked the daring of older boys like Josef or Shimek or the curiosity of younger ones like Jacob. Besides, he had an older sister who watched out for him. But there was another reason Romek never went to the other side.

He looked Jewish.

Jacob was the first down the ladder. He knew the way into the sewers. Then it was Zivia's turn and then Romek's, and for them this was an adventure. They hadn't been out of their flat for months. Next came Jacob's Aunt Gerda, but she found it awkward stepping down the ladder. Then Jacob's father went, followed by his mother, who was nine months pregnant and with a belly so big she couldn't face the ladder and had to climb down backwards with her hands behind her, feeling blindly along the railing. By the time she got to the bottom rung, she was practically sitting on her husband's shoulders.

Jacob knew of a small compartment and this was where they set themselves up. The only thing they brought with them was old blankets. When his mother was on her back on a bed of blankets, Jacob took his father through the sewers until they were directly below the Church of the Virgin Mary. Then he took him up the hole to meet Father Kasinski. Samuel had known about the kindly priest, but not about his son's baptism or the Hail Marys.

Jacob's father explained their predicament and Father Kasinski listened intently. He promised to give them potatoes, onions and cucumbers from the garden beside the church. He said the priests grew more food than they needed and had plenty to spare. He also said he would give them meat, but it was pork sausage. Jacob's mother was indignant when she saw it.

"*Treif*," she said. "I can't eat this!" But Samuel insisted and he tore the biggest piece for her.

Jacob didn't know anything about foods to be avoided like pork and ham. The first time he tried ham was the sandwich made by Father Kasinski and it was delicious. He couldn't get enough of it. He couldn't get enough of any kind of meat Father Kasinski gave him. To refuse food because it was *treif* didn't make sense when they were starving, and when his mother was about to give birth in the sewers it didn't make much sense to his father either.

Father Kasinski used a rope to lower the food in buckets, but was careful because the Gestapo, Polish police and Jewish police were always watching. He lowered blankets and saucepans and cups and plates. And the most important thing of all. Water. It was always done at a set time. When the bucket arrived, all six members of the Klukowskys and Zaltsmans would be waiting for it. Then the rats would appear. They would come from everywhere. Sometimes they were so quick they got into the food before anyone could touch it, and it didn't matter if you beat them with a stick or threw a pan at them. So Jacob's father had an idea. When the next bucket of food arrived, he hung it from a pipe running across the ceiling of the compartment that had become their home. This was the only way the rats couldn't get at it. Jacob, Zivia and Romek watched the rats stand on their hind legs and reach for the food with their menacing teeth and their pointed noses. They even jumped to try to get at the food. They were so big.

The buckets also collected their waste and so, a bucket would come with food, another would come with water, and an empty one would come for waste, and this was how they lived. The two families were huddled in a space that was little more than a cave with cobwebs, mud and the ever present rats. When it was time for the baby, Father Kasinski lowered a bucket filled with steaming hot water.

Jacob had never stayed in one place for long since mastering the sewers. He was always on the go, travelling through the pipes, walking along the ledges below his tenement building in the ghetto and below the Church of the Virgin Mary. But not now. Father Kasinski told them all to stay put right below the church until the baby arrived.

One morning they heard voices from the chapel. It was full of people, which meant it was Sunday. They were the voices of people praying and some of the prayers Jacob knew. *"Ave Maria, gratia plena, Dominus tecum."* He found himself mouthing the words and these moments were pleasant, his only pleasant moments in the filth and darkness of the sewers. His father said they had turned into human rats living below with real ones, but what could they do? Where could they go? A cold, wet wind broke through the deadly silence with a piercing whistle and there was always the constant stench of raw sewage. The first night Jacob couldn't stand it, but by the third night he didn't know if he could smell it or not.

His mother's labor pains began on a Friday afternoon. She was on a bed of blankets with more blankets spread across her, and when her pains started, Jacob's Aunt Gerda stuffed a rag into her mouth because one scream and someone would hear. The only person who knew about them was Father Kasinski. Even the other priests didn't know. Six hours into her labor, Jacob's father said they needed candles. Jacob figured the baby was coming, and with candles they could see better, but no. It was the Sabbath, and his father wanted to light candles. He sent Jacob scurrying up the ladder.

As always, Jacob had his stick with him and he used it to push on the bottom of the manhole cover, but it wouldn't budge. He looked below and heard the voices of his father and his aunt and the garbled moans of his mother, who was soon to give him a little brother or sister. So he pushed again, harder this time, and the cover moved. It was the first time he ever pushed it open by himself. There was no Shimek. He went to see Father Kasinski and returned with a handful of candles from the church, and when the candles were lit his father spoke in Hebrew.

"Barach attah Adonai eloheinu melech ha-olam. Ashe kideshanu bemitzvotav ve-tsivanu lehadlik ner shel shabbat."

Jacob would always remember this Sabbath. It was the last one his family would spend together.

His mother, drenched in sweat from head to foot, was panting and crying into the rags stuffed between her lips to deaden the sound. Then, in the middle of the night, an explosion came from far away, but maybe not that far. It was hard to tell. And then there was a second explosion. Everything shook and rattled, and not only the pots and saucepans that Father Kasinski had sent them, but even the pipes. Jacob's father thought it was an earthquake. He sent Jacob up the ladder again.

Father Kasinski was staying near the door of the kitchen leading to the alleyway beside the church, and when he saw Jacob he knew why he had come.

"Listen to me. The Germans know Jews are in the sewers. You aren't the only ones. They are dropping grenades into the manholes. They want to kill you or at least get you out of there but they don't know where you are. What is happening with the baby?"

Soon, Jacob said, and back he climbed into the sewers.

By now his mother was on the verge of passing out. His Aunt Gerda was wiping her brow with wet towels, making sure the rags between her lips stifled her moaning. Then finally, mercifully, her muffled cries stopped. It was a boy. Aunt Gerda cut the umbilical cord and washed the tiny baby with damp cloths. She wiped its eyes, nose and mouth, and Jacob couldn't believe how small it was. Little more than a doll. It started crying and was so weak that it was almost a cry without a voice attached. Aunt Gerda closed the baby's mouth with a soft "shh" and rocked the newborn in her arms. She moved him under his mother's breast, but Jacob's mother had no milk. Aunt Gerda tried grinding some of their food into water, but the baby wouldn't take it. He just cried and cried.

'Shh ... shh ... shh."

It was Sunday morning and by now they had been a full week in the sewers. There was singing from the church and then the singing stopped. Everything stopped. There was the sound of stomping feet and loud voices.

Jacob wanted to see what was happening. Armed with his stick, he climbed up the steel ladder and pushed away the manhole cover. He got to his feet, replaced the cover over the opening, and wearing Shmuel Zelinsky's coat went into the alleyway beside the church where he peered through a side window.

German soldiers were inside yelling at the priests and the

soldiers were angry. One of the priests was Father Kasinski. There was more shouting, and then the people sitting on the benches were ordered to get up and go, leaving the soldiers alone with the priests. There was more talking and more shouting. Two soldiers took Father Kasinski by the arms, and marched him into the kitchen and then out the side door to the alleyway. Jacob hurried behind the church so they wouldn't see him, and watched from around a corner of the building.

One of the soldiers struck Father Kasinski across the face, and there was something so hostile about it that it didn't seem real. But Jacob could see it happening before his eyes. Then he realized that this wasn't a soldier who had hit Father Kasinski, but the young Gestapo officer who always patrolled near the wall. After an approving nod from the soldier, the Gestapo officer – just a boy – hit Father Kasinski a second time. Now the soldier was yelling and Father Kasinski kept saying that he didn't know what he was talking about. Then the soldier took out his pistol. He waved it in the priest's face and even from a distance Jacob could see the terror in Father Kasinski's eyes.

The soldier and Gestapo officer talked some more and then the soldier put his pistol back into his holster. The two Germans escorted Father Kasinski to the front of the church, one on each arm, and by this time more soldiers had gathered around. They shoved Father Kasinski into the back of a car. Jacob saw the edge of Father Kasinski's black robe caught in the door, fluttering in the air as they drove off in a cloud of dust.

He never saw him again.

Jacob ran back behind the church, pried open the manhole cover, and went down the ladder into the sewer where he found Aunt Gerda holding the baby. His mother was whimpering, his father was holding onto her and weeping, and Zivia and Romek were both crying. The only one not crying was the baby.

"*Yit'gadal v'yit'kadash sh'mei raba*," his father said through his tears.

Aunt Gerda wore the sorriest face Jacob had ever seen and he had seen some sorry faces in the ghetto. "The baby wouldn't stop crying and the soldiers were there. I'm sorry, Jacob. He would have died anyway."

Jacob's father finished the prayer and then he pried the still baby from Aunt Gerda's arms. He gave a long lingering look, planted a kiss on its forehead and covered its face with the blanket. Jacob's eyes followed his father as he walked along the ledge to where the water was deepest. He saw him put his baby brother into the water and watched as the solitary figure disappeared beneath the surface into the dank darkness of the sewer.

The next day the soldiers returned. They opened the manhole cover, went down the ladder and found the six of them. Immediately, the soldiers covered their faces and complained about the stink. *"Verfluchte Juden,"* they said. Nudging them with the butts of their rifles, they marched the group up the ladder. One by one. They wouldn't let any of them help Jacob's mother, who was still bleeding from the birth.

It was August and the air was hot. When they emerged from the sewer none of them could open their eyes because the sun was too bright. Jacob's eyes hurt so much that he had to cover them with his hands and even his skin hurt with the sudden heat. He looked at his father, but the man he saw just then wasn't his father. Jacob didn't see a tailor and a fixer of sewing machines. He didn't see a man who could make the crooked line of a shirt straight by merely putting it on. What he saw was a broken man in tattered clothes with a dead face of stone.

The Germans said the ghetto was now *Judenrein*. Free of Jews. They called the Jews pigs and vermin, and they spit on them. Jacob wanted to know what happened to his friend Father Kasinski, but he didn't dare ask. He was too frightened. The next day Jacob, his parents, his Aunt Gerda, and Zivia and Romek were all on a train heading to a new place.

Auschwitz.

Seventeen

Jack's alarm went off at seven o'clock. He opened his eyes and felt sluggish. Despite his airs, he couldn't get used to all this business about being a hundred years old. It was a number that belonged to Methusalah. None of his friends had lived that long and no one in his family. There were more centenarians than ever, but the age still came with a stigma. It meant you were ancient, a dinosaur, a relic from an earlier time that people didn't understand and didn't even want to understand. But shouldn't Jack be thankful that he had lived so long? Hadn't God saved him when so many others were taken? But God also made him an orphan at the age of five or was it four? Jack didn't know. He never knew exactly what happened to his parents or when it happened. Only that they met a horrible end.

All these years he had lived without parents, siblings, cousins. Not one single relative. It meant orphanages and homes with strangers and such deep scars that not a day went by when he didn't think about his mother and his father and the time they had together. It was so little time and even that had been a prison for them. Why would a merciful God let Jack survive only to wallow in a bog of guilt where the strands of his earliest memories tugged like ghosts reaching out day after day after day? Pulling him in to join the dead where he belonged.

He had been living like this for ninety-five years.

He left his room, headed down the hall to the elevator, and passed a door with a message taped to it. A different message was posted on this door every day. *God promises a safe landing, not a calm passage.* That was today's message. Trudy, the woman who lived there, always wore a smile.

Jack made his way further down the hall and caught the elevator where he found Eric, eighty-seven and a widower like him. He was a man who never said much, just a nod or a shrug. Jack said hello, but got nothing in return and then, a few seconds into their ride, a sign of life.

"What makes you think you're so special?" Eric said.

"Excuse me?" said Jack.

"You know what I'm talking about. You think you're the only one who suffered? You think no one else deserves any pity?"

"Pity?"

"Yes pity. What makes you think you're so special?"

"What are you talking about?"

The elevator doors opened and Eric marched off in a huff to the dining room. Jack followed him through the lobby with the yellow-brown wallpaper on the wall and the red floor that was painted like that so you could see it. The first person he bumped into was Trudy, the one who put all those messages on her door.

"Good morning, Jack," she said. "How are you today? Lovely day, isn't it?"

Trudy was always smiling, but never had much to say. Nothing of substance. It was usually the weather or the Yankees or politicians or how the coffee they served in the dining room was never hot enough, but she was a lot more pleasant than Eric had been in the elevator.

"Good morning, Trudy," said Jack. "I'll try for that safe landing."

"You do that," and she gave him a warm smile. It would be the only smile he would see all day.

The next person he bumped into was a woman he admired. Linda was a few years short of the Hundred Club, but carried herself with the dignity of a well-preserved seventy-five. She could pass for that.

"Good morning, Linda," Jack said.

"Hmmph," was all she said.

"What's wrong?"

"I'll tell you what's wrong. I heard about that story in the *Times*. Everyone has heard about it. You think you're a big celebrity? Well you're not."

Jack was horrified. The reporter, a young English grad from Columbia, wanted to know about the ghettos and the camps, so he told him. He told him about the Zyklon gas and the death chambers and the ovens. He told him about Dr. Mengele and the experiments with children. He told him about the six million.

Jack went to the far corner of the dining room, to the faces he knew at his table by the window. Fred, eighty-something and not well, got around with a walker. He always wore a scowl and Jack figured it was because no ladies ever took an interest. Patricia, a retired schoolteacher and also in her eighties, often shared stories with Jack. They talked about their grandchildren and great-grandchildren. Then there was Rachel, a friendly Jewish woman approaching ninety and recently confined to a mobiler.

"We are honored to have you join us for breakfast," Rachel said, her voice thick with sarcasm. "Thank you for educating us about the war and for telling me how to live my life."

"What do you mean?" said Jack.

"You paint yourself as the ultimate victim and you're not even Jewish!"

Jack sat down and examined his place setting. A glass of orange juice and an empty plate. A bright green napkin. And the cutlery set up nice and tidy. The waitress arrived and filled their plates with scrambled eggs and toast.

"Hey girl, no butter for me," Rachel said.

"She's new," said Fred. "She doesn't know."

Jack began to eat when Patricia of all people tore into him.

"Those things you said in that story. You shouldn't have said that. You shouldn't have said those things."

"What things?"

"That bit about ovens and gas chambers. No one wants to hear that."

"But it's true."

A voice from the next table. "Who said so?" It was Linda.

"I find that strange coming from you," said Jack, turning to face her. "You know these things happened. You're just as old as me."

Linda glared back. "I am not. I'm ninety-four and you ... as everyone on God's green earth knows ... are a hundred."

So that was it, the celebrity status that went with his one hundredth birthday, and the revelation about being a survivor.

"Linda, when were you born?" Jack asked her.

"Nineteen-forty five. Why?"

"And you're telling me the holocaust never happened? I don't believe what I'm hearing."

"It was a hundred years ago," she said. "How's your memory Jack? You don't even know what you ate yesterday."

"Are you denying it? Are you saying it never happened?"

"What she's saying is you like to embellish things. You do, Jack. You tend to exaggerate."

It was Fred. He always resented Jack because women found him charming.

"I don't exaggerate," retorted Jack. "When do I exaggerate?"

"All the time."

"Give me an example."

"I can give you six million examples."

Rachel piped up. "What upsets me most is that you're not

even Jewish and you pretend to be a victim."

"I was a victim! I still am! I've been a victim my whole life!"

"What were you doing in those camps if you weren't Jewish?"

"That's not all," said Fred. "What was all that business about soap?"

"Soap?" said Jack.

"Soap being made into lampshades."

"That was in the story," said Patricia. "And toenails made into paper ... and teeth ... human teeth ... taken from people and carved into art."

"What?" said Jack.

Patricia nodded her head.

"I never said anything like that," Jack told them.

"So where'd he get it from?" said Patricia.

"InfoLink," said Rachel.

"What?" Jack said.

"InfoLink. You don't know what it is? Well finally there is something that Jack Fisher doesn't know. My nephew told me about it. When you want to find out something you go to InfoLink. It's all there. When Allan saw the story in the *Times* ..."

"Who's Allan?" said Jack.

"My nephew. Aren't you listening? When he saw the story in the *Times* he went on InfoLink and read about soap being made into lampshades and the toenails business. What did they do with toenails anyway?"

"They turned the toenails into paper," said Fred.

"And what was that other thing about teeth?"

"They took out your teeth and carved it into art. It was sculpture."

"Yes teeth. It's all there on InfoLink. If you want to know about it just ask Allan."

"I don't know what any of you are talking about," said Jack. "I never told him anything like that. I never heard of these things. I heard about the skin and lampshades but I don't know if it was true. But teeth and toenails? What the hell is all that?"

"It was in the story," said Fred.

"Yes," said Rachel, "and if it didn't come from you where did it come from?"

"It must be InfoLink," said Patricia.

"What if InfoLink is full of crap?" said Fred.

Jack had never heard of InfoLink, but was inclined to agree with Fred. "Look," he said, "I don't know anything about this with toenails and teeth. Yes the Nazis took out teeth ... gold teeth ... they did that to everyone before they killed them ... but they didn't take out all your teeth. Why would they do that?"

"I know why," said Fred. "They took out your good teeth and used them in place of their bad teeth. With cavities. That makes sense."

Jack looked at him wide-eyed. "I think you're crazy."

"You're calling me crazy?"

The four of them, their energy sapping with every word they spoke, returned to the breakfast laid out before them. Their forks picked at the scrambled eggs. Their dentures munched on the slices of toast. And their juice glasses sat full, the fleeting sips cutting through the deadly silence.

Eighteen

"Is that Lieutenant Hodgson?"

"Speaking."

"This is Jack Fisher. You came to see me the other day about my great-granddaughter Christine."

"I did."

"I got another message from her this morning."

"This morning?"

"About ten minutes ago. If I can get hold of a nurse I'll have her send it to you. Hello? Are you there? Lieutenant Hodgson?"

"I'm here."

"Do you want to see it? This message I mean. It's one of those 3D things."

"If you got it I want to see it. You could have one of the nurses send it to me. You still have my card, don't you?"

"It's right here on my night table. She seems excited about something but she doesn't look too well."

"You know what, Mr. Fisher? On second thought maybe it would be better if I just come over there myself."

"If you like."

"I think that would be better. You're at that residence in the village?"

"The Greenwich Village Seniors Center. She's all right, isn't she? Christine I mean."

"I'll see you soon."

....

Jack sensed something was wrong when three people showed up at his door. There was Mary Lou his director of care, the mammoth Lieutenant Hodgson, and a woman he didn't know.

"Mr. Fisher," said Hodgson. "This is Kathy Sottario. She's a police officer with the NYPD."

"Nice to meet you," Jack said. She flashed him her badge.

Mary Lou asked Jack if he was all right. Then she said she would excuse herself, but if Jack wanted anything he could page her.

"Thank you," said Jack and with that Mary Lou was gone.

"We'd like to see that 3DE," Hodgson said. "Let's get that out of the way first."

Jack ushered his two visitors into the room. Hodgson shut the door behind them.

"Is Christine all right?" Jack said.

Hodgson pointed to the box. Jack flipped open the lid, pressed the button, and there she was. Christine. With some papers in her hand.

"Hello Jack. I said I'd be getting back to you. Remember? Well I hope you're sitting down because this is fantastic. I've been digging into these old records. I'll bet you didn't know they existed. I'm talking about the population registry books kept by the Judenrat. Am I saying that right? Judenrat? It sounds funny. These registries are all about the Lodz ghetto when you were a boy. They survived the war and have the names of everyone. I have here in my hands the page with your family. The Klukowsky family. Let me read it

for you. Klukowsky, Samuel Icek ... that's your father and I hope I'm saying his name right ... born in 1912 in Lodz. The address was Basargasse 24. Klukowsky, Bela Chana ... your mother ... born in 1915 in Lodz ... same address. And you Jack. It says right here ... Klukowsky, Jacob ... born in 1939 in Lodz ... same address again ... Basargasse 24. Then there's another column with the place of deportation and ... extermination. That's what it says. A lot of people from Lodz went to the death camp in Chelmno but everyone in your family wound up in Auschwitz-Birkenau. So I searched some more and this is what I found. The Official German Record of Prisoners in Auschwitz Concentration Camp. May 1940 to December 1944. You were right about those Germans, Jack. They kept records of everything. Year by year. Month by month. They have tables of ... let's see ... non-Jewish prisoners entering Auschwitz ... total typhus deaths in Auschwitz ... Jewish typhus deaths in Auschwitz ... deaths by natural causes for Jews and non-Jews ... transfers for Jews and non-Jews ...and this one ... administrative executions. They have dates for that. And there are lists ... long lists ... of names. In August 1944 more than sixty-five thousand Jews from the Lodz ghetto were deported to Auschwitz-Birkenau including you and your parents and your aunt and your two cousins. I found all six names. I have more to tell you so I put together a package and it includes a little surprise. I even gift-wrapped it for you. Consider it a belated birthday present for your one hundredth. I know you're coming to Kitchener soon so I'm going to leave it for you in our old hiding place. You know where it is. Love you Jack. Your little Christine."

When it was over, the woman officer with Hodgson took hold of Jack's hand, and it made him uncomfortable. He was never one for people touching him, especially people he didn't know.

"This is very interesting," she said. "Look, Mr. Fisher, we still haven't heard from Christine. The only one who has is you. She hasn't been in touch with her parents or her sister."

"So?" said Jack.

"Well, it does seem odd, doesn't it? That she hasn't been in touch with those who are closest to her. Doesn't that seem odd to you?"

"I don't know. Christine is a big girl. She doesn't live with them. She has her own place."

"She lives alone?"

"No. She lives with a friend."

The woman and Hodgson exchanged glances.

"A friend?" the woman said. "And who is that?"

"Her girlfriend. They have their own place. I met her once or twice."

"What is her friend's name?" Hodgson said.

"I forget," said Jack.

"Can you tell us anything about her?"

"Not really. They live together in a house."

"Is she also a teacher?" asked the woman. "Like Christine?"

Jack thought for a moment. "Maybe. I'm not sure."

Jack's eyes weren't the best, but he caught how the woman was looking at him. As if she didn't believe him.

"Mr. Fisher," she said. "We've been in touch with Christine's family and no one mentioned anything about Christine living with a friend. Now why is that?"

"I don't know. They share the rent. It's cheaper that way."

"I'm sure it is but how come her mother didn't tell us about that?"

"Emma? She's a strange woman that one."

"Christine's mother?" said Hodgson. "Why is she strange?"

"She's a nurse who thinks she invented the cure for every disease known to man. And she's old-fashioned."

"Old-fashioned?" said the woman. "What do you mean?"

Jack hesitated.

"Well?" said Hodgson.

"Emma ... she thinks two women shouldn't be living together."

"Why not?" said Hodgson.

Jack shrugged.

"And *you* think she's being old-fashioned?" said the woman, a wry smile on her face.

Jack looked at her. "You don't believe me when I tell you I don't know her name or anything else about her, do you?"

"I beg your pardon?"

"You think I'm lying."

"I didn't say that."

"You didn't have to."

She let go of his hand, and Hodgson broke in.

"Mr. Fisher," he said. "Kathy here is an investigator and an expert interrogator."

"I thought you were an investigator," said Jack.

"I am but two heads are better than one."

"You don't believe me either? You think I'm hiding something?"

"I never said that."

"So what do you need her for?"

"May I?" said the woman. Hodgson granted her a nod of his head. "Jack," she said, switching to his first name, "Lieutenant Hodgson is right. I'm an interrogator. I know about detecting and defusing deception. I studied these things. I have a lot of experience."

"So do I," said Jack.

"You don't understand. Lieutenant Hodgson brought me along to assist on the case. We have a missing person here and there's a local connection. You. We have to explore every possible lead. Every possible angle."

"So?"

"So it's important we find out everything you know."

"I told you everything I know."

"But the first time you met Lieutenant Hodgson you didn't mention anything about a roommate. Why was that?"

"He never asked me."

It wasn't going well between the two. Hodgson could see that.

"Jack," he said, "is it okay if I call you Jack?"

"I think at this point I'd prefer Mr. Fisher," Jack said, looking at the woman. "It shows respect."

Hodgson let out a sigh. "Jack ... I mean Mr. Fisher."

"You know something? I know a little about ... what was that you said before?" Jack said to the woman. "About being able to detect things?"

"Detecting and defusing deception?"

"Yes. I know a little about that too and I get the impression you two aren't telling me everything. About Christine I mean."

"Jack," Hodgson said before stopping himself. "Mr. Fisher. Look, I'm going to level with you. It's been several days now. Nobody seems to know where Christine is or what happened to her."

"You think something happened to her?"

"We don't know."

"Maybe she just went away for awhile."

"Without notifying her school? What about her classes?"

"I can't explain that."

"Jack." He did it again. "Mr. Fisher ... Kathy and I are police officers. We've dealt with this sort of thing before."

"I'm sure you have."

"When people go missing for a couple days like this ...then a few days ... then a week ... and they don't call anyone ... well ..."

"Well what?"

"We were hoping you could help us."

It was her again.

"How?" said Jack, avoiding her now and eyeing only Hodgson.

"Well," Hodgson said, "has she ever done anything like this before? Just disappeared like that?"

"Not that I know of."

"Does she have any financial problems?"

"No. Christine's very responsible that way."

"What about her friend? The one who lives with her? Does

she have any financial problems?"

"I don't know but I don't think Christine would get mixed up with someone like that. Like I said she's very responsible."

"Has Christine been seeing someone lately?" The woman again. "Somebody new maybe?"

"Why are you asking me? Why don't you ask her parents?"

"We did and they don't know anything but then Christine hasn't been in touch with them and she has been in touch with you."

She said it accusingly.

"All I got were these email picture things," Jack said.

"Mr. Fisher," she said, "we were wondering why she's been in touch with nobody else ... nobody else on the face of the earth ... but she did contact you ... and more than once now. Twice. There has to be a reason."

"I don't know."

Hodgson held up his hand, a sign to stop. He looked frustrated.

"Mr. Fisher, you don't mind if I forward this latest 3DE to my office, do you? Like I did before?"

"No. Go right ahead. I would but I don't know how to do it."

"I remember you saying that."

Hodgson tapped away on the keys and did his business. Jack marvelled at how hands as big as his could move so quickly on the keypad. Hodgson's fingers made the keys look tiny, insignificant, and it reminded Jack of his last visit when he was leaving and he put his arms on his sides. He made the room shrink.

"How is that titanium knee of yours?" Jack piped up.

"It's getting better. Getting better all the time. A little stiff now and then, that's all. But thanks for asking."

The woman broke in. "Mr. Fisher, one more thing. This package Christine left for you. She said you'll find it in your old hiding place. Can you tell us where that is?"

"Our old hiding place? That would be at the gorge."

"The gorge?"

"The Elora Gorge."

"And where exactly is that?" said Hodgson.

"It's where the two rivers meet ... the Irvine and the Grand ... in Elora ... just under the bridge."

"What bridge?"

"The bridge that goes over the Irvine River. You see there are these big posts or pillars ... they hold up the bridge ... and the spot ... our spot ... was behind one of the pillars."

Hodgson took out his pen and notebook. He started writing. "What pillar would that be?"

"The first one."

"Okay let's back up and take it from the top, shall we? The place where the two rivers meet."

"Look," said Jack, "the best place to see the gorge is Lovers Leap. From there you look off to the right and you can see the bridge over the Irvine River. The first pillar ... right behind it ... was our hiding place."

"Mr. Fisher, this is very helpful," the woman said and she touched Jack's hand again. But he drew back and she saw his discomfiture.

So did Hodgson.

Nineteen

Kitchener, Ontario, October 2039

The ice-cold beer went down nicely. It was much appreciated after the hazardous night the crew from Station No. 5 of the Kitchener Fire Department just had. They had spent three hours battling a blaze in an apartment complex on the east side of town. One of them had to be treated for smoke inhalation and another got his eyebrows singed, but the rest were all right. When the crew got back to the hall, completely spent, they showered and went to sleep, and when their shift was done they didn't go home but hit the pub. It was a good way to cool down.

"Another pitcher please."

This was as good a time as any for firefighter Brett Krust to get a little drunk because the twin cities of Kitchener-Waterloo were hosting Oktoberfest. The annual celebration, North America's biggest Bavarian festival, had just kicked off. It meant a lot of drinking and partying, and over nine days more than a million people would visit, tripling the local population. Since many families in the area had German roots, Oktoberfest was a throwback to heritage, a time for *Gemutlichkeit*. Congeniality.

Brett didn't have a German bone in his body, but he liked his beer and drinking with the guys from the hall. One firefighter from his crew, Clifford, had a son who went to school with Brett's daughter Stephanie. Both kids were thirteen and Grade 8 students at Williamsburg Senior Public School.

"What do you tell a kid who starts asking lots of questions about history?" said Clifford, sipping his brew.

"What do you mean?" said Brett.

"Jeff's taking this course about the twentieth century. He wants to know how many Jews were killed in the Second World War."

"Not enough," said Brett and they both laughed.

Brett didn't have much sympathy. Ten years earlier, after seeing thousands of Christians rounded up and killed mercilessly by Islamic fundamentalists in the Great Holocaust of Southern Turkey, he figured it was time people started paying more attention to a growing problem. He was an avid reader of a blog called The Cobra. The Cobra said that immigration of undesirables was destroying the fabric of Western society. This was nothing new. Many people had been saying that for years, but according to The Cobra, the Great Holocaust of 2029 was the wake-up call. The Cobra said if such a thing could happen in Turkey, it could happen here and people should wise up before it's too late. The Cobra said there was nothing wrong with Caucasians and that too many years of apologizing should come to an end.

"I'm not prejudiced," said Clifford.

"Neither am I," said Brett.

"There's a couple Chinese kids in Jeff's class."

"I don't have a problem with that. I mean they're free to celebrate who they are but what about us? Why can't we?"

"That's just it. We can't."

Brett didn't see the logic in that. Wellington County remained a conservative, predominantly white society that hadn't been impacted by the influx of visible minorities who for years were flocking to the big cities. Brett wanted to keep things the way they were, so he kept reading The Cobra and he even went further. He joined a group of like-minded thinkers who often got together to talk. They all read The Cobra.

Brett's daughter Stephanie never brought schoolwork to her father because he was rarely home. He was a firefighter who worked shifts, and if he wasn't sleeping at the hall he was out with the guys, so Stephanie brought her schoolwork to her mother Jennifer. When Brett got home, he found them both fast asleep. Oktoberfest was in full swing, and he and the boys had just gone through six pitchers of beer.

"Jen," he said, nudging his wife in bed. "Get up. We gotta talk."

He touched her arm. Jennifer was all skin and bone. Her blonde hair spewed over her shoulders across the pillow. She stirred.

"What?" she said.

"Has Steph been asking you about Jews?"

"What?"

"You heard me. Has she been asking you about Jews?"

Jennifer rubbed her eyes. "She mentioned something. They're taking a course at school about the twentieth century or wars of the twentieth century or something like that."

"So?"

"So they're studying the Jewish holocaust."

That was enough for Brett. His head still cloudy from the beer, he stormed into Stephanie's room and switched on the light.

"What the hell is going on at your school!" he roared.

He was mad.

"What?" Stephanie said.

He asked her again and she said they were studying Nazi Germany. The death camps. The gas chambers. The whole thing.

"Lemme see your e-reader!" he demanded.

"It's not in our e-reader."

"What do you mean?"

"There's nothing in there about it. Our teacher tells us about it in her lectures."

"What's her name?"

"Christine Fisher. She's nice."

"I don't care how nice she is but I sure as hell don't want her brainwashing my daughter with all this crap!"

Jennifer, cowering in the doorway, hated it when he came home like this. It wasn't the first time.

"You're drunk," she said.

"I'm not drunk! Well maybe a little but not as drunk as you!"

"What're you talking about, Brett?"

"I know you go over this stuff with her. And you just take it? Why don't you tell her it's not true?"

"She's learning it at school. I don't like to mix in."

"You don't like to mix in! What's that supposed to mean?"

"I figure her teacher must know what she's talking about."

Brett, eyes glassy, leaned his lanky frame against the door.

"You're drunk," she said again.

"Listen Jen, if you don't do something about this I'm gonna march into that school and tell her myself!"

"Tell who?"

"Anyone I have to! I'll see the principal if I have to!"

Their son, seven years old, was up now. He asked what was going on.

"Your father has been drinking again," Jennifer told him.

"Why you piece of shit!"

Brett wouldn't be belittled by his wife in front of the kids like that. He grabbed her by the hair and pushed her onto the bed. She was barely a hundred pounds and he didn't have to push very hard. She fell on top of Stephanie, who began to cry. She always did that when her parents fought and it set Jennifer off. Soon both of them – Stephanie and Jennifer – were crying and then the boy, too. The three of them. The little boy wanted to join his mother and sister on the bed, but Brett wouldn't allow it. He stepped in front of his son, blocking his way, his big firefighter hands on the boy's shoulders so he couldn't budge. Then he wrapped his arms around him. Tight.

"You're choking him!" Jennifer screamed. "You're choking him!" She got off the bed and tried to pry his hands away from their son, but Brett was a man and she was so slight. "Let him go! Let him go!"

But Brett wouldn't let go. She flailed away at him with those boney arms of hers, the back of her hands, the back of her wrists, pounding him with everything she had. There wasn't much flesh on her. He just laughed, but then she caught him with an elbow.

"You bitch!" Brett said and he told her to stop. But she wouldn't. "I'm warning you," he said. Finally, he had enough. With his fist clenched, he hit her in the face and she fell on the floor, the blood gushing from her nose like a river.

"Mommy!" screamed their son, rushing to her side.

The three of them – Jennifer and her two children – were huddled on the floor next to the bed embracing one another. Crying. Snivelling. Jennifer bleeding badly. Her nose looked broken.

Brett stood there, hovering over them. The man of the house. He shook his head and crossed his arms.

"This is all your fault, Jen," he said. "And that teacher of yours, Steph. That Fisher woman."

CHAPTER TWENTY

Twenty

"Jack, this will make you famous."

Mary Lou Bennett, Director of Care at the Greenwich Village Seniors Center, had the last word when it came to requests involving her residents, but there were never requests from the media. Who wanted to talk to old people in a seniors' home? But Trish Anderson did. She hosted a talk show that was syndicated across radio, television, Internet and 3D networks in North America, Europe, Australia and English-language outlets right around the world. The audience was huge. The theme this time would be racial and ethnic tensions, the trigger a sudden outbreak of violence between Sunni and Shi'ite Muslims in Nigeria, the most populous country in Africa.

An advance person from the show was preparing Jack for his interview, hooking him up to receptors for sound and 3D imaging in a lounge on the building's mezzanine level. It was a small, intimate room that had never been used for anything like this before. Mary Lou regarded Jack as her responsibility. She made sure a glass of water was on hand so he wouldn't dehydrate, and then thought orange juice was better and replaced it. This would be live. She told the show's producer that Jack was a hundred years old, that even though he was in stable health he had a problem with blood pressure and was not to be stressed, and everyone knew why Jack got invited. Ever since the article appeared in the *Times*, word was out that he might be the last living survivor of the Jewish holocaust from the last century.

Images of Trish Anderson and her other guests would be beamed in 3D format into the lounge while a small camera would shoot Jack as he talked. Jack would follow the proceedings and watch what everyone was saying. The show was in full swing when he finally got connected, the familiar face of the host coming in loud and clear.

"Thank you, Mr. Ambassador, for your comments. We have been speaking with Hans Stracht, Austrian ambassador to the United Nations. Now we go to New York and a very special guest. Mr. Jack Fisher. Hello Mr. Fisher. Welcome to Talk Back."

"Can you hear me?" said Jack, who wasn't even looking at the camera. He was talking across the room to Mary Lou.

"We can hear you," said Anderson. "Now if you just look this way. Great. We've been speaking with Austria's ambassador to the UN who said his country never had any concentration camps or at least death camps during the Nazi era. Is that right, Mr. Fisher?"

"Austria?"

"Yes Austria."

"Well I was at *Auschwitz*. That was in Poland."

"You were at Auschwitz?"

"Yes."

"When was that?"

"In 1944 and 1945. We were liberated in January 1945."

"How old were you?"

"Five."

"How old are you now?"

"I'm a hundred years old."

"Well I don't think we ever had a guest that age before. What's the secret to living so long?"

"Having a lot of patience and trying your best not to hate. But some people make it hard to do."

Anderson laughed. "So you remember being at Auschwitz. A place where some say the Nazis murdered a large number of Jews. A death camp. Is that right?"

"They did murder a lot of Jews. Thousands. Hundreds of thousands. Millions. In that one place alone. It was hell."

Hans Stracht, Austria's ambassador to the UN, was still on the air. His English was impeccable, but his accent strong. "Now hold on a moment," he said. "I too would like to congratulate this gentleman on his long life but I fear his memory is failing him a little."

"Why do you say that?" asked Anderson.

"Because there were no death camps in Austria."

"That's a lie!" said Jack.

Mary Lou pressed her hand to her chest.

"Wait a minute," said Anderson. "Mr. Ambassador, you seem to have elicited quite a reaction here from Mr. Fisher. He claims to be a former resident of a death camp at Auschwitz and he might be the last one. The last living survivor. That's what he claims."

"He claims."

"There was a camp in Austria," said Jack. "At *Mauthausen*. That was in Austria."

"Nonsense," said Stracht.

"I wasn't there but I know it existed," said Jack.

"Now listen to me," said Stracht. "Yes there was a facility at Mauthausen as this gentleman says but it wasn't a camp. It was a holding facility for enemies of the state. You have to understand. The world was at war and it was a terrible war. As with any war many innocent people lost their lives but the great majority of those deaths took place on the battlefield."

"That's not true," said Jack. "My own parents were murdered by the Nazis and that didn't happen on a battlefield. It happened at *Auschwitz*. And before we were there we were in the ghetto in *Lodz*."

"You were in a ghetto?" asked Anderson.

"A Jewish ghetto. I was born there and when I was a little boy my parents had to hide me."

"Why did they have to hide you?"

"Because the Germans would've killed me."

"A child?"

"Yes. They killed many children. Millions of them."

"They killed millions of children? Jewish children?"

"Absolutely."

"Trish," broke in Stracht. "Can I say something?"

"Just a minute, Mr. Ambassador. We've got some serious accusations coming here from Mr. Fisher and I want to explore this further. You'll get your chance. Let's go back to Austria for a minute. Mr. Fisher claims there was indeed a camp in Austria."

"*Mauthausen*," repeated Jack.

"Mr. Fisher," said Anderson. "You're an American citizen, is that right?"

"Yes I am."

"But I must say it sounds like you speak German awfully well."

"Yes I speak German. And Polish."

"Why Polish?"

"Because I was born in Poland. In *Lodz*."

"If you were born in Poland how come you speak German?"

"Because Germany invaded Poland and made everyone speak German. The city where I was born ... *Lodz* ... they changed the name to *Litzmannstadt*. Even the street where I was born ... Bazarowa Street ... got a German name. They changed it to *Basargasse*. Everything had to be in German. It would be like someone taking over America and you have to say *die Stadt Neu York* instead of New York City."

"Really?"

"Yes."

"Well I must say your German is very good. Now the Austrian people already spoke German, didn't they? Isn't that what they speak over there?" said Anderson.

"The Austrians were Nazis too," said Jack.

"Trish!" said Stracht. "I'm sorry but I can't let that go. This man has just insulted my country."

"I believe he has."

"What he just said would be like labelling all Americans as Nazis."

"What are you talking about?" said Jack. "The Austrians were no better than the Germans. In some cases they were even worse. Hitler himself was Austrian."

The eyes of the Austrian ambassador rolled. "Trish, I'm afraid there are things I must deal with here."

Anderson said to go ahead.

"First, there were no death camps in Austria. None. If this man says there was he is mistaken. There was only a holding facility for enemies of the state at a time of war. Even the United States did this with its own citizens of German and Japanese ancestry during that same war and so did other Allied countries. If you look at the historical record you will see that in many Western countries ... like the United States ... Germans who were citizens of those countries were discriminated against and forcibly confined throughout the entire conflict. The second point I want to make is that Austria was invaded by Nazi Germany."

"With open arms," Jack said.

"I must say, Mr. Fisher," said Stracht, "you have a lot of energy for a man your age."

"And you have a lot of baloney for a man your age."

Anderson laughed and even Stracht permitted himself a chuckle. Anderson took over.

"I'm getting hand signals from one of our other guests who's with the Al Jazeerah news agency. He wants to say something. Mohammad Rahman. Go ahead, Mr. Rahman."

"Thank you Trish. You have an older man here who doesn't know what he's talking about and I excuse him for that but I give him credit for coming on your program considering his advanced age. However, it's a very dangerous thing when someone can be on this show and make whatever claims he wants. I can just as easily say the State of Israel has been waging genocide against Arab people and Palestinians in particular ever since the State of Israel was created and there is all kinds of proof and witnesses to back me up."

"Indeed," said Stracht.

"I am a witness," said Jack.

"With all respect, Mr. Fisher," said Stracht, "but during all my years practising law I can tell you that if the sole witness to an alleged crime was a person one hundred years old who may or may not be in full command of his faculties, well I don't feel terribly confident that their testimony would be admissible in court. Here we have a man who's a hundred years old who has just besmirched the nation that gave the world Beethoven, Schubert, Mozart and Strauss."

"And Adolf Hitler," said Jack.

"Excuse me," said Anderson. "But a call has just come in from a sitting member of the Austrian Parliament. Mr. Karlheinz Gunther. I'm going to take that call. Hello Mr. Gunther?"

"There are some serious accusations being made here which must be corrected," said the caller.

"Now you are a member of the Austrian Parliament?" said Anderson.

"I am."

"And please correct me if I'm wrong but you're with the Freedom Party. Is that right?"

"Yes."

"Which currently serves as the Official Opposition in

that country?"

"That is correct."

"Go head, Mr. Gunther."

"Thank you. Our ambassador to the United Nations is correct when he says there were no death camps in Austria during the Second World War. As he says there were holding facilities for enemies of the state and yes Austria was invaded by Nazi Germany and not with open arms. Germany annexed Austria on its long march across Europe and did in fact invade many countries but talk about a systematic annihilation of the Jewish people at the hands of Nazi Germany is not exactly how it was although some people seem to think so. Yes many Jews did lose their homes and in some cases their possessions as did many people during that war. This happens in all wars. Sometimes to innocent people. But these claims about five or six million people being wiped out according to a plan is not accurate. We really don't what happened to all those people or even if that's how many it was. In my opinion it's more accurate to call it blasphemy perpetrated by those with an axe to grind."

"What axe is that?" asked Anderson.

"Well for religious reasons."

"Can you be more specific?"

"Must I? People of one religion get upset with people of another religion. Your show today began with a conflict taking place between Sunnis and Shi'ites. They're all Muslims. People of the same religion. And still they kill each other. In a civilized world there is no room for fanaticism and there is also no room for misrepresentation of history."

"What?" said a startled Jack.

"Mr. Fisher," said Anderson. "Can you hear me?"

"Yes."

"Do you know who this gentleman is? Our caller?"

"Not exactly."

"He is Karlheinz Gunther, a member of the Austrian

Parliament, a member of the Freedom Party of Austria which is the Official Opposition in that country. Now isn't the Freedom Party a right-wing party that's against immigration, Mr. Gunther?"

"We're not against immigration. We're against bringing in people who cause trouble."

"Would you call someone like Mr. Fisher a troublemaker?"

Anderson's question was greeted with stony silence and she let it last as long as she could, which was an eternity in a live 3D broadcast. It was broken by the sound of the Austrian politician clearing his throat.

"I think he is a delightful old man who unfortunately doesn't know what he's talking about."

"Did you hear that, Mr. Fisher? Did you just hear what Mr. Gunther said?"

"No."

"He said you don't know what you're talking about when you speak of millions of Jews being murdered by the Nazis."

"I was there. I should know."

"But you're still here, Mr. Fisher. You're still here."

"Yes I survived but my own parents were killed and so was everyone else in my family. I'm the only survivor from my entire family."

"Can you tell us how they were killed?"

"Many ways. They were shot or sent to gas chambers or they died of disease or they starved to death."

"Why would they starve to death? Didn't they have enough to eat?"

"No. Just a few crumbs. That's all. They kept us like rats. Men. Women. Children. Old people. But the children and old people were killed first. They weren't of any use so they killed them right away."

"But you were a child."

"Yes."

"How come you lived?"

"I was lucky."

"You talk about gas chambers."

"They also used ovens. They stuck people in ovens. Alive."

"Alive?"

"Yes."

"I've read about that. But did you ever see this with your own eyes?"

"We all knew it happened."

"Trish, this is very dangerous what's going on here," said Stracht, and Al Jazeerah's Mohammad Rahman agreed.

"Our Al Jazeerah correspondent Mohammad Rahman says this is dangerous," said Anderson. "Why do you say it's dangerous?"

"Because what he is saying is not true. You can just as easily say the Second World War never happened or the First World War never happened or the U.S. Civil War never happened. Just whitewash the true historical record with fanciful allegations that can't be proved or disproved. This sort of thing is what enflames people and spreads hatred and that's why it's dangerous."

"He's right," said the Austrian ambassador.

"Hold on. We have another caller and I want to take this," said Anderson. "It's a professor from the Hebrew University in Jerusalem. I'd like to welcome Esther Dorion who is with the Department of Humanities. Welcome to Talk Back."

There was the 3D image of a plump woman with a friendly face and loose-fitting clothes. She was seated behind a desk, a tall bookcase at her back.

"I've been watching your show. You have a gentleman here who says he's a living survivor of the death camp at Auschwitz and he may well be. It's entirely possible. There aren't many left but there is a huge amount of testimony from survivors which is available to anyone who cares to listen. Just last year an old woman in Switzerland ... her name was Rachel Gertberg ... may have been murdered precisely because she was a holocaust survivor."

"Murdered?" said Anderson.

"That's right. She was almost a hundred years old just like this man and she was a survivor from Treblinka."

"She was murdered by who?"

"That we don't know. We don't even know if she was murdered but her death was very suspicious. I'm sure you are aware that over the last decade ... ever since the Great Holocaust of 2029 ... there has been a rebirth of right-wing fanaticism all over Europe. There are political movements in many countries that are against immigration of any kind. I would put Austria's Freedom Party in that category and there are many more. There are also right-wing racist organizations that are dead set against Jews, Muslims, blacks, Orientals and any person of color. This is exactly the sort of thing that led to the creation of Nazi Germany over a hundred years ago and to say that Nazi Germany did not target Jews ... as well as other people ... is ridiculous. But Jews were the number one target. To say Hitler and Nazi Germany didn't plan to wipe out European Jewry ... that they didn't destroy six million Jews between 1939 and 1945 ... that's what is blasphemous. It is a fact that cannot be debated and I invite all your guests to come to the Holocaust Museum in Israel so they can learn more about it."

"There is also a Holocaust Museum in Washington," said Anderson.

"Yes there is."

"Hold on Professor Dorion. We've got another caller."

"It is *not* a known historical fact at all."

"I'd like to introduce Robert Burns from the Institute for Historical Review," said Anderson. "What exactly is this organization, Mr. Burns?"

"The Institute for Historical Review? It's a professional association of historians and academics. It's international in scope but is based in the United States. We examine the veracity of historical claims such as this man's claim about a Jewish holocaust at the hands of the Nazis."

"And who belongs to this organization?"

"Our members include respected academics from schools like Yale, Harvard, Georgetown and Princeton and they've published scores of e-books and mini-kindles and countless articles about this hoax that has been perpetrated for the past century. To say there was such an event of such magnitude is to denigrate the work and the very careers of some of America's most distinguished historians."

"But there is also a lot written about this ... event ... is there not?" said Anderson. "I mean the Jewish holocaust? I've read these books myself and there are lots of them."

"Ms. Anderson, have you ever read *Gulliver's Travels*?" said Burns.

"Yes of course."

"That's a book too. About giants and little people."

"But that's a novel," broke in the Israeli academic. "A work of fiction."

"Yes just like the Jewish holocaust," said Burns. "But it's still a book. Sometimes people find it difficult to draw a line between truth and fiction and that's the problem we have here. Just where do you draw the line?"

"You call yourself a revisionist, don't you?" said Anderson.

"No I never used that term," said Burns. "Other people use it. People who don't like to know the truth use it. If I am anything I'm a historian. But I want to add that it's not only historians who dispute this allegation. So do the American people. Just last year a poll said that eighty-two percent of the U.S. population don't believe six million Jews were killed by Nazi Germany in the last century. Eighty-two percent. That's a pretty large majority."

"Yes but another poll said half the American population doesn't believe we ever landed on Mars," said Anderson. "Yet we know it to be fact."

"Well I don't know about that but it's clear that most people, at least in the United States, don't accept all this nonsense about a Jewish holocaust with six million dead and it's not just in the United States. Polls taken in many other countries show the same thing. Sweden. Australia. Spain. Portugal. Most people don't believe it."

"All right. I want to go back to Mr. Fisher for a moment," said Anderson, "but wait. We have another caller. William Hawthrington is Professor Emeritus of History at the University of California at Berkeley. Welcome to Talk Back, Professor Hawthrington."

"I take exception to the comments made by the previous person who portrays himself as a legitimate historian when he is not. One cannot dispute that Nazi Germany tried to wipe out Europe's Jews in the Second World War. At the Nuremberg Trials right after that war it was the extensive documentation put together by the Nazis themselves as well as actual film they took that did in the defendants. We're not talking about an opinion here or a suggestion or innuendo. We are talking about facts and the facts speak for themselves. At the beginning of that conflict Europe had 9.6 million Jews and when it was over 5.7 million of them were dead."

"Mr. Burns," said Anderson, "what do you say to that?"

"Well it depends on which Nuremberg prosecutors you're talking about. The American prosecutor was concerned with Jews while the Soviet prosecutor was concerned with the genocide waged by Nazi Germany against Soviet Russia. The Soviet Union as it was called in those days lost twenty million people in that war. *Twenty million people!* How come nobody talks about that holocaust?"

"Twenty million?" said Anderson.

"He is correct," said Hawthrington. "That's the first thing he has said that's right. The Soviet Union lost twenty million people, most of them civilians, in the Second World War."

"And since we're on the subject of Nuremberg it's interesting that not all Nazis who were on trial there received the death penalty," said Burns. "Even the American-controlled judge and jury didn't see all these characters as being equally culpable. But that whole trial was a perfect example of victor's justice."

"Victor's justice?" said Anderson.

"Yes. The whole thing was put together by the victorious Allies ... the Americans ... the British ... the French. Nazi Germany was on trial because it lost the war. Another thing we shouldn't forget is that that the Second World War was over only when the United States dropped the world's first atom bombs on Japan. How come U.S. President Harry Truman was never put on trial for killing hundreds of thousands of innocent Japanese civilians? I'll tell you why. Victor's justice. Japan and Germany lost the war and the Americans won the war."

"We're getting off track," said Anderson. "Professor Hawthrington mentioned the documents and the films ... German films ... that were presented as evidence at Nuremberg."

"It was all about revenge," shot back Burns, "which happens in every conflict where there's a clear winner and a clear loser. The fact is ..."

"The Jews were the losers," said Jack.

"What was that Mr. Fisher?" asked Anderson.

"Six million Jews murdered by the Nazis were the losers in that war. Not Germany or Japan. Those countries were rebuilt right after the war and both of them became very prosperous. But the Jews were wiped out. Where are all the Jews in Poland today?"

"They are in America," said Burns. "And they help write foreign policy."

There was a lull. It was broken by Professor Hawthrington of Berkeley.

"Ms. Anderson, your guest here has just shown us his true colors. No historian would say a thing like that and it shows where he's coming from. This is the stuff of conspiracy theories of the worst kind ... and anti-Semitism ... and that is the seed of this revisionist junk that masquerades as history. Unfortunately, the masses ... and it pains me to me say this ... but especially the American masses ... are ignorant of history. Even their own history. They are susceptible to the garbage peddled by this junk salesman."

"I beg your pardon?" said Burns.

"You heard me."

"I didn't say anything about conspiracy theories."

"I suppose 9/11 was conceived in Washington by the Joint Chiefs of Staff."

"Well," said Burns, "there are many people around the world who believe that. At the United Nations ..."

"Listen," said Hawthrington, "I can't think of a more anti-Semitic organization or anti-Israeli organization than the United Nations."

"I would like to say something about the Nuremberg trials," said Jack.

"Excuse me?" said Anderson.

"The Nuremberg trials," repeated Jack.

"Yes? What about Nuremberg?"

"In November 1945 the chief prosecutor ... I forget his name ... but I know what he said ..."

"What did he say?" asked Anderson.

Jack cleared his throat. "We must never forget that the record on which we judge these defendants is the record on which history will judge us tomorrow."

At first, no one said a word. Anderson let Jack's quotation sink in.

"His name was Robert L. Jackson," said Hawthrington. "This gentleman Mr. Fisher has an excellent memory. The quote is correct." Hawthrington allowed himself a smile.

"Well," said Anderson, "we don't have much time left, I'm

afraid, and I see that every one of our callers is still with us. So Mr. Fisher we have several guests on the show today who don't think your story is true. About the Nazis murdering six million Jews in the last century. They think you're lying."

"I never used that term," said Stracht. "I just think the old man is mistaken and he can be forgiven for that. I mean, he is a hundred years old."

"I'm not mistaken about anything," insisted Jack. "I was there. I saw it. When I was in the ghetto at *Lodz* I saw the SS shoot people right on the street. I saw a man, a Jewish man, walking on the sidewalk and they shot him because he was supposed to walk in the gutter. That was the law for Jews. You had to walk in the gutter. I saw people dying from disease and starvation every day. When I was at *Auschwitz* I saw them use rifles and machine guns to kill women and children."

"Children?" said Anderson.

"Yes. They didn't care. They had no use for them. Not if they were Jews."

"You're telling us that they used machine guns on little children?"

"Yes! I saw it with my own eyes!"

Mary Lou was beginning to think Jack had had enough. More than enough.

"Mr. Fisher, you call yourself a Catholic, don't you?" said Anderson.

"I am Catholic but I was born a Jew and the first five years of my life that's what I was."

"So you converted?"

"You might say that but I didn't have much of a choice. If you were a Jew they were going to kill you one way or another."

"In ovens and gas chambers?"

"Yes."

"Now Mr. Fisher, I want to ask you about something else. What's this about skin made into lampshades?" said Anderson.

"What?"

"Skin ... from Jewish corpses ... made into lampshades. I've heard about this. Did it really happen?"

"I don't know anything about that."

"Have you ever heard these stories?"

"Yes but ..."

"So you mean it may not be true?" interjected Stracht.

"I don't know if it's true or not," said Jack. "But I never saw anything like that. I can only tell you what I saw."

"But you never actually saw someone being placed in a gas chamber, did you?" said Stracht. "Did you see your own parents placed in ovens or gas chambers?"

"No."

"Did you see their corpses? Their bodies?"

"No."

"So how do you know that happened?"

"What else happened to them?"

"A lot of things could have happened to them. They could have been sick. They could have had a fatal disease. Maybe one of them got it and it spread. Isn't that how a lot of Jews died during that time? From disease?"

"A lot of Jews did die from disease but most of them died from machine guns ... or rifles ... and gas chambers. Millions died in the gas chambers."

"Trish," said Stracht, "I'm afraid I have to go but I want to remind you and all your viewers around the world that Austria never had any death camps which harbored and tortured and murdered Jews. Even during a war my country would never do such a thing."

"There were no such death camps anywhere ... not in Europe or anywhere else," said Burns.

"But didn't they just close some of those camps a little while ago?" said Anderson. "Wasn't there one in Holland?"

"Now it's Holland," said Stracht. "Listen. Holland closed

a few wartime facilities just as several other countries did. In America do they keep those camps open where German Americans and Japanese Americans ... U.S. citizens all of them ... were incarcerated during the Second World War? Are they open now?"

"No," said Anderson.

"And weren't they shut down right after that war? Immediately after?"

"I believe they were."

"And why did the Americans do that? Maybe so the world wouldn't be reminded about it? Listen, these places you're talking about in Europe were kept open for decades after that conflict until there was no purpose in having them. But none of them ... and certainly not in Austria ... were death camps. That is a fabrication."

"What about Auschwitz?" said Anderson. "Didn't they have some kind of museum there that was shut down? And aren't they now talking about getting rid of the place for good?"

"Auschwitz was a holding facility just like Mauthausen."

"Okay. Mr. Fisher, our time is up," said Anderson. "I'd like to go back to you for a final word. The Austrian ambassador to the United Nations doesn't believe your story about the camps. Neither does the member from the Austrian Parliament and neither does the gentleman from the Institute for Historical Review. And according to one of our guests eighty-two percent of Americans today don't believe that six million Jews perished at the hands of Nazi Germany in the middle of the twentieth century. Only Professor Esther Dorion from the Hebrew University in Jerusalem and Professor William Hawthrington from the University of California at Berkeley agree with you on this one."

"So it's three against three," said Burns.

"What I want to know, Mr. Fisher, is what do you say to these men? They don't believe your story. They think you're either not telling the truth or maybe your facts are mixed up."

Mary Lou was squeezing her hands together. She had started to tense up with the first mention of gas chambers.

"I was at *Auschwitz*," Jack said. "I saw the most horrible things there. If I had my choice I wouldn't want to remember these things but living with these awful memories is my life sentence. As for the camps, of course they had camps. I was in a camp myself. An extermination camp. A death camp. *Auschwitz*. That's what it was and it wasn't the only one. There was also *Treblinka* ... *Belzec* ... *Chelmno* ... they were everywhere. All over Europe. And they were there for one reason and one reason only. To kill Jews. And they did. I should know. I was there. I am a witness."

Twenty-One

It was two weeks before Christmas and unseasonably hot for New York City. The temperature hovered around sixty-five degrees Fahrenheit – the United States being the only country in the world still using that scale – and city dwellers were peeling off their coats and jackets. Some were even wearing shorts. Hodgson found Jack sitting in the garden behind the Greenwich Village Seniors Center. Alone. In a sweater.

"Mr. Fisher?" Hodgson said.

Jack's eyes were shut. He looked to be sleeping under the blazing sun.

"Mr. Fisher?"

Jack opened his eyes. "Lieutenant Hodgson. I didn't know you were coming."

Hodgson pulled up a chair and sat down. He had a bulging envelope under his arm.

"Is your woman friend with you today?" Jack asked him.

"No," Hodgson said.

"What have you got there?"

"Some documents I think you'll find very interesting."

Hodgson opened the envelope, peeled off a few sheets of paper and handed them to Jack, who began fumbling around for his glasses. When he had them on, he started to read.

"Lodz Ghetto ... Deportations ... and Statistics." Jack looked up at Hodgson. Even when sitting, Hodgson towered over him. "What is this?" Jack said.

"These are copies of the documents Christine left for you in that package she told you about. The one at the Elora Gorge. You were supposed to go to Kitchener for a family function but you didn't make it, did you?"

"My blood pressure was acting up and I wasn't going on that train again."

"She left this for you and she left it just where you said she would. Behind the first pillar under the bridge that goes over the Irvine River. You were right. We found it, well not us, but the local police up there found it. They scanned everything so I could show you. I didn't think you'd want a mini kindle so I made hard copies."

Jack looked at the papers again. *Lodz Ghetto Deportations and Statistics.* Below the title was a list of tables:

Table A: Liquidation of Jewish Population in the Lodz Ghetto, 1942-1944.

Table B: Number of Deceased in the Lodz Ghetto, 1940-1944.

Table C: Towns in the Warthegau from which Jews were deported to the Lodz Ghetto.

Table D: Jews Deported to the Lodz Ghetto from Western Europe in 1941.

Table E: Timeline of Deaths and Deportations in the Lodz Ghetto.

Jack stared into space. Unblinking.

"Are you all right?" Hodgson said.

Jack didn't say anything.

"How about we go through this together?" Hodgson said.

He moved his chair in closer. The two began poring through the documents one by one, starting with Table A. Hodgson did the reading.

"January 16th to 29th, 1942. Number of victims ... 10,003. Place of Deportation slash Extermination ... death camp in Chelmno. February 22nd to April 2nd, 1942. Number of victims ... 34,073. Place of Deportation ..."

He left out the word *extermination*.

"Death camp in Chelmno."

He went down the list until he came to the entry for August 9th to 29th, 1944.

"Number of victims ... 65,000 to 67,000. Place of Deportation ... Auschwitz-Birkenau."

"I was in that group," Jack said. "And my parents and my aunt and my two cousins."

"It says here that 72,000 people were transported to Auschwitz and from that number only 5,000 to 7,000 survived."

"I survived."

"Table B. Number of Deceased in the Lodz Ghetto 1940 to 1944. In 1940 there were 160,320 people in the ghetto. A total of 8,475 died and of that number 41 were shot."

Jack was nodding his head up and down, listening to the numbers.

"In 1941 there were 145,992 people in the ghetto. Some 11,456 died of whom 52 were shot. In 1942 there were 103,034 people in the ghetto and of those 18,046 died. And 43 were shot. The total number of deaths in the ghetto for those five years was *approximately* 43,000. That's what it says. Approximately."

Hodgson went to the next table. Table C. Towns in the Warthegau from which Jews were deported into the Lodz Ghetto. "What is War-thuh-go?" he said.

"*Warthegau*," Jack said, speaking like a German. "That was the part of Poland that was incorporated into the *Reich* in 1939."

"The what?"

"The *Reich*."

Hodgson had a blank look on his face.

"The *Reich*," Jack said again.

"Jack, I don't speak German."

Hodgson seemed to be apologizing, but Jack didn't buy it.

"*Warthegau* is what Germany took over," Jack said. "*Reichsgau Wartheland*."

Hodgson had pressed a button and he knew it, but what hit him just then wasn't Jack's frustration at his not knowing about the Reich, but the fact Jack didn't sound at all like a man whose mother tongue was English.

"There's a list of towns here," Hodgson said. "Ka-lees? Is that how you say it?"

Jack looked at the list. "*Kalisz*. I knew people from *Kalisz*." His finger went down the names of the towns. "And *Kutno* ... and *Lask* ... *Lodz* of course ... there were many from there ... *Poznan*."

Hodgson shuffled through the papers.

"Here," he said. "Timeline of Deaths and Deportations in the Lodz Ghetto. January 16th, 1942 to May 15th, 1942. It says ... large-scale genocide begins. That's what it says. *Genocide*. Some 57,064 Jews from the Lodz ghetto are deported to the death camp at Chelmno."

He stopped.

"It says genocide," he said.

"That's what it was."

Another document had a list of ghetto inhabitants with the Polish names of Jack and his family among them – Samuel Icek Klukowsky, Bela Chana Klukowsky, and Jacob Klukowsky, all of them at 24 Basargasse. In Lodz.

"Well what do you think?" said Hodgson.

"I'm shocked these records exist."

"Christine got them for you. The sheer number of people killed. It's mind boggling." Hodgson looked at the papers again. "Over a period of five months in 1941 more than 57,000 people were sent to the death camp at Chelmno. That's more people than were killed in the holocaust. In the whole thing I mean."

"You mean 2029?" said Jack.

Hodgson nodded.

"Let me tell you something," said Jack. "There is only one holocaust and it wasn't in 2029. Why, 57,000 was a drop in the bucket. We're talking about six million people. *Six million*."

"Jack, I have to tell you something and I know you're not going to like this. But I find a number like that hard to fathom."

"Why?"

"How do you kill six million people? Especially back in those days."

Jack brushed his hand against the envelope as if swatting a fly. "It's all right there," he said, pointing to the papers. "It tells you ... 57,000 Jews ... they were all Jews ... were sent from Lodz to Chelmno. What do you think happened to them when they got there?"

Hodgson was shaking his head.

"And that was only one place. There were more. Many more."

Jack slipped off his glasses and stared into the sky. "I watched the news last night and a boy was gunned down in the street. They tried to interview his mother but she couldn't say anything. She just lost her son and the only thing she could do was cry. I didn't know this woman but I could feel her loss ... her pain ... from her sobbing."

"I know what you mean."

"Yes I guess you do but that was only one death. Sometimes you hear about a bomb that goes off and maybe ten people are killed. Just like that. Then they have those big bombs that reach their target and a hundred people are killed. Blown to bits. Now imagine you have this enormous room that can hold a thousand people if you pack them in tight ... so tight they can barely move. You lock the door and then you drop poison pellets through openings in the ceiling and in the walls and the pellets release cyanide gas. For some ... a little child ... it doesn't take long to die ... for an old woman a little longer ... and for a young man even longer than that. But soon everyone in that room is dead and when they open the door they find them in a pile. The smallest ones ... the children ... they were the weakest ... and when everyone was trying to escape the gas the stronger ones climbed on top of the weaker ones and that's how they found them. The bodies of the strong young men are at the top of the pile ... the women and the old people are under them ... and the little children are at the bottom. That's how it was at *Auschwitz* and a thousand people are dead. They could kill twenty thousand a day like that. And they did."

Hodgson was numb, but Jack wasn't finished. He sniffed at the air.

"It's a beautiful day," he said. "There isn't a cloud in the sky. And it's so blue up there. Have you ever seen such a blue sky? When I was at *Auschwitz* you would never get a day like this even if the weather was perfect. Even if it was a day like today."

"What do you mean?" said Hodgson.

"Just what I said. The sky was never clear."

"Why not?"

Jack took another sniff. "There is so much you don't know," he said. "But I guess it's not your fault. It's our fault. It's my fault."

"What are you talking about?"

"It's my fault for not telling people. I kept quiet all these years. I didn't even tell my own grandchildren about it. Not until Christine. I was trying ... hoping ... to forget."

"Why wasn't the sky clear?"

"Because of the smoke."

"What smoke?"

"From the incinerators. They were burning the bodies. The thousand people, remember? The crematoria. That's why there was always so much smoke. You could see it and you could smell it. All the time."

Hodgson was staring Jack in the eye.

"I saw it and I smelled it," Jack said. "Every day. That's what happened to all those people from *Lodz* ... and *Kalisz* ... and *Kutno* ... and *Lask* ... and *Poznan* ... and *Warta* ... and *Zgierz* ... and *Klodawa* ... and *Chodecz* ... and everywhere else on that list of yours."

Hodgson checked the list again. "What was that last one you said?"

"Chodecz."

"You're right. Here it is. They're all here."

"You know nothing about this, do you?" said Jack.

"About this?"

"You never learned about it in school? When you were a boy?"

"No. Not really."

"And you're an American. A New Yorker."

"That's right."

"This is exactly what Christine has been fighting all these years."

Hodgson had the envelope on its edge. It sat on his lap, his big hands going up and down the sides. Up and down. Up and down. "What I don't understand is why," he said. "Why did they want to kill all those Jews? For what possible reason? What did they stand to gain from it?"

"You mean the Nazis?"

Hodgson nodded.

"Lieutenant, what do you know about Nazis? And Hitler? What do you know about him?"

"What I know ..." Hodgson said more to himself than to Jack, "is from old movies. At least, those that went digital. But they were just movies."

"The Nazis were a lot more than movies."

"But that still doesn't tell me why. Why did they do it?"

"Lieutenant Hodgson, can I tell you something?"

"What's that?"

"I think you're a nice man. A decent man. But you are the victim of an ignorant people."

"I beg your pardon?"

"Ignorant people. Americans ... Westerners ... people all over the world. They are ignorant. We have a whole generation of people who know nothing about the human condition and that's the danger. That's why it can happen again."

"What do you mean?"

"I mean people don't know and what's worse they don't even *want* to know."

"They don't want to know what?"

"The truth."

Hodgson eased his huge frame back into the chair.

"Lieutenant Hodgson," said Jack, "you're a police officer and I'm sure you've probably seen a lot of bad things in your day."

"I have."

"Do you ever ask yourself why these things happened?"

"All the time."

"Now you know how I've lived my life for the past ninety-five years."

Twenty-Two

Colton Brock was six-four and 245 pounds. Chiselled. They called him Coal and it fit. He was all rock and no emotion except for rage, and it came in a torrent. When he fought on the street, it was in blue jeans and black boots that were laced up his shin. The boots were heavy and did a lot of damage, especially the way he kicked with those steel-pipe legs built through merciless hours in the gym. But in the ring he was bare-chested and barefoot, and he wore shorts. Money was at stake and they wanted to see what he looked like – the sculpted torso, the rippling arms, the tapered back, and those two pillars of muscle that he stood on. If he had boots in the ring, the bouts would have been over much faster. A flurry of jabs and uppercuts and the odd roundhouse with his right would soften his opponent and prepare for the final blow, more often than not a well-placed kick to the side of the head. Coal had cracked more than one skull that way. The boots – jackboots – were perfect for it, but in the ring there were rules; an open battle was waged within the confines of a prescribed space, the only weapons your hands and feet and any other part of the body you want to risk. No three-minute rounds or anything like that. It was a brawl, but organized. Structure but not too much structure. Coal preferred fighting in the street where there were no rules at all, but you couldn't make a living there. One did carve a reputation, however.

His opponent today was of similar size, two raw specimens in the super heavyweight division about to battle, and there was great anticipation leading up to the match. Both men were undefeated, and large sums of money were wagered. Coal was the favorite, but at 3-2 not by much, and he was surprised with the odds because he had little respect for this man. He had never fought anybody good, not really good like Coal, who for two years now had been destroying everyone they threw at him. The fight was held in an intimate arena for 1,000 people who forked over money to witness the spectacle of two professional fighting men pulverizing each other. Before things got regulated, the bouts were illicit affairs in an abandoned warehouse in the Jersey backwoods. But that attracted organized crime, so they opened it up with official sanction. As headliners for the night, Coal and his opponent would each take home a handsome stipend, the winner a little extra. There was no referee. Only an announcer.

The bell sounded and it started like a boxing match with the two behemoths sizing each other up, feigning moves to one side and then the other. But their hands were bare, not even taped, open and constantly circling in front of their bodies. Their feet never stopping. Their brains strategizing about what to do next. And, of course, they could use their legs, too.

Coal knew this man liked to begin with his right, either a punch or a kick. It could be high or it could be low and if he did lead with his right, a punch or a kick, it might be a fake to set up with his left. Then again, maybe not. Coal allowed this to go on for a minute or two, waiting for his chance. He waited and waited, and then the man made his move. He leaned to his left and brought his right arm back to deliver an uppercut, but Coal saw how he planted his left foot on the mat, bracing himself for a kick. Not an uppercut. Coal knew what was coming. He swerved his head to the side and the big foot came up high just off his ear. No contact. Not even close. Now the man was off balance. He had just lunged full force with his right leg, hit air and had to come down for a landing. And he did. All his weight was on his right foot, his other foot far to the side.

It meant there was an opening.

Coal jammed his knee into the unprotected groin and the man went limp, but before he hit the mat, Coal hit him again. Twice. He delivered a one-two exchange, first with his right fist flush in the face, and then the follow-through with his left into the abdomen. *Boom! Boom!* One knee, two blows, and it was all over. But no. As Coal backed away to a corner, the man ordered his body to climb up off the mat, and he staggered to his feet. That was the trouble with big men. They didn't know when to stay down. You had to destroy them physically and if that wasn't enough then destroy their will. Coal looked at him. He was reeling, his head teetering, his arms hanging weak at his sides. A simple jab would put him away now, but all these people had paid good money to watch the match and it was going to be over quickly. Too quickly. Coal the showman decided to give them what they wanted.

He sniffed. Heavy. A bull ready to charge. Pushing off the ropes in the corner, he was three steps into his run when he leapt from his left foot and then led with his right shoulder into a 360-degree turn. His ripped body twirling backwards in mid-air. Coming out of the turn, he unleashed a ferocious, flying kick at precisely the right moment. His naked foot was a guided missile and it struck its target. The side of the head. There was a wicked smack and the air sapped from the man's lungs like a balloon just pricked. He went down. A pool of blood and fragments of teeth were on the floor beside him.

"Winner of the match. Colton 'Coal' Brock!"

It was a good night's take, but to Coal the money wasn't for a few minutes of action. It was for two years of fighting without a single loss. It was for all those scrapes in the street where he earned his mettle. It was for forty weeks as a Navy Seal, which taught him everything there was to learn about underwater demolition, close-quarters combat, land warfare and firearms. Coal was a natural swimmer and this was the perfect career for him. It was the first time he had ever found anything that satisfied him physically as well as mentally.

He had left school early only to get into trouble with the law. Nothing major. Petty thefts, a few fights. He was young and couldn't get his mind wrapped around anything useful, at least, not until the Navy Seals. They made him complete. They made him a force. But two months short of completing the program, he had killed a man with a kick to the head in training. He wasn't supposed to hit him that hard, but he did and the man, just a kid really, went into a coma and never recovered. It was an accident. To make matters worse, his victim was black – a boy of eighteen. Coal was red-flagged as a crazy who couldn't control himself. He was released and no charges were laid. Now what to do? He was a fighting machine and the options were few.

Only once did he ever get hurt on the street – hurt bad – and it was a kick to the head, but it wasn't so much the force of the blow as the boot. The man who helped him off the pavement that day was a runt named Cobra Creeley. Cobra wasn't his real name, but that's what he went by. He was about a foot shorter than Coal and a hundred pounds lighter.

But more dangerous.

He had a tattoo on both his arms just above the elbow. The same tattoo on each. It was the body of a snake, at the front its mouth wide open with fangs exposed, ready to consume the tip of its own tail. On his back between his shoulder blades was another tattoo, a bigger one – King Cobra – with the forked tongue of the snake painted a bright blood-red.

"You got beat by an inferior," he told Coal. "You're wearing shoes with a soft heel and he had jackboots. That was the difference. If you want I can get you a pair."

The boots were made of tough, black leather and went up the leg over the calf. They were pliant, offering freedom of movement, and looked good. Why this Creeley character took such an interest in him, Coal didn't know, but just like he said he got him the boots and they worked. After that, Coal always wore them on the street.

Coal was a man of few words, but when you were his size and of his cut, you didn't need many. Creeley was different. Small and nothing to look at, he was a fast talker with lots of ideas who made up for his lack of brawn with his street-smart ways. He knew what made people tick. He knew that if you dig deep and liberated whatever it was that drove them, they would be indebted to you. In Creeley's mind, the core of every man was frustration at not being able to deal with life's basic instincts, which were programmed into our DNA from the beginning. All he had to do was unlock it, and his key was a blog that he wrote called The Cobra. He built up a following, and over time it grew into an ezine with thousands of subscribers who paid to hear what he had to say.

One thing led to another and Creeley introduced the big man to his friends. Some of them were physical types, who like Coal came from the military, while others had done time behind bars. The common ilk was that all of them were white and diehard nationalists. At first it was a social thing, a chance to mix and exchange stories. Coal's story was that he was a Navy Seal and got tossed out because he was too mean.

"If it was a white kid you killed nothing would have happened to you," said Creeley. "There are lots of accidents. Same thing with the marines. It happens all the time and they try to hush it up but you killed someone who was black. That was your mistake."

Coal started going to the meetings. They weren't all skinheads, but some were and like Creeley most of them had tattoos. Coal wasn't into that. He always treated his body with respect. No disfigurations for him and, aside from the crucifix around his neck, no jewellery either and when they told him why he was no longer a Seal, he bought it. Why else would they dismiss the best fighting man in the unit?

"You got shafted," Creeley said. "The military isn't for you and you know why? It's too organized. There are too many limits. Too many restrictions. That's not for a man like you. You have potential but you have to be free to realize it. What you need is a path with some structure. But not too much structure."

It was through them that Coal discovered the pro fighting circuit and he liked that. He was good at it and could even make money, more money than he ever had before, and money had always been a problem for him. He would have time to train and Creeley would be his manager of sorts. Ex officio. Structure but not too much structure.

They said the white race was the superior race and history has shown this to be true. History has made that abundantly clear. Everything America accomplished that was great was on account of white Christian men and women, God-fearing people who knew their place in the bigger scheme of things. This is not to denigrate anyone else. We are not racists. We just look at the facts and the facts are plain to see. A better world is a world where the ones who pull the strings are those who are most able. Some will lead and more will follow. That has been true with every civilization. Those who are born to lead shall lead and any other way is a road to certain disaster. It was all there in The Cobra.

Coal bought it all.

"Now you're the champion," Creeley said. "You beat them. Every one of them. No matter what happens to you for the rest of your life they can never take that away from you. At this point at this time you are the best."

Creeley made Coal feel good about himself and not many

people did that before. So on the night of his victory, Coal offered to buy drinks with his winnings. There was a group present and their women were on hand, too. One of the girls mentioned a show that went viral around the world. It was called Talk Back, and there was something about an old Jewish man who talked about extermination. Coal hadn't seen it, but Creeley had.

"He says he was a witness," Creeley said.

"To what?"

"He talked about death camps and bodies burning in ovens. He called everyone on the program a liar and they were all experts. Educated people. Politicians. They had a man from the United Nations on it and hell he tore a strip off him too and called them a bunch of liars because they didn't believe his story."

Coal listened.

"Now this is the sort of thing that causes trouble," Creeley said. "A lot of trouble."

Twenty-Three

Cathy Trachter was an investigator with the Waterloo Regional Police. She had risen quickly through the ranks since joining the department fresh out of police college, beginning as a fourth-class constable who patrolled the quieter areas of Wellington County. That was all they would give her. But she soon got to see the seedy side of life – a domestic that went wrong, a robbery that erupted into a knifing, or even the occasional shooting. But shootings were rare and homicides rarer still. Not in these parts. However, Waterloo Region was a huge area to patrol and sometimes there were missing persons. The Missing Persons Report for Christine Fisher was nothing out of the ordinary.

Christine Fisher was last seen on December 3rd, 2039 at approximately 4:30 p.m. She was leaving Williamsburg Public School where she was a teacher through a side-door exit that led to the parking lot.

The Missing Persons Report also had other crucial information.

Date of birth – April 11th, 2014.

Age when last seen – 25.

Gender – Female.
Race – Caucasian.
Height (Metric) – 170 cm.
Height (Imperial) – 5 ft. 7 in.
Weight (Metric) – 65 kg.
Weight (Imperial) – 145 lbs.

There were details about Build, Hair Color, Hair Description, Facial Hair, Eye Color, Eyewear, Features, Clothing, Personal Effects and Location Description. According to the Personal Effects, when last seen she was carrying her bag and at least one book. A hardcover book.

Whenever a person went missing, the first few days were the most critical, especially the first forty-eight hours. After a week, police would hedge their bets that the person either disappeared willingly – maybe to leave a bad relationship or escape from financial problems – or was the victim of foul play. It was rarely the latter. Not in Wellington County. But this has been going on for two weeks now.

In this case, the missing person was a schoolteacher who was only three years older than Cathy. Being a teacher meant that she was well educated with a position of responsibility in the community. She had a stable place of work, and judging by the preliminary investigation, no financial troubles. She didn't take drugs, was a light drinker at best and didn't mix with unsavoury types, so off the top there was no reason to assume she met with foul play. At least, not from someone she knew. The chances of meeting with foul play at the hands of a stranger always existed, but they were slim and in Wellington County very slim indeed.

It was Sunday and there had been a light dusting of snow overnight, just enough to cover the ground in a thin, white blanket. Cathy was looking for a missing dog, of all things. The dog was a full-grown Collie last seen in Elora, in the park immediately west of Church Street. It had been missing for almost twenty-four hours and the family was frantic. Cathy stopped by the house and talked to the two despondent children. They said they had looked everywhere and couldn't find their beloved Ranger, a medium-sized dog with the pointed snout typical of Collies and white fur around the shoulders.

"Did you look by the gorge?" Cathy asked them, but they said the dog never went near there.

"I'll check it out."

She parked her car in the clearing by the bush and strolled to the edge. Lover's Leap Lookout. It was a fancy name, but Cathy didn't know of any lovers who ever jumped. In fact, over the past fifty years there had been only two suicides at the gorge. The first one was a middle-aged man who had been taking depressants after a medical condition. He got his things in order, wrote a letter to his best friend, stopped by the gorge, scaled the barrier and jumped. It had happened at the turn of the century. The second one was many years later. A young woman had just split with her husband after a quarrel and took her life. Just like that. It was more spur-of-the-moment than the first one, but neither incident demanded much of an investigation because both times it was obvious what had happened.

There was no sign of the dog in the park. No sign of anything. When Cathy got to the edge, she looked down. It was a cold December morning and the snow made everything pretty, but it would be gone before the day was over since the forecast called for mild temperatures that afternoon. Cathy peered over the railing and thought she saw something at the bottom. An article of clothing? Maybe a scarf? She wasn't sure, but it was red. That was easy to see because of the snow.

She took the path along the edge to the wooden stairway that led down the steep slope to the river. When she got to the bottom, she came back the other way by the water. There it was again. A red scarf. That didn't mean much. Not by itself. Anyone could have dropped a scarf or had it blown away if it wasn't tied securely, but a little further along was something else. A shoe. She picked it up. Size 8. Navy blue with a fashionable bow imbedded in the leather. It was a woman's shoe.

Woof. Woof.

The barking wasn't from a dog marking territory or asserting authority. It was a soft unassuming bark just to let you know it was there. The dog was downriver back by the Irvine Street bridge. Cathy put the shoe down and followed the sound, and then she saw it. A Collie. Not too big. Not too small. White fur on the shoulders.

Woof. Woof.

She got closer and the barking grew more intense. Cathy put her hands up in front of her. "Easy boy. Easy boy. I bet you're Ranger, aren't you?" She dug her hand into her pocket and fished out a biscuit. When looking for dogs, biscuits were always good things to have. "Here boy. I got something for you." The dog sniffed and approached her cautiously. Cathy went down on one knee with the biscuit in her hand. "Here boy. C'mon."

The Collie took the last few steps, sniffed the biscuit again, leaned in quickly and lapped it up. Cathy patted its soft fur and checked the collar. It said Ranger. She took out another biscuit. The dog lapped that one up, too, and started licking her hand. Then he barked.

"What's wrong, Ranger?"

He ran back along the river's edge to the spot where Cathy first laid eyes on him, and when he got there he stopped and began to bark again, but not like before. This time the barking was louder. Ranger had found something.

From a distance it looked like a collection of old clothes that had washed up by the side of the river, but when Cathy got closer she saw that it was more than that. The face was battered and scratched and there were rips all over the clothing, but they weren't the kind of deliberate rips you find from a knife or some other weapon. These were more typical of rocks and branches. And a very long fall.

Twenty-Four

Jack was resting, half-asleep, when he heard a knock at the door. He stirred and put on his slippers. It was Trudy from down the hall with something in her hand.

"Hello Jack. And how are you?"

"Fine."

"You know you shouldn't lock yourself up today. You should get outside and get some of that fresh air. It's going to be just wonderful. You need that vitamin D. Can't forget the sunshine."

Jack didn't know how old Trudy was, but figured she was in her eighties. Standing barely five feet tall, she was skin and bone, ninety pounds if that. She spent a lot of time in the lounge and was always the last one to leave her table in the dining room. She would sit and talk with whoever was there, even people she didn't know. She just liked to talk.

"I always take my calcium and my zinc," Trudy said. "Every day. You should too. It makes your bones strong."

"Is that what you came to tell me?" said Jack.

"No. I found this on the floor under your door. It's a letter. Your name is on it."

"It was under my door?"

"A nurse probably put it there. I got one once and that's what they did. The letter came to reception downstairs and then someone brought it up and put it under my door."

"Thank you, Trudy."

That was all Jack had to say, but she kept standing there as if something more would happen, still hanging on to his letter.

"Well what's your message today, Trudy?" Jack said. He had to say something.

"Want to come and see?"

"All right."

The two walked down the hall to Trudy's room. She stood beside the door as if unveiling a work of art.

Growing old is mandatory. Growing up is optional.

"That's nice Trudy," Jack said. "It's true."

"Yes it is. Oh here's that letter."

Jack thanked her again, returned to his room and shut the door behind him. The letter came by special delivery, and he hadn't received a letter like that in years. But there was no mistaking the name in big letters on the envelope. JACK FISHER. GREENWICH VILLAGE SENIORS CENTER. 142-7th AVENUE SOUTH. NEW YORK, NY 10016. He stared at it just to make sure, and then sat on the chair by his night table, and opened it. It was handwritten. Neat. Dated December 15, 2039.

Mr. Fisher:

I saw you on Talk Back the other day and your performance made me sick. Who put you up to it? Was it the Jews and if they did how much did they pay you? How pathetic that an old kike like you gets a platform to tell these lies and they let you insult respectable politicians and ambassadors and historians who are trying to clear up all this crap about the Jewish holocaust which is a myth that never happened. Too bad they didn't fry you when they had a chance so you couldn't come over here and pollute this great country of ours with the poison of your blood line that goes back to the Crucifixion. You "children of the Devil" (Book of John, 8:44-47). You "brood of vipers" (Book of Matthew, 12:34). Even your own people know what they are. "His blood be on us and on our children" (Book of Matthew 27:25).

Where did you hear all this crap about Nazi death camps and concentration camps? From Jew writers and Jew academics? From Jew bankers who steal our money then charge us for the privilege? I know my history. The Nazis were trying to lead Europe out of the ravages of the Great Depression which was an economic plot hatched by Jews so they could maximize their return on interest which they charged Christians through their role as money lenders. It goes back to ancient times. In 1543 Martin Luther wrote On the Jews and Their Lies ("Von den Juden und ihren Lügen"). Why do you think he wrote it? To tell the world about the danger of the Jews. He said "The Jews are a base whoring people that is no people of God and their boast of lineage, circumcision and law must be accounted as filth. They are full of the Devil's feces in which they wallow like swine." Why would he say this if it wasn't true?

Hitler knew about the danger posed by the Jews and tried to do something about it and yes he put Jews away but he never tried to wipe them out. He just wanted to keep their Jewish hands off our money. He showed them more kindness than they deserved and after they killed him and began indoctrinating our schools with their own version of the facts the story of Hitler got changed and the myth of the Jewish holocaust was created. In fact, all the Jews were deported to Russia. That's what really happened to them. They didn't disappear. If they disappeared, how come they're all over the world now? This proves the Jewish holocaust is a myth propagated by Jews so people would feel sorry for them and give them Palestine which is exactly what happened after the Second World War and then the Zionist Imperial State of Israel arrived on our doorstep as the new Satan.

Why God let someone like you live to be a hundred years old

I'll never know. Maybe to remind us how dangerous you and your scheming kind really are. Keep looking over your shoulder, you dirty Jew dog vermin brainwashing bloodsucking leech and know that I take consolation in the knowledge that one day you and yours will rot in hell.

There was no name on it, no signature at all, but at the end was a drawing of a snake and it looked like a cobra with the wide flared neck. Jack put the letter down and blinked. Was this real? Or a dream? He looked at his hands. They were holding a letter. He could feel the paper in his fingers. He rubbed it a few times, then his eyes went back to the beginning and he started reading again.

I saw you on Talk Back the other day and your performance made me sick.

Jack didn't have to read the whole thing again because the words were seared into his memory. So what should he do? Tell Mary Lou? Or just forget about it and throw it away? But he couldn't do that. He had never received a letter like this before, and it was because he went public and told what he knew. He decided to call the police.

"Hodgson here."

"Lieutenant Hodgson? This is Jack Fisher."

Silence.

"Lieutenant Hodgson? Hello? You there?"

"Hello Mr. Fisher."

He seemed distant.

"I just got a letter you should know about," Jack said.

"A letter?"

"From a neo-Nazi."

"What are you talking about?"

"I got a letter. You want me to read it to you?"

Before Hodgson could reply, Jack started reading. He got through the first paragraph and the 'children of the devil' and the 'brood of vipers' when Hodgson said to stop.

"That's pretty nasty stuff you got there."

"There's more."

Jack read him about Martin Luther's *On the Jews and Their Lies*. Hodgson told him to stop for the second time.

"I get the idea," he said. "Now listen to me. I want you to hang on to that letter and keep it somewhere safe. Where you won't lose it. Can you do that? You say it came how?"

"Special delivery."

"Paper?"

"That's right."

"With your address on it?"

"Yes. Whoever sent this knows where I live."

"I better see this for myself."

"You don't believe me?"

"I didn't say that."

"You think I'm making this up? That's what everybody thinks. That my whole life is an invention. Did you see the show? Talk Back?"

"No I was working that night but I heard about it."

"What did you hear?"

"That you gave a pretty good accounting of yourself."

"It's nice to know somebody thinks so."

Silence again. Longer this time.

"Look, Mr. Fisher, I have something to tell you. Some news."

Jack could tell from the sound of Hodgson's voice that it wasn't good. He waited. But nothing was coming from the other end of the line. Then Hodgson cleared his throat.

"Mr. Fisher?" Hodgson said.

"It's about Christine. Isn't it?"

"Yes but first let me ask you a question. What can you tell me about the Elora Gorge?"

Twenty-Five

Elora, Ontario 2018

Christine pushed her nose through the railing and gazed out onto the gorge. Right away her jaw dropped. She had never seen anything like this before.

"Wow!" the little girl exclaimed.

Her mother Emma wasted no time prying her away from the railing. "Christine! What are you doing? Get away from there. Take my hand and stand back here with me!"

"It's okay Mommy. There's a fence."

"Christine's right. There is a fence. It's solid."

Christine's grandfather Bill was standing behind them with his son Will, Christine's father. Both of them were thinking the same thing. But not Emma. She glared at the two men – her husband and her father-in-law.

"You're both crazy," she said, and promptly marched her four-year-old daughter away from the railing.

"Mommy I can't see from back here. I want to see. Can I go

on the ledge?"

"On the ledge? Are you kidding? Of course not. Why would you want to do that?"

"To see better."

"Oh my God."

"I want to Mommy. I want to see if I can do it. I want to balance. I bet I can. I do it at school."

"What are you talking about?"

"I do it at school. I walk in a straight line with my arms out. Like this."

Christine put her arms at her sides and walked as if on a tightrope. She was looking down while she did it.

"See? I can do it! I want to walk on the ledge! I can do it!"

Jack was there, too.

"Christine, you're a little daredevil," he said. "Nobody ever goes up on that ledge. It's too dangerous. That's why the fence is here. Why don't you come with me and your great Grandma and we'll take you on the path where the ground is higher and you can see from over there? What do you say to that?"

Christine turned to her mother. "I want to Mommy! Can I? Can I go with Great Grandpa Jack? Can I?"

Jack was a year short of eighty. His son Bill had two grandchildren – Tiffany and Christine – and Jack called them 'the girls'. Christine spent most of her time copying her big sister, who was three years older. Christine was in kindergarten and every day was an adventure, but seeing the Elora Gorge was the biggest adventure yet.

"I'm going with Great Grandpa Jack!" she told her mother as she let go of her hand and latched onto Jack's.

"You come with us now, Christine," Jack said. "This way it's higher so you can see better. You'll get a real good look at the gorge. I promise."

Christine and her great-grandparents took the path that twisted its way along the edge of the park.

"It's such a beautiful day," she chortled, and it made her great-grandmother Eve laugh out loud.

"You're such a sweet little thing. Why don't you come live with us in New York? You'd like it there. We'd spoil you."

"Where is that?"

"A long way from here. It's another country."

"What's a country?"

Eve looked at her husband Jack. "You want to tackle that one, dear?"

Jack knelt down and took Christine's hands in his. "Christine, the world has a lot of countries."

She stared into his eyes across the seventy-five years separating them. "Why isn't there just one?" she said.

"That's a good question. I don't know. Maybe if there was just one country people would get along better."

"Don't people get along?"

"We get along. You and me. But not everybody does."

"Why not?"

Jack stood up and scratched his head. He looked at his wife. "The kid's four years old. What am I supposed to tell her?"

"Just tell her the truth."

He tried again. "Well it's like this. You see, there are different types of people in the world."

"Are you a different type of people, Great Grandpa Jack?"

"Different from you? No."

"Then why do you live in another country?"

"You're a step ahead of me, Christine. Well, let's see. Where I live isn't really that different from where you live which is right here but some countries are different. Different from here I mean. The people look different and they act different. Sometimes people fight over those things. It's silly but they do."

"Jack, you shouldn't be telling her things like that!" Eve said.

"Why not?" said Christine.

"Now look what you started," Jack said. He pointed to the

gorge. "Look out there, Christine. See how it's a lot higher over here? You can see a lot farther. You see that bridge over there? You see all the cars going over it?"

"I see them."

"You see the water down below?"

"Yes."

"Well a little further up this river you have two rivers that meet and that's why this great big gorge is here."

"The rivers meet?"

"That's right."

"Wow!" said Christine, who was close to the railing again, poking her nose through it. "How deep is it down there?"

"I don't know but it's a long way down."

Christine had her hands on the bars now. "Can I walk on the ledge over here?" She turned around. "Mommy's not looking."

Jack knelt down again. His knees were getting sore. "No you can't do that. Nobody walks over there. It's too dangerous. Why do you want to do that anyway?"

"To balance. I do it at school. Watch me!"

She stepped back from the railing and just like before walked with her arms at her sides.

"That's very good, Christine, but you're still on the ground. Over there on the ledge you wouldn't be. It's too dangerous."

She stopped walking and looked up at him. "Great Grandpa Jack, why is this place here?"

"Why is what here?"

"The *gorj*."

Jack looked at Eve for help.

"God made it," said Eve.

"Why did he make it here?" said Christine. "Why didn't he make over there? Or why didn't he make it at my house?"

"That would be dangerous," Eve said. "That's why God made it here."

"But isn't it dangerous here?"

Jack laughed. He was standing right behind her now, his hands on her shoulders. "Christine, you are a very smart little girl. Did you know that?"

"I know."

"How do you know?"

"People tell me. I know a lot."

"What do you know?"

"I know I like looking at this ... *gorj* ... because it's big and pretty. There's lots of trees and water and birds. The birds don't fall. I bet they walk on the ledge."

"They do but they can also do something you can't. They fly. If they fall off the ledge they just fly away. But only birds do that, Christine. Not people."

"I want to fly too. How long has the *gorj* been here?"

"It's older than you and older than your parents and even older than your Grandpa."

She turned around and looked up at him. "Great Grandpa Jack, are you the only one as old as the *gorj*?"

That brought a chuckle. "I guess so," he said.

"You know why I like it here?"

"Why?"

"Because there's no countries and no one is fighting."

Again she stuck her nose through the railing, licking her lips. Then she whispered under her breath, but only to herself, so no one else could hear.

"I still think I can do it."

Twenty-Six

Soon after they had moved to New York City, Jack and Eve took in a Midnight Mass at St. Patrick's Cathedral, and the moment he stepped inside it took him back to the first time he ever visited a church. The Church of the Virgin Mary in Lodz. That was the day he had met Father Kasinski. The little boy who knew only the ghetto had been awed by the great open space, the beautiful stained-glass windows, and the faces of the disciples staring back at him. But even that glorious church was nothing compared to St. Patrick's. This palace had enormous stone columns climbing up to the heights with huge chandeliers hanging from the ceiling.

Christine's family was in New York to spend Easter with Jack and Eve. Sitting next to her great-grandfather in the mammoth cathedral, Christine couldn't get her mind off the sheer enormity and detail of the place. She wanted to know everything. When it was built. How long it took. The dimensions of the sanctuary.

Jack told her that work was suspended during the Civil War. The cornerstone was laid on the Feast of the Assumption – August 15, 1858 – and for years afterward nothing happened because Americans were too busy killing themselves. That was how he put it. Work resumed in 1865 and the church eventually opened in 1879. Over the next one hundred and fifty years a number of renovations and improvements took place.

"Christ the Lord has risen," said the archbishop presiding over the mass on this Easter Sunday. He spoke of the increased attendance during the past week and of the extra crowds who came on Ash Wednesday before prodding those present as to where they were the other fifty-one weeks of the year. It made Christine chuckle. There were references to the Crucifixion, burial and resurrection from the books of Matthew, Mark, Luke and John. When it was done and the crowds began to spill out, Christine had her arm around Jack.

Jack was her link to the most insane madness the world had ever seen, but his scars were revealed to her only in glimpses. There was the time at the train station in Kitchener when the sounds took him back to his arrival at Auschwitz, and then the time at the Confession box. That, too, was in Kitchener. The family had gathered for a Sunday morning service, and when it was over the line for Confession formed.

"Got anything to confess, Jack?" Christine said. She stepped into the box and shut the door behind her. A few minutes later, she came out. "That was good. I got some things off my chest. Now it's your turn."

Jack was reluctant.

"Go ahead," she said.

He stepped in and closed the door. Not thirty seconds went by before she heard him screaming and pounding from the inside. She pushed the door open and found him sweating. She asked him what was wrong.

"I had my back against the wall. There was no room to move in there."

"You were screaming."

"I was trapped."

He said it had been like that ever since he was a boy. It had been like that in school and sometimes even in his own bedroom. He didn't like feeling trapped. Now here in St. Patrick's Christine was thinking about that time at the confession box. She hadn't taken Jack to Confession since then and wouldn't do it today. When the Easter service was finished, they went back to Jack's home on the Upper East Side. A brownstone.

"Jack, have I ever told you how lucky you make me feel? Because I know you never had the things that I have. Like my family around me all the time. What was it like for you?"

"Lonely."

"But people took you in. They cared for you."

"The family that raised me treated me like a son but I wasn't their son and I knew perfectly well why they took me. They felt sorry for me. Everyone was sorry for me because I was an orphan. Every morning I would wake up thinking they'd all be gone and the house would be empty."

"Why?"

"Because I thought they were going to leave me."

"Why would they do that?"

"Because everyone left me."

"That was different."

"Not to a little boy it wasn't. Even when I got married I thought your great-grandma was going to leave me."

"No!"

"It's true. I did. It was hard for me to think someone would really stay with me. You have to understand, Christine. I was just a little boy when all this happened. My earliest memories were the ghetto and *Auschwitz*. One day my parents were with me and the next day they weren't. They were gone. Just like that and I was all alone."

"Jack."

"I never saw them again. That's why it was so lonely. You see, it's lonely when the only thing you have of your family, the one and only thing you can hang onto, are thoughts."

Twenty-Seven

Kitchener, Ontario 1947

The teacher's name was Miss Tacini and the 'c' was soft. *Ta-seeni.* But when Jack tried saying it, it came out *Ta-cheeni.* He was having trouble with English because his tongue didn't work like an English tongue. In Polish, a 'c' was always *'ch,'* but there was no always in this language. It was bad enough being with students two years younger; they had put him back two grades upon his arrival.

"Good morning, Jack. How are you today?" she would say to him and he would reply *"Good mor-neeng Mees Ta-cheeni."* Immediately, the chuckles and heckles would begin.

Jack was different from the other children, but then he had always been different. When he was a little boy, he wasn't even supposed to be there. He was hidden. A Jew born in the ghetto of a Polish city that was suddenly German. Then, when he and his cousins were discovered, they were sent to a camp to die, only Jack didn't die. He survived. Two years in an orphanage in

Holland and he got sponsored by the Jewish Congress and came to Canada where he was adopted by a family in Kitchener. Their name was Fisher.

Jack was eight years old, but all the other children in his Grade 1 class were six. Language shouldn't have been an issue for him since he was more advanced than any of them – he could speak Polish and German, and was more than capable in Dutch – but here everyone spoke English. It was the only language that mattered.

Two years after the war ended, on November 11th, a discussion came up in class. It was Remembrance Day in countries of the British Commonwealth. Miss Tacini asked the children what they knew about the war and for all of them the responses were in terms of their parents or older siblings.

"My Daddy's younger brother was a soldier."

"My Mom worked in a factory."

"My sister always listened to the news on the radio."

Then it was Jack's turn. He was older, his memories more ingrained.

"I lived in the ghetto. We barely had enough to eat."

Someone asked what the ghetto was.

"It was where they kept Jews. My parents had to hide me because the Germans would have killed me if they found us."

"Now now, Jack," Miss Tacini said.

"Why would they have killed you?" a boy asked.

"The Germans killed all the Jews. They starved us to death or they burned us in ovens or they put us in gas chambers."

Miss Tacini held her hands up. "Jack, we're not going to talk about such things."

"He asked me."

"I know but we're talking about soldiers. We're not talking about things *like that*."

"But that's what happened. I was born in a ghetto then we went to Auschwitz and my parents were killed. Everyone was killed there. They were murdered."

There were gasps from the other children.

"Jack, I'm telling you again that we are not to talk about such things. We don't want to hear about things like that. Do you understand?"

The little girl next to Jack nudged him on the shoulder. "Is it true?" she said.

Miss Tacini overheard and shook her head. "No, of course not."

"He's making it up?" the girl said.

"I'm afraid he is."

Jack was about to say something when she put her finger across her lips, a sign to hush up, and she meant business.

"Now," she said, "does anyone know why we have Remembrance Day on November 11th?"

No one knew.

"That was the day the war ended but not the war just past. I'm talking about the Great War. World War I. It ended on November 11th, 1918 and ever since then we have celebrated Remembrance Day on this day and there's something else you may not know. Did you know that the city where we live ... Kitchener ... used to be called something else?"

No one knew.

"It was called Berlin. Berlin is a big city in Germany. Canada was one of the countries that fought against Germany in World War I and during the war someone decided to change the name to Kitchener."

Jack raised his hand. Miss Tacini was reluctant to let him speak again.

"What is it, Jack? I hope you're not going to ..."

"Kitchener used to be called Berlin?"

"That's right."

"Are you sure about that?"

"Of course I'm sure. I've lived here all my life. Why the look on your face?"

Jack couldn't speak. His brain, his whole body, was suddenly numb. He decided right then and there what he would do. When school was over, he would go straight to the train station. Not home.

Berlin was the biggest city in Germany and the center of the Third Reich. It was also where he was supposed to meet his parents. That is what his father had told him. When they were on the train to Auschwitz, his father said they would meet at the train station in Berlin if they got separated. It would be their point of contact. The train station in Berlin. That is where they would meet, at Track No. 1. Later, he was told that both his parents, along with his Aunt Gerda and his cousins Zivia and Romek, all perished in the gas chambers. But he was only five years old and it made no sense that the most important people in his life would leave him just like that. Gas chamber or no gas chamber.

He never forgot what his father said to him.

Jack's regular bus arrived. He asked the driver how to get to the train station and the driver said to cross the street and take another bus in the opposite direction, then switch to yet another bus and head downtown. Jack did as he was told. The terminal was on Weber Street West, immediately south of Breithaupt.

"This is it," the driver of the second bus said. "You catching a train?"

"I'm meeting my parents," Jack said with a confident smile.

"There's only two tracks so it won't be hard to find them. Where are they coming from?"

"Berlin. I mean I'm meeting them in Berlin. At the station."

"Kid, Berlin is in Germany."

"Didn't Kitchener used to be called Berlin?"

"Yes a long time ago. Is that what you mean?"

Jack said it was.

"Good luck. I hope you find them."

The terminal was busy with scores of men in business suits

and hats. Most of them were carrying briefcases or luggage. There were few women. As the bus driver said, the terminal had only two tracks, so Jack marched to a bench by Track No. 1 and sat down. It was four-thirty in the afternoon. An hour went by, and two trains came and went. When the first one arrived, Jack got up and searched as the passengers scrambled off the train. He eyeballed every one of them. It was a mad rush. If his parents were on this one, he didn't want to miss them, so he climbed up on the bench to see better but no luck. It was the same with the second train.

The Fisher family always had dinner at six o'clock. Of course, they were expecting him after school, but he didn't phone and he didn't leave a message. What on earth would he tell them? That he was meeting his real mother and father and had to leave them now? That he was grateful for all they had done, but he had to be with his parents? Surely they could understand that.

Another train arrived at six-fifteen and, like before, there was a flurry as people rushed through the doors. Everyone was in a hurry. At seven, after yet another train left the platform, a porter in uniform approached him.

"Are you lost, son?" he said.

"No sir."

"You waiting for someone?"

"I'm waiting for my parents."

"What train are they on?"

"I don't know. All I know is I'm supposed to meet them here."

Jack looked up at the porter. "Kitchener used to be called Berlin, didn't it?" he said.

"Yes. A long time ago. What's that got to do with it?"

"My father told me to meet them at the station in Berlin. That's here. Isn't it?"

The porter put his hands on his knees, his eyes level with Jack's. "What's your name, son?"

"Jack Fisher."

"Where do you live?"

Jack gave him the address.

"How old are you?"

"Eight."

"Do your parents know you're here?"

"They told me to meet them."

"I see. So nobody's at home then?"

Jack didn't say anything.

"When did they tell you to meet them here?"

Jack mumbled under his breath.

"I didn't hear you. What did you say?"

"I said three years ago."

"Three years ago? What do you mean?"

Jack didn't know how to begin.

"Does anyone know you're here?"

Jack shook his head.

"Somebody must be worried about you."

"Kitchener used to be called Berlin, didn't it?"

"Yes but what's that got to do with anything? It's not Berlin now. It hasn't been for a long time."

"How long?"

"I don't know. Must be thirty years."

"Thirty years?"

"That's right. It's been Kitchener for a long time. Since long before you were born."

Jack was thinking.

"You got a phone number at that house you live in?" the porter said.

Jack said he did. He gave him the number.

"I'm going to call. You stay right here. All right?"

"Do you know when the next train is coming?"

The porter checked his watch. "In twenty minutes but it's not coming from Berlin I can tell you that."

"If you don't mind I'd like to wait. Just to make sure. I'm not bothering anyone, am I?"

"No you're not bothering anyone but I think somebody must be worried about you and I'm going to straighten that out right now. You stay here."

The porter left to make the call. There was one more train coming before Jack would have to go home. One more train. Maybe that was the one.

Twenty-Eight

Auschwitz, August 1944

Jacob's Uncle Israel was always dead. He didn't know what he looked like or how old he was, only that he was dead. It was the only thing Jacob ever knew about him. Shmuel Zelinsky was dead, too, but Jacob didn't know that when he saw him covered in newspapers in the lane on Bazarowa Street or Basargasse as the Germans called it. But he knew he was dead when he saw his body thrown onto the truck the next day. If he had any doubt what it meant, it became abundantly clear the day he saw a man shot for walking on the sidewalk instead of in the gutter. The man was warned and kept walking defiantly, so they shot him and he crumpled like one of those pillowcases Jacob and Shimek filled with apples when they returned from the Aryan side. Blood poured from a hole in the man's head as he lay in the gutter where he was supposed to be. But in the boxcar death got even closer.

Jacob was with his mother and father, his Aunt Gerda, and his cousins Zivia and Romek. They had been loaded onto the train at Lodz with countless others. Huddled on the floor next to his mother, Jacob didn't know how many people were in that car. All of them were Jews and they were packed so tight no one could move.

The stench was terrible, even worse than the sewers had been. Once the doors slid shut and the train started to move, he could smell it right away. Shit. It was everywhere. They had been given one open bucket for everyone in the car, maybe a hundred people, but when the bucket overflowed there was nowhere to go, so they went in their pants, they went on the floor or they went on the person next to them. It didn't help that the air was thin and hot, and you couldn't breathe. Children cried and women moaned and the old collapsed with no place to fall and everyone was scared because they all knew about Chelmno.

After a few hours, an old woman died and then an old man died. "Another one," someone mumbled. They were sitting in the boxcar with corpses, and the longer the journey the more corpses there were. The smell kept getting worse and worse. At one point the train stopped, the doors opened, and two Germans with rags over their noses appeared. They wanted to get rid of the dead. "*Verfluchte Juden,*" they said. Someone pointed to the bodies and a voice cried out about them being tossed from the train, but one step inside the car was enough. The two Germans turned around and shut the door behind them.

A narrow slit was the only way to see outside, but not for the children. There were only five or six of them – Jacob, Zivia and Romek, and perhaps another three – but it was hard to tell because all the people looked alike after awhile. It was one huge mass of brown and stink and vomit and shit, and no one wanted to move because you might touch one of them even when you were one of them yourself.

It seemed forever in that boxcar. Finally, after two days, maybe three, the train screeched to a halt. There was the sound of dogs barking, loud banging on the doors, and voices screaming *"Heraus! Heraus!"* The doors slid open and a man in striped clothes, little more than a skeleton, jumped into the car. *"Hast du gold? Hast du gold?"* He was asking for gold in Yiddish and someone said he was crazy, but Jacob had gold. He hid the Russian coin Father Kasinski gave him in the heel of his shoe. The *chervonets*. Maybe if he gave this man his gold coin he could get something to eat. He raised his hand and started to holler, but nobody heard him or noticed him.

Two Germans carrying rifles followed the crazy man into the car, grabbed him by the shirt and threw him out, and then they started pushing people through the opening. They ordered everyone out, but it was a long drop to the platform. An old man on his hands and knees peered over the edge, afraid to move, and was tossed from the train like a sack. He hit the pavement hard and when he was slow to get up the Germans who were already on the platform started kicking him. He told them he had to pee, so they stood him on his feet and rolled his pants down to his ankles, exposing him to everyone, and then they laughed and told him to go ahead. He stood there shaking before the pee trickled down his leg and gathered in a puddle at his feet.

Jacob climbed out of the boxcar with his mother and father, and the first thing that hit him was this crude stench in the air, but it wasn't like the stench from the boxcar. It was different. He didn't know what it was. It had been raining and the ground was still wet. There was muck everywhere and strange people in striped clothes standing around aimlessly and dogs sniffing and barking. When everyone was off the train, they were told to stand on the platform.

Jacob was next to his parents, and beside them were his Aunt Gerda, Zivia and Romek. Just then one of the SS started pointing. All the men were ordered into one line and the women and children into another, and it wasn't long before the women began to scream and the children began to cry. As he was being led away, Jacob's father reminded him about what he had said in the boxcar, about meeting at the train station in Berlin at Track No. 1. He looked over his shoulder at Jacob as a German shoved him with his rifle. It was a long look – the same look he gave his dead baby son in the sewer. When all the men were taken away, the Germans ordered the women and children to separate and then the bedlam got even worse. A woman with a baby in her arms wouldn't let go of it. One of the SS tugged on the baby and still she wouldn't let go, so he hit her across the face with his rifle, grabbed the baby and threw it to the ground. Then the worst thing Jacob had ever seen. Absolutely the worst. The man turned the gun on the baby and fired. Just like that. The baby exploded. There is no other word for it. The woman started to scream. Hysterically. He pointed his gun at her and fired again.

Everyone saw it and everything went quiet.

Another SS ordered Zivia and Romek to one side – to the left – while Jacob's Aunt Gerda was ordered to the right. Romek was crying for his mother, and Zivia had her arm around him, saying that things would be all right. Then the SS who was making the selections told Jacob's mother to go to the right with her sister. He pointed his rifle at Jacob and said to go to the left with his cousins, but Jacob didn't want to leave his mother. The man raised his rifle and stared at him, and without any warning smashed the butt of his gun on Jacob's left shoulder. Hard. Square on the bone. Jacob dropped to the ground. His shoulder, his whole arm, felt as if it had been ripped off. The man stood over him and pointed the gun at his head. Jacob looked up at him.

"*Ave Maria, gratia plena, Dominus tecum.*"

It was the first thing that came into his mind.

"*Was?*" said the German.

"*Benedicta tu in mulieribus, et benedictus fructus ventris tui, Iesus. Sancta Maria, Mater Dei, ora pro nobis peccatoribus, nunc ete in hora mortis nostrae. Amen.*"

Jacob lowered his head and made the sign of the cross. The German still had his rifle pointed at him.

"*Wie heist du?*" the man said.

"*Mein name ist Jacub.*"

The German lowered his rifle.

"*Bist du Katholisch?*"

"*Ja. Ich bin Katholisch.*" Jacob looked over to his mother and his aunt. "*Und meine Mutter und meine Tante.*"

The German touched Jacob's blonde hair and studied his features. Jacob could feel his eyes examining his face, his nose, his cheeks, his mouth. He could feel his breath on him. The German called another SS over and the two of them talked, and when they were done talking, the one who had hit him motioned for Jacob to go with his mother and his aunt.

To the right.

A few minutes later, everyone in the line on the left – children, old people, women – were led away. Jacob didn't see any children in his line. He was the only one. Then everything happened very quickly. German women with needles were grabbing people at random and sticking the needles into their arms, and when it was his turn, Jacob pulled back and looked around to see where to run, but there was no place to go. One of the women snatched his arm and jabbed the needle into him. It stung, and when she took it away, it left a number. *A-25073.* Then another woman started to shave their heads. Jacob's mother had her head shaved and so did his Aunt Gerda, but when they were about to shave Jacob's head, the SS man, the same one who had hit him, said to stop. He said something to the woman with the needle, and she let Jacob be.

They were marched into a long building and told to take off their clothes. Everything. At first the women hesitated, but then they went ahead and stripped, and soon Jacob was standing naked next to his mother and his aunt and they, too, were naked. The women tried covering themselves up with one hand over their breasts and the other between their legs. Jacob put his hands across his middle. They were led into a large empty room and told they were going to shower, but someone cried out that they were going to be gassed. Jacob thought he was about to die. It wasn't the first time that day. He thought he would die when the SS pointed the rifle at him and again when the woman came at him with the needle and now a third time. His mother held him tight, the doors closed, people screamed and for one horrifying moment the terror in that place was so thick and palpable that there wasn't a single breath. Then the showers turned on. Cheers erupted and the cheers were even louder when the doors opened to let them out.

They were told to put their shoes on, which was good because Jacob had the *chervonets* in his heel. No one knew about it. Not even his mother. They were given baggy striped clothes and led outside, but that strange smell was still in the air. Jacob looked up and saw the black smoke rise into the sky.

Twenty-Nine

Jack's alarm went off at seven. He was uneasy because of the dream. He knew now that it was a dream, but it seemed so real. He was with Christine and it was strange because she was all grown up while he was a little boy and what made it even stranger was that they were at the camp. They were sleeping side by side in the barracks, sharing a bunk up on the third row. It was always the third row. That was their place. The siren went off at four o'clock as it did every morning and then they gathered outside for inspection, but no one else was there. Only the two of them. When it was over, they went back into the barracks to busy themselves. Packing down straw on the bunks and later, peeling potatoes and cleaning bricks. In the middle of the afternoon, they got their meal. Crusty bread with water. The Nazis called it soup. In the dream, Jack the little boy was bored to death.

"I want to play," he said. "I want to play with the other children."

"There are no other children," Christine said. "You are lucky."

"I want Mama and Papa."

"They're gone but don't worry. You have me."

"Where did they go?"

"They died in the gas chamber. Everyone is dead. All of them. The only ones left are you and me. We're lucky. You don't know how lucky we are."

"I want ..."

"Sha, Jacob. Sha."

"But ..."

"Sha. Sha. Hust."

"Where are they?"

"Es vet gornit helfen."

"I want Mama and Papa."

Christine held him close.

"Listen to me, Jacob. We are alive you and me. We're alive! Let's drink to it. *Le chayim!*"

"Le chayim!" Jack said. He didn't even realize he had said it, but he heard himself. It was the first thing he said that morning. He was tossing back and forth in his bed and then he rolled over thinking Christine was in the bunk beside him. He reached out for her, but no one was there.

"Christine," he said out loud.

He got up and washed his face. His body ached from the arthritis and the worst thing was that damn shoulder of his. He was hungry. When he was ready to go, he opened his door and went out to the hall. He wasn't thinking right and didn't even close his door. Halfway down the hall, right in front of Trudy's room, he realized his mistake.

Good friends are like stars. You don't always see them but they are always there.

That was Trudy's message for today and where she found all these sayings Jack didn't know, but she had a different one on her door every day. He turned around and headed back to his room and it was weird because something was pulling him there. Like a magnet. He had never felt that way before, but of course, he left his door open. That was it. He had to shut his door. Make sure it was locked.

He pushed the door closed and then he saw it. Scrawled in the middle of the door was a swastika. The size of his hand, even bigger than that. Neatly drawn. The lines straight, thick and black. Even the space inside the lines was filled with black. Whoever did it had taken their time. Jack kept staring at it and then he put his hands on his mouth and started gasping for air. He took a breath and couldn't get it out. He tried again. He couldn't breathe. He was choking. He slumped against the door frame and cried for help.

CHAPTER THIRTY

Thirty

New York City, 2038

The day of his arrival someone told Eustace that no one else had a name like his. And they were right. He had a room on the second floor of the Jewish Home for the Aged in New York City, even though he was Seventh-day Adventist. His condition had deteriorated to the point where they were talking about putting him in the palliative ward. He had dementia and Parkinson's and heart disease, and they didn't give him long, but he had suffered from these ailments for years and was still hanging on. He had always been obese and the single hardest thing for him to do was climb out of bed. He needed help with that. The report said he was anti-social, had a short fuse and would fly into a rage at the slightest provocation. There had already been two incidents. He had attacked a member of the cleaning staff when he objected to the antiseptic she was using, and had to be restrained. It took three men to subdue him. The other time he had thrown his food tray at a nutritionist who was trying to get him to eat. But it's not his fault, they said. It's a symptom of the condition. He has to be monitored. The Jewish Home for the Aged was supposed to be a short-term thing until a bed became available elsewhere.

Shirley Rosen was two doors down the hall and she didn't like Eustace. She found him loud and coarse and overbearing, but that wasn't the worst thing. The worst thing was the smell. He stunk. There was a staleness about him, as if he never had the inclination to shower. On more than one occasion, she had heard him screaming at the staff when they were trying to coax him into the bath. He always reeked, so she did her best to stay away from him. Shirley was a hundred and one years old, and at this stage in life she didn't have time for such things.

Like Eustace.

The nurse was coming in with her daily meds – the regular course of blood thinners, beta blockers and Lactulose. Shirley suffered from chronic constipation and joked that laxatives were her middle name. Today was especially bad. She hadn't gone for four days and the pressure was so bad she couldn't eat. It was too painful.

Everyone knew that Eustace and Shirley mixed like oil and water.

The man who came to visit less than a half hour before visiting was over said he was a friend of Shirley's. He said he knew her from the old neighborhood, but he was a young man in his thirties and never said what neighborhood that was. He told the nurse Shirley might not recognize him at first, but would come around soon enough. He brought a box of cookies. It was a cold day and he was wearing a bulky sweater. He didn't bother to sign in.

"Hello Shirley, you sweet girl. Remember me?"

She didn't, but why would she? She had never seen him before in her life.

"How are you?" he said.

"Fine."

"These are for you," and he gave her the cookies.

"Thank you."

He started with small talk about the weather and she kept trying to place him, figuring she must know him from somewhere. But nothing registered. He certainly seemed to know her, however, and he also knew about her problem with Eustace.

"You should give him another chance. He's not such a bad guy. He just has a lot wrong with him."

He found it hot in her room, so he rolled up the sleeves of his sweater past the elbows. She could make out the beginning of the snake tattoos on his arms.

"I have a lot wrong with me too," said Shirley, "and I'm older than he is so I don't have much pity."

He laughed. "How about I bring him in and try to get you two to be friends?"

Shirley didn't like the idea, but didn't want to be rude. "You'd be wasting your time," she said.

"Maybe not."

The man marched into Eustace's room and Shirley could hear them talking since it was only two doors away, but she didn't know what they were saying. Still, she knew it would be a waste of time. Eustace was impossible. She had no use for him.

Soon visiting hours would be done for the day, a busy time for the nurses who were near the end of their shift and going over patient files at their station down the hall. Shirley closed her eyes and tried to nap. Sometimes a few minutes here and there were enough to recharge her, and then all of a sudden there he was. Eustace. She knew it was him even before she opened her eyes. It was the smell. There was no mistaking that fetid stench. He was standing over her, beside her bed, a scowl on his face. The man who came to see her – the visitor she couldn't place – was just inside the door.

Shirley had her mind on Eustace and didn't notice the man taking out his mini. He tapped the little screen and some names came up. He touched the last one and it was deleted.

Her name.

"You think I'm fat?" Eustace said and Shirley could only look at him stone-faced.

"Excuse me?" she said.

"You think I'm fat and ugly, don't you?"

"What are you talking about?"

"Don't lie to me."

Before Shirley knew what was happening, the door to her room was closed. The man who came to see her, the man who just brought Eustace in, was handing this maniac a pillow.

"Go ahead," he said. "They can't hear you now."

With that, Eustace lowered the pillow onto Shirley's face so it covered her eyes, her nose and her mouth. Then he leaned over and put all his weight, all his bulk, behind it. Everything he had. He pressed down hard and Shirley couldn't breathe. There were stifled gasps, and arms and legs trying desperately to do something, but to no avail. Shirley was an old woman flat on her back and he was a big angry man standing over her with seething blood rushing to his face, adrenaline filling his veins. He kept pushing and she kept struggling and the more he pushed the stronger he got. It didn't take that long. When she finally stopped moving, he eased up on the pillow and took it off. He stared at her dumb-founded.

"What's the matter with you?" he said. "Say something! Say something!"

He started screaming obscenities at her and the nurses outside in the hallway all stopped what they were doing. Two of them rushed into the room.

"Oh my God!" one of them said.

Eustace was standing there with the pillow in his hands. Shirley motionless on the bed. Her eyes wide open and still. Not breathing. No one else was in the room. The man who came to see Shirley was gone.

Thirty-One

Jack opened his eyes and saw a woman in a blue smock hovering over him.

"Hello Mr. Fisher. You feeling better?"

"What?"

"You had a little tumble."

He raised his head and looked around. "Where am I?"

"You're in the hospital. You're here for some tests."

"Hospital?"

"They brought you to emergency a couple hours ago but you're going to be all right. No worries."

The nurse wiped his brow with a damp cloth. He heard voices in the background. People were talking about him. Something about his *condition*.

"Why am I in the hospital?" he said. "I'm all right."

There was a man's voice.

"Hello Jack."

It was Lieutenant Hodgson and he had that policewoman with him. They were standing at the foot of the bed, Hodgson a good head taller than she was.

"Hello Mr. Fisher," she said.

Jack looked at Hodgson. "What are you doing here?"

Only then did Jack realize something was attached to his nose. A tube was feeding him oxygen. He was hooked up to intravenous and a monitor beside the bed was recording everything. Hodgson had his notebook and pen with him. He looked at the nurse and then came closer.

"Jack, everybody is worried about you," he said. "They want to make sure you're all right."

"Why? What's wrong with me?"

The woman officer piped up. "Mr. Fisher? You remember me? Kathy Sottario? NYPD?"

Jack gave her a nod. "You're the expert interrogator," he said and she smiled.

"Mr. Fisher?" It was the nurse in the blue smock. "You've never had any heart trouble, have you?"

"Me? No. Why?"

"We just want to make sure. That's why you're here. Do you recall how you were feeling when you fell?"

Jack remembered the dream with Christine. He got up and went into the hall, but forgot to close his door. He passed Trudy's room, then turned around and came back.

"I couldn't breathe," he said and he mentioned the swastika.

"We saw it," said Hodgson. "You got that letter and now this."

"Why would someone do that?" Jack said.

Hodgson shook his head.

"Mr. Fisher, you say you couldn't breathe," said the nurse. "Did you experience any pain in your chest by any chance?"

"I don't know but I couldn't catch my breath. Is that what caused this?"

"What?" said the nurse.

"The *swastika*?"

He said it like a German.

"The what?" the nurse said.

"*Swastika.*"

"What?"

Jack looked at Hodgson.

"He found it on the back of his door," Hodgson told the nurse. "It was from Nazi Germany."

"What's that got to do with anything?"

"It may have a lot to do with why Jack is here. It really upset him."

"Why?"

Jack was hooked up to the monitor and the oxygen was connected to his nose, but Hodgson could still see the exasperation on his face.

"It was a shock to his system," Hodgson said.

"That'll do it every time," said the nurse. "Any shock to your system could do it but it has to be a severe shock." She spoke over her shoulder to another nurse standing behind her. "He seems to have no history of angina or angina pectoris but he does have a problem with high blood pressure."

"For a man his age that's not bad," the second nurse said.

"Mr. Fisher." The policewoman again. "The reason Lieutenant Hodgson and I are here is because of what you found on your door. Do you have any idea how it got there?"

Jack shook his head.

"Look, Mr. Fisher," she said. "I have to ask you a question and it's not a question I want to ask you but I have to. You understand?"

"What question?"

She and Hodgson exchanged glances. "It isn't possible that you put it there by any chance, is it?"

Jack looked her in the eye. Even deeper than that. It penetrated.

"What?" he said.

"That you may have put it there yourself?"

"Why would I put a *swastika* on my door?"

She shrugged. "I don't know. To make a point."

"To make a point? To make what point?"

"I don't know."

Jack's rage started boiling through the surface. "How could you say such a thing!" he said. "And to *me* of all people!"

She put her hands up and said to calm down. He was getting flushed.

"Don't you understand that a *swastika* means murder and death and torture and millions of innocent people being exterminated like they were fleas? Why would I make a *swastika*?"

She shrugged again, uncomfortable with his outburst.

"I'm sorry, Mr. Fisher. I didn't realize how strongly you would feel about this."

"You didn't realize how strongly I would feel about this? Do you have any idea what the holocaust was all about?"

"You mean the Great Holocaust?"

"No I don't mean the Great Holocaust! All holocausts are great or they wouldn't be called holocausts! I'm talking about *the* Holocaust! Six million Jews!"

Jack just glared at her.

"Look," she said. "I realize a lot of people have suffered at one time or another."

Hodgson broke in.

"Jack," he said, "no one came here to argue with you about what people know and don't know. Kathy is a police officer and a highly respected person on the force. She's a great cop."

"An expert interrogator?" Jack said. The sarcasm was thick.

"I'm sorry if I offended you, Mr. Fisher," she said.

"I think she just apologized to you," Hodgson said.

Jack made a grudging sigh.

"Look," said Hodgson, "we don't know exactly what happened to you yet but whatever it was got triggered by something." The nurse who was attending Jack agreed. "And when you saw your door I can imagine how you felt."

"You can?"

"Well ..."

"I was dreaming about Christine and it was a crazy dream. It was just the two of us. We were together. At *Auschwitz*."

"Where?" said the nurse.

Jack was getting really frustrated now.

"Jack, we told you what happened to her," Hodgson said. "Remember? Christine I mean?"

Jack's head sank back into the pillow. He opened his eyes wide. Now he remembered. They found her at the bottom of the gorge.

"I never told you something," he said.

"You never told me what?" said Hodgson.

"She had Tay-Sachs disease."

"What?"

"It's a disease. A Jewish disease."

"What are you talking about?"

Another nurse was coming over.

"Just a minute," Hodgson told her. "Just a minute." He leaned over Jack. "What are you talking about?"

"It wears you down. There's no cure."

"What do you mean a Jewish disease?"

"Jews have it more than anyone else. Christine ... comes from Jews."

Hodgson brought his face in closer. "Christine had a disease?" he said.

Jack nodded.

"What do you mean it wears you down? How?"

Jack remembered the day he found out about it. It was a bad day. A terrible day. Ralph had phoned and told him and then there was a flurry of calls. Ralph. Bill. Bill's daughter-in-law Emma, the nurse. She was the one who provided the details.

"She was in her early twenties when she got it," Jack said. "And it's all my fault."

"What do you mean, Jack?"

The nurse said they had to take him away for tests now, but

Hodgson wanted more time.

"You said it wears you down?" he said. "How?"

"It wears down the muscles. It's a progressive disease and there's no cure. She had it. She got it in her early twenties. Right out of the blue. We had no idea. Lately it's been getting worse."

Hodgson was saying something to his colleague Kathy, while the nurse standing behind them was growing impatient. Hodgson told her he still needed another minute with Jack.

"Jack, listen to me. We didn't know anything about Christine being sick. How come you never told us?"

"She didn't want people to know."

"So she had this disease and there is no cure? And it was getting worse?"

"Yes."

"And she was depressed about it?"

Jack said she was.

"You know they found her at the Elora Gorge."

Hodgson waited for Jack's reaction, but then Jack already knew this. They had told him. Jack moved his head up and down. He knew.

"It would appear that she fell," said Hodgson. "That is ... unless she didn't."

"What do you mean?"

"I mean based on what you're telling me now ... maybe she didn't fall."

"What are you saying?"

Hodgson bit his lip. "Maybe it wasn't an accident," he said. "Maybe ..."

"Maybe what?"

"Maybe she jumped."

Jack shook his head. "No," he said. "Christine would never do that."

"We have to consider every possibility."

"She would never do that! You don't know her. Not Christine.

Not in a million years would she do something like that!"

He was shouting again and the nurse told him to calm down. She said they had to go. She got behind the bed and started wheeling Jack away, and as she did he lifted his head and turned to Hodgson.

"Not in a million years would she do that! Not Christine."

Thirty-Two

Jack didn't know much about God when he was in the ghetto at Lodz and he didn't know much about him at Auschwitz. When he was a little boy, the one thing evident about God was that he had been forsaken in such places and they were the only places Jack knew. His Aunt Gerda always mentioned God when she talked about her dead husband. *"Yiskor Israel,"* she would say. May God remember Israel. Jack was glad that God remembered his Uncle Israel because he didn't. The man died of tuberculosis. A lot of people died of it. They said Shmuel Zelinsky died of tuberculosis and so did Shimek's grandfather and if people didn't die from tuberculosis then they died from other diseases like dysentery or typhoid. But TB was the big one and whenever there was a death someone would mention God. Jack's father would recite the Mourner's Kaddish.

"Yit'gadal v'yit'kadash sh'mei raba."

It said how God was great and that he had created the world, but if the ghetto was the world he had created Jack didn't see what was so great about him. Before going to Auschwitz they would celebrate the Sabbath every Friday night and every Friday night God was mentioned. *"Baruch atah Adonai Eloheinu melech ha-olam."* God was blessed. King of the universe.

Jack's universe was the ghetto.

When he found out about Christine's Tay-Sachs disease, he didn't resort to prayers or think about God except for maybe asking him why. What had she done to deserve this? Emma explained how the disease led to deterioration of the central nervous system. The symptoms could be everything from slurred speech to hand tremors to dizziness. No one noticed anything like that with Christine, but the doctor made his diagnosis and there was no doubt.

They said Tay-Sachs was carried by one in every thirty Jews of Ashkenazi origin, those from eastern Europe. It appeared in little children, even babies, and sometimes it meant an early death. Late-Onset was rarer still. It had to do with chromosomes and a missing enzyme, but at least this type wasn't fatal. You could learn to live with it. There was no cure, but one thing they did know for sure was that over time it would get worse.

Sometimes Christine told Jack about it when she called or wrote. Not those crazy 3D things, but letters she would send him in the mail. She used to do that a lot before she got him that box. She said the first time she noticed anything was while teaching a history lesson at school. She was writing with an e-wand and then her hand started to shake and she dropped the wand. So she bent over to pick it up and her fingers wouldn't move. After that there were little things. She would be talking to someone and miss a word or run into trouble with alliteration. Later still it started to affect her balance and it was all because of him. Jack. That was what he thought. He didn't know it then, but he was a carrier of the disease, too, even though he didn't have symptoms. But he was the one who had passed it on. It had to do with mutations in the genes. No other person in the family was affected. Only Christine.

Thirty-Three

Hodgson called the procedure a functional MRI and said it was becoming common in police investigations. He said Christine's case was a natural for it because of the Elora Gorge. Christine had known about the gorge for a long time and so had Jack. They were both there when she was a little girl, and later Christine would go on her own when she was older. It was a place of retreat, so Hodgson wanted to know more about it, especially if there was a chance Christine committed suicide. He didn't like that word – it was an ugly word – but a young woman was dead and police on both sides of the border were determined to find out what happened to her. That was when Hodgson asked Jack to take a brain scan.

The way Hodgson explained it, many people had repressed memories. If someone was abused as a child, they might push it from their mind to the point where they no longer remembered, but technology was showing that such memories could be hidden, lurking in the deep recesses of the brain. A functional MRI could reveal what they were.

"We know the brain can block an unwanted memory,"

Hodgson said. "There is a biological basis for it. By stimulating your memory we can sometimes jolt your subconscious into recalling something you may have forgotten. It could help us learn what happened to Christine."

"Will it hurt?" Jack asked and Hodgson said no.

After it was confirmed that Jack had not suffered a heart attack, Hodgson got the go-ahead. Doctors at the hospital said Jack was under stress, that he should try and relax, but the police had unfinished business and Jack was still the only person Christine had contacted.

St. Vincent's Hospital in New York had an fMRI machine. It stood for *functional magnetic resonance imaging*. After signing the consent form, Jack had to empty his pockets, take off his shoes and remove anything with metal – his watch, his wedding ring, his glasses, his belt. He was asked if he had seen a dentist recently for dental implants and he said no. He was given paper slippers for his feet. Then Hodgson and a woman named Fatma – Jack had never heard such a name before – led him down a hospital corridor to a room housing the fMRI machine. Hodgson said Fatma was the technician who would operate the scanner. Jack asked her what kind of name that was and she said it was Egyptian, and that she had studied at Alexandria University before coming to the United States. When they got to the room with the scanner, they met someone else.

"This is Dr. Jordan," Hodgson said. "He's a psychologist with St. Vincent's and he also teaches at Columbia. We're lucky to have him. He knows a lot about the brain."

"Hello," said Jack. "Are you a medical doctor?"

"No," was all the man said.

Then they got down to business. Hodgson explained that once inside the scanner, Jack would be subjected to stimulation. Those were the words he used. *Subjected to stimulation.* Jack would see and hear things, and all the while his brain would be scanned as he reacted, and it would only take fifteen minutes.

But Jack couldn't wear his glasses because the machine worked with magnets, and metal was taboo.

"I can't see too well without my glasses," Jack said.

"You'll have to do what you can," Jordan said. He said anything Jack saw would be displayed through a mirror reflection of images inside the scanner and anything he heard would be magnified by headphones. Once the headphones were applied, Jordan and Fatma helped Jack onto the long platform that fed into the scanner. They put him on his back, making sure his head and body were secure.

"You understand why we're doing this?" Jordan said.

"To see if there's anything I know about Christine that I forgot," said Jack.

"That's right. You know how it works?"

Jack had no idea.

"We take brain imaging scans and then identify the neural systems that suppress memory."

"That means you read my mind?"

"Something like that."

The long platform carried Jack into the big donut hole inside the scanner. It was dark. The machine began to whir and the next thing Jack knew he was looking at a photograph of the Elora Gorge. It wasn't sharp – he didn't have his glasses – but he recognized it. There was the river with the rushing water and a few seconds later something else – a photo of the rapids where the river breaks into two streams. He recognized that, too. Then it stopped being a photo and the water started to move and everything came to life. There was the waterfall with all the rocks at the bottom and even sound. Jack could see the water and hear it.

Then Christine appeared, first in a photo as a little girl, then in another photo as a teenager, then yet another one when she was older and this time she was waving. And moving! She had come to life! She was waving at him and talking. He could hear her voice.

"Hi Dad! Hi Mom! Hi Grandma and Grandpa! Hi Jack!"

The power of this strange machine suddenly dawned on Jack. It was something that could tear his heart out, and the more he saw and heard the less aware he was of being inside the machine at all.

Then there were more photos with different angles of the Elora Gorge and an aerial shot that made it look huge and then everything began to move. For all he knew, Jack was standing right at Lover's Leap looking over the edge. There was Eve talking and waving with Christine, the menacing gorge behind them, and Christine was just a little girl. She was talking about getting up on that railing. No don't do that, Jack wanted to say. Only the birds can do that. Suddenly, Jack felt his whole body shift forward. Eve and Christine were getting further and further away from him.

"Come back! Come back!" he cried.

The next thing he knew there was bright light everywhere and he was staring into the face of Jordan.

"Mr. Fisher?"

"What? What? Where are they? What happened to them?"

"They were only pictures. And a video. You were watching a video."

"That was a video?"

"Yes."

Jack collected himself. It was like waking from a dream. He stared at the ceiling and blinked. His eyes were wet.

"There was significant alteration in the neural circuitry linking the prefrontal cortex to the hippocampus. Especially with that last one."

It was Jordan's voice.

"Are you all right, Jack?"

Hodgson.

Jack had tears in his eyes.

"Are you all right, Jack?"

Hodgson's face was looking down at him.

"What?" said Jack.

"Are you okay?"

Then he realized where he was. The machine. They had pulled him out.

"Was that fifteen minutes?" Jack said. "It didn't seem like fifteen minutes."

"It wasn't," said Hodgson. "We're not finished yet. I just want to make sure you're all right."

Hodgson had a damp cloth in his hands and wiped Jack's brow. "That was quite an experience for you, wasn't it?" he said.

"Yes," said Jack. "It's kind of tight in there but you forget all about it when you see the pictures. And the video. You forget about everything."

Now Jordan was talking to Hodgson and the Fatma woman. He said something about *voluntary memory suppression* and the *right frontal cortex* and other things Jack didn't understand.

"Did you learn anything about me?" Jack said, looking up at him. He was still on his back on the platform.

"Possibly," said Jordan, his face buried in his mini.

Hodgson said they were going to put Jack back in, but this time they would show him other things. He said some of them might be disturbing, but the whole point was to study how he reacted and try to get at those suppressed memories.

"Are you ready?" Hodgson said.

The machine started to whir and the long platform carried Jack back inside again. The first picture he saw was an old black-and-white photo. Jack didn't have his glasses and had to squint, but then it got clearer. A German soldier had his arm raised and people were piling furniture onto the road. Jack thought it was the Lodz ghetto. The next photo was also black and white. Two German soldiers were kicking a man in the street and the soldiers were laughing. Then there was a photo of children begging in a laneway. The one after that was grainy and hard to make out, but it was a crude caricature of an unshaven man with a bulbous nose, and below it the German words *Wer beim Juden kauft ist ein Volksverrater.*

Whoever buys from a Jew is a traitor to his people.

The photo after that was of men in uniform standing beside suitcases. Machine guns were propped up against each other. The men looked grim and Jack knew who they were. An *Einsatzgruppen* murder squad. They were the ones who did the systematic killing of men, women and children, and then something even worse – a photo of naked women and children, some of the women with infants in their arms. They were standing in an open ditch just before being shot.

Jack swallowed.

Then it was a photo of converging railway tracks and in the background a long black building with a tower in the middle. The entrance to Auschwitz-Birkenau. The one after that had the gate to Auschwitz with the sign *Arbeit Macht Frei.*

Work will set you free.

Then Jack saw a photo with scores of corpses piled on top of each other in a huge open pit. There were hundreds of them. Then, as with the earlier pictures of the gorge and Christine, things started to move, but this time in black and white. Workers were pushing limp bodies into a massive ditch. It was a mountain of bodies. Then a woman was leading a group of people on a tour. She was pointing to the gas chambers, explaining in German how they worked. Then back to still photos. Children, little more than skeletons, were standing in striped clothes, looking straight at the camera. Then a shot of bodies – what was left of them – in open ovens. The next one was a simple photo of a handsome man in a white cloak. He had a narrow gap between his teeth, his hair was neatly combed, and he was smiling. Jack looked at him and tried to focus. The next thing he knew they were pulling him out. Fatma was removing the headphones and Jordan was standing over him with his mini. Jack, still flat on his back, his eyes straight ahead, was staring up at the ceiling. He could hear them talking.

"Those things were horrific," the woman said. "I've never seen such gruesome things in my life."

"Jewish holocaust. A hundred years ago."

"And those are actual photographs? And videos?"

Jack saw Jordan turn his head to the side.

"I think we got what we wanted," Jordan said.

"Good."

It was Hodgson.

Jordan looked down at Jack. "You knew that man, didn't you?"

"*Der Todesengel*," Jack said.

Jordan helped Jack sit up. He still wasn't steady.

"I'm sure he recognized that man," Jordan said to Hodgson. "Do you know who he is?"

"Someone Jack wants to forget," said Hodgson.

They had Jack on his feet now and were holding onto him. He was shaky.

"They called him the Angel of Death," said Hodgson. "He was a doctor who did experiments on children. Especially twins. I looked him up."

Jack raised his hand.

"Lieutenant Hodgson?" he said.

"What?"

"It wasn't just twins."

Thirty-Four

Auschwitz-Birkenau, August 1944

Konzentrationslager Auschwitz was a massive camp surrounded by tall trees of white bark, pockmarked with dabs of black. It looked like the work of a paintbrush. In Polish, the birch trees were called *Brzezinka* – the name of a local village – and in German it was *Birkenau*. The nearest town was Oswiecim or *Auschwitz* in German. This place of death would become known to the world as Auschwitz-Birkenau.

The walk from Auschwitz to Birkenau was only three kilometers, but it took a long time for the children because they were little and hungry and tired. There were also distractions to slow them down. Along the route they could see slivers of blue sky slipping through the branches, but smoke always got in the way. Off in the distance were long skinny things hanging from trees in a clearing, and when the children got closer they could tell that these things were people with ropes around their necks. But they weren't the kind of people Jacob saw every day. They weren't even like the corpses he had seen thrown onto trucks in the ghetto. The heads were all tilted to the side – some one way, some the other – most of them with their tongues sticking out as if they were trying to lick their cheeks. Many had their eyes open. One of the children on the walk, a little girl who was even younger than Jacob, pointed and shrieked when she saw them. The German woman in charge – the *Kapo* – told her to be quiet and slapped the girl with the back of her hand.

At Birkenau they were sent straight to the barracks. Jacob was assigned to his place. The top bunk on the third row. There were two to a bunk and only children were in this building. The boy who shared his bunk said his name was Jerzy. He was ten years old and from Kalisz. He was taller than Jacob, his body little more than a stick. Jacob had never seen a person like him before with bones protruding from skin as if they wanted to break out but couldn't.

Jerzy had big round eyes – expressionless eyes – and a head and face so gaunt that Jacob could see every line and bump on his skull. He was shaved, but his hair had started to grow back. Jerzy looked at Jacob's blonde mane with fascination and stared at his shoes. He said Jacob was in trouble because they would take his shoes. Jacob immediately thought of the *chervonets* in his heel.

"I have an idea," Jerzy said.

He told Jacob that if they each exchanged one shoe, no one would take anything from them because they didn't take your shoes if you didn't have a pair. So Jacob gave him his left shoe, but kept the right one because that was where he had the gold coin. In return, Jerzy gave Jacob his left shoe. It was an old wooden clog that was very uncomfortable and at least two sizes too big. Then Jerzy told Jacob how lucky they were to be in the top bunk. Jacob asked him why.

"Everyone gets diarrhoea but if you're on the top no one is above you so you don't have to worry."

When Jacob heard that, he started feeling sick to his stomach. Jerzy said it wasn't so bad and put his arm around him. Jacob didn't like the feel of it.

"Tomorrow I will show you around," Jerzy said.

That first night the *Kapo* came and it wasn't the woman who had led them on the walk from Auschwitz, but a burly young German boy. A teenager. He told everyone to go to sleep. Jacob whispered something to Jerzy about food, and Jerzy only smiled and shook his head.

After the *Kapo* left, Jacob tried to sleep, but couldn't. How do you sleep in a place like this? There was hardly any air and they hadn't been given a thing to eat. Still, it wasn't as bad as the boxcar because the musty smell was better than shit and while two to a bunk was cramped it wasn't like the train from Lodz.

As the night wore on, Jerzy kept putting his arm around Jacob and Jacob kept brushing it off. Jerzy would rest his arm on Jacob's back or caress his neck with his hand, and no matter how many times Jacob pushed him away, he kept doing it. Then sometime in the middle of the night the *Kapo* returned. He climbed up on their bunk and roused Jerzy, and then the two of them went back down and were gone. Early in the morning, Jerzy came back. He dropped himself beside Jacob and in a few seconds was snoring.

Jacob had to use the latrine, which was out in the back of the building. The latrines were little more than holes side by side in a long wooden slab and this, too, was better than the boxcar where all you got was a single bucket for a hundred people. But it was here where the horrible truth of Birkenau was revealed to Jacob. On the way to the latrine, scattered all around the floor, were bodies of little children. All of them were naked and their bones stuck out like Jerzy's. Their ribs stuck out, their shoulders had sharp corners with no meat on them, and their skulls looked less than human. Some had their eyes open, staring dead and glazed into space. The smallest one was a little girl who couldn't have been more than two. Jacob felt the bile rise from his stomach and he vomited all over his feet. All over his right good shoe and all over the left wooden clog he got from Jerzy.

He couldn't sleep after that. Up in the bunk he put his head on the straw, trying to look away from Jerzy, but he didn't want to close his eyes because they might come and do to him what they did to those children. He couldn't get their faces out of his mind, especially the little girl. She was so small. Soon Jerzy had his arm on him again.

Later all the children in the barracks were summoned for roll call. Jacob didn't know how much time had elapsed since his visit to the latrine because time was different here, different from anywhere he had ever been before, even different from the ghetto. Time didn't move at all. As they walked from the building, Jacob asked Jerzy where he went with the *Kapo* during the night.

"You have to do something for them or they will kill you," Jerzy said in a whisper. "And I'm still alive. What are you going to do, Jacob?"

Outside the building they were told to line up. Yet another line. A man in a white cloak who was standing with the soldiers seemed important because the soldiers listened to everything he said. He approached each child one by one. He looked at a boy and pointed to the right. He looked at a girl and pointed to the right again. Then he came to a girl who was taller and older than the others, but didn't weigh any more than they did. She was another stick. Her lips parched and dry, her skin peeling away, she had open wounds festering on her arms and chest. The man examined her quickly and pointed to the left. He did this with all the children – some to the left, some to the right – and with each one he was exactly the same. Without emotion. Then he came to Jerzy. One glance and he pointed to the right. Finally, he came to Jacob. The two soldiers beside him had their rifles at the ready. The man asked the soldiers why this boy still had his hair, but before they could answer his hands were running through Jacob's golden locks. His fingers weaved in and out though the strands of hair and the way he did it made Jacob feel like a piece of merchandise. Then he took Jacob's chin between his thumb and forefinger, and lifted his head. The man said this boy doesn't look Jewish.

"*Ich bin katholisch*," Jacob said.

The man told him to lower his pants.

In the ghetto Jacob often saw the young Gestapo officer who patrolled near the wall, but the officer always took him for a Polish boy and never bothered him. Not once. It was that same officer who later hit Father Kasinski. With the German soldier standing beside him, the Gestapo officer, little more than a boy himself, suddenly became very powerful. A figure of authority. He struck Father Kasinski with no hesitation. The Gestapo officer was part of a food chain. The Jews were at the bottom, the Poles were next, and then came the police, the Gestapo, the soldiers and the senior officers. All the Germans had guns and they used them. Jacob saw it happen in the ghetto and he saw it here. A soldier had turned his rifle on a mother and her baby. They wouldn't think twice about shooting him. But the man in the white cloak was at the very top of the food chain. The soldiers listened to anything he said and followed his every command.

Jacob started to tremble.

The man looked him in the eye and with a snap of his fingers again told him to lower his pants. His hands shaking, Jacob loosened the string belt of his striped pants, but before they fell to his knees he grabbed his bare penis with his fingers and pushed the skin up over the end. The man bent over to inspect him. He still wasn't satisfied. He snapped his fingers again and ordered one of the soldiers to check Jacob himself, but the soldier didn't want to touch him. Not down there.

"*Doktor*," the soldier pleaded, but the man insisted. His voice was firm and impatient.

The soldier handed his rifle to the other soldier. He bent down and brought his face in close. Jacob could feel the breath on his naked skin. He could feel it on his bare stomach. The soldier didn't want to touch him. Jacob was standing there holding his penis between his fingers, the skin rolled up over the top, every bone in his body trembling with fear. He couldn't stop the trembling. The soldier did the inspection and Jacob – four and a half years old – knew his life was hanging in the balance. The soldier kept looking at him and Jacob kept shaking. He had no control over the muscles in his fingers or in his arms and legs, but still he held onto himself. Finally, the soldier looked away and glanced over his shoulder at the man in the white cloak.

"*Er wird is nicht beschnitten,*" the soldier said.

He is not circumcised.

The man nodded. He told Jacob to do up his pants and then he pointed to the right. Jacob did as he was told. He was still trembling.

Thirty-Five

Kitchener, Ontario, November 2039

"I'm Stephanie's mother. Jennifer Krust. Are you the history teacher?"

She was in her thirties, rakishly thin with wild blonde hair and deep blue eyes that wore a tired, pained sadness. Everything about her looked scattered – her clothes, the way her purse bulged as it hung over her shoulder, her unevenly applied lipstick.

"Yes that's me."

"Christine Fisher?"

"That's right. Nice to meet you, Mrs. Krust. Please. Come in and sit down."

The school had already heard from her husband about the course Christine was teaching. *An Overview of the Twentieth and Twenty-First Centuries.* He said he wanted to speak to the principal and when he connected with her he didn't pull any punches. He told the principal that Christine was brainwashing his thirteen-year-old daughter and not only that, but he accused her of bringing to class doctored photographs showing horrible things which she claimed had happened to Jews during the Second World War.

"He wasn't very nice," the principal told Christine. "He was a crude man and he wouldn't let me get a word in. Then he got really heated and started yelling at me. Cursing the school. Cursing you. Cursing me for letting this happen."

It was only Christine's second year of teaching, but she had sat down with enough parents by now to know how to read them and her first impressions were usually right. Five minutes with this Mrs. Krust was all she needed. She was a stay-at-home Mom, not particularly well educated. Two children. There was Stephanie, who was in Christine's Grade 8 class, and a younger brother of seven. There was also a husband, a firefighter who wasn't around much. And one more thing. She was afraid of him.

"What is your husband so angry about?" Christine asked. "And if he's so concerned about it why didn't he come and see me himself?"

"Well ... he has a bad temper," she said. "I told him I would go."

Christine had a responsibility to look out for her pupils, but she was a schoolteacher, not a social worker. There were limits.

"I'd be happy to talk to him," she said, trying her best to be diplomatic. Always take the high road with parents. "I'm sure he's a reasonable man who is only interested in your daughter's welfare."

The woman turned away, avoiding eye contact. Her tongue skimmed along the edge of her teeth, smudging her lipstick more than it was before. She didn't look the type who wore lipstick much, and if she wasn't anorexic, she was dangerously close.

"You don't understand," she said and began to fiddle with her purse. "You see ..."

"What?" said Christine.

She took a deep breath and played with her purse, opening the zipper, closing it, opening it again.

"What is it?" said Christine.

"Brett ... my husband ... he has a bad temper and when he gets angry about something there's no telling what he can do. He can fly off the handle."

"You mean he's violent?"

"He can be."

Christine was thinking. She had to be careful here. Kid gloves treatment. "Has he ever been in trouble with the law?" she asked.

"Well he's a firefighter. He knows the police and they know him."

"I see."

That wasn't reassuring.

"Listen," Christine said. "Can I get you a glass of water? Or a cup of coffee?"

"Coffee would be nice. Thank you."

Christine needed a few minutes to clear her head. This woman was troubled and the problem wasn't her daughter and it wasn't even the history course. The problem was her husband. When Christine returned, she was thanked for the coffee.

"Mrs. Krust, I have an obligation to ask you a question," Christine said. "Are you in any way concerned for your daughter's safety? Stephanie's safety?"

"You mean here? At school?"

Christine gave her a nod.

"No. Why should I be worried about that?"

"And what about at home?"

She hesitated. She shook her head from side to side and there was something about the stilted way she did it that said she didn't mean it.

"So what is it about my history class your husband is so upset about?" said Christine.

"It's all this stuff."

"What stuff?"

"You know. About the Jews."

"What exactly?"

She looked unsure, as if walking on hot coals. Maybe that's how it was at home. And she was so skinny. Christine wondered if they had enough to eat, but her daughter Stephanie wasn't like that.

"My husband reads this newsletter. It's written by some person called The Cobra."

"What about it?"

"Well there was this article about ... what's it called ... the Protocol of ..."

"Protocol?"

"Something about the elders ..."

Christine thought for a moment. "The Protocol of the Elders of Zion?" she said.

"That's it! So you've heard of it?"

Christine had heard of it. "Yes," she said. "I know what it is. I believe it has something to do with a Jewish conspiracy theory. Something like that, right?"

"It goes back to the early 1900s."

"Uh-huh."

"Well Brett and I were talking over dinner and he was telling me about it. It seems it stems from this business about Jews working with the masons."

"Uh-huh."

"These Protocols ... whatever they're called ... got spread all over the world."

"You seem to know a lot about it."

"Not really but Brett told me. You see he reads a lot and he belongs to this group."

"Group?"

"Yes."

"What group?"

"Well they think this Protocols stuff is right and the Jews want to take over everything. I mean they already control a lot, don't they? And they're worried about Muslims too and I can understand that. I mean isn't that what 2029 was all about?"

"You mean the Great Holocaust?"

She nodded her head up and down, and it was the first confident gesture she had shown since coming in.

"They were killing Christians just because they were Christians," she said.

"They claimed the Christians were trying to convert Muslims," said Christine. "It was a horrible thing."

"But they were targeting Christians, weren't they?"

"Yes they were but what's that have to do with Jews? Jews had nothing to do with that."

"Well do we really know? I mean some people think they're all in it together. Brett thinks so."

She started fidgeting with her purse again. Opening the zipper. Closing it.

"What do *you* think?" Christine said.

"I don't know but he reads a lot and like I say he goes to these meetings and when he comes home he tells me about it."

"Can you tell me anything about this group?"

"Well they think white people know best."

"Aren't Jews white?"

"That's why he says they're dangerous."

"Your husband thinks Jews are dangerous?"

"Yes ... well ... they're not Christians."

"So this is about white Christians then?"

"I guess so but it's more than that ... more than just color ... you have to believe in Jesus."

"I see."

"Brett's talked to our kids about it ... Stephanie and our little boy Billy ... he's seven. What I mean is he tells them about the bible and what it says about Jews."

Christine was trying to keep her emotions in check. She felt sorry for this woman. "So what's all this crap have to do with me?" she said. She didn't mean to say that, but *crap* is what came out.

"Look ... it's Ms. Fisher, right?"

"That's right."

"Let me put it this way. If you taught this Protocols business in your class I imagine some people would be upset about it. No?"

"I think some people would be upset about that. Yes."

"Well what about the Jewish holocaust?"

"What about it?"

"Some people are pretty upset about that too."

"Are you?"

She began fidgeting again, more than before. Her parched, boney fingers kept playing with that purse of hers.

"Yes I'm upset. My husband is angry about it and he's causing me a lot of grief. Do you understand what I'm saying?"

Christine nodded. Gentle now.

"So you're asking me to change my history curriculum to accommodate your husband?"

This woman, this Mrs. Krust, leaned over and for the first time in the interview looked Christine right in the eye.

"I'm asking you," she said. "I'm begging you."

She stopped. She was on the verge of tears. She zipped open her purse and wiped her eyes with a tissue. The purse was wide open now and there was a knife inside it. A kitchen knife. It was as plain as day.

"Why do you keep that in there?" Christine said.

She snapped the purse shut.

"Look I'm not a political person," she said. "I couldn't care less about politics. As long as Stephanie stays out of trouble and is getting decent grades that's fine with me."

"She is getting decent grades. She's not at the top of the class but she's doing all right. I don't have a problem with her."

Christine was still looking at the purse. It was zipped up, but there was a knife in there and this woman didn't want to talk about it.

"Look ... my husband ... Brett ... he isn't happy about this and he wants to go to the school board."

"He would do that?"

She said he would. Christine leaned back in her chair and checked the time. She had other parents to see.

"I don't have long," she said and then she smiled. "Lots of meetings." The woman didn't smile back. Christine wondered if she was capable of it. "It seems to me that the crux of the matter here is what I'm teaching in my class. This stuff as you put it about the Jewish holocaust. It did happen, you know. It's part of history."

"I don't know if it did and I don't know if it didn't and to tell you the truth I don't even care."

"You don't care?"

"No. But what happens in my own household is something else again and I'm really starting to reach the breaking point with Brett I can tell you that. He's my husband. He's the father of my children."

"I know that."

"He's not the easiest guy to live with but he's been getting more difficult."

She wanted to say something else. Christine could see that.

"What is it?" Christine said.

"Well I guess what happens in my home is none of your business."

"If it involves changing my course it is my business."

"Look ... I have an idea."

"What's that?"

"Couldn't you just include some other stuff in your course? What about that?"

"Other stuff?"

"I mean what if you showed the kids what other people have to say? I mean people who don't think all this happened. Maybe that would give it more balance."

"You want me to bring your husband into the class so he can talk to them about it?"

She shook her head. "I don't think that's a good idea."

"Or maybe this Cobra character? What about him? You think I should download a copy of his work and circulate it to give my students more balance?"

"Could you?"

Christine, shaking her head now, was incredulous. She had come to the end.

"You want to know what I think, Mrs. Krust?" she said. "About this problem and about your husband?"

"What?"

"I think your husband is a coward."

"What!"

"He must be. To treat you the way he does and to make all these crazy insinuations about how I teach history to my Grade 8 class. Tell me, why do you keep a knife in your purse?"

"What are you talking about?"

"You have a knife in there. I saw it. Why do you keep a knife in there?"

She didn't say anything and then she went pale. Stephanie's near anorexic mother became white as a ghost.

"I think I have to go," she said and got up from the chair.

Christine tugged on her sleeve. Once. Twice.

"Why do you keep a knife in there?" she asked again.

"Why do you think?"

"For protection? From your husband?"

She didn't say anything, but she didn't have to.

"I really have to go now."

Christine got to her feet.

"Look, Mrs. Krust. Can I call you Jennifer?"

No response.

"There are people you can talk to. People you should see. They can help you. I can give you a name and maybe your husband can go and he can talk to them too."

She shook her head.

"No. No. I don't want to do anything like that. But *you* could help me. If you can just make some changes to how you teach this. Make it a little more *fair*."

"More fair?"

"Yes. Then all this might go away."

"It will? I don't think so."

They started walking to the door.

"I guess we haven't really settled anything, have we?" said Christine. "Your husband knows you came to see me, doesn't he?"

She said he did.

"Well you're going to have to tell him something and what you're going to have to tell him is this. I have absolutely no intention of changing a thing about how I teach my course. I've already been through this with the school and the school board and I teach the course the way I teach it."

It wasn't what she wanted to hear. She looked up at the ceiling, her arms limp at her sides, the clothes hanging from her body as if from a mannequin in a showroom window. She was that skinny.

"Then I don't know what I'm going to do," she said. "But I just can't go on like this."

CHAPTER THIRTY-SIX

Thirty-Six

"You ever hear of Sigmund Freud?" said Hodgson.

Jack was gazing out the window from the second-floor lounge of the Greenwich Village Seniors Center. Hodgson had just arrived and deposited himself in the armchair next to him. The chairs were identical, but Hodgson's was being taxed severely with his huge frame and bulk. The moment he planted himself there was a loud *crunch* from the springs.

"Who? Freud? He was a famous psychologist, wasn't he?"

"He was a neurologist. The father of psychoanalysis. He developed a lot of theories about defence mechanisms and how we repress memories and things like that. Between you and me I think the guy was a little nuts with all his ideas about sex. But this business about memory suppression is real."

"And you think I did that? Suppress my memory?"

"Yes."

Hodgson had Dr. Jordan's report with the results of Jack's brain scan. Dr. Jordan had assigned a number to every photo and film clip that Jack saw inside the scanner. Beside the numbers were readings.

"Now let's see," said Hodgson. "If I can only get through all the mumbo-jumbo." He started reading from the report.

'With the onset of the presentation of stimuli in the form of photographs to the subject, the fMRI images demonstrated immediate abnormal activation in the hippocampus suggesting that insufficient activation of the prefrontal cortex could be an indicator for suppression of unwanted traumatic memories stored in the hippocampus. The level of neural activity was further heightened with the presentation of moving pictures and ensuing digital formats.'

Hodgson had a pained expression on his face. "I'll be damned," he said. "You know what's one of the worst things about my job? Reading doctors' reports and the more degrees they have the worse they are."

"Does Dr. Jordan have a lot of degrees?" said Jack.

"Many. Lucky for me he called back after I left him a message."

"What did he say?"

"He said there was an increasing level of neural activity in your brain as the photos proceeded from shots of the Elora Gorge to shots of Christine. Then when you saw the movies your neural activity increased even more. The one with Christine waving at you and calling your name generated a lot of activity. Neural activity I mean. That's not surprising. You probably felt like she was right there in front of you."

Jack said he did.

"But this is interesting. The clip after that showed your wife and Christine but Christine was just a little girl. There was a huge jump in your neural activity with that one."

"When she wanted to get up on the railing?"

"Yes. When you saw that your brain waves went through the roof."

"So what does that mean?"

"Let me try and explain it to you. You see, there are different parts to the brain. The left and right frontal cortex is the part that represses memory. Then you have the hippocampus which is the part that remembers your experiences. Our friend Freud said unpleasant experiences we want to forget are still with us. Hiding somewhere in the brain. With this fMRI we try to stimulate those memories and hopefully trigger something. We use this in criminal investigations all the time. Like homicides. Some character murders somebody then they go and dispose of the body. Maybe they hide it under a pile of leaves in the forest. We show our suspect pictures ... 3D videos ... whatever ... anything about where that body was found ... and sometimes we can tell if they're lying. It's much better than what they used to do with polygraphs."

"You think I'm lying about something?"

"No I didn't say that. In your case we're just trying to learn more about Christine and her fascination with the Elora Gorge. She seems to have had that ever since she was a little girl."

"She always loved going to the gorge."

"Why?"

Jack thought for a moment. Even when Christine was a child, she couldn't get enough of the place.

"It was big and peaceful," he said.

"Peaceful? As in no pressures?"

"I guess so."

"So later after she became a teacher and people got on her nerves she would go there to get away from it all?"

"I guess she did."

"But according to Dr. Jordan's data your neural activity almost went off the chart when you saw the clip of the gorge and Christine was there. When she was little." Hodgson went into the report again. "Don't do that. Only birds can do that."

"What?" said Jack.

"That's what you said when you were in the scanner. You were talking out loud. We recorded it."

"I said that?"

"Yes you did."

Hodgson read from the report.

'With the presentation of sample no. 8 in the first series the subject exhibited severe stress-related disorder which suggests that insufficient activation of the prefrontal cortex could be the basis for inadequate suppression of unwanted traumatic memories stored in the hippocampus.'

"Dr. Jordan?" said Jack.

"To put it in English, Jack, this stuff about Christine when she was a little girl wanting to go on the railing obviously left its mark on you. Can you tell me about that?"

"Christine was always a daredevil."

"How do you mean?"

"She wasn't like her older sister. Tiffany was careful about things. But not Christine. She was the opposite. When she was little she was all ready to climb up on that railing. She wanted to walk on it."

"She wanted to walk on it?"

Jack nodded. "And she would have if we let her."

"Why did she want to do that?"

Jack bit his lip and looked off into space. Hodgson took note. "She wanted to see if she could balance herself," Jack said.

"You mean on the railing?"

"Yes. That's why I told her only birds can do that."

Hodgson took his time with what he wanted to ask next. "So Christine always had this fascination about walking on the railing that overlooked the gorge?"

Jack said she did.

"And they found her there," said Hodgson. "That's where they found her."

With that, Jack's eyes started to well up.

"Jack, listen to me. There's a police investigation going on into Christine's death. From what we know at this point it's one of two things. Either she fell ... or she jumped."

Jack was staring into space.

"Did you hear what I said?"

"I heard you."

"Well?"

Jack looked straight at Hodgson. "She didn't jump. She wouldn't do that."

"What about this Tay-Sachs disease? She was depressed about that. Anyone would be."

"She still wouldn't do it. Not Christine. Oh she was a risk-taker all right. That was her nature. But she wouldn't go and jump like that."

"Tell me more about her being a risk-taker."

"She would go the limit. If someone dared her to do something she would just to make a point. Once when she was nine or ten she climbed up a tree. Some boy said no one could climb it, that it was too high. Well that was all Christine had to hear. She had to show him so she did. She climbed the tree right to the top but then she couldn't get down. They had to get someone with a ladder to bring her down."

Jack stopped. He was reminiscing.

"It was a big one too. A birch tree. A tall birch tree."

Hodgson saw the abrupt change in him, like a switch being turned. He was staring straight ahead, his eyes glassy, as still as death.

"What is it, Jack?"

"*Brzezinka.*"

His hands started to twitch like those of an old man suffering from Parkinson's. Jack may have been a hundred years old, but Hodgson didn't think of him that way. As being old. His eyes weren't good and his hearing wasn't sharp, but his mind was clear and more than that, he was keen. There was nothing stale about Jack. But here he was twitching to no end.

"What was that word you said?" Hodgson asked.

"*Brzezinka* is Polish for birch," said Jack. "In German it's *birkenau. Auschwitz-Birkenau."*

"Auschwitz?"

Jack blinked and then he came out of the trance that was holding him.

"Lieutenant Hodgson," he said. "I think that's the first time you said it right."

"What does all this have to do with Auschwitz, Jack?"

"The birch trees. *Auschwitz* was full of birch trees. That's where the name *Birkenau* comes from. In Polish it's *brzezinka."*

"So let's back up a minute and see what we have here. You have a little girl who is fascinated by this gorge. She wants to go up on the railing. She's a kid who likes to do things and doesn't worry about the consequences and even when she gets older she's still fascinated with the gorge. She was alone and figured what the hell? I always wanted to get up on that thing. Here's my chance. So she did."

"Maybe but ..."

"Either that or she went there with the intention to jump and that's suicide."

"No. Not Christine."

"How can you be so sure? You don't know exactly how she was dealing with this disease. You said yourself she would get dizzy. She would lose her balance."

"Maybe she lost her balance."

Hodgson was stymied. He sat back in the chair and it went *crunch.* "Jack, you have to understand something. We may never find out what happened to Christine at the gorge that day. We may never find out."

"It was an accident. It had to be. Christine was a lot like me but she wasn't stupid."

"What do you mean she was like you?"

"I took risks. My whole life was a risk. But I didn't always have a choice."

"Let's get into that, shall we? The second series of stimuli in the scanner. You remember what we showed you?" Hodgson went into Dr. Jordan's report again, and then he took out a few photos. "There was this one."

He showed Jack the black-and-white photo of people stacking furniture on a roadway with a soldier ordering them around. Jack looked at the picture. Then Hodgson took out the photo of German soldiers kicking a man in the street. Jack leaned in closer. Hodgson showed him another photo.

"Is that the hospital in Lodz?" Jack said, squinting. "The building in the back?"

"I don't know."

Jack looked confused.

"What is it?" said Hodgson.

"There's something about that building."

Hodgson moved on to another photo with a group of children begging, and then to the caricature of the haggard Jew with the big nose. Jack stared at them and said nothing. Then Hodgson showed him the photo of the murder squad with their machine guns.

"Dr. Jordan's numbers indicate a pretty big increase in neural activity with this one," he said.

Jack shook his head.

"This one too," said Hodgson.

It was the photo of naked women standing in a ditch, some of them with little children in their arms. About twenty of them were in the picture, all facing to the left, and at the far right a woman cradling an infant in her arms was rushing in to join them. Behind them strewn about the ground were articles of clothing.

"With that one ..."

"Those poor people," Jack said. "Those poor women and those helpless children. I could have been one of them. I should have been one of them." And just like that he broke down. The tears came from his eyes in a flood. "All my life all this guilt. Horrible guilt that I shouldn't be here." Jack buried his head in his hands and wept.

Hodgson put his arm around him.

"I have no right!" Jack said, sobbing. "Why am I here when so many died? How did I get to be a hundred years old? To suffer so long. Why did this happen to me?"

"It's all right, Jack," Hodgson said. "It's all right. I know how you feel."

"No you don't. How could you? How could anyone know? People don't even think it happened. No one believes me. But it did happen. I was there."

"I know you were."

"Do you? Really?"

"Yes."

"And that monster. *Der Todesengel.* Mengele. I knew him the bastard. He murdered so many children but nobody believes me. Nobody believes me."

"I believe you, Jack."

Thirty-Seven

Jack's ninetieth birthday was a family celebration, but it would be his last one with Eve. It wasn't long afterward that she had her aneurysm and died. They had been married over sixty years. It meant that Jack was suddenly living alone in his Upper East Side brownstone, and despite daily visits from his son Ralph, not doing very well at it. During this time the Great Holocaust of 2029 took place. Like everyone else Jack followed the news and was horrified with the massacre of Muslim converts to Christianity by fanatical Islamists in southern Turkey. Pretty soon any Christians at all were being slaughtered. It all happened over a period of six weeks. Christians were being targeted by roving gangs who resorted to guns, knives, axes, even hand grenades. The growing army of radicals would toss the grenades right into residential neighborhoods and blow up homes. Most of the Arab world ignored the story or downplayed the extent of carnage, but everywhere else the killing of innocent masses was widely condemned. *The Great Holocaust* became part of the language.

It was then that a 3D documentary began to generate interest. The documentary wasn't about the Great Holocaust,

but something else. It presented a convincing argument about
what had befallen European Jews in the last century. Central
to its theme was Auschwitz. The documentary began with a
dramatization of Rudolph Hess, commandant of Auschwitz-
Birkenau, signing an affidavit on May 14, 1946 in which he stated
that two million Jews had been gassed at the camp between 1941
and 1943. The actor who portrayed him – with his long face,
heavy eyebrows and square jaw – even resembled the real Hess.
As he signed the form, faint music played in the background, and
then Hess was taken away. His confession was said to have been
obtained under torture. The actual paper with his confession
would go on display decades later at the Holocaust Memorial
Museum in Washington, D.C.

Then the music got louder as the scene shifted to a plaque
unveiled at Auschwitz. The year was now 1948. Actual footage
from the time was adapted and modified to digital 3D. The words
on the plaque said that four million people had been killed at the
site between 1940 and 1945, a figure provided from the Soviet
Union at the Nuremberg International Military Tribunal in
November, 1945.

Then, with the music louder still, it was Auschwitz in 1990, the
year when the original plaque was replaced with another plaque.
The words on the new plaque said the Nazis had murdered one
and a half million people at the site, most of them Jews.

Auschwitz faded away and a huge 3D graphic of a red cross
appeared. With the music still building the narrator said that,
according to the International Committee of the Red Cross, an
estimated 135,000 registered prisoners had died at Auschwitz.
This figure came from Nazi Germany's Death Books confiscated
by the Red Army immediately after the Second World War. The
Death Books had been turned over to the Red Cross by the Soviet
Union after the fall of communism in 1989.

Then another dramatization. Richard Glueks, head of Nazi
Germany's Concentration Camp Inspectorate, was busy at work

in his Berlin office. The camera showed him from the back and focused on his record books, which opened up to reveal that 103,429 inmates at Auschwitz-Birkenau – a little more than half of them Jews – had died of typhus between 1942 and 1944. The image of Glueks slowly dissolved with the voice of the narrator saying that, according to microfilmed records from the Russian Archives, the total number of people executed at Auschwitz was 1,646, most of them Poles. Of this total, only 117 were said to be Jews.

The documentary moved to its closing segment, a tour of present-day Auschwitz. The museum was still open to the public, but the rest of the site had been closed, which meant that few people were visiting anymore. The tour was accompanied by a running commentary, along with footage of what remained from the buildings. But now the music was very different. It began so softly you could barely hear it, and then it became clear. *The Blue Danube.* The strings playing in perfect unison, Strauss's celebrated movement swept the viewer away as the voice of the narrator carried the film's message to its final crescendo.

There was one building where, the narrator said, Zyklon gas was used to disinfect clothes from severe outbreaks of lice. There were the remains of two crematoria where the bodies of those who died of typhus were burnt. There was a building where elaborate theatrical productions were staged to entertain those staying at the camp. There was the excavation of what was once a swimming pool, of all things. The documentary concluded with this statement: 'The manipulation by media over the course of almost one hundred years about what really happened at Auschwitz is the greatest crime of deception and deceit the world has ever seen.'

Coming on the heels of the Great Holocaust of 2029, the documentary gained traction and before long many people all over the world accepted it as the last word on Auschwitz. It was used to justify a book called *The Great Hoax* which made a compelling argument about how the Jewish holocaust never really happened. This was the book Christine had tossed into the Elora Gorge. The Upper Grand District School Board would later add a children's version of it to the reading list for her course *An Overview of the Twentieth and Twenty-First Centuries*.

The Great Hoax inspired a feverish debate in Germany's parliament, the Bundestag, about whether or not to close the old camps for good. Many said that the camps were perpetuating a lie. In time, the camps in Germany did close down. One by one. The first was Buchenwald, prompting a protest at the Buchenwald Memorial by a handful of Jews from the nearby town of Weimar, but no one took much notice. That was followed by the closing of Bergen-Belsen, and again, local Jews staged a rally at the Jewish Monument which had been erected at the site in 1946. But the rally created a furor that flew right in the face of those same protesters because words inscribed on the monument referred to 'thirty thousand Jews' exterminated in the camp.

"That is a far cry from six million," said a reporter covering the story. "And it's twenty thousand less than the number of Christians who were killed in the Great Holocaust."

Then Ravensbruck closed and Dachau, and both times protests by Jews were met with little fanfare. Then all the other camps in Germany closed. Flossenburg. Neuengamme. Sachsenhausen. Dora-Mittelbau. The movement to close the camps spread to other countries, first to the Ukraine where Janowska was closed, and then Belarus where Koldichevo was closed. Then it was Kaiserwald in Latvia, Sered in Slovakia, Natzweiler in France, Theresienstadt in the Czech Republic, and Mauthausen in Austria. Before long, all the camps in Italy, Croatia, Slovenia, Serbia, Macedonia and Bulgaria closed as well. Then it was the camp in Holland – Westerbork. Some of them were bulldozed right away and others later. Soon the only ones left were in Poland.

The first camps to close in Poland were Stutthof, Majdanek,

Plaszow and Gross-Rosen. There were no protests. Not one. They were followed by Chelmno, Treblinka, Sobibor and Belzec. The camps with their museums and memorials were said to be bad for business. What was once a source of tourism revenue was now met with increasing indifference. The Polish government could no longer make a case for maintaining them since the cost of upkeep was high, the cause unpopular, and donors nowhere to be found. By the time Christmas of 2039 approached, only one camp had not been bulldozed into oblivion.

Auschwitz.

Thirty-Eight

The somber procession wound its way along the narrow road that meandered through the small cemetery in Kitchener. It was easy to get lost with all the twists and turns, but the driver of the hearse knew the route. Many people came to Christine's funeral. The mourners included her Grade 6 students and teachers from Williamsburg Public School, members of the Upper Grand District School Board, close friends, city councillors, a reporter from the only daily newspaper in town, and the entire staff of the community weekly *The Reflector* where Christine once worked. There were also families who were interviewed by Christine for the obituaries she wrote, and of course, the Fisher family.

Christine's sister Tiffany, her little girl in her arms, wept by the open grave. Her father Will, his head hung low, was grieving quietly under his breath. Christine's grandfather Bill, Jack's older son, kept shaking his head from side to side as if this couldn't be real. Christine's mother Emma, a woman who had seen much suffering as a nurse in the trauma ward at the local hospital, would emerge as the strongest. When everyone was gathered around, the priest started to read.

"Turn thou the key upon our thoughts, dear Lord and let us sleep.

Grant us our portion of forgetfulness, silent and deep.
Lay thou thy quiet hand upon our eyes to clear their sight.
Shut out the shining of the moon and stars and candlelight.
Keep back the phantoms and the visions sad. The shades of gray.
The fancies that so haunt the little hours before the day.
Quiet the time-worn questions that are all unanswered yet.
Take from the spent and troubled souls of us their vain regret.
And lead us far into thy silent land that we may go
Like children out across the field of dreams where poppies blow.
So all thy saints and all thy sinners too wilt thou not keep
Since not alone unto thy well-beloved thou givest sleep."

When the priest finished, Emma with her husband Will at her side, opened a book. Her voice, the voice of a broken mother, was weak but it did not crack.

"I'll lend you for a little time a child of mine.

For you to love the while she lives and mourn for when she's dead.

It may be six or seven years, or twenty-two or three,
But will you till I call her back take care of her for me?
She'll bring her charms to gladden you, and should her stay be brief
You'll have her lovely memories as solace for your grief.
I cannot promise she will stay, since all from earth return,
But there are lessons taught down there I want this child to learn.
I've looked the wide world over in search for teachers true,
And from the throngs that crowd life's lanes, I have selected you.
Now will you give her all your love, nor think the labor vain,
Nor hate me when I come to call to take her back again?
I fancied that I heard them say, 'Dear Lord, thy will be done.
For all the joys thy child shall bring, the risk of grief we'll run'."

The graveside service was brief, just as Christine would have wished. The priest concluded with a short prayer.

"Eternal rest grant unto them whose earthly lives are past.
Perpetual light shine on them. May they rest in peace at last.
Eternal life grant unto them whose laughter now I've lost.
Whose presence and whose smiles I miss but never mind the cost.
Eternal joy grant unto them whose sufferings now are through.
Their pain and illness finally gone, their minds and hearts renew.
Eternal peace grant unto them, my friends and foes together.
Forgive them all their trespasses. May they rest in peace forever.
Amen."

The Fisher family took a step back, and the casket was lowered into the ground. There were hugs and tears and long, enduring embraces that didn't want to end, and later at the family's home an awkward gathering that was almost perverse with the absence of Christine. No one said much of anything, and the next day Jack was back home in New York. Ralph stayed with him in his room the first night, but then Jack told him to leave.

"I don't need a babysitter," he said. "I'll be all right."

But Jack wasn't all right. He kept asking himself by whose law had his great-granddaughter been taken. Christine was only twenty-five years old, a schoolteacher with her whole life ahead of her. She would have married and had children and some day grandchildren and here was Jack at a hundred. What more could there be for him? Surely he wouldn't live much longer now, but he was alive and his little Christine was dead. Where was the reasoning in that? But Jack had never seen much reason in his life. Nothing ever really made much sense. Things just happened and you dealt with them.

Not thirty minutes after Ralph was out the door, Jack was sitting alone in his room at the Greenwich Village Seniors Center, staring at that little box Christine got him the previous Christmas. Now Christmas was coming again. It was almost a year to the day. Her gift was some newfangled thing that let you send and receive 3D messages to anyone you wanted. Anywhere in the world. All you needed was their identity code. It would take his blood pressure, heart rate and other things that measured his health, but Jack didn't care about his health anymore.

He couldn't explain it, but something was pulling him to that box and maybe it was because she bought it. He got up, flipped open the lid, pressed the *receive* key and there she was.

"Hi Jack. How are you? You must be getting tired of hearing from me like this but I have something to tell you. I hope you're sitting down."

Jack's mouth was ajar. He just came from her funeral the day before, and now here was Christine standing in front of him. Talking to him as if all was well with the world. He took her advice and sat on the edge of his bed.

"You remember how you told me about your experiences in the Lodz ghetto and at Auschwitz and then I found those old records the Germans kept? They were meticulous record-keepers and I hope you forgive me for saying this but in a way it's a good thing because everything they did is there for the world to see. How can anyone deny it? That's why you're important, Jack. You are the last living person who can tell the world what happened. You are the last witness. After you there is no one else. You have a duty ... an obligation ... to tell everything ... everything you can remember about what happened to you. Now about what I wanted to tell you. Are you ready? When you were that little boy in the ghetto ... Jacob Klukowsky ... hidden by your parents Bela and Samuel so the Nazis wouldn't find you ... you had two friends named Josef Karasik and Shimek Goldberg. Remember them? You would sneak over the wall or through the wall and steal apples and pears from the shopkeepers in the market. You stole other things too so your family could eat. Those boys were eight years older than you and Shimek was the one who helped you with the manhole cover so you could get into the sewer. Until you could do it by yourself."

Christine stopped talking and lowered her head.

"Shimek didn't survive. He died in the gas chamber with his family. I found all their names in the record books."

Then she looked up and a smile came to her face.

"But Josef did survive! He survived! Just like you, Jack, and just like you he was the only one from his family who made it. After the war he wound up in a camp ... a DP camp they called it ... in Austria. It was called Bindermichel and it was in Linz. Then he went to an orphanage. I have the records right here. It was in the mountains near Salzburg. Later he was brought to America by the Jewish Congress. He lived in the Bronx, then got married and moved to Cleveland and he must have learned a lot about food when he was in the ghetto with you because he ran a grocery store with his father-in-law and they did very well. He died in 2017. He was eighty-six."

Christine stopped talking again. She caught her breath and the smile returned.

"Josef Karasik had children and grandchildren. One of his granddaughters is a woman named Emily Silver. She is fifty years old and lives on the Upper East Side not far from you in one of those brownstones like the one you had with Eve. She knows all about you, Jack. Her grandfather told her the stories and I hope you don't mind but I gave her your identity code. She wants to meet you but first she's going to send you a 3DE. What do you think of that? I love you, Jack. Your little Christine."

Thirty-Nine

Auschwitz-Birkenau, August 1944

Jacob had to go to the latrine and he hated going back there. Every time he went he saw the bodies of new children. He didn't know how they got there or what happened to them. Some of the bodies were so bruised and broken with arms and legs twisted backwards, bones sticking through the skin and in one the head missing its eyes that it didn't matter what happened to them. It got to the point where Jacob resisted the urge to go – to pee or move his bowels – and he started feeling sick. Jerzy was quick to tell him that he couldn't get sick because if they found out then he wouldn't pass the next selection.

"Come with me," Jerzy said. "I want to show you something."

Jerzy had already told him what was going on here. He told him about the gas chambers where they put hundreds of people at a time, shut the doors and turned on the gas until all of them were dead, the lot of them piled in a heap with the strongest men on top and the smallest children at the bottom. He told him about

the ovens where they burned people alive and then disposed of
them all. He told him about the barbed-wire fence around the
outside of the camp and how it was charged with electricity, so
if you made a run for it your life would end right there on the
fence. And he told him about Kanada.

It was a huge yard with watchtowers at the four corners. In
the middle were piles – mountains – of the things they collected.
Blankets. Thousands and thousands of blankets. Baby carriages.
Hundreds and maybe thousands of those, too, but no sign of
babies anywhere. Pots and pans and trunks and clothes and even
food. Mountains of all these things. The women who worked
there weren't sick, but healthy and well-fed with color in their
cheeks. All these things were taken from Jews after they arrived
at the camp. The belongings were sorted and the people were
sorted and then most of them went straight to the gas chambers.
But Kanada was a place of plenty named after a country far away.

Jerzy wanted to take Jacob to another place, so they could
play a game. The game was called *Amuzierung zu den leichen
bringen*, which was German for 'tickling the corpses'. You had to
speak German, of course; any words in Polish and they would
beat you and some children were beaten to death for using other
languages. Jacob didn't want to see another corpse, but Jerzy told
him this one wasn't like the bodies at the latrine. This one was at
the wall where they shot people with a single bullet to the head.
It wasn't messy, he said, and they weren't children, but adults and
that was better because there was more to tickle.

The body of a man was in the yard. He had been executed
that very morning. A black hole was in the middle of his
forehead, but apart from that and the dried blood on the ground
everything about him looked intact. Jerzy lifted one of his arms
and pretended to tickle him in the armpit and then he laughed.
He lifted his other arm and did the same thing. Then he spread
his legs apart and tickled him between them. He laughed the
loudest at that.

"Now you do it," he said.

Jacob didn't want to, but Jerzy knew Jacob wasn't well, that he had diarrhoea from holding it in for so long, and that if it got worse and they found out he wouldn't make the next selection. Then they would send him to the gas chamber and burn his body in the crematorium. Whatever was left would go up in the smoke that filled the air. It had happened to many children who were there one day and gone the next and Jerzy said it would happen to him, too.

"You do it," said Jerzy.

Jacob was younger and smaller than Jerzy and though Jerzy was just a stick he was still the stronger of the two. Jacob had trouble moving the dead man's arm. It was too heavy. It made him think of the time he saw the body of Shmuel Zelinsky buried under the newspapers in the lane back in Lodz. He tried to get that coat off by slipping one arm out of the sleeve and then the other. This was like that. Like lifting a rock.

When he had the arm out to the side, he dropped to his knees and tickled the corpse in the armpit. Jerzy laughed, but Jacob didn't see anything funny about it. The man was dead. He had a bullet in his head. His brain shattered. He had a wife and children and parents and they would all be crying for him unless they were dead, too. Then Jerzy pointed between his legs.

"Go ahead," he said.

Again Jacob didn't want to, but he did as he was told. He moved the man's legs apart and tickled him. Down there. Jerzy laughed and Jacob allowed himself a sly smile, but only for Jerzy's benefit. Jacob didn't want them to know he was feeling sick.

"You see," Jerzy said. "It's not so bad."

Jacob didn't know how many people were killed at the camp, but it was a lot. Jerzy told him how the trains brought more in every day. Jews from all over Europe. After their arrival they were split into one group that went straight to the gas chambers and another group that went to work, but most went to the gas chambers. That was where the children went, usually with their mothers. That was where the old people went and anyone deemed unfit for work. Jerzy said the people were told they were going to the showers, but it was really a gas chamber. The SS would shut the doors and drop cyanide pellets through holes in the roof.

Jerzy said they could kill twenty thousand people a day like that. Jacob didn't know how many people that was. The boxcar that carried him from Lodz to Auschwitz had a hundred people – that was what they said – and was so crowded you couldn't move. A thousand was more than that and Jerzy was talking twenty thousand. Every day. It was a lot. They were gassed, cremated and disposed of like in a factory assembly line, Jerzy said. After the bodies were burnt, the ashes were used for fertilizer, but Jacob didn't know what that was. Jerzy said the *Sonderkommandos* at the crematoria took gold teeth from the corpses and then melted the gold down. The people's belongings – blankets, baby carriages, trunks, everything else – all got sorted at Kanada.

Jerzy called Birkenau a *Vernichtungslager*. An extermination camp. It was too big a word for Jacob, but Jerzy knew what was going on and how to stay alive because he was still there while many others had been killed. And every night in the middle of the night the *Kapo* came for him and every night when Jerzy got back he went to sleep.

One day during the morning roll call the *doktor* who had told Jacob to drop his pants at the selection line came to visit. He was with two SS. He pointed to Jacob and said he wanted him. As soon as Jacob saw him, the shivering began. Jacob went with the two SS and the man in the white cloak to another building. They took him to a room, and then the SS shut the door and left them there. Inside the room were two girls, a little older than Jacob but not much, and it was weird because they looked exactly alike. Jacob had never seen such a thing before – two children who could have been looking at each other in a mirror. The man in the white cloak saw Jacob's reaction and laughed.

"*Meine lieben kinder,*" he said to Jacob and the girls.

He told the three of them to sit and then he gave them candy. He patted Jacob's hair and ran his hand down the arm of one of the girls. There was a knock at the door.

"*Doktor Mengele?*"

The man in the white cloak said to come in and three men, all in white cloaks just like his, entered the room. They shut the door and started talking. A few minutes later there was another knock and another man came in, but not in a white cloak. He was wearing the same striped clothes as Jacob. Jacob took one look at him and knew he was a Jew. He was skinny, but not as skinny as Jerzy with bones sticking out everywhere. He had coffee for the three Germans, and as he presented each of them with a mug he said in a respectable manner "*Doktor.*"

They were all doctors. The men ignored Jacob and the girls while they talked, but Jacob understood much of what they said because they spoke German. Jacob thought it odd that the man called Doktor Mengele addressed the other doctors in the same way that he addressed him and the girls. *Meine lieben kinder.*

My dear children.

They talked about how the war was going. They talked about the Fatherland. They talked about Jews and Gypsies and Slavs, and then the man they called Doktor Mengele motioned to Jacob and in front of the others he said "*Der blonde polnische Junge.*" The blonde Polish boy. A moment later and he said *Versuch.* Experiment. Jacob didn't know this word until Jerzy told him about it. Jerzy told him what Doktor Mengele was doing to the children he was saving from the gas chambers. He told him how, before Jacob's arrival, there had been an outbreak of a disease called spotted fever and they couldn't contain it, so Doktor Mengele ordered every person in the whole block of barracks that was infected – seven hundred people – sent to the gas chambers.

After hearing about the twenty thousand, Jacob didn't think seven hundred was much, but then he thought of the boxcar and how crowded it was with a hundred people. This was seven times that.

The man they called Doktor Mengele was kind to the two girls. He kept patting them and smiling at them. At first, Jacob thought he was their father, but he couldn't have been because they looked exactly alike and nothing at all like him. It was about the *Versuch*.

Experiments.

Jerzy told Jacob that *Der Todesengel* – that was what he called him – was the most dangerous person at *Konzentrationslager Auschwitz*.

When the doctors were finished talking, they took Jacob and the girls to a room with sinks, tables and tools. There were knives, needles and tubes with things sticking out the ends. Jacob didn't know what they were for, but he remembered what Jerzy had said and he started to tremble again. He couldn't stop it.

The man they called Doktor Mengele sat the girls down on two chairs and told them to wait. He turned to Jacob. He said he would give him chocolate if he did as he was told and didn't create a fuss. He asked him if he liked chocolate and Jacob said he did even though he had never tasted it. Then the man they called Doktor Mengele picked Jacob up under the arms and put him on a table. He made him take off his shirt. He said the chocolate was coming. Then he jabbed a needle into his arm. That was all Jacob remembered.

When he woke up in his bunk, the pain in his stomach was so bad he thought he would die. It felt like knives with twisted edges tearing his insides apart. For two days, maybe three, he couldn't eat. Not a thing. It hurt too much. All he had was water and even drinking water hurt. Then he started to eat again, just a little at first, and then some more. Not that they gave him much. The amount of food at the camp was even less than what the Germans had provided in the ghetto, but soon the pain began to subside and then he had to go to the latrine again.

He went out to the back where bodies of children were all over the floor. It was always like that and there were always new ones. One of the new ones was a girl a little older than him. Maybe she was six. She had thick blonde locks and her hair looked alive, but her body wasn't alive. There were small, round holes in her chest and splotches of dried, black blood between her legs and long streaks of blood running down her legs. Jacob looked closer and realized it was one of the girls who was in the room with him and the man they called Doktor Mengele. It was her. He didn't know what happened to the other one.

Forty

"Hello Mr. Klukowsky. My name is Emily Silver and Josef Karasik
of Lodz was my grandfather. What a pleasure to meet you!"

She was portly with heavy jowls and full, round eyes. Her
hair was neatly coiffed, she had a touch of makeup on her cheeks,
her voice wrapped in deep respect.

"I must tell you before I go any further that your great-
granddaughter Christine is a wonderful person. She really is. She
called and I had no idea who she was and then she mentioned
your name and I knew immediately this would be one of the most
important 3DEs of my life. How she found me I don't know but she
did and I can only guess she's been doing a lot of digging to get this
far. We haven't really met ... not in person anyway ... but after that
first call we exchanged a few 3DEs and now I feel like she's a good
friend and I look forward to speaking with her again. I feel I've
known her a long time but then our families go back quite a bit,
don't they? Well I don't know how to begin. My grandfather spoke
a lot about you and your adventures together during the war. I was
born in 1989 and I remember as a little girl he would sit me on his
lap and tell me about this brave little boy he knew in the ghetto.

In Lodz. His name was Jacob Klukowsky and he was four. I was probably about four myself when he first told me about you. He wanted us to know. Oh excuse me but my grandfather ... my Zayda ... had three children ... two sons and a daughter ... and his younger son who was the middle one in the family is my father. His name is Howard Karasik and he's still alive. He's seventy-eight and thank God in good health. My mother is alive too. Her name is Sheila and she's seventy-six."

Jack was glued to the box. It was as if his life was unfolding before him through this woman he had never met. Josef Karasik's granddaughter. And did she really call him Mr. Klukowsky?

"My Zayda told us what it was like in the ghetto. How there was never food and how so many died of disease and how people were taken away for no reason and you never saw them again. Being born when I was and living my whole life in America it's pretty hard to get a handle on what it must have been like. I mean I've always had everything handed to me on a silver platter. Even my name is Silver!"

She laughed and her jowls shook like they would never stop shaking. But it was a good laugh. A hearty, honest laugh.

"My Zayda was a hard-working man. I'm sure like you he learned a lot of values in the ghetto and later at the camp where they sent him. He went to Chelmno and lost everyone in his family there. His mother. His father. His brother and his two sisters. All of them. They were all gassed. I'm not even sure how he got out. He always said he was lucky. But you! He talked so much about you! About the little four-year-old boy Jacob Klukowsky and how fast he could run when he knocked over the fruit stalls and how he could make a hole in the wall using a knife and fork. He said you were so brave. That you risked your life to get food for your family and later how my Zayda got beat up by a policeman and you didn't want to go with him anymore."

She laughed again.

"He called you a pisher. I'm sorry but he did but you were

only four years old and he was twelve so that's what you were to him. But he had a lot of respect for you. For your courage and the way you did things. He said you were a good partner and sometimes he was happy to get out of the Aryan part of the city with one pillowcase filled with fruit ... that's what you used, right? ... but you would take two because those rich machers wouldn't know the difference."

The laugh again.

"Well I keep rambling on but I want you to know what an honor it is to get the chance to speak with that brave little boy who left such an impression on my Zayda when he was in the ghetto. My Zayda died a long time ago. In 2017. Over twenty years now. I can't believe it's been that long. I was twenty-eight when he died so I knew him very well and I loved him. He was a wonderful man. My grandmother ... my Bubby ... is gone now too but she almost got to ninety. She was eighty-nine when she died. But Christine tells me you just turned a hundred! Mazel-tov! How satisfying it must be for someone from the ghetto and the camps to reach a hundred. To have such memories as a little boy and then overcome all that and have such a rich life with children and grandchildren and even great-grandchildren. Christine says you even have a great-great-grandchild. Mazel-tov! I can't wait to meet you. I live on the Upper East Side and know you're at the Greenwich Village Seniors Center. I'd love to come by to say hello. Maybe we could have lunch? I know a nice deli in Greenwich. Do you like pastrami or corned beef? It doesn't matter. You could get soup and potato salad but it has to be on me. I insist. I want to tell you about my family and the grandchildren your friend Josef left behind and I want to know what you've been up to for the past ... what is it ... ninety-six years? Maybe we'll have two lunches! That would be nice. Or you could come and visit us and meet the family. They would all be so honored to meet you. Please send me a 3DE and we'll talk some more. I'm really looking forward to meeting you. Say hello to Christine for me. I'd love to meet her. Good-bye for now."

Forty-One

Brett Krust was really worried about his kids. Both of them. Even little Billy who was only seven. Brett knew it wouldn't be long before his precocious Stephanie discovered boys. Maybe she already had. Billy, six years younger, looked up to his sister and Brett figured he better set an example with her or he'd have bigger fish to fry with the boy later. Their schooling was always left to their mother, but when Jen came home empty-handed after meeting with Stephanie's teacher, he figured it was time to act.

The Cobra made everything so simple. He talked about securing the dignity of the gene pool and Brett liked how he put that. *Securing the dignity of the gene pool.* If races were supposed to mix, then all of us would have been brown from the beginning, but we weren't. We were different and there was a reason. The Cobra talked a lot about *dilution*, and how the traits and characters of one race could dilute that of another. It was all right if you were on the bottom rung – what he called the *mongrel* among us – but if you were at the top, then all this inter-mixing could yield only one result.

Your gene pool was diluted.

This is exactly what has been going on, and the white race was suffering because of it. All its values were under attack. Democracy was threatened with tribalism. The family unit was under bombardment, and just being a Christian meant that you had to apologize for it. This new philosophy of *miscegenation* – the mixing of the races – would be our downfall, and soon the mongrels would dominate.

What happened in Turkey in 2029 with the Islamists massacring all those Christians in the streets was the barometer. That's what the Cobra said. It could, *it would*, happen again.

There weren't many blacks in Wellington County, which was fine with Brett. It was one reason why he wanted to raise his family in Kitchener and not a big city, and while there were some Orientals in town, at least they kept to their own. But Jews, despite their small numbers, always seemed to have their hand in things. And to make matters worse, they were white.

Don't just think – intervene! That's what the Cobra said. It was his call to action. Brett read him all the time. He also read *The Great Hoax*, a powerful argument that showed how six million Jews dying at the hands of Nazi Germany a hundred years ago couldn't possibly have happened.

He knew what Christine Fisher looked like from the 3DEs she sent her students, and after getting her schedule from Stephanie, he found out what time her classes finished. He picked a day when he was off work, so he could show up at Williamsburg Senior Public School and set the record straight. And that was what he did. With the book in his hand, he planted himself in the hallway outside Christine's last class of the afternoon. The door opened and the kids poured out, including Stephanie.

"Daddy, what are you doing here?" she said.

"Go home," was all he said.

But where was the teacher? When the kids dispersed, he peaked through the door and there she was, still at her desk at the front of the class. Reading. Brett stuck his head in and cleared his throat.

"Can I help you?" Christine said.

With his lanky frame, he ambled in and then stopped. "I'm Brett Krust. Stephanie's Dad," he said.

He saw how her jaw dropped when he mentioned his name.

"Oh," was all she said, and then, "I met your wife."

He walked into the room and looked around. He had never been here before. Not once. There were posters on the walls. Indians with headdresses. Fur traders in canoes. Soldiers with guns slung over their shoulders.

"So this is where Steph gets her history, huh?" he said.

She didn't say anything. He looked around some more. The desks were set up in rows, everything neat and tidy, and on a table under the window were piles of discs and kindles and mini-kindles. Then Christine saw a book under his arm.

"I think you better read this," Brett said.

"What is it?"

He came closer and showed it to her. Christine grimaced when she saw the title. The book was against everything she stood for. A sad and hopeless disguise of the truth.

"I am familiar with that book," she said.

"Steph told me it's on the list for your course but you don't use it. Why not?"

She shook her head. "No that's not correct. That book isn't suitable for Grade 8. The one they put on the reading list is a children's version but that's not suitable for my kids either."

"Why not?" he said again.

She felt like spitting. That would have been appropriate. And if not on the book, right on him. But she held back. She had to think of his daughter.

"Because just like that one in your hand ..."

He waited for her to finish the sentence.

"What?" he said.

"I find it offensive. It insults my intelligence as a history teacher but even more as a human being."

Brett smirked. "You think you're so high and mighty, don't you?" he said. "You think you're smart but you're not. All you're doing is confusing these kids with all this garbage you teach them."

"Garbage?"

"That's right. About this Jewish holocaust business. You're supposed to teach history and you don't even do what the school tells you to do. Someone like you shouldn't be teaching at all."

"I think you better leave."

"I'm not going to leave."

Christine knew about this man and the kind of man he was. But she didn't know if she should be afraid. "What do you want?" she said, and he held up the book.

"I bet you haven't even read it, have you?" he said.

"I don't have to read it."

"It's all here in these pages. Empirical evidence that what you claim isn't true."

She saw how proud he was at using such a word.

"This is real," Brett said. "It's real but what you teach them isn't. It's only what you think. What kind of teacher would do something like that? I'm gonna get you expelled."

She almost laughed. "Teachers can't be expelled," Christine said. "They can be suspended but only in extreme situations."

"*This* is an extreme situation."

He was pathetic.

"I'm gonna leave this book with you and I want you to read it from cover to cover," he said. "Then maybe you'll understand about all the harm you're doin' to these kids."

That was enough to put Christine over the edge. She could only take so much. She got to her feet and walked across the front of the classroom to him. Nose to nose.

"You're telling me about all the harm *I'm* doing to these kids?" She forgot just then about being afraid and let the words roll. They just came out. "Let me tell you something, *Mr. Krust.*

You have a lot of nerve coming to *my* school ... *my* classroom ... trying to lecture *me*. You worthless piece of shit who beats his wife and kids and tries to keep them as ignorant as you are."

He stood there frozen, his mouth ajar, the color rising through his face. If a man ever spoke to him like that, he would pay. Big time. But a woman? Jen could be difficult, but she wouldn't have the guts to say such things. Not to him. He moved the book from one hand to the other. One of his fists was clenched.

"What are you going to do?" Christine said. "Hit me? You're good at that, aren't you? Hitting women. Try it and I'll lay a charge against you and you'll never put on your firefighter uniform again. And I don't care how many cops you go drinking with."

Christine felt good. Relieved. She had never talked to anyone like that before, let alone a stranger, but he wasn't really a stranger, was he? She knew exactly who he was and, not only that, what he was. This man standing in front of her was none other than the Enemy.

Brett felt like hitting her. He did. He could feel the rage boiling inside him. All bottled up. Ready to explode.

Christine went back to her desk, sat down, and resumed her reading. But nothing would register in her brain. Not a word. At first she tried pretending that he just wasn't there. Ignoring him would be the ultimate degradation. She let the seconds pass, but they were slow seconds. Deathly slow.

He still had the book in his hands and she wondered if he would throw it at her or maybe throw it through the window. Vandalism was in tune with his makeup. It wouldn't be the first time. He was the kind of man who did things and thought about his actions later. If he thought about them at all.

He started walking over to her desk. Methodically. And with every step he took her heart picked up a beat. What if she had to defend herself? But no. When he was standing directly over her, her chest pounding and ready for anything he might muster, he dropped the book onto her desk, turned around and left.

Just like that.

She would never see him again.

The Lie sat there soiling the surface of her desk, polluting the air in this place of learning, and Christine got an idea. She grabbed the book and her bag with her portable e-book reader. There were hundreds of titles in it. Then she left her class and rushed through the hall of her school to the parking lot. She was in a frenzy. She climbed into her car and threw everything into the seat beside her. She had charged the power cell that morning with just enough mileage for this trip. Christine was always frugal that way. Never one to waste. She got behind the wheel and waited for the onboard computer to recognize her.

'Hello Christine. Driving conditions are ideal today.'

The car started itself and she was off. She took Regional Road 22 out of town, crossed the Conestoga River and headed north through the rolling hills and farmers' fields, the silos and barns, the signs advertising fresh maple syrup and the lonely cows on either side of the road. The hills soon gave way to flat open land and she liked the fact she could get lost in the country in fifteen minutes flat. Up a bit more and the image of a deer appeared on the screen of her dashboard. The voice of her computer came on again.

'Be careful. It's not far off the roadway, about two kilometers up number 22.'

Sure enough, a moment later the deer appeared at the side of the road, but one glimpse of the car and it ran off, disappearing through the grasses. Christine watched and then there was that familiar sign – 'Christ died for the ungodly' – and further up the road another sign. It marked the boundary of the town of Salem, or as it more accurately noted, the Historic Hamlet of Salem. A few minutes longer and she pulled into the next town.

Elora.

Forty-Two

"She must have FT'd the message," Hodgson said. "That is the only possible explanation."

"What's that?" said Jack.

"What's what?"

"What you said. *Eff-tee?*"

"She Future-Timed it. You can do that."

Jack had no idea what Hodgson was talking about.

"Look. She wants to send you a 3DE. Even a series of 3DEs. So she shoots herself ..."

"She shoots herself?"

"You know what I mean. She records herself digitally. Video and audio. It's all 3D. She sends you a message right away and the next one she sends whenever she wants. She can set it up so it comes at two in the afternoon the next day or in the middle of the night. She can send you ten 3DEs and have them arrive at the same time every day for the next ten days or at different times. They can arrive whenever she wants them to arrive. In a week. A month. Whatever."

"But I got it after she ..."

"I know. She must have set it that way. I guess she had her reasons."

Hodgson had joined Jack in the lounge at the Greenwich Village Seniors Center. He was on edge today.

"Jack, I didn't come here this morning to tell you how to FT a 3DE. I came to tell you that we found something. About Christine."

"What?"

"You were right," Hodgson said. "She didn't jump."

"I told you. So it was an accident."

"No."

Hodgson looked even bigger now. Bigger than before. His tie hung loose around his neck, the flesh bulging from inside his shirt collar. His jacket was crumpled. He had been up half the night speaking to the Canadian police in Kitchener.

"But if it wasn't suicide and it wasn't an accident then what was it?" said Jack.

Hodgson put his head down. "She was murdered," he said.

"What!"

"I'm sorry, Jack. I know this is hard. But she was murdered. Someone pushed her."

"I don't understand."

"Jack, when Christine went to the Elora Gorge that day she was just like that little girl who wanted to see what it would be like up on the ledge. That little girl who always wondered about it. And she did it. She climbed up on the ledge."

Jack's mouth was open, his eyes staring wildly at Hodgson.

"But someone came behind her and pushed her. She was murdered."

"Murdered?" was all Jack could say and it was only a whisper. He brought his hand to his mouth.

"There was a witness. A ten-year-old girl was in the park and she saw Christine. She saw her throw a book into the gorge and then she saw her standing there by the railing. She watched her get up on the ledge."

"She really did it?"

"Yes," said Hodgson. "But she didn't jump. The girl saw a man come behind her and push her. Into the gorge."

"Oh my God!"

"I'm sorry. I know how hard this is for you."

"But who? Why?"

Hodgson put his hand on Jack's arm and gave him a friendly tap. Once. Twice. Three times.

"We pretty well ruled out foul play from the beginning because it looked like a suicide or an accident. One or the other. But then they found this girl. She gave the police a description of what she saw."

"But who would want to kill Christine?"

This wasn't the first time Hodgson had to tell someone about the murder of a loved one, but never a one-hundred-year-old man. He planted his size fifteen shoes in front of him and leaned over so his face was only inches from Jack. He watched how Jack was breathing.

"Are you all right?" Hodgson said.

Jack nodded his head. "Tell me what you know."

Hodgson said that before going to the gorge that day, Christine had stopped at the Elora Mill Inn to eat. In the dining room. It was called the Gorge Lounge. He even told him what she had – a salad, a dish of tomatoes with chickpeas and spinach, a glass of wine. He said she left in a hurry and had a book with her. *The Great Hoax.*

Jack was shaking his head from side to side. "They made her put a children's version of that thing on her reading list," he said.

Hodgson told him that the local police went to see the waiter who had served Christine in the dining room at the inn. The waiter saw the book on the table.

"There was some conversation between the two of them and he asked her what she was reading and she showed him. She told him she was going to throw it into the Elora Gorge. From there she walked to the park and went straight to the gorge. Right over to the railing. Lover's Leap Lookout?"

"Lover's Leap Lookout," said Jack.

"She threw the book into the gorge. They found what was left of it and there wasn't much and then she climbed on the ledge. She stood there with her arms at her sides and that's when this character came behind her ... and pushed her."

"Who was it?"

Hodgson leaned back into his chair. This type of thing was never easy.

"His name is Brett Krust. He has a 13-year-old daughter. The girl was in Christine's history class at Williamsburg Senior Public School."

"What!"

"He's a firefighter. Apparently there was a lot of trouble in the household over what Christine was teaching his daughter. He went to the school to see the principal and made a scene. Later his wife ... the mother ... Jennifer Krust ... met with Christine. She asked Christine to stop teaching the course the way she was teaching it. You know. About the holocaust."

Jack was shaking his head again.

"Christine refused," said Hodgson.

"Did she threaten Christine?"

"No I don't think so. You see ... judging by the police report ... this woman has been on the receiving end of an abusive husband for years. She was scared of him and so were their kids. Now Jack, there's more. He's got this connection to this group. Seems to be a whites only kind of thing."

"What are you talking about?"

"Jack, this Brett Krust character is a wacko. They went into his data files and looked at everything. I only know what I got from the Canadian police but they found all this material he kept at his fire hall and even more at his home."

"What did they find?"

"Interesting stuff."

"Like what?"

Hodgson whipped out his notebook and flipped through the pages. "He saved all these articles going back to the 1900s. He had a library. Stuff written by George Lincoln Rockwell. The guy who founded the American Nazi Party. Stuff from old neo-Nazi organizations. The National Alliance. The Heritage Front. Aryan Nation. And something called the Hammerskins which operated out of Texas. And I'm sure you know after the Great Holocaust of 2029 there was a resurgence with some of these groups and others like them."

Hodgson put his notebook down. He pursed his lips together, crossing his big arms.

"And one more thing I want to tell you about. There's this newsletter."

Forty-Three

The elevator doors closed and Jack found himself alone. His head, his mind, was all a blur. He felt only emptiness. His little Christine wasn't just dead, she had been murdered. His mother and father were murdered. His Aunt Gerda was murdered. And so were Zivia and Romek and his baby brother who never even had a name. Murdered. All of them.

And now Christine.

His destination was the dining room on the main floor, but when the elevator doors opened, nothing looked familiar. No yellow-brown wallpaper on the wall. No light fixtures hanging from the ceiling. No red paint on the floor. Everything was a dull grey. He walked into the hall not knowing where he was.

"Where am I?" he said out loud, but no one was there.

He started walking, but didn't recognize anything. Meandering along, looking this way and that, trying to get his bearings. It was deathly quiet. Up ahead was an opening leading off the hallway and then a wall of glass with a sign. He went to see what it said. ACTIVITY CENTER. The door was open and he looked through it, but it was only an empty room with tables spread about and chairs stacked on top of each other in the corner. No one was inside.

Confused, Jack went back into the hallway. There was another room, smaller than the first, and a sign was here, too. SPECIAL EVENTS. He went inside and it was just like the other one with a few tables and chairs, but no people.

"What's going on here?" said Jack. "Where am I?"

Then he heard what sounded like thunder from down the hall. Jack followed the noise, which kept getting louder and louder. *Chug-a-chug. Chug-a-chug.* What was it? He felt dizzy, his head pounding, his eyes blurry. His legs wobbling, he leaned against the wall and used it for support. He put his hands flat against the cold wall behind him and his breathing got heavy. He could still hear it.

Chug-a-chug. Chug-a-chug. Chug-a-chug.

The sound was getting louder and louder.

Chug-a-chug! Chug-a-chug! Chug-a-chug!

"What is it! What's that noise!"

He put his hands over his ears and opened his eyes and right there in front of him was a huge swastika on the wall and another one on the ceiling. Yet another one was on the floor. There were swastikas everywhere. Dozens. Hundreds of them. Their black arms twirling. Going round and round and round. All of them together. Like pistons.

CHUG-A-CHUG! CHUG-A-CHUG! CHUG-A-CHUG!

Jack was surrounded by all these swastikas. Stepping on them. Breathing them into his lungs. He started to gag with his arms flailing about and then the swastikas became snakes, their dancing arms turning into serpents with hideous heads at the end. One of them wound itself around his neck and started squeezing the life out of him. He put his hands onto its slithery body and felt the cold, wet scales in his fingers. Then its massive head jutted out right in front of him. Staring him in the face. A cobra. The mouth wide open with fangs ready to strike.

"Help me! Help me!" cried Jack.

The next thing he knew, two women were getting him off the floor. They had blue robes just like the staff at the Greenwich Village Seniors Center.

"Are you all right?"

"What?"

"You fell," one of them said. "Right here outside the laundry room. Are you all right?"

"Where am I?" said Jack. He looked around, bewildered. "Where are the snakes?"

"Easy now. You got lost. Disoriented. You're in the basement."

"The basement? I'm in the basement? How did I get here?"

"You probably came out of the elevator and thought you were somewhere else."

"The elevator?"

He looked around. There were no swastikas. No snakes. Only bare grey walls.

"You're Jack Fisher, aren't you? From the sixth floor?"

"What?"

"We'll take you to your room and get a nurse."

Forty-Four

Hodgson keyed in the name Brett Krust of Kitchener, Ontario, which got him into the Canada-United States Police Information Exchange System. It was a massive but effective databank that for police purposes treated the border between the two countries as if it didn't exist. And for police investigations it didn't. Now he had access to Canada's police data on crime. Everything he wanted. There were no convictions for Brett Krust, but there was one charge of assault against him laid by his wife. It had been stayed. Once she took out a restraining order against him. But there was also something else. Not a conviction or even a charge, but information. He was a member of The United Front, a group based in Atlanta, Georgia with chapters all over the world. There was nothing to show how many members it had, but its publications were printed in different languages – English, German, Spanish, French, Italian and Russian.

The United Front had grown out of the old National Alliance, which was once cited by the FBI as the best-financed, best-organized, white nationalist group in America. But by the year 2010, its membership had dwindled to less than a thousand. After the Great Holocaust of 2029, however, it returned with a new name and new executive. A radio program and an ezine called Voices of Dissidence had a string of regular contributors. One of them known as The Cobra wrote about survival of the white race and how it was under attack. The Cobra said blacks, Jews, Muslims, Orientals and anyone not white and Christian were a problem for America. The Cobra said the Jewish holocaust never happened because it was impossible for that many people to have been murdered back in the 1940s.

"Kathy, I want you to find what you can about whoever writes this column The Cobra for The United Front."

Kathy Sottario had not endeared herself to Jack, but she was helping Hodgson with the Christine Fisher file. When it came to research, she was a crack investigator who could find things faster than anyone else.

"Have you got a name?" she asked Hodgson.

"No. Just The Cobra. I've been through some of the columns but I can't find a name anywhere. You might start by learning what you can about this group. The United Front."

"I'll get right to it, Lieutenant."

"And if you do get a name see if there's anything about him in NCIC."

The National Crime Information Center was the central database for tracking all crime in the United States. The very next day Kathy knocked on Hodgson's door.

"His name is Jon Creeley," she said. "No 'h' in Jon. He lives in Jersey."

"Go on."

"Like you said he writes a column called The Cobra and it's widely circulated through The United Front. It gets translated into several languages but not once does he ever identify himself. He's just The Cobra. However he does radio broadcasts and those get translated too so I managed to tap into some of the internal correspondence between the ezine editor in Atlanta and the translator who actually lives in Frankfurt but everything the translator does is sidetracked through London."

"London?"

"That's right. Germany has tougher laws than England for stuff like this so I'm guessing he doesn't want to show any German connection. No German-based 3DE identity code. No German address of any kind."

"How did you find that out?"

"I have my ways."

"Okay. Anything else?"

Kathy started reading from her mini.

"NCIC showed three Jon Creeley's in the state of New Jersey who are still alive and have criminal records. The first Jon Creeley is in his seventies. He's long retired. Back in the 1990s this guy got convicted of auto theft. The second Jon Creeley is fifty-six, a digital strategist who did six months for possession of child pornography in 2027. That's all it shows."

"What exactly is a digital strategist?"

"It could be anything. Someone who adapts data into 3D or builds new platform technologies from older formats."

"I see. And the third one?"

"The third Jon Creeley is younger than those two. Thirty-six. His occupation is listed as fight promoter."

"Fight promoter?"

"That's right. For the past four years he's been one of the backers of a professional martial arts circuit that stages fights. Bouts. It's organized and legit but he seems to have his finger in a few pies because he manages one of the fighters himself. A guy named Colton Brock who is known as Coal. He's the champion. Undefeated. An ex-Navy Seal who once killed a guy in training and got discharged. No criminal charges were ever filed."

"Hmm. It was military."

"It was military. But here's the thing. This Jon Creeley character was known to the police before he ever got involved in the martial arts circuit."

"How?"

"Jon Creeley had a conviction for fraud in 2026. Another conviction for embezzling in 2028 and for that he got six months. He served his time at Attica and got paroled but later was charged with parole violation but he never did any more jail time. In 2030 there were charges for common assault on a minor ... teenage girl ... but the charge was withdrawn."

"Uh-huh."

"Four years ago in 2035 ..."

"Yeah?"

"He was questioned about a homicide."

"A homicide?"

"That's right. Albert Freedman was a ninety-five-year-old man who was found murdered in his apartment on the upper East Side. His superintendent found him. Massive trauma to the body. He was badly beaten and was either choked to death with a cane ... it was probably his own ... or else he died of a snapped vertebra."

"Snapped vertebra?"

"Broken neck."

"Nasty. Why one or the other?"

"The police report wasn't clear about the cause of death. And the file is still open on that one. Nobody was ever charged. The place was ransacked. Money gone. Stuff like that. It looked like a robbery."

"But no ninety-year-old is going to put up much of a fight. Why did they have to kill him?"

"He was ninety-five."

"Okay. Why did they have to kill him?"

"I don't know."

"So what's this got to do with Jon Creeley?"

"Well that's just it, Lieutenant. Jon Creeley ... the fight promoter Jon Creeley ... was questioned by police. On the night of Albert Freedman's murder he was seen on the street outside the old man's apartment. They let him go. There was nothing to implicate him. But there's more."

Hodgson leaned over.

"There was a story about the old man who was murdered ... Albert Freedman ... in *The Jewish Post.* That newspaper is still around. Not cyber. Newsprint. There's not many of those anymore."

"No."

"Well this story said Albert Freedman was a holocaust survivor. A Jewish holocaust survivor."

"Kathy, give me that again."

"I said this man Albert Freedman was a holocaust survivor. At least according to this story."

"And he was ninety what?"

"Ninety-five."

"When was that? When was he murdered?"

"Four years ago."

Hodgson did the math. "So if he was alive today ... he'd be ninety-nine."

Albert Freedman, a murdered man, was born one year after Jack. A holocaust survivor.

"I suppose it could've been a robbery gone astray," Hodgson said. "Heat of the moment. Stuff like that."

"Unless they wanted to kill him," said Kathy.

"But why would someone want to kill a ninety-five-year-old man?"

"I don't know."

Forty-Five

The taxi deposited Jack in front of the three-storey brownstone on East 88th Street. It was near the Jewish Museum, a few blocks from the Gracie Mansion. The driver offered to help him up the stairs, but Jack said no. He had a cane. Ever since he turned ninety – ever since Eve died – people have been saying that he needed a cane, as if her death rendered him incapable of walking on his own. But now there had been two incidents at the residence, both of them falls, so he had a cane. He tipped the driver, marched up the steps and rang the bell. A woman's voice said she'd be right down. Jack waited and then there she was. Emily Silver. The woman he saw on the 3DE.

"You must be Mr. Klukowsky," she said with a smile.

Mr. Klukowsky? Jack had never been called that before. It sounded strange. He returned her smile with one of his own.

"Please," he said, "you can call me ..." He stopped himself and thought about it. "You can call me Jacob."

"Jacob," she said, extending a hand. "What a pleasure. What an honor. Please come in. And watch your step."

She noticed the cane and he saw how she noticed it. Then she apologized for living on the second floor and for there not being a lift. She said she would help him up the stairs, but Jack said no.

"I have a cane," he said.

"Yes I know you do."

"But it's not my cane. It's society's cane. I don't really need it but everybody seems to think a man my age should have a cane so I have it to make them happy."

She said something about him being a hundred years old. He dismissed it as no big deal.

"Lots of people get to be a hundred these days," Jack said. "But two hundred? Now that would be something. That's what I'm working on now."

She liked him right away.

No one else was home. She said her husband was at work and they had two sons, both at college out of town. She said she owned a hair dressing salon and drew customers from well-to-do women on the Upper East Side. Business was good. Even though she was the owner, she worked Saturdays – her busiest day – but took Wednesday off, which was today.

"I guess I was lucky," Jack said.

"No I arranged it like that. If you couldn't have come today I would have taken another day off. Meeting you was more important than going to work."

She brought him coffee and cookies, and said she wanted to have him for dinner one evening to meet the family, but thought it better this time if it was just the two of them. She mentioned Christine and said what a lovely girl she was. Jack hadn't told her what happened. He didn't know how to begin. Then she began talking about her grandfather. Her *Zayda*. Jack listened and then he started telling her stories from the ghetto about himself and Josef Karasik, but she seemed to know them all.

"My *Zayda* told me everything," she said. "He always talked about you. What a brave little boy you were. But what I don't know is what happened to you after the ghetto. After they took you away."

Jack told her about the sewers and how his baby brother was born there and died there. How his Aunt Gerda had to suffocate him because he wouldn't have survived and how she had to do it or the Germans would have found out about them, but they did anyway. He told her about Father Kasinski and what he did for the family. He told her how he, his parents, his aunt and his two cousins all went to Auschwitz and how he was the only survivor.

"That's what I want to know," Emily said. "How did you survive Auschwitz? Children didn't survive that place."

Jack said two dozen children, including him, were liberated by the Red Army in January, 1945. He said they were from many countries – Poland, Belgium, Holland, Czechoslovakia, Hungary. Then she said something about how the Russians never got credit for helping defeat the Nazis.

"That's true," Jack said and then he shook his head. "They raped the girls, you know."

"What do you mean?"

"When they came to liberate us. Some of the older Jewish girls. The Russian soldiers raped them. There was no one to stop them. I thought they were beating them up. What did I know?"

"I never heard that before."

"It was a war."

Jack said he had been at the camp since August 1944 when he arrived by train from Lodz. He told her about the boxcar.

"How did you survive? You were just a little boy."

Jack said it was a long story, but if she had the time he would tell her.

"For you Jacob I have all the time in the world."

He liked being called that. No one had called him Jacob for so long that he had forgotten what it sounded like, but his parents called him that. Or something close. *Ya-coov*. She went to bring fresh coffee and when she returned she wanted to hear the story about how he survived.

"One thing your grandfather and I both learned in the ghetto was this," Jack said. "Even people who want to harm you have a price. They can be bought. Josef ... your grandfather ... used to buy them by selling them cigarettes. I learned a lot from him. He was a rascal."

Emily laughed and her eyes started to tear up.

"You want to know how I survived Auschwitz? A boy who wasn't even five years old? I turned five on December 1, 1944, a few weeks before we were liberated. There was no birthday party for me."

She smiled.

"I survived because I took what people taught me and used it."

"Tell me," she said. "I want to know."

"When I got to the barracks at Birkenau ... they called it Auschwitz II ... I shared my bunk with an older boy named Jerzy. He told me everything that went on there. Everything. Birkenau was hell. Even a little boy four years old can recognize hell when he sees it. Every night the *Kapo* came for him. He was a German ... seventeen ... eighteen ... and I still remember what he looked like. He wasn't tall but husky and he was a lot bigger than me and he was a lot bigger than Jerzy. He took Jerzy away every night and did what he wanted to him. I didn't understand any of that at the time. All I knew was that every night the *Kapo* came for Jerzy and a few hours later Jerzy came back and he was always tired. One night the *Kapo* took him away and Jerzy never came back. I never found out what happened to him. He probably wound up in the gas chamber unless the *Kapo* killed him. I don't know. Anything was possible. But a couple nights later the *Kapo* came and this time he wanted me."

Emily put her hand to her face.

"I opened up the heel on my right shoe and showed him my *chervonets*. It was a gold coin from Russia. Father Kasinski gave it to me. Naturally the *Kapo* wanted it but I told him I had lots of them. I told him I hid a coin at the bottom of every latrine out

in the back and there were a lot of latrines there, at least thirty
of them, but I only had room for one coin in my heel. He didn't
believe me so I told him if he left me alone I would show him
a different *chervonets* the next night. He would know because
it would have a different year inscribed on it and that's what
happened. Every night I showed him a gold coin with a different
year on it. One time I heard Mengele and the other doctors
talking and I knew the war wasn't going well for the Germans.
It was just a matter of time, they said, before the Allies defeated
them so I told the *Kapo* when the war was over I would share all
my gold coins with him. I promised to give him half of them. If
he would just leave me alone."

"But you said you only had one gold coin," Emily said.

"I did have only one gold coin but when I was a little boy
living in the ghetto my father showed me how he changed the
nameplate on sewing machines. You see, he was a tailor and he
fixed everyone's sewing machine. All the Jews wanted a Singer
sewing machine and all the Germans wanted a *Pfaff*. It was a
different make. German, of course. The name was painted in gold
letters on the black base, then it was covered with this transparent
lacquer. My father showed me how to sand off the lacquer,
repaint the black, then paint the name 'Singer' in gold and recoat
it with the lacquer. He was a very enterprising man. He made
sure every Jew got a Singer sewing machine and every German
got a *Pfaff*. Nobody could tell the difference. They just looked at
the nameplate. So no matter what kind of sewing machine he
had he made sure all his customers were happy. I used that same
kind of reasoning with my *chervonets* at Birkenau. You see, I had
a friend. A *Sonderkommando*. They were Jews who helped burn
the bodies. Some of them were just as bad as the Nazis but this
man helped me. He took me where the ovens were and put my
chervonets in for a few seconds. That was all we needed to heat it
up. Then we took it out and etched a new year in it with a carving
knife. We did it together. We did that every day until the *Kapo*

was convinced I had a mini Fort Knox hidden in the latrines out in the back."

"But why did the *Sonderkommando* help you?"

"I appealed to his sense of Jewish pride. He could see this little Jewish boy who was fooling this dumb German and he took a lot of pleasure in that. But I had to promise to give him the *chervonets* when the war was over and I did."

"You gave it to him or you just promised?"

"I just promised. One day the *Sonderkommando* went to the gas chamber but by that time I had the *Kapo* in my hip pocket. He couldn't wait for the war to end because he thought he was going to be rich."

Jack chuckled and Emily burst into a smile. She liked the story.

"I appealed to his greed and it worked but he wasn't the only person like that. There was another *Kapo* in the barracks, a German woman, and she was the only one who didn't hit us. She liked children. She was Catholic and considered herself a good Christian so with her I appealed to her sense of Christianity. I knew all the prayers ... in Latin ... and I used to recite them for her. Sometimes we did them together. Sometimes we even sang them. She would bring me things. Like bread or soup that really tasted like soup. Or extra clothes to keep me warm. She was the only one who didn't hit us."

"So you used her the way you used the young German *Kapo* and the way you used the *Sonderkommando*?"

"I used Mengele too."

"How?"

Jack took a sip from his coffee and asked if he could have another cookie. Emily said he could eat them all. She said she had lots.

"It was because of Mengele that I knew things were bad for the Germans. I didn't know anything about the Allies but I knew if they were fighting the Germans they were my friends.

Mengele and the other doctors said the Allies were winning the war and one day it would be over. Mengele was a real Aryan. He worshipped children with blonde hair and blue eyes. I had blue eyes. I can thank my mother for that."

"But you didn't have blonde hair. You said Father Kasinski dyed your hair. With peroxide."

"Father Kasinski did dye my hair with peroxide but he also showed me *how* to dye my hair with peroxide. The nice German woman ... the *Kapo* in the barracks ... the good Christian who thought I was a Catholic just like her ..."

"She gave you peroxide?"

"Yes. They had lots of it for the Germans. Not for the Jews or the other prisoners. But she liked me and helped me dye my hair."

"And Mengele?"

"If he ever knew I was dying my hair he would have sent me straight to the gas chamber. No question about it. He used to check my hair all the time. He'd look through it and check the roots but it was always blonde so with him it was a matter of aesthetics. The aesthetics of the Aryans. He thought children with blue eyes and blonde hair were beautiful and he thought I was Polish. Not Jewish. He would have killed me if he knew I was Jewish."

"So you fooled them all. You. A little boy of four years old. You fooled everyone."

"I don't think of it that way. I was just trying to stay alive. But I was fortunate to meet certain people. I was fortunate to have a father like I did. I was fortunate to have met Father Kasinski and I was fortunate to know Josef. Your *Zayda*. He was a good friend. He taught me a lot."

Emily clasped her hands together.

"There is something I want to tell you!" she said. "Almost forgot. I belong to an organization. It was started a long time ago by children of survivors but there aren't many members anymore. You go one generation and two generations and people start to lose interest. Even Jews. But today with all the trouble in Poland and this talk about closing Auschwitz ... it's the last camp ... the only one they haven't got rid of. Well we had a meeting and they want to have a rally to protest the rising anti-Semitism in Poland ... you hear about it every day ... and this move to close Auschwitz. They can't do that. When they closed the museum people stopped going there and if they get rid of what's left then nobody will think it ever existed. That's all people have to know and then ..."

"They will say that it never happened," said Jack.

"They want to send the bulldozers in just like they did at Belsen and Treblinka and Sobibor and all the others. We can't let it happen, Jacob. *You* can't let it happen. After you there won't be anyone left."

Jack was thinking to himself. That was what Christine said. "Where are you going to do this thing?" he said.

"At the Statue of Liberty."

"The Statue of Liberty?"

"Can you think of a better place?"

Jack couldn't. "What do you want me to do?" he said.

She said it would be good if he could say a few things about what happened at Auschwitz. What he saw there. There would be a lot of people and her group could help him prepare his comments.

"One of our members used to write speeches for the mayor," she said.

Jack said he would think about it. Then she clapped her hands together.

"Jacob! I almost forgot. I have pictures. Do you want to see them?"

"Pictures?"

"Of Lodz."

"Yes I'd like to see them."

She left the room and came back with a stack of digital photos.

"They can do these in 3D now but it's not the same. I had them reproduced just like they were in the old days. I got them from my *Zayda*. They were his. They were black-and-white photographs from way back but we had them digitized and now they're good quality but they're still black and white."

Emily handed them to Jack one by one.

"I recognize that," he said. "That's *Hamburgerstrasse*. That was the headquarters of the Jewish police and oh my God that's *Bazarplatz* or Bazarowy Square. They used to do executions there. We didn't live far from there. And that bridge. I remember that bridge!"

Then she showed him another picture. He stopped and squinted, closed his eyes, rubbed them. He looked at it again. It was a picture of a three-storey building. He sat up and his face went pale.

"Are you all right?" Emily said.

Jack didn't say anything, but his mouth was wide open.

"Are you all right? Can I get you something?"

"It's true what they say," Jack said and it was only a whisper.

"What's true, Jacob? What's true?"

"What they told me ... about the brain ... how it can suppress memory."

"What are you talking about?"

He looked at the picture again. "Oh my God," he said.

"What is it?"

"Let me see that." He took the photo in his hands. "That's the hospital in *Lodz*."

"That's right. That's what it says on the back. You remember it?"

"Oh my God. Oh my dear God."

Forty-Six

The Lodz Ghetto, September 1, 1942

Jacob's parents knew another *Kinderaktion* could happen at any time. It had been two years since the last one. Jewish children were still allowed to live in the ghetto with their family, and while it wasn't a good life at least they were together. But they knew it wouldn't last. Today, however, Jacob's mother Bela was really excited. Her sister-in-law Miriam, Samuel's youngest sister, had just given birth to her first child.

"Jacob, we're going to the hospital to see the baby," she told him. "You, me and your father. Get your good shoes."

In three months Jacob would be three years old and he was looking forward to it. He knew his birthday was on December 1st and his father kept telling him how far away that was. He remembered him saying it was six months away, then five months, then four and now it was only three. Every day it got a little closer. But today they were going out, which was always an event, and it was even more than that because they were going to see a baby.

Jacob's new cousin. A little girl. She was only a few days old.

"Her name is Esther and she's very tiny," Jacob's mother said. "Like a doll."

Jacob had never seen a newborn baby before.

The three of them put on their best clothes and marched out the door of their building at *Basargasse 24*. It used to be called Bazarowa Street, but now it was *Basargasse*. Jacob didn't know why the name changed, and when he asked his father Samuel just shrugged and told him to learn the new one. The hospital was a few blocks away and they had to walk, but it was a long way for Jacob. He fussed and fidgeted and kept saying it was too far and they should turn around and go home.

"We're going to see a baby," his mother insisted. "Your new cousin Esther. Don't you want to meet her?"

Once they began walking Jacob didn't care if he met her or not, and after two blocks he started complaining. He was too tired and couldn't go on, so his father picked him up. Jacob wrapped his arms around his father's neck, and he liked that. It felt safe. His father carried him the rest of the way and Jacob hoped that after they saw the baby and left the hospital he would carry him home, too.

When they got to the hospital, they found it cordoned off and there was a big commotion out in front. A lot of people were standing on the street behind a line of ropes, wanting to go inside, but no one was allowed. German soldiers and SS were shouting commands and screaming at everyone. They looked angry.

Trucks pulled up to the entrance and stopped. People were coming out of the hospital and the soldiers were pushing them into the back of the trucks. Some of the people they were pushing were old – old men and women – and they all looked sick. One old man could barely walk, another had his arm in a sling, and a woman with frizzy white hair was hunched over, her hand on her back.

Someone said they were emptying the hospital of all the patients and that the people were going to Chelmno. There was crying and moaning, and Jacob was scared. Then shots were fired and with each one he cringed. He was standing on the street outside the hospital with his parents, tugging on his mother's leg. Then he saw doctors and nurses being herded out the front door and loaded onto one of the waiting trucks.

"There is my sister!" said Jacob's father and he began calling her. "Miriam! Miriam!"

Jacob recognized his aunt who was in a pink nightgown. She heard her brother's voice and started looking for him, and Samuel was about to call her again when one of the soldiers told him to shut up. The soldier nudged him in the side with his rifle. At the tip was a bayonet.

"She just had a baby," Samuel told him. "Why are they making her leave the hospital?"

The soldier nudged him again and told him to shut up. He pointed the bayonet at him. He said if he didn't shut up he would shoot him.

Jacob watched as his aunt, still frantically looking for the familiar voice of her brother, was loaded onto a truck. She was with other young women and one of them was crying for her baby. She wanted her baby. A soldier told her to shut up.

Soon only one truck remained. It stood but a few feet from the hospital building. There were lots of young soldiers in uniform standing around. Then all the people who were bunched up beyond the rope looked up. Someone pointed and yelled.

"What are they doing?"

Two soldiers were on the third floor by an open window. A second later and something fell out the window and dropped into the truck below. It was a baby. The soldiers had pushed it out the window. Its tiny, naked body crashed into the metal frame of the back of the truck with a thud. Women standing behind the ropes started screaming, and Jacob never heard screams like that before. Never. He squeezed his mother's leg.

Then another baby came down and this one was wailing

as it fell. When it hit the truck it stopped wailing. Then there was another one and another one after that. More women were screaming now and the screams were even worse than before.

"Murderers!" someone cried.

A few SS were with the soldiers and the SS were young. Just boys. One of them said something to a soldier, who nodded his head up and down. Then the SS planted his feet on the sidewalk and stuck out the bayonet of his rifle. He looked up to the open window.

A baby came down and it was wailing louder than the others. The SS pointed his rifle in the air and caught the baby right on the tip of his bayonet. Blood poured all over his bayonet, down the barrel of his gun, and onto his sleeve before dripping onto the sidewalk. He cursed, gave his bayonet a jerk, and tossed the bleeding baby – what was left of it – into the back of the truck. There was a signal from the window, the SS said to go ahead and another baby came down. It, too, was wailing. Again he pointed his rifle in the air and caught the baby on the tip. The blood streamed out and just like before he deposited what remained of the baby into the back of the truck. They dropped yet another baby, but this time the SS missed and the baby landed on the pavement with a dull thud. Jacob shook when he heard the sound. The baby didn't move. It stopped crying. One of the soldiers picked it up by a leg and threw it into the back of the truck as if it were a chicken.

"Where is Esther? Where is Esther?" screamed Jacob's father. "My sister's baby!" He was getting hysterical and Jacob never saw his father like that before. His mother yes, but not his father. Jacob was shivering with fear and he couldn't stop it.

The same soldier who spoke to his father earlier glared at the Jew who was standing on the sidewalk with his wife and son. He marched up to him and told him to shut up. He said this was the last time he would tell him. Then he pointed his rifle at Jacob and cocked the trigger. The soldier said if he didn't shut up, he was going to shoot his little boy in the head.

Forty-Seven

Jack heard some racket from the hall. He opened his door, and saw a group of doctors and nurses a few doors down. A woman was crying and two of the nurses were consoling her. Jack had never seen the woman before. He went down the hall and no one paid him any attention, but Trudy's door was half-open, so he looked in. Trudy was on her bed with a sheet over her, the tips of her toes sticking out the end.

Jack walked into the room. On the wall over a dresser were family photographs, and there was one of a young Trudy – Jack recognized her right away – and her husband. The date across the bottom said July 18, 1972. There was a cross on the wall with a picture of the Virgin Mary, the baby Jesus on her lap. The dresser was full of pages scattered about with scribbling all over them. Every page had a saying.

Never take life seriously. Nobody gets out alive anyway.

We don't stop playing because we are old. We grow old because we stop playing.

If you are 19 and lie in bed for a year and don't do anything, you'll turn 20. If you are 87 and stay in bed for a year and don't do anything, you'll turn 88.

These were the sayings Trudy put on her door every day, and along with them were the sources where she got them from. In the middle of the dresser was a page with today's date and saying.

The elderly don't have regrets for what they did but for what they didn't do.

"Excuse me," said a doctor.

Jack didn't know him.

"Are you a friend of Trudy's?"

"I'm just down the hall," said Jack. "What happened?"

"Massive heart attack. It was very sudden."

"When?"

"About an hour ago. Maybe less. Her daughter found her in the bed. It looks like she died in her sleep." The doctor put his hand on Jack's shoulder. "She was a friend of yours?"

"I knew her."

"I'm sorry."

Jack headed for the door and a moment later they were wheeling Trudy out on a stretcher. The woman, Trudy's daughter, was still crying. Jack stood in the middle of the hallway feeling numb, but this kind of thing happened all the time. Old people lived here. Trudy's door was still half open. He looked at today's message again.

The elderly don't have regrets for what they did but for what they didn't do.

Jack stood there thinking about it. He stood there a long time. Trudy was right.

"Thank you Trudy," he said.

Forty-Eight

"Lieutenant?"

It was Kathy.

"What is it?" said Hodgson. He was in his office, his face buried in paperwork. All this technology and still they could never get rid of paper. It had been going on for years. Decades even. As long as he'd been on the force.

"I have more on our friend Jon Creeley."

Hodgson motioned for her to come in and said to shut the door. She remained on her feet.

"Well," said Hodgson. "What've you got?"

All she did was smile.

"Is it something funny?" he said.

The smile disappeared.

"No Lieutenant. It's not funny. In fact it's pretty scary. But here it is."

She handed him a file. More paper. He sighed.

"Can't you just tell me what it says?"

"Sure," she said.

Kathy picked up the file and opened it.

"The other day I told you about Albert Freedman. The old man? Ninety-five? The holocaust survivor?"

"Yes. I've been thinking about him ever since."

"Well there was another case, Lieutenant. More recent. Two years ago an old woman drowned in the Hudson River. They called it suicide. They said she jumped from the George Washington Bridge. Jon Creeley was questioned for that too. Same guy. He was driving a cab and gave the woman a lift the night she died. According to the statement he gave to police she told him to stop halfway across the bridge so she could get out and look at the lights from Manhattan and then she told him to leave so he did. That's what he said. Later that night they found her body in the river."

Kathy put the report down.

"Lieutenant, there were stories about it with the woman's name and age. She was ninety-seven. Her name was Miriam Abraham."

"Hold on, Kathy," said Hodgson. "The GW Bridge? There are railings on that thing five feet high. How does a ninety-seven-year-old woman climb up on a railing and jump off?"

"I have no idea."

"And you're saying Creeley was questioned in this case *and* the other one?"

She nodded.

"So how come no one picked up on it?"

"Two police forces. Here and Jersey. But here's the thing, Lieutenant. *The Jewish Post* did a piece on her too. This woman ... Miriam Abraham ... was also a holocaust survivor."

"What!"

"She was a holocaust survivor too. Ninety-seven years old. Then there was Shirley Rosen."

"Who's that?"

"Another woman. A hundred and one years old. She lived at the Jewish Home for the Aged not far from here and was murdered last year. By another resident. Some guy with dementia named Eustace Smith. He put a pillow over her head and suffocated her in her own bed."

"I remember that one."

"Yes."

"So what's that got to do with ..."

"Their 3D surveillance caught the image of a man who came to visit her the night she died. I think it's Jon Creeley."

"What do you mean you think?"

"There was no police report or record of him or anything like that but after the first two I looked into ... Albert Freedman and Miriam Abraham ... I found some digital images of him so I started looking for anything I could find about holocaust survivors ... *Jewish holocaust survivors* ... who were either murdered or died under unusual circumstances and Shirley Rosen's name came up. I read about what happened to her and called the Jewish Home for the Aged. I told their security people about our investigation and they let me look at their surveillance video from the night she died."

"And?"

"Lieutenant, all I have to go on is the image but I'm pretty sure the man who came to see her that night was Jon Creeley."

"It was?"

"Yes. And another thing. Shirley Rosen was a holocaust survivor too."

Forty-Nine

Hodgson didn't want Jack going anywhere alone. A man his age shouldn't go anywhere alone at the best of times. But certainly not now. Hodgson knew about the incident in the basement and how Jack got disoriented. It happened at night, a few hours after he had told him about Christine. Jack was on frail ground, and always at the back of Hodgson's mind was the fact that he was a hundred years old.

"You got that hate letter and then you find a swastika on your door," Hodgson said. "That's two things that have happened to you. And then there's Christine. Have you considered the possibility that all these things might be connected somehow?"

"What are you talking about?" said Jack.

"This Brett Krust ... who pushed Christine into the gorge ..."

"They caught him, didn't they?"

"Yes. He's in custody now."

"So what's the problem?"

"It's just that ..."

"What?"

"Hell Jack! I don't want you to get yourself killed!"

It was the first time Hodgson had ever raised his voice with him, but Jack was a stubborn old coot. And now he wanted to take the ferry to Liberty Island. He said there was a news report about the planned rally at the base of the statue, he was mentioned, and now someone wanted to interview him down there. Jack had arranged to meet the person that afternoon.

He was planning to go by himself.

"This rally will be the first time I ever speak in public about what happened to me when I was a boy," Jack said.

"You were on that show Talk Back."

"This is different. The Mayor is going to be there. There's going to be all kinds of people. I have to do this."

"But why the interview today?"

"They want to talk to me about the rally. Everyone will see it."

That is exactly what worried Hodgson, so he decided to tell Jack a little more about Brett Krust and the group he belonged to. The United Front.

"They're wackos and they have chapters all over the world and one right here in New York. These people talk to each other all the time. Do you understand what I'm saying?"

"No."

"Do I have to spell it out for you?"

But Hodgson didn't want to tell Jack everything he knew. He didn't want to upset him any more than he already was. Hodgson didn't want to tell him what Kathy Sottario had learned, that Krust had been in touch with The Cobra. He first contacted the editor of the ezine Voices of Dissidence in Atlanta, and working through that person then got hold of Jon Creeley. Kathy tried and failed to break into their exchanges, but she did know there was direct contact between the two and that was enough for Hodgson. Hodgson also didn't want to tell Jack what they now knew about Creeley. That he was a man who had been questioned about the murder of a holocaust survivor in 2035. And again two years later when another survivor had apparently drowned in the

Hudson River. Then there was the woman in the Jewish Home for the Aged. She had a visitor who looked like Jon Creeley on the night she was murdered. According to Kathy, it was him. All three of these people were holocaust survivors, and it made Hodgson wonder how many survivors were left.

He could think of only one.

"Jack, I want to put an officer on you. For precaution."

Jack said it wasn't necessary. But Hodgson knew the chances of sticking a cop on Jack were slim. With budget cuts and manpower stretched to the limit, an old man in a seniors' home wasn't going to merit the resources of a police officer around the clock. And why? Because some crazy police lieutenant figured people were going around murdering holocaust survivors?

Not likely.

"Lieutenant Hodgson, can I be straight with you?" Jack said.

"Sure."

"What else can the world do to me? I'm just an old man. But now I have a chance to do something and tell people. I promised Emily Silver I would speak at her rally and I'm going to and if I don't do this interview today I might as well not go to the rally either. But it's important. So this afternoon I'm taking the ferry to Liberty Island to do that interview."

Jack looked at Hodgson. Straight in the eye.

"And I'm going there whether you like it or not."

Fifty

The last ferry from Battery Park to Liberty Island ran at 4:30 every afternoon and left the island at 6:00 sharp when everything closed down for the night. The reporter had arranged to meet Jack at 5:00 outside the entrance to the monument. They would do the interview, leaving ample time to make that last ferry back to the mainland. There was no way Hodgson would let Jack go alone, so he came along and would have liked to bring some backup. But there was no backup. It was just the two of them.

This was Hodgson's first time on water since his knee replacement and it didn't take long to see that anything other than stable ground wasn't good for the new joint. The knee, his right, didn't feel solid like the left one.

It was the last ferry of the day, and it being the middle of December, the crowds were sparse, which was good because fewer people were on board. On the other hand, it wasn't good because there was more space with everything out in the open. On the ferry to the island Hodgson kept looking around. Checking.

"There's a big guy at the back," he told Jack. "A real muscular fellow."

"I saw him," said Jack. "He's big but not as big as you, Lieutenant. I bet you have a hundred pounds on him."

Jack had a cane with him, 'society's cane' he called it, but lately it had become less of that and more of his. With two falls at the Greenwich Village Seniors Center, he was now on a watch list, and those who deal with such things every day know that the third fall is always the worst. After getting off the ferry, it was a good walk to Liberty's entrance. The pair of them stood out – Hodgson for his gargantuan size and Jack because of the stark contrast in a slight old man standing next to such a behemoth.

"You must be Mr. Fisher."

The reporter, a young woman with a small 3D camera perched on her shoulder, said they would do the interview by the entrance so she could get shots of the statue in the background. She didn't pay any attention to Hodgson, which was fine with him, but Jack was a man who valued introductions.

"This is Lieutenant ..."

Hodgson stuck out his hand. "Jack Hodgson," he said.

"Lieutenant?" said the reporter.

"I'm a good friend of Jack's and sort of looking out for him."

Hodgson had done scores of media interviews, homicides mostly, and these things became awfully mundane over the years. Do you have any suspects? We're following up on every lead and if we find anything of interest to the public we'll let you know. Was there anything about how the body was found that can tell you why this crime may have been committed? As I said we're following up on every lead but that's all I can say right now. It was like a scripted scene from a 3D drama, each side saying their lines by rote, but they both had jobs to do. Hodgson knew the reporter didn't want him interfering with the story, and would rather he wasn't around at all.

"I'll just stand back here," Hodgson said. "I won't be in your way." He retreated to the edge of the walkway running around the octagonal base supporting Lady Liberty.

The wide neck and broad shoulders of the strapping Adonis who was at the back of the ferry were bursting through the leather jacket. He was ripped. All muscle. On the trip to the island he and the nondescript character beside him had spotted the old man with the cane and the bulky colossus by his side. Colton Brock had been in enough bars and brawls to recognize bouncers and bodyguards, and could tell Hodgson was neither. But he didn't know he was a cop. When all the passengers disembarked from the ferry, he and Jon Creeley made sure to keep their distance from the pair, and by the time they hit the walkway on the island they had split up.

The interview didn't begin until camera angles were studied and meter readings taken, and then the reporter and Jack went over the questions to be asked. So it was 5:15 before things got under way. It took only ten minutes and if Jack was lucky one minute would make air time and two might go cyber. The interview done, there was barely a half hour before the last ferry would leave the island. Not much time to make the long walk back for a one-hundred-year-old man with a cane.

Hodgson was standing off the edge of the walkway near the water, a good distance from where Jack and the reporter just finished the interview, and didn't notice someone creeping behind him. Before he knew it, an arm with the weight of a tree trunk wrapped itself around his chest and came up under his left elbow, pushing it up and over his shoulder. The first thing that occurred to Hodgson was to get his own arm down and fast. For a man six-five and over three hundred and twenty pounds, it shouldn't have been a problem. But not this time. Hodgson couldn't move his arm. Whoever was standing behind him was just too damn strong.

Hodgson's shoulder hurt, and if his arm went up any more his shoulder would pop and he would be toast. Up ahead he could see the reporter parting ways with Jack and then Jack all by himself at the entrance to the monument when a stranger approached him. Hodgson recognized the man immediately. It was Jon Creeley. He had seen Kathy's images of him – in 2D and 3D – and there was no mistake. It was him.

"What do you want?" Hodgson said to whoever was behind him.

Nothing.

"Do you realize you're assaulting a ..."

Two fingers dug deep into his armpit and Hodgson started going numb. Whoever was behind him knew the body's pressure points, but Hodgson couldn't pass out. Not now. Jack was standing there with Jon Creeley.

"What do you want?" Hodgson said again.

Nothing.

The next thing the dazed Hodgson knew, he was being led away with that muscular arm encircling his chest. He still couldn't see who it was. The man, his equal in height, marched him over to a bench and sat him down. Then he took the spot beside him and draped his tree-trunk arm over his shoulders as if the two were good friends. Hodgson was about to get a look at him when those big fingers dug into his armpit again, and he blacked out. The last thing he saw was Jack and Creeley walking through the entrance into the base of Lady Liberty.

Fifty-One

The man had come out of nowhere and started talking with Jack. He said he was going to take him up the Statue of Liberty. He said there wasn't much time because it would close soon. He had two tickets that would allow them to go to the observation deck and then on to the crown at the very top.

"Why do I want to go up there?" Jack said.

"It's a free ticket."

Jack wondered where Hodgson was, but Creeley told him not to worry. He said he spoke to his friend and that his friend would wait for them.

"You spoke to him?"

"Yes I did."

"He knows we're going up there?"

"Yes. Of course."

"But why do I get a free ticket?"

"We know who you are and about the rally. We thought the least we could do was give you a ride up Lady Liberty. It's all about freedom, right?"

Then they were at the turnstiles. Creeley stopped to have a

word with the attendant, who looked Jack's way and gave him a friendly wave. Jack thought nothing of it and waved back. Creeley handed over the tickets and the two of them went into the elevator. No one was with them. The place was closing soon.

"Do you work here?" Jack asked Creeley, as the elevator doors shut.

"Yes."

"But you're not wearing a uniform."

"For security we don't wear uniforms anymore."

"But the person who took our tickets had one."

"He works inside. I work outside. On the grounds."

The cramped elevator made Jack uneasy. He was never comfortable in close quarters.

"How long does it take to get up there?" he asked.

"Not long," said Creeley. "People take the stairs but there's too many stairs for a man your age. I figured we would take the elevator. But when you're inside the crown I'm afraid you have to climb some stairs. It's the only way to get to the top."

"Are there a lot of them?"

"You mean stairs?"

"Yes."

"Don't worry. I'll be with you."

When the elevator stopped at the observation deck, Creeley led Jack by the arm. Another attendant had the two of them scanned, and then he checked their tickets and reminded them about the closing time.

"Thank you," said Creeley.

Jack looked up at the winding, spiral staircase in front of him. "I can't go up there," he said.

"Sure you can," said Creeley and he gave him a little nudge.

Jack took the first step and then the second and the third, and with each one there was a sharp *clunk* from his cane. After a dozen steps, he had to stop to catch his breath. This wasn't going to be easy.

"Are you sure this is the only way up?" Jack asked Creeley.

"Yes," Creeley said with a nod. He gave Jack a moment to rest before nudging him in the side again. "Keep going," he said.

Jack went up another twenty steps and another twenty after that. The winding staircase was steep, always turning to the inside, and going around and around like that made him dizzy. Jack would grip the handrail and step up, first one foot then the other, and follow with his cane. *Clunk. Clunk. Clunk.* After a few more minutes and another two stops on the way, he was dead tired. He started to sweat and was worried about his blood pressure getting the better of him.

"I can't do this," he said.

"Keep going old man."

Creeley was two steps below him. By this time his jacket was off and he had it draped across his shoulder. One of his arms was on the railing. That was when Jack saw the tattoo of the snake. Something wasn't right.

"Who are you?" said Jack.

"A friend."

"I don't know you."

"But I know you."

"What are you talking about?"

"Keep going."

Higher and higher they went and the steps kept coming at them. This spiral staircase was turning into a marathon. Jack's breathing was getting shorter and shorter, and if not for the cane he wouldn't have made it this far. He had to stop again.

"I can't do any more," he said.

"Yes you can. You're a determined old man. You can do anything you want." Creeley nudged him in the side. "Keep going."

Jack took another step. *Clunk.* And another. *Clunk.* A few minutes more and he felt his legs were ready to give. Then there was a noise. Someone was bounding up the stairs from below. Far below. The sound of feet clomping and clanging on the metal steps reverberated up the staircase.

"Coal is that you?" Creeley called out.

It was almost an echo.

"Yes," came the distant reply.

"Did you take care of him?"

"He's not goin' anywhere."

"What are you talking about?" said Jack.

Creeley was one step below him now. He looked up at Jack. "Your friend. He's not going anywhere."

The sound of someone coming up the stairs kept getting louder and louder, and Jack thought just then about hollering for help. But he didn't have the energy. He was breathing too hard. Besides, no one else was there anyway.

"Look. I can't do this anymore," he said through his teeth, but Creeley nudged him yet again. He wouldn't let him stop.

Clunk. Clunk. Clunk.

"Go on. We'll be there soon," Creeley said.

This is insane, Jack thought. Why was he doing this? It was only the two of them, but someone was coming up the stairs and it was someone this man knew. Jack kept doing Creeley's bidding, going up those stairs one by one. Each step taking a little longer than the last.

Clunk. Clunk. Clunk.

Jack didn't know how many steps he had climbed, but there must have been one for every year of his life – even more than that – and the relentless sound of feet bounding up the stairs was getting louder and louder by the second. Jack stopped again.

"Look," he said, "I don't know who you are or what you want but I can't do this anymore. This is way too hard for me. Thank you for the free ticket but I'll have to come back another time."

He turned around only to find a hand planted on his shoulder.

"You're not going anywhere old man," said Creeley. He pointed up the staircase and then he placed both his hands on Jack's shoulders. "Keep going."

Jack bit his lip. "It's going to take me a long time to go up there," he said. "I don't want to slow you down."

"That's all right. We have all the time in the world you and me."

Back they went trudging up the staircase. One step at a time. Jack constantly clunking with his cane, Creeley edging him on.

Finally, mercifully, after what seemed an eternity, they were at the top. Inside the crown of Lady Liberty's head. There was a small, circular platform with room for maybe ten people at most, a handrail around the edge, and narrow openings to look through. There was nothing in them but air. Each opening was big enough for a person to pass through. A small person. Like Jack.

"What do you want?" said an exhausted Jack. "Are you going to throw me out? Is that it?"

Creeley just smiled.

"Now why would I do that? That wouldn't be very smart. No. You see I brought you here because you always wanted to go up the Statue of Liberty. It makes you feel like an American and you are an American, aren't you? Of course you are. But that was a long climb and you're an old man. You shouldn't have done it but you're stubborn. It was too much for you. You collapsed. I called for help. When they arrived it was too late."

Creeley shrugged.

"You're the one who sent me that letter," Jack said. "It was signed with a snake. Like the snake on your arm."

Creeley nodded.

"And you painted that swastika on my door. Didn't you?"

Creeley said yes. He said how easy it was to get into the building. He laughed. Then he stopped laughing.

"I know about the girl," he said. "The teacher. She got what she deserved."

If his heart was telling him what to do, Jack would have stuck that cane of his right down this character's throat or hit him with it as hard as he could. But Jack was old and he knew he was old. He looked Creeley in the eye.

"What is it old man?" Creeley said.

"I haven't come this far only to die at the hands of someone as insignificant as you," Jack said.

Creeley was not a complicated man. He knew when people were in trouble they got desperate. It was always like that. When Coal fought in the ring, his opponents got into trouble and became desperate and desperate people make mistakes. That makes them weak and vulnerable. When the old man Albert Freedman had his apartment invaded he got desperate and wanted to fight and when Creeley's henchman had the old woman Miriam Abraham perched on the railing of the GW Bridge she got desperate, too. She struggled and kicked. But Jack didn't look like that.

He didn't look desperate at all.

"Jack! Jack!"

It was Hodgson. There was a hurried exchange of voices from below. Two, maybe three of them. It was hard to tell.

When Hodgson came to, he had found himself on the bench with his left wrist handcuffed to the railing under the seat, his body twisted awkwardly. He had been tied to the railing with his own cuffs. Embarrassing. Using his free hand, he went through his pockets and found everything there – his wallet, his badge, his gun. Nothing was missing. Then he bent down low to check his watch – a quarter to six – and remembered that the last thing he saw was Creeley leading Jack into the base of the monument. That was enough to get his adrenaline going. He swung his body around and inserted a finger from his free hand under his watch. Then he pressed a button to activate his emergency police line.

"Lieutenant Jack Hodgson. NYPD. Detective Bureau."

He told them what happened and gave his coordinates. The Port Authority Police were going to send a boat over right away and it couldn't come soon enough. Jack was alone in there with Creeley.

And so, the third voice from down the staircase was that of a Port Authority officer who had freed Hodgson from the bench and was now coming up the stairs with him. But he was a younger man and much faster than Hodgson. Coal heard them. He stopped and turned back to head down the staircase. One glimpse of the imposing Coal and the Port Authority cop reached for his gun, but Coal was too fast. With a lightning move he kicked the gun away, and a second later his black, leather jackboot was in the man's face. There was a crunch and a gasp, and the young cop fell back head first over the spiral staircase, crashing to the metal steps below.

Hodgson was trudging up the stairs behind him and figured something bad just happened. Then, the moment he laid his eyes on Coal, he knew this was the person who had handcuffed him to the bench. So now it was one big man against another, but there the similarity ended. Hodgson was slow and fat, while Coal was a machine of muscle and split-second reflexes.

It wasn't a good place for a gun, not a spiral staircase with twisting metal and the chance of a ricochet, so Hodgson reached for his pepper spray. He would spray Coal in the face, but again Coal was too quick. His arm came out of nowhere and knocked the little canister away, and with his other hand he plastered Hodgson right in the ribs. If they had been on level ground and not a spiral staircase, Coal would have solid footing and would follow with a kick to the head. That would have finished Hodgson for good. But the shot to the ribs was enough. The wind knocked out of him, Hodgson went down in a heap.

Coal turned around and started springing back up the staircase. A few seconds later he was at the top with Creeley and Jack. The three of them.

Jack was on his own.

Creeley wasn't much to look at. He was even shorter than Jack and just as lean. No wonder no one had noticed him on the ferry. Standing next to the imposing Coal, he had looked smaller still. But Coal? He was all muscle and thick. Like a rock. Jack caught something else about him, too. He wore a cross around his neck.

"My friend Coal used to be a Navy Seal," Creeley said. "He knows how to kill someone and make it look like natural causes."

Jack was in trouble. It wasn't the first time. Back in the ghetto when he was a little boy his life was in danger every day. He was only three, four years old then. If the Germans found him, that would have been it. But he had help. His parents. And at Auschwitz things were even worse. Any time, any hour, they could have sent him to the gas chamber. Or shot him. It could have happened the day he arrived. Or at the selection line by the railway track. Or when they made him drop his pants and the SS examined him. It could have been Mengele. He had ample opportunity to kill him whenever he wanted. No one would have known. Or cared. And who was there to help him? Jerzy? Not really. He showed him the ropes maybe. But Jack had to help himself.

"What do you want?" said Jack.

"What do I want? To get rid of people like you. You're not the first but you are the last. After you this will be all over."

"I don't know what you're talking about."

"You don't? Come on old man. We've been getting rid of people like you for years. We find them and hunt them down and make it look like an accident and most of the time it does. Albert Freedman was on my list and I took care of him. It was messy but I took care of him. Miriam Abraham was on my list too and I took care of her. She was easy and so was Shirley Rosen. I know all the names."

He took out his mini.

"And you're the last one. The last one on the list. After you there won't be any list."

He touched the little screen and Jack's name appeared. One tap and it was gone.

"What list are you talking about?" said Jack.

"The list ... with the names ... Albert Freedman ... Miriam Abraham ... Shirley Rosen ... Rachel Teischman ... Lilly Gold. They were all here in New York and Jersey but there were others.

Lots of them. Levi Braun in Montreal. Arthur Swadron in LA. Rose Weisbrod in Paris. Rachel Gertberg in Switzerland. They were all on the list and every year the list gets shorter. Now there's only one name left. Yours."

Creeley took a step forward and knocked Jack's cane out of his hand.

"You won't be needing this anymore," he said.

The cane hit the floor with a *clunk*.

Jack could figure it out. When it was over, Coal would get out of there and so would this character or maybe this little twirp would even call for help himself. He would tell them he didn't know anything about Hodgson or anything about Coal for that matter. All he would know was that he was taking Jack Fisher up Lady Liberty as a gesture of appreciation, but in his excitement the old guy expired.

He was a hundred years old.

But back at the death camp Jack was only five. How does a child of five survive when everyone and everything around him wants him dead? By using his wits. His brain. By making friends of his enemies because he had something for them. Something they wanted.

"I have a proposition for you," Jack said.

"What do you mean?" said Creeley.

Jack leaned against the handrail and lifted his right foot. He shook the heel of his shoe, swayed it this way and that, and then grabbed it with his fingers and gave it a twist. The heel slid open. "Here," he said and he took out a coin.

Creeley came in closer.

"This is a *chervonets*," said Jack. "It's from Russia and it's gold. It's worth a lot of money."

Creeley looked at Jack and back at the coin. "Gold?" he said.

"See for yourself."

Creeley took the coin from him. It was thick and heavy.

"I can get you more of these," Jack said. "I have lots of them and they're worth a lot of money."

"How much money?"

"To find that out we'd have to go to a bank ..."

"I'm not goin' to no bank."

"All right. A pawnbroker then. We can go to a pawnbroker. Or you can go by yourself. Why don't you take this one and find out what it's worth?"

"Why should I believe anything you say?"

"Why shouldn't you? Look, these coins are very rare. There's only a handful of them left."

"You're lying to me," said Creeley.

"Why would I tell you lies?"

"To save yourself."

"Think of it as a negotiation. How many of these do you want?"

"How many have you got?"

"Look. You see the date inscribed on it? You see how old it is? This coin is over a hundred years old."

Creeley checked the inscription. "It's older than you," he said. "How many have you got?"

Jack put his hand to his brow. "I keep them in a safety deposit box but I haven't been there in a long time. It's hard to remember."

Creeley was playing with the coin between his fingers. It looked real enough.

"It's from Russia," Jack said. "It was minted in the 1920s. You see the letters on it? SSSR? You see the coat of arms? That stands for the seven republics of the Soviet Union but later there were fifteen republics. That's why this one is so rare."

Creeley was studying the coin.

"A coin like this went for a hundred thousand dollars in an auction," said Jack.

It sounded like a good amount.

"And you keep it in your shoe?"

"It already saved my life once."

"How did it do that?"

"Greed is a powerful emotion."

Jack saw that Coal was staring at the coin, too.

"A hundred thousand dollars?" Coal said.

"Yes," said Jack. "And I have more of them. But if something happens to me ..."

"You keep them in the bank?"

It was Coal again.

"Yes and I'm the only one who can take them out. They won't let anyone else do it."

Jack could see what was going on with Coal now and so could Creeley.

"He's lying," Creeley said. "We'll take this one and split it. Half for me and half for you."

Jack saw his opportunity.

"Don't be a fool," he said to Coal. "You do all his dirty work and if something goes wrong do you think he'll be there for you? He risks nothing and you risk everything."

"That's how it is," said Coal and he was still staring at the coin.

"Think what you could do with a hundred thousand dollars," Jack said to him. "And that's just for this one. I have others. A lot of them. And I can get them for you. We're talking a lot of money here and you don't have to give him anything. Nothing."

"What?" said Creeley.

"He doesn't want to share anything with you. He'll just pocket the hundred thousand and you'll go to jail. What's to stop him?"

Coal looked at Jack and back at Creeley, and then he stuck out his hand. He wanted the coin, but Creeley wasn't about to give it to him. Not if it was worth a hundred thousand dollars. So Coal grabbed him. He had one hand around Creeley's wrist and the other on his elbow.

"You're breaking my arm!" Creeley cried and with all the grappling he dropped the *chervonets*. It went down the spiral staircase. Bouncing from one step to the next to the next.

Cling. Cling. Cling.

"You idiot! Now look what you did!"

Coal lost it. No one talked to him like that. No one. He made a fist – a huge fist – and hit Creeley square in the face. Creeley went down. He wasn't moving. He looked like he was dead. Then Coal turned to Jack and still there was the sound of the *chervonets* bouncing down the steps. It seemed to go on forever.

Cling. Cling. Cling.

Now it was only Jack and Coal standing there. Just the two of them.

"I see that you are a Christian," Jack said. "You can still save yourself, you know."

Coal looked at him.

"Tell me," said Jack and he was staring at the cross around his neck. "How do you reconcile what you do with being a Christian? You're Catholic, aren't you?"

Coal nodded.

"You wear a crucifix to identify yourself as a Catholic but do you even know what it means?"

Jack switched to Latin.

"Ave Maria, gratia plena, Dominus tecum. Benedicta tu in mulieribus, et benedictus fructus ventris tui, Iesus. Sancta Maria, Mater Dei, ora pro nobis peccatoribus, nunc ete in hora mortis nostrae. Amen."

Coal wasn't moving a muscle. He was as still as the rock he was carved from.

"I'll tell you what it means," Jack said. "You praise Mary and God and Jesus and then you ask Mary to pray for you. As a sinner. You have sinned but you can still save yourself."

Coal looked confused.

"Let me help you," Jack said. "I can help you. But only if you let me. You have to let me."

He extended his hand and thought Coal was about to take it. But Jack would never know with the rustle from the stairs and the sudden sound of stomping feet.

"*Uhhh!*"

The pocket taser was a powerful weapon. It zapped Coal in the middle of his chest. Hodgson had aimed from three steps down and his aim rang true, but then the target was a big one. Still, Coal somehow stayed on his feet.

Hodgson got up on the platform and was going to taser him again, this time from up close, but Coal was a man who always did the unexpected. Anyone else would have stepped back to avoid absorbing more voltage. But not him. His arms in front, he dove straight for Hodgson. Right through the air. He was a big man who could cover a lot of space quickly. He would take Hodgson's legs out from under him and even with this he used the element of surprise. He wouldn't strike with his stronger hand. His right. No. Coal would lead with his left.

With his body in full flight, Coal's left hand clipped Hodgson's knee with just enough force to topple him. But it was Hodgson's right knee. His titanium knee.

Coal's hand was broken.

There were bodies all over the floor. Creeley was still down and not moving a muscle. Hodgson's right leg had crumpled and he was on his side. Coal was flat on his chest, gripping his left hand, the fingers hanging like putty.

The only one standing was Jack.

Coal tried to get up, but his hand wouldn't support him. Hodgson, on his feet now, pointed his taser at Coal yet again. Then he thought better of it, took out his gun and cocked the trigger.

"That guy is a monster," Hodgson said.

"You know, you didn't have to do that," Jack said to him as he looked down at Coal. "I had him. I had him."

Hodgson shook his head from side to side. There was a trace of a chuckle.

"Are you all right?" he said.

"I'm a little tired. Can you help me find my coin?"

Fifty-Two

The doctor pushed the bigger weight, the three-hundred-pound marker, to the far end of the old balance scale. Then he gave the smaller weight a little poke with his finger.

"Congratulations Lieutenant. Three hundred and eighteen pounds. That means you lost nine pounds since your last visit. Another forty-three pounds and we'll be at our goal of two-seventy-five."

"Why is it always we?" said Hodgson.

"We learn that in medical school. First thing they teach you is identify with the patient. So how did you lose those nine pounds? Are you following the chart?"

"You mean fruit and vegetables? Easy on the red meat?"

"What about exercise?"

"I've been doing a lot of stairs."

The doctor told Hodgson to get off the scale. He asked if he's been to the gym. Hodgson said no.

"Doc, you ever been to the top of the Statue of Liberty?" Hodgson said.

"As far as the elevator takes you."

"That's not what I mean. To get to the top you have to climb a hundred and eighty-six steps and it's a winding staircase. I ran it."

"You ran it? What was it? A police fundraiser?"

"If it was my fundraising days are over."

"Well Lieutenant, whatever it was I suggest you do it another five times."

"I beg your pardon?"

"Five more times will get you down to our goal. As far as your knee is concerned it's just fine but you pulled something. A ligament. Try to stay off it as much as you can. When it heals I suggest you hit those stairs again."

Hodgson sat down and slipped on his size fifteen shoes. He had a cane beside him, the same one he used after the knee replacement.

"Doc, believe me when I tell you this but I'm never going up those stairs again as long as I live."

Armed with the good news about losing some weight, Hodgson left the doctor's office and went outside the building where a police car was waiting for him. Kathy Sottario was behind the wheel.

"We have to hurry, Lieutenant," she said. "The Port Authority is expecting us with their boat in twenty minutes. Shall I?"

"Go ahead."

She turned on the siren and they sped down to the docks.

Jack was already on the ferry with Emily Silver at his side. It was the day of the big rally and he was the man of the hour. When they first boarded the ferry, she had introduced him to all the members of her group. One woman whose grandparents died in the gas chambers at Auschwitz wanted to touch him and even kiss him. And she did. She said she could feel the presence of her grandparents in Jack. Jack didn't know what to say. Everyone kept peppering him with questions. They wanted to know what it was like in the ghetto and the camp.

"It's funny how people are interested all of a sudden," Jack said.

"You're the last survivor," said a woman who wasn't even part of Emily's group. She was just a person on the ferry. But she saw Jack on television.

"Until a few weeks ago no one seemed to care," said Jack.

The woman asked him what he thought about the government of Poland wanting to close Auschwitz and what he thought of the anti-Jewish incidents fomenting in that country.

"What are you going to talk about at the rally today, Mr. Fisher?"

Emily stepped between the woman and Jack. "Please," she said and took him by the arm.

Flying overhead was a helicopter carrying the Mayor of New York City. He would be speaking at the rally. There was a rumor going around about Jack receiving the key to the city, but Jack didn't know anything about that. Besides, he wasn't even thinking about the rally. He was thinking about Christine.

The ferry pulled in to Liberty Island. Emily took it upon herself to be Jack's escort and today he needed one. She had all her papers with her, including the speech they had prepared for him. One of her group had met with him at the Greenwich Village Seniors Center to get the necessary background. The speech was written, Jack approved it and it was even printed in big type, so he could read it at the rally. Tables were set up with refreshments at the east side of the monument, and over a hundred chairs were arranged with a special section reserved for dignitaries and media. There was a lot of media. Emily also brought some bottled water, so Jack's mouth wouldn't get dry.

They had thought of everything.

Jack was introduced to the Mayor, who shook his hand, and the two of them posed for pictures. Then everyone sat down and the Mayor marched up the steps to the podium. He got behind the lectern they had set up. There was polite applause and he started to speak.

He talked about Ellis Island and the millions of people who

began a new life in America at this very spot. He said many of them were Jews. He said the lucky ones were those who arrived before the Second World War in the last century to set down roots. He spoke of their contributions to American society and rattled off prominent names from science, medicine, the arts, business, even politics. Then he spoke of the horrors of Nazi Germany and the great crime committed against the Jews of Europe.

"Today one hundred years after the beginning of the Second World War we are honored to have with us a man who is also a hundred years old."

There was light applause, which began with Emily's group, and then it spread through the crowd. The Mayor smiled and with a nod acknowledged Jack, who was sitting next to Emily on the podium. Jack was uncomfortable in the spotlight, but he had something to tell these people. Something important. The Mayor continued.

"Jack Fisher whose real name is Jacob Klukowsky was born on December 1, 1939 in the Polish city of Lodz. Earlier this month he turned one hundred and I want to take this opportunity to wish him a belated happy one hundredth birthday."

Another nod to Jack and more applause.

"Two months before Jack was born Nazi Germany marched into Poland, beginning the war. As a little boy Jack lived in the Jewish Ghetto in that city. All Jewish citizens of Lodz were confined to a special area and deprived of the basic necessities of life. Many of them were notable people from the community. But now their businesses were taken from them. Their valuables were taken from them. Their very life and freedom was taken from them. This is what happened to Jews all over Europe. Jack spent the first years of his life living as a hidden child in the ghetto because if he was found he would have been taken from his family and they never would have seen him again. But they couldn't hide forever and soon he and his family along with many other

Jewish families were sent to Auschwitz, the biggest death camp the Nazis established. It was a place where countless numbers of people ... numbers we can't even imagine ... were sent to their death. Such camps were set up all over Europe in the countries that Nazi Germany invaded. At the time the United States was not yet in the war but after Pearl Harbor we did enter that war and we entered it for good reason. To fend off the evils of Nazism and Fascism. We sacrificed many young American lives in that conflict so we may live with the freedoms we enjoy today."

The Mayor introduced the president of Emily's organization, who said a few words before introducing Emily. She talked about all the camps shutting down, first the museums and then the sites themselves, and how most of them have since been razed by bulldozers and in her words "removed from the face of the earth forever." The only one that still remained, she said, was Auschwitz and now it, too, was in danger of being torn down. She told Jack to come forward.

Jack stood up. He had his cane. He was wearing his best shirt, the French cotton one with the long, button-down sleeves and the gray lines running up and down. He hadn't worn it since his birthday. He also had a jacket. It was a special day.

"Ladies and gentlemen, this man beside me was a friend of my grandfather in the Jewish Ghetto of Lodz," Emily said. "My grandfather was also a survivor of the Holocaust. He died in 2017 and I miss him terribly. He often spoke to me about this brave little boy Jacob and I must tell you right now I can feel the presence of my grandfather as I stand next to this man. Please welcome Mr. Jacob Klukowsky."

There was a spattering of applause and then all was quiet.

The microphone was inches from Jack's mouth at exactly the right height for him. The speech they wrote with the big type was laid out across the lectern. Everything was just the way it was supposed to be. He looked at all the people who came. He didn't know who most of them were. He looked out to the water and the skyline of Manhattan.

"Thank you Emily," he said with an appreciative nod. "And thank you Mr. Mayor. For the past ninety-five years of my life ... ever since I was one of a handful of children who were liberated at Auschwitz in 1945 ... I have not lived as Jacob Klukowsky but as Jack Fisher. I agree with everything the Mayor and Emily said. That the camps should remain open so the world will know what horrible things really happened there. It is a crime to remove them. A terrible crime. But I'm afraid I can't read the speech they want me to read to you. You see a few days ago I had an article published."

He raised his head.

"Imagine having your first article published at the age of one hundred."

There were chuckles.

"I have this article with me now and instead of the speech I want to read it to you."

Jack pulled out a newspaper from inside his jacket. Across the top of the front page were the words *The Reflector*. He opened it, adjusted his glasses, and began to read.

"My great-granddaughter Christine Fisher was born in 2014 in the town of Kitchener, Ontario in Canada. She was the second daughter of Will and Emma Fisher who are long-time residents of the community, the younger sister of Tiffany, and the proud aunt of Tiffany's little girl Rebecca."

Jack looked out at the crowd. There were so many people.

"Rebecca who is here today is my great-*great*-granddaughter."

He went back to his article.

"The Fisher family has lived in Kitchener since I arrived there in 1947 as an eight-year-old boy with no family. Christine's grandfather Bill is my son. I want to tell you about Christine. When she was a little girl she loved to read anything she could and her favorite subject was always history. That's why she became a history teacher. Christine grew up in Wellington County which is a beautiful area with a lot of history and she knew its history. She knew about the first mill that was built in the 1800s and she knew who built it and how much it cost. Even when she was a little girl she knew how to do research.

"She was fifteen when I first told her what happened to me. About being a hidden child in the Jewish Ghetto in Lodz and being sent to Auschwitz. A death camp. When you're a little child death should be something that only happens to old people but for me growing up the way I did death was a constant companion from my earliest memories. I saw more death as a four-year-old than anyone should see in their lifetime. I've never talked in public about this before because the memories were too horrible and raw and I wanted to forget them. Some things I did forget. But I was wrong not to tell Christine about this. I was raised as a Catholic and all my family in North America is Catholic. And then Christine found out I was born a Jew and that Jews were persecuted and murdered in the most horrible genocide the world has ever seen. Six million lives were lost and many of them were children. The only thing Christine knew about what happened to Jews during the Second World War was what she learned in school. Which was nothing.

"She wanted to change that and any student who was lucky enough to have her for a teacher was sure to learn their history. All of us should know history because to understand the present you have to understand the past. And we should learn about the good things as well as the bad because this is where we come from and this is how we learn from our mistakes. I am a hundred years old and one thing I know is that people who don't learn from their mistakes are destined to repeat them. It is the story and legacy of the human race.

"For those few years that Christine taught history at Williamsburg Senior Public School she was always fighting with her school board. They didn't want her to teach about the Holocaust. Some of them didn't even think the Holocaust happened. Now I'm not talking about the Great Holocaust of 2029 which was only ten years ago. More than fifty thousand people ... innocent people ... were killed in that terrible episode and the children of all those victims deserve better than to have it forgotten. They deserve better. If we don't tell people what happened then who in the year 2129 will believe it?

"They say I am the last living survivor of the Holocaust of the Jewish people from the last century. I may be and it brings me no pride. You see, the Holocaust has nothing to do with pride but everything to do with shame. I am an old man and some might even say wise. I don't know about that but I have learned a bitter lesson from my great-granddaughter and it's this. We ignore the past at our own peril."

Jack raised his head and looked over to Emily Silver and the Mayor, and then he looked out at all the faces before him. In the front row were the people from Emily's organization. The offspring of Holocaust survivors. One row back were Lieutenant Jack Hodgson and Kathy Sottario of the NYPD. Near the two of them were Mary Lou Bennett from the Greenwich Village Seniors Center, along with some of the residents – Eric, Linda, Fred, Patricia, Rachel. His dinner mates. Jack saw his son Ralph and his family, and he saw Christine's parents, her sister and her little niece.

As he took in the members of his family, he was thinking what a great victory it was to be here with all his descendants. That is exactly what it was. A victory. His eyes began to well up and for a moment he couldn't speak. But he wasn't finished.

Hodgson saw the difficulty he was in and stood up on his feet. Like Jack, he had a cane with him. He called Jack's name and said to wait. Mary Lou Bennett also got up. The two of them marched to the podium and joined Jack behind the lectern. Standing on either side of him, they each put an arm around him.

"Good afternoon everyone," said Mary Lou. "My name is Mary Lou Bennett and I'm the Director of Care at the Greenwich

Village Seniors Center where Jack lives." She turned to Jack. "I'm sorry to interrupt but we have a little surprise for you."

She pointed to the very back where a group of children were now standing.

"Jack, these are Grade 8 students and I know your great-granddaughter Christine also taught Grade 8. These students are beginning a new segment in their studies today. They are starting their history program. Their teacher thought it would be a good idea for them to have their very first class here so they could listen to you."

Jack wanted to say something, but could only mouth 'thank you' because the words wouldn't come. Hodgson gave him a hug and people started to clap. Then Hodgson spoke.

"I am Lieutenant Jack Hodgson of the NYPD. Over the past few weeks I have come to know Jack Fisher very well and I can tell you he is one of the most remarkable people I have ever met. He is a courageous man and a man of great dignity. I am honored to call him my friend. Oh I almost forgot."

With that, he stuck a hand into his pocket and pulled out a coin. The *chervonets*.

"I believe this belongs to you."

Jack wrapped his fingers around it and pressed it to his chest.

"And now," said Hodgson, "I know Jack wants to finish reading his article to you from the local paper where his great-granddaughter once worked. She wrote the obituaries in this paper. It's called *The Reflector*. Jack lost her a few weeks ago in a horrible tragedy."

A hush descended on the gathering. Hodgson and Mary Lou knew all along what Jack was planning to do. With both of them at his side, he returned to his article, clutching the *chervonets* in his hand.

"I have learned a bitter lesson from my great-granddaughter and it's this," Jack said. "We ignore the past at our own peril. I might be a hundred years old but the little boy Jacob Klukowsky who was a hidden child in the ghetto and who was sent to the death camp at *Auschwitz* still lives in this frail body. His memories live. His love for his mother and his father lives. His love for all the murdered members of his family lives. And this is what it's all about. The value of a single human life.

"Christine once said that if they made a movie about me it should be called *Indifference* because indifference is how the world treats the memory of six million Jews who were killed by the Nazis a hundred years ago. The world has forgotten them. Some people don't even want to believe this crime ever happened.

"On the last day of her life Christine went to a place she loved and tried to do something she wanted to do ever since she was a little girl. She wanted to stand up on a railing so she could look out over this great natural wonder called the Elora Gorge and see how beautiful the world can be. The beauty that only a child of four can see. A world with birds and trees and rivers. A world where there is no misery and no suffering and no misfortune. I was denied these things when I was four years old and I take solace from the fact that my little Christine wasn't. She was a courageous person who fought the scourge of indifference with everything she had. She even gave her life for it.

"Christine Fisher was born in 2014 and she died in 2039. But it was the world's indifference that killed her. She was a child of the Holocaust."

AUTHOR'S NOTE

My father used to take me to the local Jewish bakery where this kindly woman behind the counter would serve us. I remember seeing numbers on her arm, but I was just a boy and didn't know what those numbers meant. Later I found out. One day in the not too distant future there is going to be one person left. One survivor. This is what *The Last Witness* is about. I want to thank some people who were helpful to me in my research. The 'readers' who offered valuable advice and comments on my early drafts include Ray Argyle, John Robert Colombo, Jennifer Dale, Barry Lane and my good friend Cam Campbell who took time to read when he was suffering from ill health but wouldn't live to see the final product. Special thanks must go to real-life child survivors of the Holocaust – Anna Cheszes, Anita Ekstein, Etti Miller, Jack Veffer, Gershon Willinger, Miriam and Roman Ziegler, the other members of their group at the Baycrest Centre in Toronto, and social workers Paula David and Peggy Solomon who allowed me to intrude on these most intimate gatherings. Elly Gotz is another survivor who provided me with key details and facts that helped me make my flashbacks accurate. I also want to thank technology wizard Chris Kata for showing me what the near future is going to look like, Jack Jebwab for revealing the sad state of Holocaust knowledge, my agent Ken Atchity for having faith in me and my work, all those who read the manuscript prior to publication and did reviews, and eminent historian Sir Martin Gilbert for being so kind and helpful when I told him about my idea. Lastly, I want to thank my wife Dorothy for her understanding when I disappeared for long stretches of writing and research to explore this most deadly time of human history. It is something we must never forget.

Dear Reader,

Without you none of this would be possible, so I want to thank you for reading my work and I would be eternally grateful if you would take a minute or two to review the book on Amazon. No matter what authors tell you, we do want to know what our readers think.

Sincerely,
Jerry Amernic

JERRY AMERNIC

Jerry Amernic is a writer who lives in Toronto. He has been a newspaper reporter and correspondent, newspaper columnist, feature writer for magazines, teacher of journalism, and media consultant. Alas, while wearing all these hats he has suffered from a chronic condition which he calls his 'fiction addiction'. It is fed by his insatiable appetite for history and then by inserting the characters he creates into the story. His first novel, *Gift of the Bambino*, was published in 2004 and will soon be re-released as an e-book. *The Last Witness* is his second published novel, and very soon another historical thriller called *Qumran* will be released, to be followed next year by *Medicine Man*.